A. K. SPALVA

THE RED DOVE

SOME STONES ARE
BEST LEFT UNTURNED

Published by Mystic Feather Publishing

ISBN: 978-3-9525554-3-9

Editor: Allison Williams / unkindeditor.com

Cover design & art: Jeff Brown / jeffbrowngraphics.com

Interior formatting: Mark Thomas / Coverness.com

To my parents and to Elina,
without whom this book would never have been written.

I am all-powerful Death, which destroys the world, and I have come here to slay these men.

—The Bhagavad Gita, Chapter 11, Verse 32

PROLOGUE

"*The Red Dove's almost…here.*"

The entire song, from start to finish. The others stared, their mouths wide with shock.

All eyes turned to Boris. After calling Tihomir a coward and daring him… would he recite it too? Or would he chicken out?

A chilly wind blowing through the forest saved Boris from his predicament.

"I'm cold," Jasna said. "And I have to go home."

"Yeah. It's getting late," Boris said quickly. "See you all tomorrow." He hurried away, careful not to look anyone in the eye.

Tihomir still stood with his fists clenched, until he and Sofija were the only ones left.

"Are you coming?" she asked.

In silence, they followed the dirt road separating farmer Vuković's wheat fields and the big forest. Sofija shivered. It was early July, but the air was freakishly cold. They could have gotten home faster through the woods, but Tihomir had told Sofija it was too scary in there. At the time, she had fought not to laugh at how easily frightened he was. But today, with distant thunder rumbling in the stormy sky, even she wouldn't have set foot in that forest.

Tihomir limped, wincing at every step. Sofija looked at his bruised leg and his skinned knee, where the blood still hadn't fully dried. Why did Boris insist on such rough games, anyway? Now, if something came for

Tihomir…he wouldn't be able to run away!

She stomped her foot and willed the bad thoughts away.

"How could you recite the whole song?" Sofija asked. Tihomir was always so shy, so helpless. Unable to get out one sentence without stuttering. What had gotten into him?

"I-I d-d-d-do-don't kn-kn-know. I-I-I'm sc-c-cared n-n-now."

Sofija quickly faked a smile. "But see, nothing happened! No Red Dove! Maybe Boris made up the whole thing."

"G-g-granny w-w-wouldn't l-lie."

She had forgotten about his grandmother. But couldn't she be wrong? Why were only Boris' grandparents and Tihomir's granny scared of the Red Dove? If it was so dangerous, wouldn't everybody know about it?

"D-d-don't you t-t-turn r-right h-here?"

Sofija looked up. She had almost walked past the fork in the road. "Oh, yeah. Get home safe! See you tomorrow."

CHAPTER 1

Just how many court files has Dad stashed away here? Amanda lifted a stack of papers from another storage box, and a small envelope slipped out and floated to the floor. She picked it up and held it under the old lightbulb.

Cyrillic letters. *Mom must have misplaced it. I'll show her later.* She stuffed it into her jeans pocket.

She turned her attention back to the stack of papers. *Arguments for the prosecution… Arguments for the defense… Witness Testimony… Expert Witness Testimony… Diagnosis… Psychopathy! Finally!*

She leaned against a pile of boxes and wiped her forehead. Who knew you could stuff so much of a family's life into an attic?

She spotted a box labeled 'Amanda,' peered inside and pulled out a white dress. That was a surprise. Her mother had kept her communion dress. She hadn't seen the inside of a church for ten years, at least. *Maybe Mom is hoping for some grandchildren to wear this?*

She fished around and found another white dress, of heavier cloth and with intricate red embroidery. A Croatian folk costume, a gift from her grandparents when she was four or five—the last memory she had of them. Or of any extended family—her mother had no siblings and her father's brother and parents had died in a car crash before she was born. Only her grandmother's wristwatch had survived, miraculously untouched by the surrounding destruction. Her father had given it to her on her sixteenth

3

birthday, when she was 'old enough to take good care of it.'

Amanda looked at her wrist. This watch, the Croatian dress and some old photographs were all she had left of her family. She shook off the loneliness creeping up on her and checked the box again.

No way. She took out a worn, leather-bound notebook. *I thought I lost it.*

Her phone rang.

"Hi Tom!"

"Hey darling! How's it going?"

"Just spent two hours combing through the attic for Dad's court records."

"That sounds as fun as my client portfolios."

She clamped the phone between her ear and shoulder while she folded the dresses back into the box. "I found four cases where he was an expert witness, hopefully on the psychosis of the defendant."

"Couldn't you have just asked him?"

"Those cases are from almost a decade ago. He wouldn't remember his exact testimony."

"I guess…by the way, a letter came for you. From Chicago Lakeshore Behavioral Hospital."

"It's probably about the internship. Did they accept me?"

"You want me to open your mail?"

"Sweetie, it's not a top-secret order from the president. I'm not the FBI. Not yet anyway."

"All right, give me a sec…"

She stuffed the notebook and the court files into her backpack and climbed down the attic ladder. Tom said, "Okay, here we go. 'Dear Ms. Dawson, we are pleased to inform you—'"

"Yes! I knew it!"

"Modest as always."

"Naturally. Anything important in there?"

"Let's see…uh, yeah. Didn't you say you're starting on the 22nd next month?"

"Yeah?"

"They're saying 'We look forward to welcoming you on the 15ᵗʰ of June 2009 and to—'"

"Great. One less week of vacation. Oh hi there Maxwell! Did you finish your 16-hour nap already?"

"Wow, he's awake?"

"I know, doesn't happen often. I like to call him a 'low maintenance' cat. Any other lovely surprises in that letter?"

"Not really. Except… Are you sure this is really a good idea?"

"Why? Didn't you do an internship?"

"Not in a mental hospital! What if something happens to you?"

Amanda swallowed a burst of laughter. "You sound like my ever-worried mother. It's an internship. What do you think I'll do? Fight hordes of stampeding inmates? Come on, you know how internships work. I'll be sorting papers and bringing everyone coffee. You know, 'valuable work experience.' I just hope they'll let me take a peek at the patient files."

"But if you want to become a star profiler, shouldn't you intern for the police? Or at the FBI directly?"

"Profilers don't chase criminals themselves; they analyze the criminals' psychology. So I don't need experience on police procedure, I need psychology experience."

"Fine…I'm just worried, okay?"

She dropped the stack of court files on her desk. "That's sweet of you, but I think I can handle pushing papers around."

"All right, all right. I better get back to work."

"Ah, another Saturday spent in your portfolios, huh? Have fun!"

"Yup. Slackers don't get anywhere at Citi. Bye, I love you."

"Love you too."

Amanda put her phone on silent. *All right, let's see what Dad had to say on serial killers.*

*

When she checked her watch again, three hours had passed.

Seriously? I only got through two of them. Maybe I'm taking too many notes. But she figured, when her criminal psychology final came up, the more notes, the better. Maybe her notes could be useful even after that, if she ever had to testify in a similar case.

She opened her backpack to get another file, when she saw the notebook she'd found. She took it out and opened the first page.

"Amanda Dawson's case book" it read in artsy handwriting.

She laughed. 'Case book,' what a joke. But this notebook did mark the beginning of her obsession with criminology. Back when she was only thirteen. It had all started in her father's study room.

"Dad, what are you reading?" she had asked him.

"A case file on a murder. And you?"

"Almost the same thing," she said, holding up Agatha Christie's *A Murder Is Announced.* "Do you know it?"

"No. I deal with this subject enough in my job. No need to spend my free time on it, too."

"Cool! You help the cops catch killers?"

"No," he laughed. "Psychiatrists aren't detectives. We just get asked to testify in court sometimes."

"Don't the police need smart people to find the killer?"

"They do, but it's different. See, in books like yours, the killer always uses some clever and elaborate scheme. This fools everyone, including the police. Except, of course, Sherlock Holmes, or whoever the star of the story is. Real murderers aren't like that. Most crimes are relatively simple, and the police know who did it. The challenge is finding enough evidence to convict. Criminals usually don't meticulously plan fancy murders like in books. In fact, most criminals aren't all that smart."

"Huh? Why?"

"Because someone smart wouldn't need to become a criminal to get things like power or money. He could get that through equally harmful, but legal means. You know, like...arms dealers. And politicians."

"What about people like Jack the Ripper? He killed lots of people and nobody caught him, right?"

"Those are the ones you should be very afraid of. Criminals who are intelligent and ruthless, who commit evil methodically and with no discernable motive. Lucky for us, such people are rare."

"You seem to know a lot about this, Dad. Is this what you do? Studying evil people and how they think?

"No, no. My specialty is psychoses. But there are people who study that, they're called 'criminal psychologists.'"

"Awesome! Do they solve murders?"

"Sometimes. But they study the criminal, not the crime. Studying a crime mostly involves talking to witnesses and examining a crime scene. It's as much science as it is art. Studying criminals themselves is different. At its worst, it means studying, interacting, and even 'understanding' arsonists, murderers, rapists and serial killers."

"That sounds so cool!"

He shook his head. "Amanda, I can tell you from personal experience, studying this sounds 'so cool' only until you come face to face with it. When you look someone in the eye and find only a bottomless void, staring back at you."

Amanda wasn't listening anymore. Why bother with boring things like geography or math if she could literally be studying evil? She pestered her father for weeks, until he finally got her *Mindhunter*, the first book among many she read over the years about serial killers, sexual predators, and psychopaths. In her childish hubris, she had even started this 'case book' to jot down notes as she read. She chuckled as she flipped through the old pages. 'Ted Bundy—Confessed to thirty-five murders. Would kill again if set free?' She had filled half the booklet with those TV-detective scribbles, until she realized it was simpler to just make those notes in the margins of the books directly.

How far she'd come since those days. Now she was well on her way to turning her fascination into a career.

Her thoughts were interrupted by a deafening noise from outside. *Dad's home, huh?*

She put her notebook on the desk and went downstairs. "Hi Dad!"

"Hey Sweetie! How are you?" He gave her his usual bear-hug.

"Great! Heard your car from a mile off. I thought you sold the Porsche?"

"*Draga*, you know your father." Her mother emerged from the kitchen. "When he sells a car…"

"…It's only to buy an even louder one." she replied in Croatian.

"Sofija…if you're going to make fun of me, you could at least do it in a language I understand," her father complained. "Especially when you have no trouble speaking English."

"Sorry, Edward. Force of habit." She embraced him. "I need to speak my mother tongue when I get the chance."

*

As always, dinner looked delicious. Amanda had already picked up her fork when she noticed nobody was eating. She looked over to her mother, eyes closed and hands folded, quietly whispering her prayer. Each time Amanda came here, she forgot about this little part of dinner. She put down her fork and waited with her father. When her mother opened her eyes, she looked touched they hadn't started yet.

"You know you don't have to wait for me! The food is getting cold."

"It's okay, Mom. No need to break this little tradition."

"Then let's eat before it gets even colder."

Not even two minutes in, her mother asked, "How is Tom? How has it been since you two moved in together?"

So the quizzing starts this fast, huh? "Same as usual, I'd say."

"He still insists on paying the rent all by himself?"

She shrugged. "Yeah. Since he was the one so intent on getting the apartment, he says it wouldn't be fair to make me pay for it."

"Technically, making *me* pay for it," her father winked.

"For which I would've been grateful, Dad. You know that. Though, technically, even with my tuition, you still had enough money for that new Porsche, so…eh." She exaggerated a shrug.

"Cheeky girl."

Her mother shook her head. "Did you and Tom talk about the future yet?"

"You mean like marriage? Not really."

"That's something you should discuss soon; you're already living under the same roof!"

"Your Catholic sensibilities are showing, Mom. But I get what you mean. I don't know why he hasn't popped the question yet. Then again, I'm not sure I'm ready for it, either."

Her father's expression grew somber. "I'm not sure I'm ready to call myself grandpa yet, either."

"Not happening anytime soon, Dad."

"But things are still well between you, right?" her mother asked.

"Don't be silly Mom, I love Tom."

"I'm just worried you two might grow apart, what with him being so busy with his job."

"That's an understatement. He's even working on the weekends lately. But we still find time for each other. He's taking me skydiving next week."

"Dear God. What if something happens?"

Amanda sighed. "Mom, relax. The plane won't crash, and the parachute won't fail. Literally thousands of hours of engineering and testing have gone into these things. I'll be fine."

"Yes, but couldn't you have chosen something safer? Like a romantic dinner?"

"Heck no. A day where you come home with unwrinkled clothes is a day wasted, as far as I'm concerned. That's what I love so much about Tom. He's the only one able to keep up with me, not one of those couch potatoes who never do anything outside their comfort zone."

Her father chimed in, "And despite that desperate need for wrinkled clothes, you've decided to spend the weekend visiting your old folks. I can't help but be touched. Even if it was mostly to tear up the attic for my old court records."

"Hey! I *did* come to visit you guys. Also, 'tear up the attic' sounds so dramatic. Mostly, it was just digging through dust and cobwebs. But I did find a few cool things. Like my Croatian dress, my old notebook, my—Oh yeah, Mom, almost forgot…" Amanda reached into her pocket and retrieved the letter. "I found this in one of Dad's boxes."

Her mother's face turned pale, as if Amanda had pulled out a leukemia diagnosis. Sofija stood up so abruptly, a glass fell from the table and shattered on the floor. As Amanda dodged the spray from the liquid, her mother ripped the letter from her fingers.

"Mom, what's—"

Without another word, her mother clenched the letter into a ball and ran from the room.

*

What the hell was that?

Amanda lay in bed, mulling over what had happened. She had never seen her mother act this way. On the contrary, she had always admonished Amanda for impulsive behavior. Why this overblown reaction?

A meow interrupted her thoughts. She looked down and saw Maxwell staring up at her.

"The bed is not that high. Jump up on your own. I've got some thinking to do here."

Another drawn-out meow was the cat's reply.

"You seriously are the laziest creature in existence." She heaved the cat onto the bed. "And you've gained weight."

While caressing Maxwell, Amanda thought back to the letter. The paper had been musty and yellow with age. Given the Cyrillic script, it was probably from back when her mother lived in Yugoslavia. Over twenty years ago. How could something so old make her panic so much? The only thing Amanda could think of was an affair, but her mother was far too pious for that.

And if it was so incriminating, why would her mother keep it? It had to have sentimental value, obviously. But then, shouldn't she be happy her daughter found it?

Her cat meowed disapprovingly when she moved him out of the way and got up.

"Sorry, Maxwell. But this is bugging me."

Amanda went to her parents' bedroom and found the door closed. She knocked. "Mom? Are you in there?"

She opened the door. It was dark inside. That meant her mother was downstairs.

Probably reading one of her sappy romance novels by the chimney.

She was about to close the door when something caught her eye. Barely illuminated by the light from the hallway, two crumpled pieces of paper lay on her mother's nightstand. She stepped closer. The Cyrillic characters were unmistakable. The handwriting was unique—flowing and elegant, as if its author had studied calligraphy.

She could just make out the same handwriting on the creased paper next to the envelope, meaning her mother had come here to read the letter after storming off from dinner.

Amanda listened carefully. She was alone. Her hand froze over the paper. This was obviously *very* private. Her conscience told her to go see her mother and ask for permission. But what if her mother refused? Then Amanda would never find out what was inside.

She picked it up and turned on the small lamp on the nightstand.

> *My dear sister,*
> *I hope you are in good health and that this letter finds its way to*
> *you. I hoped to write you sooner, but survival has been a struggle*
> *this past year, as it probably has been for you.*
> *   I know you will not forgive me for what I have done. Neither will*
> *I ask for your forgiveness until I see you in person. Unfortunately,*
> *I cannot make the trip to you—an injury has left me unable to*
> *travel.*

If you ever find it in your heart to see me again, you will find me in the village of Priboj, in the southeast of our country, near Vranje.

I love you and I hope that one day, I will be able to make amends.

With the greatest affection,
Mirko

'My dear sister'? Her mother had always insisted she had no siblings. And the envelope left no doubt—the letter was clearly addressed to her. Amanda had an uncle somewhere! An uncle her mother had lied about for twenty years.

But what was so scary about 'Mirko' that her mother would hide his existence for so long and then react to his letter in such a terrified way?

Whatever it is, I'm going to find out.

Amanda opened the door to the living room and opened her mouth, but stopped herself when she saw her mother, kneeling on a cushion, holding her rosary and forming silent words. She leaned against the doorframe and waited patiently while her mother moved her fingers along the rosary, bead by bead.

This had always impressed Amanda. There were so many prayers, it took almost half an hour to do the whole rosary. Her mother once told her it was very soothing and allowed her to meditate on her faith, but Amanda had tried it as a kid and felt like the boredom would kill her.

Back then, her mother was always taking her to church. Amanda's father wasn't religious, and it always annoyed her how he was free Sunday mornings, while she had to sit on a wooden bench every week.

When she was eleven, she finally worked up the nerve to tell her mother she didn't want to go anymore. She still remembered her relief when her mother had agreed. Mom was a very devout Catholic, but seemed to understand it was pointless to force her daughter into it.

When she saw her mother was finished, Amanda gently knocked on the open door.

"Oh, hello *draga*. I did not notice you there."

"Didn't want to disturb you," she said in Croatian. No need to for her father to overhear this conversation.

"Thank you. That's very considerate of you."

"Do you have a minute?"

"Sure honey, what is it?"

"Tell me about Mirko."

Her mother grimaced and shifted uncomfortably on her cushion. "You read the letter? Without my permission? How could you?"

"Unbelievable. Hey, remember when I was a kid? On those Thanksgivings and Christmases when I wondered why my friends were having huge family reunions while we were all alone? Yeah, you sat there, telling me that 'sadly' we didn't have any family to spend those holidays with. You lied straight to my face! And now that I find out it was all BS, yet *you're* mad at *me*?"

Her mother's hands anxiously fumbled the crucifix she kept around her neck.

Yeah, I hope you feel uncomfortable. You deserve it. "Everyone else in your family is dead. Your brother is all you have left and you pretend like he doesn't even exist? For over two decades, now? Because of some stupid family feud? Is that what's going on? Is that your justifi–"

Tears were streaming down her mother's face. Amanda had never seen her so crestfallen, clutching her crucifix as if she would die if she let go.

"Mom, I'm…I didn't mean to…I'm sorry."

Her mother struggled to suppress a sob, trying to make it sound like a cough. "No, you are right. I deserve this."

Amanda watched her mother wipe away the tears, not sure how to make it up to her now. "Mom, I'm really sorry. I didn't know this was such a painful topic for you."

"You have no idea…But even so, it was a sin to lie. I am sorry. I should not have been so petty."

"What happened?"

Her mother remained silent for a long time. "It's a long story. Why don't you sit down?"

CHAPTER 2

What you read in the letter is true. I did have a brother called Mirko. We grew up on a small farm with a tiny plot of land. My mother stayed home while my father sold jewelry and trinkets. He worked hard and traveled often, sometimes for weeks, barely sending home enough for us to survive.

But no matter how bad things were, Mirko was always there for me. Once, when I was 11, Mother had sent me to buy a loaf of bread. On the way home, some local boys spotted me and bullied me for the bread. I refused. We had nothing else to eat. They threatened me and shoved me. Luckily, Mirko was playing nearby. He fought alone against three and was badly bruised, but he still sent them home crying. He was a strong boy. I could always count on him.

It all started to go wrong when I was fifteen. With increasing competition, Father was having trouble selling his baubles. We had to start growing our own food. It was really difficult, Amanda. The soil on our land was poor and we had no farming experience. Our harvest was meager and when winter came, we often went to bed hungry.

We worked as hard as our bodies would allow, all throughout the year. Sometimes, we even considered missing church. For my parents, this was nothing short of blasphemy. We *never* missed church. But we were growing desperate.

Mirko's and my school grades suffered, too. The work was hard and long and we could barely concentrate. Mirko especially—he only slept a few hours a day, using the extra time to make us more money. He tinkered with simple jewelry out of wood, yarn and stones, whatever he could get his hands on. Father even praised Mirko for the trinkets he made and promised to sell them along with his other wares. Naturally, Mirko never saw any of the returns. We needed every coin.

Mirko grew bitter over this. Eventually, he told me his suspicion: That Father's trade hadn't just dried up—that he was wasting all the money on gambling or drinking. Mirko had no proof, of course, but he said he had examined the local shop prices and that it was impossible for Father to make so little that we were close to starving all the time.

A few days later, I was about to go to bed after another long day, when I saw Mirko enter our father's room. Maybe it was the way he walked, but something felt wrong. I hid myself and eavesdropped.

Mirko openly confronted Father, asking him why we never had any money.

At first, Father was confused and asked Mirko what he meant.

Mirko answered, "I've been going around town lately. I know what sells at what price, I know you should easily make enough. So, I am asking: Why is there never any money?"

I heard my father get up. I felt as if my heart would stop.

'What are you implying?' my father asked.

I prayed to God to make Mirko stop and apologize, but he kept going,

"We are starving! That's what I am implying! Making us work in the fields like mules doesn't change that. Don't you think it's time you stopped drinking or whatever it is you do and start taking care of our fam—"

Mirko suddenly stopped talking and I heard a loud 'thump'. Then, I heard a belt being taken off. And then…awful whistling sounds, and Mirko's agonized cries. Over and over, Father flogged him and screamed, "You come in here and run your mouth off? To your own father? You disgusting insect! You useless piece of trash! Do you know how much I work my back off, just to keep you fed, you worthless worm?"

I thought Papa would kill Mirko in his rage.

"Spare not the rod! If only I had listened to the words of our Lord sooner. I was too soft on you, but this ends now!"

When it finally stopped, I heard Mirko's whimpers and Father's heavy breathing.

"Another word from your filthy mouth, and I will kick you out on the street like the dog you are."

Father left the room, passing mere inches from the corner where I was hiding. I was so frightened—if he had seen me, he probably would have hit me too. I waited for a bit, then went into the room. Mirko was still on the floor, trembling and moving in a strange way, trying to soften the pain. Blood was dripping from his ear. I tried to comfort him, to ask him why he had challenged Father so brazenly. He didn't reply. He struggled to his feet and limped out of the room.

The next day, Mirko vanished, without telling my parents, without even telling me, or leaving a note. We knew he had run away—Several things in his room were missing. I was scared for him, but also disappointed. How could he leave without even saying goodbye to me? What had I done to deserve his scorn?

Weeks went by without a single word. Mother and I were worried sick. Then, finally, we received a letter. It just read, 'Do not wait for me. I will not return. Farewell.' The stamp showed it was from the southeastern part of Yugoslavia, over 500 miles away. What is today Serbia. We never figured out how my brother had gotten so far on his own, but the message was clear: He had abandoned us to our fate. And still, not a single word to me.

Mother broke down in tears and father said that Mirko might as well rot and die.

The winter that followed was even harsher than the ones before. Without my brother, Mother and I worked ourselves to the bone. And we really felt the lack of extra income from Mirko's trinkets and toys. We sometimes went for days without so much as a bowl of soup.

In those days, I also thought of running away. I kept thinking, *What if Mirko is right? What if our father is using all our toils to finance his vices?* One evening, my curiosity got the better of me. I pretended to go to sleep and waited until my parents had gone to bed. Then, I sneaked into Father's room. With nothing but a candle to give me light, I found his satchel, where he kept his papers.

I spent over two hours reading Father's notes and studying his earnings. By the time the candle burned out, I had found nothing to suggest he was being wasteful. His trinkets and baubles were simply not selling, just like he said. He was making so little, he could not have gambled or drank it away even if he wanted to.

Mirko was wrong.

In that moment, my heart turned to stone for him. He had wronged his father and reaped the result. Then, in his hurt pride, he had abandoned us like a coward. We were starving and he would not even write me a proper apology or farewell.

A year later, he finally bothered to send me the letter you found in the attic. But this was too little, too late, and I never wrote back.

After two more years of endless work, Father's trade finally picked up again. This allowed me to finish my education and get a job at the university, where I eventually met Edward. But my parents and I came very close to starvation, Amanda. All because Mirko left us at the worst possible moment. Since then, I have never spoken with him again.

*

Amanda was surprised by how suddenly her mother's tale ended. "That can't be all, right? Why would you hide this for so many years? It's sad, but it's no reason to storm off from dinner."

Her mother stared off into the distance, seemingly lost in thought.

"Mom? What aren't you telling me? Where's Uncle Mirko now?"

Her mother looked up, as if she was asking heaven for guidance, and took a deep breath. "No."

"What?"

"I'm sorry, but I will not speak about this anymore."

"Come on, you can't be serious. Don't I deserve to know about my family?"

"There is too much at stake here. I know it's unfair to you, but it's for the best."

Amanda massaged her temples, trying to keep her cool. "Okay, first, you lie about my uncle for twenty years, then when I find out, you leave me with half the story because it's 'for the best.' What are you worried of? That I might talk to him? You can't hate him that much."

"It has nothing to do with hate. It is for your own good."

"The hell? What kind of a bullshit reason is that?"

Her mother's eyes narrowed. "Watch your tongue."

"He's my family, too! You can't just keep him from me because you're still mad at him!"

"Amanda, enough."

"Fine, screw this! I read the letter, remember? I know where he lives—a village called 'Priboj', near 'Vranje.' Mark my words, I will find him. I'll go through every damn phone book in the whole *country* if I have to. And if that won't do it, I'll fucking visit the place myself!"

Her mother's face twisted into shock and fear. "Don't do that."

"Why not? I want to know about Mirko and you won't talk, so I'll just do this the hard way."

"Please, Amanda. Don't do that."

The meekness in her mother's reply stopped Amanda in her tracks. "Why not?" she asked again, calmer.

Her mother lowered her eyes, deep creases furrowing her forehead. Amanda waited for a few seconds, then stood up abruptly, ready to leave.

"Wait!" Her mother ran her hands down the beads of her rosary. "If I answer your questions, will you stay here?"

"Huh?"

"If I tell you everything, will you stay here, in the United States and not go to Serbia?"

"What, I'm not allowed to visit him?"

"There's no need. Mirko is dead."

"What? Since when?"

"1995."

"That's ages ago! If he's dead, why didn't you tell me about him sooner?"

"Do you really *promise* that you will not go to Serbia?"

"Good grief, what has got you so spooked about Serbia? Fine, I promise. Now speak up already."

Her mother took a deep breath. "All right. I'll trust you…In 1998, I found Mirko's letter by accident, a bit like you did today. Reading it again, I decided I couldn't keep hating him to my dying day. God taught us to forgive. Following his letter, I traveled to Vranje. But, his village, Priboj, was apparently so small, it wasn't on any wasn't on any of the maps I bought. So, I went to Vranje city hall. The clerk told me that Priboj was actually a city, about 200 miles to the northwest. When I showed her Mirko's letter, she asked her coworkers, but none of them could help me.

"I began to worry that the village might have been abandoned since Mirko wrote to me. With no alternative, I wandered the city, asking random passers-by if they knew where Priboj was. Nobody had heard of it. Finally, a young man told me the name sounded familiar. His grandmother had once told him something 'bad' about it. He gave me her address and said I should go ask her.

"When I arrived, I found her working in the garden. I introduced myself and she seemed friendly. But when I mentioned Priboj, she began shrieking, calling me a Satanist and that I would bring doom to everyone. When she paused for breath, I asked her to calm down and told her I was only looking for my brother.

"She yelled, 'Go! Go away! Your brother is dead! Stay away from Priboj or it will kill you too!'

"Mirko, dead? Impossible. I asked her if she knew him personally, or where she had heard this. She replied, 'Everyone in Priboj died three years ago. The Red Dove has taken them all.'"

Her mother crossed herself. "Finally, I understood what she was so frightened of. I thanked her for telling me and fled back here on the first flight I could take."

"Um. What?"

Amanda waited, but her mother didn't reply. "Okay, you 'fled' from Serbia because an old lady told you your brother was dead?"

"It was not his death that made me flee. It was what killed him."

"What? This 'red dove' thing?"

Her mother nodded, but again stayed quiet.

"And? What is this red dove supposed to be? Don't make me drag every little detail out of you."

"I am sorry. It is still hard to speak of it." Her mother closed her hands around her crucifix. "When I was a child, way before I had to work in the fields, I often played with the other children from my town. We had our favorite spot, a secluded place where the forest met the fields.

"One day, Boris, our 'leader' and a troublemaker, told us about the Red Dove. Many of us had never heard of it. Or it was just a myth, something our grandparents used to frighten us. 'Be good, or the Red Dove will come and take you.'

"But Boris said his grandmother had sung a strange song when she was knitting one day. When she started singing it a second time, his grandfather stormed into the room and screamed at her, telling her to never sing 'that cursed song' again, or that she would end up 'bringing the Red Dove down on all of us!'"

Her mother's face grew sour. "How I wish his grandfather had entered the room sooner, before she could sing it in its entirety. She must have been senile, maybe sick with Alzheimer's. I can see no other reason to do something so stupid.

"But the harm was done. Boris immediately wrote down the song and showed it to us. Whoever lost the games we played, he decided, should sing a part of the song as a test of courage. Lucky for all of us, even he wasn't brave enough to sing the whole thing.

"My shy friend Tihomir panicked. He said his grandmother had told him the Red Dove was a curse from the evil one and that that song should never be uttered, not even in part. None of us took it seriously. Tihomir was always easily frightened and Boris loved making fun of him. He started teasing Tihomir, telling him he was a weakling and would never become a real man. Everyone started laughing, including...including me. I did it to fit in. Even though I agreed with Tihomir. I did not want to be the odd one out."

Tears pooled in her mother's eyes. "What happened that day…it was all my fault. Tihomir was my friend, he trusted me. When everyone was laughing at him, he looked to me for support and all I did was stand there and laugh with the others. His expression that moment haunts me to this day. If only I had not been such a coward! I am certain it was my laughing that pushed him over the edge.

"Tihomir closed his eyes, clenched his fists and sang the cursed song. Or rather, shouted it. In its entirety. Just to make us all stop laughing.

"That evening, when Tihomir and I walked home together, was the last time I saw him. The next day, we learned in school that he had gone missing. It took the authorities a week to find him in the forest. We were children, so nobody told us anything. But we still heard the rumors. He was found with his limbs crushed and his throat torn open. The police blamed his death on a madman. We children knew better, but we were so afraid of the Red Dove, none of us told the police, or even his mother, what had really happened."

She crossed herself and wiped away another tear. "That's why, when the old woman in Serbia mentioned the Red Dove, I knew what fate had befallen Mirko and the other people in the village. I don't know why it took Mirko, but if it came for him, it could also come for me. After all, what if I angered it when I laughed at Tihomir for being scared? Getting any closer to it would have been suicide. So, I ran. And I have tried to forget Mirko ever since. That is the entire story."

Amanda blinked. She knew her mother would never joke about something like this, but she still half expected her to burst out laughing and admit she made it all up.

"*Draga*, I am sorry I lied to keep this hidden from you. I know you wanted to meet your uncle and that this is not the answer you wanted, but I hope this at least gives you some closure. Now please, don't force me to talk about this anymore." Her mother stood up and left the room.

Amanda looked after her. After a minute of trying to process what she had just heard, she said, "Are you fucking kidding me?"

*

The next day, after a lukewarm goodbye to her mother, Amanda flew back to Chicago.

"Home, sweet home," she said as she opened the front door. "Honey, I'm back!"

"I'm in the living room."

Amanda found Tom sitting in the middle of the floor, surrounded by a circle of papers and folders.

"Um…You know you have a desk, right? Is this some protective charm against evil IRS spirits?"

"I wish. Tax forms are comparatively easy. These are the client portfolios I still have to go through."

"Sounds fun."

"Just wait. There'll be profiling cases you'll have to work on over the weekend as well."

"At least then we can both build paper fortresses in the living room." She stepped over the circle of papers and kissed him. "You have dark rings under your eyes."

"Thanks darling. That's what I love to hear when I finally see my sweetheart again."

"I'm serious. Another night at the bar?"

"When you say it like that, it sounds like I'm an alcoholic."

"No, but…" She caressed his hand. "You can go overboard."

"What am I supposed to say? It's necessary…"

"…for networking, I get it. I'm just saying, take it easy. This will catch up with you eventually."

"Yes, Dr. Dawson."

She nodded "That has a nice ring to it. I can see why my dad likes his title. Maybe I should do a PhD after all."

He smiled. "Speaking of which, how was your weekend?"

"Exhausting."

"Why? I thought you got along well with your parents?"

"I do, but…" She told him about the letter she had found, about Uncle Mirko, and her mother's ridiculous fears.

"That's quite a story," Tom said.

"To be honest, I'm still not sure if this isn't some elaborate joke. Then again, she seemed so frightened…I've never seen her like that."

"You have to admit, though, it's a bit eerie the old woman mentioned the Red Dove."

"Eerie? Are you serious? It's a stupid coincidence, or this whole thing would have turned out differently. If the old lady had raved about a blue penguin, my mother would have given this senile nonsense the laughter it deserved and then asked somebody saner about where to find that village. God, I can't believe she ran away for something so stupid."

"But the old lady didn't rave about a blue penguin. Isn't this pretty extreme to just be a 'stupid coincidence'?"

She rolled her eyes. "The old lady only mentioned the same red dove because she grew up with the same damn stories my mom did. Like Bloody Mary around here. But I guess I shouldn't be surprised—she also believes a guy 2000 years ago was born from a virgin and rose from the dead like a zombie. If you believe that just 'cause a guy in a robe tells you so, you'll believe anything, including evil bogey doves that come down and eat naughty children."

"Didn't know you were one of those atheist hardliners."

"Usually, I'm not. But Mom's hysterical reaction to this fairy tale is beyond ridiculous. It's actually a bit embarrassing, believing in stuff like that at her age."

"A kid died after reciting that song. Wouldn't that creep you out?"

She sat down on the sofa. "The kid just got unlucky—the victim of a child molester or psychopath or whatever."

"Okay, fine. But why are you so upset? Even if the old woman is wrong about the cause, the village is gone. The city clerk confirmed it, right?"

Amanda's eyes lit up. "Hang on…*Is* the village gone? All we have is the word of some bored government clerks and a senile grandmother. But villages don't just disappear. Maybe it—and my uncle—are both still around!"

23

"Well, it's possible. However, small villages *are* sometimes abandoned, not to mention there was a war in Yugoslavia in the 90s and—Oh god, that look in your eyes…what are you up to?"

"Isn't it obvious?" She winked. "I'm going to meet my uncle!"

CHAPTER 3

Tom scratched his black hair. "Alright, slow down. Say for the sake of argument he really is alive, how would you 'meet' him?"

"Easy. Even if he still lives in the same tiny village, he probably has a cellphone by now. I just need to find his number. 'Hello Mirko, nice talking to you. I'm your niece!' Oh, and then, I can offer to book his flight here. That would be the greatest surprise of Mom's life. Mirko and I, ringing the doorbell, her opening, not expecting a thing…Oh, just imagine the look on her face!" She scrolled through her phone. "All right, let's see. My uncle's place was close to…Vranje." She jumped up and grabbed her laptop.

"You wrote down the place name in your phone? Were you planning to look up your uncle from the beginning?"

"Not really. But I suspected the letter might come in handy, so I took a picture."

Tom raised his eyebrows. "That's pretty disrespectful of your mother's privacy."

"He's my uncle too, you know. This letter is the only thing I have of him."

"But the letter was addressed to your mother."

"And that means I shouldn't be allowed to take a picture of it?"

Tom drew a breath as if to say something, but then shook his head and turned his attention to the papers around him again.

Amanda pulled up a Serbian telephone book. 'Mirko Matijević, Priboj' got no results. *That would have been too easy, I guess.* She decided to try Vranje's city hall. *Maybe they've become more competent since then.* As the phone rang, she could feel her heart beating fast, like when she had gone on her first date with Tom.

A clerk answered in Serbian, "Vranje city hall, how may I help you?"

"*Dobar dan*, I am looking for information on one of the villages in your precinct."

"Yes? Which one?"

"Priboj"

"That's a city to the northwest of here. I believe you have the wrong number."

"No, not the city. A small hamlet, unfortunately also called Priboj, near Vranje."

"I'm sorry, I've never heard of it."

"It's really, really small. Not even included on most maps."

Amanda heard typing on a computer.

"There seem to be no records of it."

"Could there be some mistake? I am certain it exists."

"Hmm…Well, some records were lost when our office burned down, a decade or so ago, before everything was digitized. If it's not on most maps, it's also possible it was never even registered as a village."

"Damn. All right, thanks for your time."

"*Zbogom.*"

She hung up. "Ugh. Why couldn't this just be nice and easy?"

Tom looked up. "Did you just call Serbia?"

"Yeah?"

"Since when do you speak Serbian?"

"Croatian and Serbian are almost the same language. It's even called 'Serbo-Croatian'. It's kind of like you meeting a Brit—You can both tell where you're from, but you can still understand each other, more or less."

"Huh. Interesting. No luck?"

"Nope."

Tom shrugged. "Look on the bright side, you tried."

"Who says I'm giving up?"

"Sorry, don't know why I ever thought that. Don't let me stop you."

She leaned back and twiddled her thumbs. What her mother had done was ask random people on the street. It was inelegant, but Amanda had to admit she also couldn't think of anything better—if this was still 1998, that was.

She pulled out her phone again.

"Look who's calling," Greg answered his phone.

"The one and only."

"That is a very suspect phrase! How do I know it's really you?"

"Are you seriously paranoid enough to believe the real Amanda was kidnapped and you're being contacted by a shadowy government organization?"

"No, shadowy government organizations would at least be fun. It's the calls by salespeople and missionaries that get me."

She giggled. "Are you in the habit of buying vacuum cleaners or your religion on the phone?"

"Hell no! Do you think I'm that stupid? But when I'm focused, being interrupted by imbeciles raises my blood pressure. And my doctor says I should avoid high blood pressure."

"Yes, absolutely. God knows what would happen if you ever went above 180."

"The world must never find out. So, to what do I owe the pleasure? Did you stumble on your secret picture of me and were so charmed by my rugged good looks, you decided Tom just isn't good enough anymore? Not very nice of you, but don't worry, I understand."

"Ah, Greg. I'm glad your megalomania is burning as brightly as ever."

"What can I say? I grow more impressive by the day. But seriously, how are you? It's been ages."

"Yeah, sorry for not being in touch. You know how it is finishing undergrad."

"Tell me about it. Congratulations, by the way."

She smirked. "How did you know I passed?"

"From the fact that you were stuck in your books all the time? When you weren't visiting random courtrooms to observe wacky murder trials, that is."

"That wasn't random. I may have ended up in the wrong courtroom, but that only happened twice, tops."

Greg laughed. "So what are you doing now?"

"Nothing much. Just relaxing before my internship in June."

"Ah, the mandatory unpaid internship for your resume, eh?"

"Exactly."

"And what will your CV say you were doing while actually being eye candy for your managers?"

"Thanks, Greg. There's a compliment hidden in there somewhere. It'll be an institution for the criminally insane."

He whistled. "You're really going all-out on that profiler thing, aren't you? Even your internship is geared to impress your federal overlords. But not a bad plan, actually. And having a renowned psychiatrist as your dad can't hurt, huh?"

"Hell no! I'm not some bimbo who needs her daddy to get her a job. He didn't even know about the internship 'til I told him."

"But why? Your dad's pretty famous, right?"

"I wanted to get that internship on my own merits, or not at all."

"You know you don't get any bonus points in life for making it needlessly hard, right?"

"Sure, but I have my pride, you know?"

Greg laughed. "Oh yes, you certainly do."

"Anyway, enough about the internship. Are you busy right now?"

"Still got a neural network to work on, why?"

"Wait, aren't you always complaining about how your assignments are too easy to bother doing?"

"They are. Perfectly trivial, in fact." He sighed. "But alas, this one counts towards my grade. And my scholarship requires those to be stellar."

"You could have just gotten a loan, you know? Weren't you just saying how there's no bonus points for making life needlessly hard?"

"Why would I be in debt when I can just be smart?"

"Ah, Greg, never change, I beg you. Anyway, since it's all so easy, can you put your IT mumbo jumbo aside? I have a job for you."

"Cool. Will you pay me?"

She grinned. "I don't have to. You still owe me, remember?"

"Actually, no. I don't recall being indebted to you."

"Who got you your first date with Barbara?"

"That…was over a year ago. And it didn't exactly last."

"Seventeen days, if I remember correctly. But that wasn't my fault, right?"

"Right. And what, you making that one phone call to arrange an awkward date means I have to do your bidding now?"

"Yes."

"You argue your case with truly forceful eloquence."

"Oh come on, Greg. Pretty please? I'll buy you dinner at 3rd Coast when the job's done."

"Excellent choice, now we're talking! What do you need?"

She sat up. "Okay, so, I learned something exciting yesterday—It turns out I may have an uncle."

"Good for you."

"Actually, it's not, because I don't know jack about him. That's where you come in."

"Uh…Wait a second. You're paying for dinner and calling in a favor a year old, just to make me look up your uncle? Can't you ask your parents?"

"No. Mom won't talk."

"Ahaaa, Amanda's investigating a juicy little family feud, huh? Sounds fun. So, what exactly do you want me to find?"

Amanda shrugged. "Anything. Everything. Whatever you can dig up on him."

"Great! I always love specific assignments. Do you know anything about that uncle, aside from 'he exists'?"

"He was born in 1951. He first lived in Croatia but at the age of 18, he moved to Serbia. Mom thinks he died in 1995, but she's probably wrong."

"And his name?"

"Probably Mirko Matijević."

"Um…how do you spell that?"

"M-i-r-k-o, M-a-t-i-j-e-v-i, and then a 'c' with an apostrophe on top."

"Gosh, what a name. Anything else you can tell me?"

Amanda tried to remember the letter. "No, I think that's it. Except…yeah, he moved to 'Priboj', near a place called Vranje, in the South-East of Serbia."

"So, almost nothing to go on. Cool. You have strange hobbies, if I dare say so myself."

"One is not responsible for one's passions, only for one's actions."

"How profound. Did you get that from a fortune cookie?"

"What? No! I came up with it myself."

"Then maybe you should write to whoever makes all the fortune cookies. I'm sure they'll appreciate your wisdom."

"Thanks, fantastic advice. So back on topic, will you do it?"

"You realize it's unlikely I'll find anything, right?"

"Yeah, I know. But if he's still alive, I have to find him."

"Alright. Fingers crossed, then. I'll be in touch."

"Thanks Greg! See you."

Tom turned around on his office chair. "Did you seriously just call Greg?"

"Yeah, he'll look into my uncle for me."

"I got that, but did you *have to* invite him out for lunch?"

"That's kind of something you do when you ask for favors from busy people. Look, Tom, I know you don't like Greg, but he's the only one I know who could pull this off. And one of my best friends. Without him, I would never have passed Calculus."

"Yeah, yeah. But are you sure he sees you the same way? As a friend?"

"Yup. Pretty sure."

"He tried to ask you out, remember?"

"How long are you going to be hung up on that? He didn't know we were together. Can't fault him for trying. Besides, it was almost two years ago. He's moved on."

"Alright, if you say so…"

"Yes, I say so, because I know him. Also, you could show a bit more trust in me, you know."

"I know, I know, I'm sorry. You know I can't help it, given how crazy I am for you."

She stepped over the circle of papers and kissed him. "Smooth talker, you."

*

The next morning, when Amanda got up, Tom had already left for work. She had just finished her cereal when her phone buzzed.

Meet me at 3rd coast in two hours.

She grinned. Greg was fast as ever. Now she just had to hope he had actually found something. When she entered the café, she found him at their usual table. As always, he had his laptop open in front of him.

"Hey Greg."

They hugged and he sat back down. "Heya. That's quite a…vibrant top."

"What can I say? I like red."

"Don't get me wrong, it looks great on you. But it's strong. Rather eye-catching, if you will."

"Aw, so it's just my clothes that are eye-catching?"

He looked her over as if he was studying an obscure art piece. "Eh, I guess the rest is passable."

She playfully slapped him. "Jerk."

After the waiter took their order, Greg smiled. "This brings back memories. Been a while since we were here for one of your emergency tutor sessions. 'Save me Greg, the evil Math is coming to kill me!'"

"Calculus was never my strong suit, okay? Sue me. Now quit stalling. What's up?"

"Your uncle, obviously…I know you were hoping I'd find his address or phone number, and I really tried, but it's impossible. Online phone books are no help, cause his name's way too common. As for that place you said he lives in, Priboj—turns out, there's a city in southwest Serbia with the same name. Just to illustrate what you wanted me to pull off here—that's like asking someone who doesn't know English to find a guy in America called Jack Brown who lives in a 'small town called Philadelphia.'"

"Damn. That bad, huh? Well, guess it was hopeless from the start."

Greg smirked. "Yeah, if you had asked anyone else, that is."

"You found something?"

"As a matter of fact, I did. Not really what you wanted, but I think you'll find it interesting, nevertheless. Can you read Serbian?"

"Yeah. Mom taught me to read the Cyrillic alphabet."

"Great!" He turned around his laptop. "Using machine translation, I figured this was a forum post on where to get nice jewelry on a budget. Check out the paragraph I've marked."

Heya! If you live near Vranje, every first Saturday of the month, a lot of local farmers and loggers sell their stuff in Soderce. Ask for jewelry made by Mirko, from Priboj. Bought a bracelet for my wife several years ago and she's still wearing it. The beads are made of wood, but arranged and polished so nicely, you'd think they're pearls. It was super cheap too, so it's well worth checking out!

Amanda's eyes went wide. "That's amazing! Mom told me Mirko had a knack for making jewelry. It's got to be him! Can we contact whoever wrote this?"

Greg shook his head. "Unfortunately, this website has long since shut down. This is an archived version I managed to dig up. I tried finding the guy, obviously, but he never reused his account name, so it was hopeless."

"Damn. It says he bought a bracelet for his wife 'several years ago.' When was this post written?"

"1999. You can tell by how crappy the website looks that this was the early days of the internet. Your uncle is supposed to have died in 1995, right?"

"Yeah. 'Several years ago' could mean anything." She looked up. "You didn't find anything else?"

"No. Hey, are you even aware of how hard this was to find? I burned several hours on this."

"I can imagine. Thanks a lot, Greg. This at least confirms the village exists and that my uncle still lived there in the 90s. Gives me hope that the village didn't just up and vanish for no reason."

"Well, it could still have been destroyed in one of those many independence wars. 1995 fits the timeline perfectly."

"There was more than one?"

Greg wagged his finger. "Tsk tsk tsk. You're half Croatian. You should know more about your country's history, young lady."

"Okay, first, I was born here. I've never even seen Croatia. So, it's not 'my country'. Second, it was hard enough having to study US history without adding Eastern Europe into the mix."

"I see. As always, it seems to fall to me to fill the gaps in your knowledge."

"Why, thank you, esteemed Professor Greg. By the way, is there any subject you *don't* know better than everyone else?"

"Maybe. But it's like Tachyon particles: Theoretically possible, but so far never observed in the real world."

"All right, enough bragging. Let's hear it."

"The gist is—After the first world war, the Austro-Hungarian empire was broken up. A few Slavic regions that used to be part of the empire were now independent. They merged into a single state, later called Yugoslavia and—"

"Greg, I know about Yugoslavia and that Croatia used to be part of it. I'm not that clueless, you know?"

"My apologies. I'll skip ahead. Yugoslavia was made up of several "states," a bit like the US. In the 80s, after the economy tanked hard, these states began demanding more independence from Serbia. Especially in Croatia and Bosnia, this led to armed uprisings by ethnic Serbs, many of whom still remembered the attempted genocide under the Nazi-controlled 'Independent State of Croatia' back in the 40s.

"The Serbian government supported these armed uprisings with their own military. Attempts at peace were made, but because of bureaucratic BS and dumb political power plays, the whole thing devolved into several different wars, lasting over a decade.

"The war in Bosnia was the worst, killing close to 100,000 people. The Serbians shelled the capital of Sarajevo for three whole years. Then came various massacres, often targeted at civilians, including one where Serbian militants slaughtered over 8000 people. NATO got involved and bombed Serbia, forcing a ceasefire. This was a bit controversial, since NATO had no UN security council authorization for this and I heard they broke international law, but I'm a bit murky on the details."

Amanda picked up the last piece of her burger. "Wow, your knowledge has limits?"

"No, I just sometimes have to pretend it does so people don't feel too bad about themselves."

"How gracious of you. So, who would have destroyed the village, then? NATO?"

"Eh, possible, but unlikely—a tiny village in the middle of nowhere, not even close to Bosnia or Croatia? Doesn't sound like a good military target. Then again, times were crazy, so who knows."

She nodded. "Still, this gives me hope my uncle's still around. I'll just have to keep digging."

"Suits me fine. Means I can get back to my neural nets."

"Have fun with that. And Greg, thanks for everything. You really helped me on this one."

"Don't mention it. Good luck. Let me know when you find your uncle."

*

Amanda was sitting on the sofa when Tom came home. "Hi sweetie," she greeted him.

"Hi. What's the occasion?"

"Huh?"

He nodded at the wine bottle and the empty glass on the coffee table. "That's a $150 Cabernet Sauvignon."

"Oh it is? Sorry, just took the first one I found. Pretty good, I admit."

"'Pretty good,' huh. If the sommelier who recommended this heard you... So, what's up that warranted opening a bottle? Did Greg manage to find your uncle?"

"No. At least, not yet. Opened the wine 'cause I had to think something over. Say, can we postpone the skydiving?"

"If we must. But why? I was really looking forward to it."

"I'm flying to Serbia."

Tom's mouth dropped open. "I'm sorry, what?"

"Greg managed to confirm that the village exists and that my uncle lived there. I called Vranje city hall again, but they keep insisting the village isn't in their database. I've tried to think of alternatives, but I can't do anything from here. So I'll do what Mom did and go over there myself, talk to people. Someone has to know where the damn village is."

"Amanda, this is nuts. You don't even know the place. Not all countries are as safe as America, you know?"

"Actually, Serbia's homicide rate is five times lower than America's. Also, if you're worried about safety, what are we doing in Chicago? 500 murders and 1500 rapes last year alone."

Tom rolled his eyes. "Whatever. Not going to argue with you of all people about crime statistics. All I'll ask is—are you sure this is worth it? Our skydiving is one thing, but you're looking at a thousand bucks and two lost days for the flight alone. How are you even paying for this?"

"Since you're paying for the apartment, I have quite a lot of Dad's money left over. He said whatever I didn't spend was, quote 'for me to use as I see fit'. Well, I see fit to use it for this."

"Wouldn't you rather spend this on something we can both enjoy? With that amount of cash, we could go on a really nice vacation together."

"Relax. You're acting as if I'm just going to blow all my savings here. Don't worry, there'll be enough left over for us to do something nice when I'm back."

He gave an exaggerated sigh. "Okay, okay, do whatever you want."

"Come on Tom, don't sulk. I promise I'll make it up to you. I know you were looking forward to that skydiving, I was too! But this is more important. I know you can't stand your relatives, but I want to at least meet mine."

"Yeah, I know. I just think you're going overboard, but I can tell I won't talk you out of it anyway. Knowing you, you've already booked everything, right? Will you at least tell me where you'll be staying? In case something happens?"

"Sure. It's a nice little family-owned bed & breakfast. I'll forward you the name and address later."

"Thanks. When's the flight?"

"May 19th."

"That's the day after tomorrow. What are you in such a rush about?"

"Why wait? I'm excited, okay? Besides, it's only a month until my internship and I don't know how long this will take."

"Are you at least going to tell your mother about this?"

"What? No, of course not. Then the whole surprise visit with my uncle would be ruined."

Tom frowned. "Doesn't your mother deserve to know you're going there? She begged you not to, after all."

"No. She'd only interfere because she believes in fairy tales. Don't worry, she'll thank me later when I dispel those delusions and bring her back her brother."

"Again, you don't even know if you'll find him alive, or at all. What am I even supposed to say if she calls and asks to talk to you?"

"Tell her I'm out, I don't know. Make something up."

"You want me to lie to your mother?"

"Tom, this is important to me. Please."

He shook his head. "This feels so wrong. I think we're both going to regret this."

CHAPTER 4

Amanda decided to take a small bag. The longest she planned to stay in Serbia was a week, so no point in lugging around a huge suitcase. As for toiletries, some basic makeup and her toothbrush would have to do. Together with her laptop, she packed her old 'case book.' After all, half of it was still empty, and what was this if not another case?

She looked at her teddy bear on the bed. *Sorry Snuggles, you're too big to take along.*

Tom arrived home soon after.

"Finally, you're home." she kissed him.

He motioned to the packed bag. "You've been busy."

"Better be prepared, you know. How was your day?"

"Wasn't too bad. Except the drive home. Police had to reroute traffic. A friend from work texted me and said there was a shooting in broad daylight."

"Ha! See! Told you, the crime stats are bad."

"Come on. This happening downtown is pretty exceptional. But if you think it's so bad, see it as a challenge—once you become a profiler, you can start bringing down those statistics."

"Sadly, no. Sorry, but Chicago's crime rate will stay sky high. My job won't be to 'clean up the streets'. Most murders here are the work of gangs. A psychological profile won't help."

"So what's the point of it then?"

"What's the last serial killer in Chicago you remember?"

"I don't remember any. Not everyone is into this as much as you are, you know?"

"Exactly. Because of the work of FBI profilers. The only serial killers here most people remember are John Wayne Gacy and Richard Speck. And if the police had been more educated in criminal psychology back then, maybe even these two would have been caught before racking up their insane body counts."

"Are you seriously saying the police are so clueless that all they would have needed to stop those serial killers is having a psychology book thrown at them?"

"They sure could have used one. Gacy's killing spree especially went on way too long."

"I don't know…you might be overvaluing academic knowledge. As I learned working for Citi, experience and intuition often trump textbook theories."

"Yeah, until they don't. Look at Ted Bundy. He killed more than thirty women over four years. Yet, the police with all their 'experience and intuition' couldn't stop him and when they first captured him, it was by dumb luck. Even though it was obvious who they needed to look for."

"From today's perspective, sure. Hindsight is always 20/20."

"It's not hindsight, it's science. Looking at the women he raped and murdered, and how he left them, it was almost certain that he was a sexual psychopath, organized personality, white, in his mid-20s to 30s, good-looking, charismatic, intelligent, educated and coming from a broken family, probably suffering parental abuse. It's perfectly trivial, really."

"Is that what the murder of these girls is to you? Some scientific equation to brag with?"

"Oh, good grief, drop the moral grandstanding. What do you want me to do? Weep and wail over some girls I don't know? That's not helping. What will help is what I will do in the future—getting monsters like that caught as soon as possible. At least that will bring justice to the victims and their families."

"Don't you think you should show at least a bit of empathy for the victims?"

"And what has that ever accomplished? I'm seriously getting tired of people who think it's a virtue to get all emotional and 'compassionate' over other people's misfortunes. Those nitwits who do nothing but sit in front of their TVs and newspapers, just waiting for a new tragedy to come along, so they can come out of the woodwork with their dumb candles and flowers and start holding their stupid vigils. Sometimes before the damn bodies are even cold. It's grotesque, really."

Tom blinked a couple of times. "Wow, Amanda. Didn't know you were that cruel. Are you condemning people for grieving, now?"

"Give me a break! The relatives are grieving. The rest are just indulging their fetish to pretend they are oh-so-good people. All the while doing jack shit to solve the real problem. See, the killer doesn't care how many people pray for the victims or how many flowers they put on those 'shrines'. He'll just keep killing. My work will do more than all those 'deeply affected' candle burners put together."

"But what do you want them to do? Not everyone can work for the police and hunt down serial killers."

"No, but it would help if they educated themselves on what to look out for, volunteered for neighborhood watching, or heck, just reported suspicious sightings to the police. But that takes actual effort or even going up against a real killer. None of these lazy cowards would ever think of doing something like that."

Tom put his hands up in the air in an 'I-give-up' gesture. "Let's drop this, okay? Have you had dinner yet?"

"What? Ah, no," Amanda replied.

It was Tom's turn to cook. While he was chopping some onions, he asked, "Say, Amanda. Will you be free on the evening of Monday, July 6th?"

"I guess, yeah. Haven't made plans this far into the future. But keep in mind I'll have started my internship then and they might ask me to stay late."

"Can you make sure they don't?"

"I'll try. What are you up to?"

Tom turned around and smiled. "Company dinner. The kind only the real bigwigs get to go to, usually. This time, I'm invited.

"Congratulations."

"And we get to bring a plus one! You can wear that dress you look so gorgeous in, the one you don't wear nearly enough."

"That's because it's not an everyday type of dress."

"And this is not an everyday dinner, either. They booked out Alinea for it!"

"Wow." She knew Alinea, considered *the* best restaurant in Chicago. And the most expensive. "If they invited you, they're really happy with you, aren't they?"

"Well, you remember that case I managed three months back? With that big client who wanted to jump ship, but ended up staying because of my intervention? They're still talking about that. I saved them a huge loss. This invitation might mean I'm on the execs' radar. I need to make a good impression during that dinner."

"Aha." Amanda grinned. "Now I understand. You want me to look smashing for the occasion so you'll be noticed."

"You always look smashing."

Amanda laughed. "All right sweet-talker, I'll ask the hospital to make sure I get the evening off."

"Fantastic!" he said and kissed her.

After dinner, Tom continued working on his portfolios, while Amanda went back to planning her itinerary and double-checking that she had everything packed. When she finally checked her watch, it was already past eleven.

She went over to Tom, who was studying a long and boring-looking paper. "Tom, I'm heading to bed. Are you coming?"

Tom didn't look up. "Are you going to sleep already? Sorry, I still have some stuff to do. Don't wait up on me."

Amanda smirked. Sometimes, Tom just couldn't take a hint. She turned around his office chair to make him face her. He looked like his mind was still on his portfolio, not understanding what just happened. She sat on his lap, swung her arms around him and gave him a long, drawn-out kiss.

"That's not what I meant by 'I'm going to bed,'" she said in a luscious voice.

She winked and stood up, walking towards the bedroom and opening her top, button by button.

"Amanda, um. I really should, I mean I have to finish …"

She looked back, cocked her head to the side and flashed a seductive smile. "We won't see each other for a while. So…" She unhooked her bra. "You can either spend time with your portfolio…" she let the bra fall to the floor. "…or with me." She left Tom sitting in the living room. She heard him stand up and follow her.

"Honestly, Amanda. You will be the death of my career one day."

*

Amanda was still sleeping when Tom kissed her cheek. She turned and saw him dressed in a dark blue suit, white shirt and matching tie.

"Hey handsome," she said and sat up. "Sorry, didn't notice you get up."

"Some things never change."

She kissed him. "I'll miss you."

"I'll miss you too. Before I go, I got you a gift. I was planning to give this to you in a more relaxed and romantic way, but seeing as you're rushing off to Serbia…" He turned on the light, opened the drawer of his nightstand and took out a small, black case.

She sat up and took the box. It was smooth, made of shiny satin. Her heart raced. Was this what she thought it was? The box seemed too large for it, but maybe it was just for dramatic effect. Was she ready for this? What would she answer if there actually was *that* in there? Her hands trembled as she released the golden latch.

No ring. Instead, there was a necklace. It was shaped like interwoven leaves of silver and in the center was a sparkling blue stone.

"Oh my god, it's…beautiful."

"You really think so?"

"Yes! It's stunning! The silver looks amazing."

"It's actually white gold and the gem is sapphire."

She ran her fingers over the surface. "Oh Tom, I can't accept this. It must be worth a fortune."

"It's yours, and yours alone. I'm not taking 'No' for an answer."

She flung her arms around him and kissed him.

"Thank you. But what's the occasion for a gift like that?"

"Well," he said, his chest swollen with pride. "I just felt like it. Will you try it on before I leave?"

She went to the mirror and fixed the necklace around her neck. Tom put his arms around her. "Amanda, that looks absolutely gorgeous on you. Blue like the deep sea. Just like your eyes."

She smiled and looked at it from every angle, admiring the intricate workmanship and glittering reflection of the blue gem. Normally, this wasn't her style. She wasn't the type to fawn over jewelry like some gold-digging bimbo. But she had to admit Tom had great taste. The way the stone sparkled and shimmered was mesmerizing.

Tom checked his phone "Okay, I've dragged it out to the last minute. I'm sorry, but I really need to go."

She embraced him one more time. "I'll never stop wearing it. And I promise, I'll be back in no time!"

"I'll hold you to that promise." He gave her another kiss. "Have a good flight, and good luck finding your uncle!"

"Bye! I love you!"

She heard the door close. As the adrenaline rush subsided, she wasn't quite sure how to feel. After two years together, it felt a bit disappointing that he still hadn't decided to ask her to marry him. On the bright side, like this she didn't need to figure out whether she was ready for this yet.

She turned back to the mirror. The necklace really was beautiful, but she wondered what had prompted Tom to buy this. No matter how good his salary was, this gift had to hurt his wallet. And Tom wasn't the type to make impulsive decisions. Had he bought it because she'd agreed to accompany him to that company dinner? Was he decorating his trophy wife?

She laughed and shook her head. What was wrong with her? Her boyfriend gave her a beautiful necklace and she was trying to make it nefarious.

The alarm on her phone rang, telling her it was time to get ready.

After boarding the plane, Amanda took out *The Anatomy of Motive*, written by FBI profiling legend John Douglas. She had read it four times already, but the last time had been several years ago. After a few hours of reading, she was surprised how much of it was obvious to her now, even oversimplified.

She put the book in her lap and looked outside. There was nothing but the endless blue of the Atlantic.

"Your soda, ma'am."

"Ah, thanks. Can you tell me when we'll land?"

"We should land in Vienna in three hours."

"Thanks."

As she took the glass, she noticed the flight attendant's eyes darting between her face and her chest. She sighed inwardly. She didn't mind when guys checked her out. She did have her pride, after all. But it was always so unappealing when they were this obvious about it. It made them look like underdeveloped apes, somehow.

She waited for the flight attendant to leave, then took out her notebook to go over her itinerary again. In Vienna, she would have to wait two hours before taking her connecting flight to Skopje airport, in the Republic of Macedonia. Once there, she could take a bus to the main station and from there another bus to Serbia, straight to Vranje.

She wondered how many more hoops she would have to jump through to meet her uncle. *Uncle Mirko*. It had a nice ring to it. Would he hug her? Or slam the door and tell her to get lost? Even if he agreed to come back with her, how would her mother react? Hopefully, it would be tears of joy, but what if she still hated him? Or even freaked out about that red dove stuff?

*A red dove...*the symbolism really was strange. Doves were some of the most harmless critters around. Pigeons, or *rock doves*, were found in every city. White doves even symbolized peace. All the creepier, then, to turn it into some sort of evil monster.

She took a sip from her soda and thought back to that song from her mother's story. Even if her mother still remembered it, she would obviously never agree to share it. Damn shame. Amanda would gladly have sung it a dozen times. Maybe it would have dawned on her mother that the entire red dove thing was just one big pile of horsesh—

The plane shook and dropped several feet in altitude. People gasped and a baby started crying. The pilot's voice came on, "Ladies and gentlemen, we are experiencing heavy turbulence. Please remain seated and ensure your seatbelt is fastened."

Amanda tightened her belt. Had this seriously just happened while she was insulting some fantasy monster? She chuckled. Unlike her mother, it would take more than a silly coincidence to scare her away.

Best not offend it again though. Wouldn't want the plane to crash, right?

✱

When she landed in Skopje, Amanda was ready to fall asleep just about anywhere. Her watch told her it was 5:18 AM in Chicago. Meaning she had been up for twenty-one hours and sitting in an airplane for eighteen of them. She had tried to take a nap, but been kept awake by the uncomfortable seats and the obligatory, constantly screaming toddler. She wondered how those frequent-fliers types managed sleep in conditions like that.

After clearing customs, she went to an ATM machine and withdrew some Macedonian cash. She adjusted her watch to local time. 12:46 PM. Which meant she had missed her bus into town. *God forbid a plane ever arrive on time.* The next bus to Skopje was an hour later, but she was in no mood to wait that long and signaled to the nearest taxi.

"Can you take me to Skopje bus station?" she asked in Croatian. She didn't know what the language in Macedonia was, but the taxi driver nodded and lifted her bag into the trunk. *Guess I'm not going to be speaking English for a while…*

When they arrived, she was surprised by how big Skopje's bus station was. She bought a ticket to Vranje and after a lot of confusion and almost boarding the wrong bus, she found the right one moments before it left.

Amanda fought hard to stay awake. If she slept now, she'd miss her stop, and have trouble falling asleep later. The landscape wasn't making it easy.

Whenever she looked out the window, she saw the same monotonous fields and forests, with the occasional village in-between.

She wondered why there weren't any faster means of travel. Humans managed to land on the moon 50 years ago, a big rock in a vacuum 240,000 miles away. Yet, they still hadn't managed to build flying cars.

The bus came to a halt, and the driver informed her that this was her stop. She stepped out onto the 'Vranje bus station', an unimpressive rectangle of concrete where buses were arriving, picking up people, and driving off again. Before setting off to the B&B, she remembered that Serbia used a different currency than Macedonia. She withdrew yet more money and hailed the first available cab.

Even though Vranje had close to 100,000 inhabitants, it felt small, like a village that had simply kept growing. The roads were narrow and she saw no buildings taller than five stories. Every single house had the same roof color—a faded, brownish red.

The taxi drive only took a couple of minutes. Amanda paid the driver and rang the doorbell. A broad, bearded man opened the door and motioned her inside.

"Ah, welcome! *Dobro došli!*" he greeted her with a booming voice. "You are from the United States? And yet you write Serbian so well. It's great, really great. Let me show you to your room."

He took her past a dining room and up to the stairs. Her room was small but looked clean and the bedsheets were neatly folded. After the journey she had just gone through, it felt like heaven.

"*Hvala Vam,*" she said.

"My pleasure! Will you join my wife and me for some *rakija* downstairs?"

"Some what?"

"Rakija! Spirit, distilled from fruits."

"Oh, ah…sorry, that's very kind, but I'm really tired after my trip."

"I understand. Then maybe tomorrow! If you need something, I will be downstairs." He closed the door halfway, then reopened it. "Oh, and welcome to Serbia!"

CHAPTER 5

The next morning, she stood in front of the poorly lit mirror and fiddled around with her makeup. The dark shadows under her eyes were annoyingly hard to hide.

"Thou shalt take off your makeup before going to bed, Amanda…"

She had slept over twelve hours and still felt tired. She wondered how business types managed to fly all over the place and not pass out in their boring meetings. Did you just get used to it? Or was there some weird trick to it, like gurgling lemon water or something?

She glanced back at the bed—it looked so inviting. But sleeping wouldn't get her any closer to her uncle.

She went downstairs and was promptly greeted by the owner's booming voice. "Good morning! Did you sleep well?"

"Yes, thank you. Still exhausted from the journey, though."

"I understand. People from America are tired when they come here." He nodded enthusiastically. "Will you join us for some *rakija* now? It will wake you up!"

You really like that drink, don't you? "I'm sorry, it's really kind of you to offer, but alcohol makes me tired and I really should get going."

"No problem, no problem. Are you heading out now? Do you need directions?"

"Yes I am, and…say, do you know how to get to a village called Priboj?

Not too far from here?"

He stroked his beard. "Priboj...Priboj...No, I don't think I ever heard that name. But there are hundreds of small villages around here. You should ask around. Somebody will know."

"Thanks. I'll do that."

He gave her instructions on how to walk to the city center and gave her his number, in case she needed something. She thanked him and went outside.

Now then. Here I am, in Vranje. It was a strange feeling. Her mother had walked the same streets, in search of the same place. Like her mother, she had no better plan except asking random people. Unlike her mother, it would take more than ghost stories to make her give up, though.

While walking to the city center, she asked anyone she came across. Most had never even heard of Priboj. The few who had didn't know where it was.

By the time she came to a small park, Amanda was getting desperate. She had asked at least thirty people already and was no closer to an answer. She sat on a bench to catch her breath. Looking around, she saw the bus station she had arrived at yesterday. *Huh. It was this close to where I'm staying? The taxi driver totally ripped me off.*

An old man sat down on the bench across from her. *All right, let's keep going.* She walked over. "Excuse me?"

"Yes?"

"Sorry for disturbing you. Would you happen to know a village called Priboj?"

"Priboj...Priboj...Yes..." The old man began scratching his head. "Yes, I have heard it before. Somewhere..." His voice trailed off and he stared into the distance. "Oh yes, I remember."

"Do you know where it is?"

"It is nowhere. Priboj was destroyed, no?"

"What? How? When?"

"Mh...Long ago...I think in the war? Or, no. Something else. The village was here one day, and then"—he gestured—"poof! No more village." Creases appeared on the man's forehead, as if he was straining all his brain cells to remember. "Hmm…There was talk about an evil spirit, yes? The whole village, dead. Yes."

Amanda suppressed a groan. Why was everyone who knew about the village mentally disturbed?

The man continued, "Yes, yes, it was all a big mystery. The newspaper said the police were in the dark. So, there were many rumors, yes."

She looked up. "The newspapers wrote about it?"

"Yes. The police had no clue. As usual!" He cackled as if he had just made a really good joke.

"Do you remember when this was, exactly?"

"Hum, hum…I think…" He fell silent again. The creases on his forehead reappeared. "I think…during the war with your people? But maybe it was later, yes?"

'Your people'? Did he mean Croatia? If so, that would be enough to get her started.

"Thank you so much, you have really helped me."

"It was my pleasure, yes. *Zbogom*!" He waved her goodbye.

Amanda wished him the same and walked away. 'The whole village, dead,' the old man had said. The same thing the old crone her mother had run into had claimed. This was bad news. But she wasn't ready to give up yet. Maybe it was just an urban legend, or if it wasn't, maybe the inhabitants had managed to evacuate.

If the newspapers *had* written about it, that gave her a far better way to get the answers she needed than asking random people on the street.

"Excuse me," she said to a young woman walking by, "Is there a library in Vranje?"

The woman nodded. It was nearby, so Amanda could walk. Less than a quarter of an hour later, she stood at the library's front desk. "*Bok*, I'm looking for old newspaper articles. Do you have any on file?"

The woman nodded. "But only for local papers. For national newspapers, I'm afraid you would have to go to the library in Belgrade. What newspaper are you interested in?"

"Anything that would cover local events during the war."

"Hmm…I think the best place to start is the Vranje Regional."

She took Amanda up two flights of stairs into a room that obviously saw little use. There were hundreds of folders stacked in bookcases and labeled by date.

"What year, specifically?"

"1995, please." She had no idea if this was the right year. 1995 was the one her mother had named, based on the ramblings of that old woman. The old man just now had mentioning the war against Croatia and according to Greg, 1995 fit the timeline. She just hoped she wasn't too far off, or she was about to spend a lot of time in this room.

"Right here," the librarian said and pointed to a section of folders marked *VR-1995.*

"Thank you. Can I take a seat somewhere here and look through it all?"

"We have a table and chairs over there. But please, make sure you put everything back the way it was and don't mix up the ordering."

When the librarian was gone, Amanda noticed she was alone upstairs. She took the first folder, marked, *January to February,* and sat down to read them.

*

With a thump, Amanda put yet another folder on the table, the fourth she'd gone through. *What a chore.* She looked at her watch and saw it was 4 PM. She had been in here for over five hours and had found zilch. Her stomach growled and her jet lag only seemed to be getting worse.

One more. Just this last one. If it's not in there, I'll come back tomorrow.

She opened *July to August* and again looked over one article after another. It was boring and exhausting to stay concentrated all the time, but for all she knew, the information she was looking for might just be buried in one tiny paragraph somewhere. She silently thanked her mother for making her study the Cyrillic alphabet, or she would never have been able to read any of this.

She flipped another page and was greeted by an ominous headline.

49

Massacre of Priboj: the mystery of the Red Dove

Her heart pounded. She went over the headline again. No, she hadn't misread it. 'The mystery of the Red Dove'? *No way. No way in hell.*

> *Police are baffled by the destruction of a small village to the northwest of Vranje. The village, Priboj, with a known population of 63, was found devoid of life by police on the evening of Monday, 10th of July.*
>
> *It appears that the entire population passed away sometime last week. 57 bodies have been found so far with many still pending identification. So far, no survivors have been found.*
>
> *Chief detective Đorđe Terzić is leading the investigation. He assured reporters that fears of an invasion by a foreign army are baseless, and that there is no indication this was a military attack.*
>
> *During their investigation, police have found several documents and drawings that mention or depict a 'Red Dove'.*
>
> *Terzić told reporters, "The meaning of this Red Dove is not clear yet, but we believe it may be of significance in this investigation." Anyone with more information on it is requested to contact Vranje police at once.*
>
> *Police have ordered that nobody try to enter the ruined village, as the investigation is still ongoing and many buildings have been deemed unstable.*

Her eyes darted over the article and found those unnerving words again. The Red Dove. Meaning the old woman her mother had met hadn't been delusional. Everyone in the village *was* dead and even the police considered the red dove important. With 'several documents and drawings' of it.

She played with her necklace as she read the article once more. *No, I refuse to believe this. There has to be a logical explanation.* The red dove part wasn't too hard—just a local superstition, like among her mother's childhood friends.

And the deaths? Some contagious disease, maybe. Or food poisoning. Since it was a small community, they had probably shared a single water or food source. Maybe a vile strain of salmonella, or botulism, or even a plague like cholera? *See? You don't need a supernatural monster to explain this!*

There was a creak behind her. Amanda jumped and twisted around. Behind her was the librarian, a stack of folders under her arm.

"Oh, I'm sorry. I didn't know you were still here."

Amanda breathed heavily. "Um yeah, you startled me a bit."

"I just have to archive this, then I'll be out of your way."

Amanda collected herself and sat down again. *Okay, calm down. Best not to speculate.* She had to know what the police had concluded. She went through the articles of the following day, then the ones on the day after that, then through all of July, but there was nothing. She moved to August, September and even October, but the result was the same—not a single word about an entire village being wiped out. She tried all newspapers the library had for July and August of 1995, but none of them even mentioned Priboj. Except for that one article, it was as if the whole thing had never happened. She didn't understand. Yes, there was a war going on, but over fifty people mysteriously dying wasn't worth more than a single article?

She leaned back in her chair. What a bummer. 'No survivors,' the article said. That meant her uncle was most likely dead, too. She hated to admit it, but Tom had been right—this was a waste of time and money. If she hurried, she could book a flight within the next few days and cut her losses. Maybe even still make the skydiving with Tom.

But there was no way she would feel satisfied like this. Yes, it was unlikely her uncle had survived, but maybe he had managed to escape whatever killed the villagers, or been away when it happened. Not all inhabitants were accounted for, after all. Why didn't she stay a day or two and keep going? The money for the flight was already gone no matter what she did, and her room here wasn't overly expensive. This was a once-in-a-lifetime thing. Skydiving could be done on any weekend.

Sorry Tom, I'm staying.

If she could find the reporter who had written the article, she might get more details about how the investigation turned out. She checked, but none of the articles named their author.

She considered calling the newspaper, when her eyes fell on someone else's name. *Đorđe Terzić*. The lead detective. She smiled. Why would she even need some clueless reporter if she could just talk to the man in charge of the investigation?

Amanda snapped a picture of the article with her phone before closing all the folders and putting them back on the shelves. As she walked downstairs, she realized something—the police back then didn't seem to know the Red Dove. Yet both her mother and the old woman she had met knew it. Meaning the legend was likely both old and obscure. Unsurprising, given how afraid everyone seemed to be of it. But then, how could she find out more about it?

"Did you find what you were looking for?" the librarian asked when Amanda got to the front desk.

"Yes, thank you. I put everything back the way I found it."

"Thank you. Anything else I can help you with?"

"No, thanks, I'm…Wait, actually, there is. Do you have any books on local folktales or stories?"

"Hmm…Yes, I think we do."

She motioned for Amanda to follow her. At one of the shelves, the librarian moved her finger down row by row. After a while she said, "I'm sorry, I can't find it right now. It might have been borrowed or misplaced."

Lovely. Why would things ever be easy?

"Can you tell me the name and author of the book?"

"Of course. *Yugoslavian Folk Tales and Legends*, by Dragan Marković."

"Thank you very much. You've helped me a lot."

"Anytime. Oh, before you go. There is a bookstore, two streets over. Maybe they have the book you want?"

"Ah thanks a lot. I'll ask there."

"My pleasure."

Amanda didn't expect much from the book; hoping to find an entry on the Red Dove was a long shot, but she wanted to leave no avenue unexplored.

The bookstore was small. But even if they didn't have it in stock, she hoped they could order it for her.

"Hi, may I help you?" the clerk greeted her.

"Yes, hi. I'm looking for a book. *Yugoslavian Folk Tales and Legends*, by Dragan Marković."

The clerk typed the name into a computer that looked like a relic from the 80s.

"No, sorry. It's out of print. I doubt anyone carries it, aside from maybe second-hand bookstores."

She thanked the clerk and stepped outside. *Okay, let's instead focus on this police officer, Đorđe Terzić.* She could always try a phone book, but she didn't even know where he lived.

For now, she would call the Vranje police station. Maybe he still worked there. She didn't want to call from her phone, though. No reason to give the Serbian police her number. She remembered walking past a phone booth earlier and walked back the way she had come.

Amanda bought herself a sandwich from a nearby supermarket to get the coins she needed. She was hungry, but she was too impatient to eat now. She found the booth, grateful that mobile phones hadn't displaced them here yet, and flipped through the phone book.

"Vranje police station, how may I help you?"

"*Dobar dan.* I need to speak to one of your detectives. I have an urgent message for him."

"Who do you need to speak to?"

She spelled out Terzić's name "D-j-o-r-d-j-e T-e-r-z-i-ć"

"Terzić? He retired years ago. Why would you have a message for him?"

"Ah, I understand. Could you tell me how to get in touch with him, then?"

"Who is this, please?"

"Sofija Matijević," she said. Her mother's name was the only one she could come up with fast enough.

53

"And what is your relation to Mr. Terzić and in what matter do you need to speak to him?"

"I'm his niece and the matter is personal."

"Mr. Terzić has no siblings," the man said, his voice as cold as ice. "Who are you?"

Amanda hung up. *Well, damn. That could have gone better. At least it seems he's still alive.*

She ate her sandwich while heading back to the B&B. It was getting late and she didn't know how safe the streets would be after dark.

The owner greeted her with his usual enthusiasm and asked how she was doing.

"So-so," she answered. "Sorry, do you have internet I could use?"

"But of course! We have Wi-Fi here!" he exclaimed with a toothy grin, as if his house was the epitome of modern technology, and handed her a slip of paper with the password.

Upstairs, Amanda took out her laptop and opened the same online phone book she had already tried to find her uncle with. Town by town, she called every 'Đorđe Terzić' there was. Luckily, his name was rare and there were only a couple of them in each place.

When she hung up the seventh call, she noticed the cheap clock on the wall giving off an annoying click every time the minute hand moved. She didn't know how she hadn't noticed it earlier, but now that she was aware of it, she wondered how she would ever fall asleep with this thing nearby.

She turned her attention back to her computer and found another Đorđe Terzić in a town to the southwest, called Bujanovac. After four rings, she heard a click at the other end of the line. A strong, raspy voice greeted her.

"Đorđe Terzić."

"Hello, my name is Amanda Dawson. I understand you used to work with the Serbian police force?"

"What can I do for you, Ms. Dousson?"

Her heart skipped a beat. *Finally!*

"I am looking for information about Priboj."

There was a long silence. Amanda remained quiet, worried about interrupting him if he started talking.

"How do you know about Priboj?"

"From an old newspaper article. It mentioned you by name as the lead investigator."

"The newspaper article you are referring to contains all available information."

"Um, were there no discoveries after the article was published?"

"No."

Amanda scratched her forehead. "So, what caused the death of seventy-three people is still unknown?"

"Yes."

"What has happened to the village, then?"

"It has been left abandoned."

Amanda was running out of questions fast. His voice was cold, as if he was trying to ditch an advertisement call. Then, she understood: To him, she was a nosy girl, maybe a reporter for a tabloid newspaper, pestering him for info on an old tragedy. Only his politeness had kept him from hanging up outright.

"Please…My uncle was in that village. Is there nothing you can tell me?"

"Your uncle?"

"Yes. I just want to find out what happened to him."

"What was your uncle's name?"

"Mirko Matijević."

There was another long pause. She knew what was going on. Terzić was testing her. It was a common trick in interrogations—remembering something so simple was effortless, but making it up would make people stumble. She bit her lip, hoping she had answered fast enough to convince him.

"My condolences."

Still not exactly talkative, but he sounded a touch warmer. She asked again, "Please, this is important to me. Can't you tell me *anything* more than what was in this article?"

"It pains me to admit it, but no. I failed in this investigation."

"And my uncle? Could he have survived somehow?"

"I remember his name. He was one of the few victims we could identify. I am sorry."

Amanda's shoulders slumped. This was it, then? Mirko was dead, and the cause of his death was still a mystery? Was this all she had to show for her trouble?

Terzić said, "If you wish to visit your uncle's resting place, I can accompany you. The village is difficult to travel to."

"Oh wow, thank you…But, why would you do that? It has to be an enormous hassle."

"Because there is nothing else I can do for you."

CHAPTER 6

The bus they had agreed on would leave in fifty-six minutes. But before leaving, Amanda wanted to try one last thing. After her success in finding Terzić, maybe she could find the author of the book on Yugoslavian folk tales in a similar way.

A search for Dragan Marković turned up a retired professor of anthropology from the university of Belgrade. It had to be him. She dialed his number, but gave up after eight rings. *Guess I'll try later.*

Amanda tossed her toiletries back into her suitcase, took a last glance around the room, then hurried downstairs.

She met the owner at the front desk. "Sorry, I need to check out right away."

"Oh, of course. A moment." He shook his head. Amanda could almost hear him thinking, *Americans...*

"That will be 2900 dinar, please."

Amanda placed three thousand on the table. "It's fine. Keep the rest. Sorry, wasn't planning on leaving this early, but something came up."

"I understand. Thank you for staying with us. *Doviđenja*! And safe travels!"

She sprinted to the park and from there to the bus station.

During the drive, Amanda pulled up the picture of the article she had snapped. It hit her how levelheaded it was. American newspapers would have gone straight for terrorist attacks or maybe UFOs and ghosts. Hundreds of "experts" and conspiracy theorists would have been interviewed on TV—

it would be headlines for weeks. Anything to milk every last dollar out of a tragedy. *All hail the consumer culture.*

As refreshing as the conservatism of the article was, though, there really wasn't much information. She did notice one thing—'The *Massacre* of Priboj.' Her own theory for sudden mass death had been some kind of disease. But 'massacre' made it sound like a bloodbath. What exactly had happened in that village? Even if this Terzić hadn't mentioned much, the police *had* to know the cause of death, right?

"Miss? We're here," the bus driver interrupted her thoughts.

Like in Vranje, all the roofs in Bujanovac were red. She wondered how nobody had ever built a single house in a different color. Maybe red tiles had been the only ones around when Serbia was built.

She looked around, but she didn't know what Terzić looked like and the bus station was crowded. A man in police uniform saw her and came over. *Is that him? No, this guy's around forty and Terzić is retired.*

"Do you need help?" the officer asked.

"No, thanks. I'm just waiting for someone."

"You sound Croatian."

"I'm not. I'm from the United States."

The officer's face darkened.

"Please show me your identification and travel visa."

What the hell?

"I didn't need a visa to enter Serbia."

"Then your identification, please."

Amanda handed him her blue passport.

He opened it and looked through it. "Your name?"

"Amanda Dawson."

"Your birthday?"

"15th of November. 1987. Is something wrong?"

"Why do you speak Croatian?"

"My mother is from there, I grew up bilingual."

"And what are you doing here in Serbia?"

"I'm a tourist. Can I get my passport back, please?"

"Ma'am, I must search your belongings. Please open your bag."

"Huh? Why?"

"A routine check."

"How is this routine?"

"Ma'am, please open your bag, or I will be forced to take you into custody."

She ground her teeth. Why was this guy harassing her like that? She zipped open her suitcase and felt nervousness creep up on her—What if she had something in there she wasn't allowed to bring to Serbia? Some stupid customs law this jerk could use against her? Amanda bit her lip and stepped back, hoping everything she had was innocuous.

The man bent down and took out her jeans, placing them on the street. *Thanks for ruining my clothes, asshole.*

From the crowd, another man came over. "Is there some sort of problem?"

The officer didn't turn around. "Official police business. This does not concern you."

"Actually, I believe it does," the man said flatly.

The officer turned around, his expression that of a man about to swat a fly. "I said, this doesn't con—" The officer froze.

"Nikolić, correct?" the newcomer asked.

"Um, uh. Yes sir! I mean, uh, I'm sorry! I didn't recognize your voice."

"So, what is going on here?"

"I, um…I suspect she may be carrying illegal goods or drugs."

"What the fu—" Amanda burst out, but a look from the newcomer silenced her.

"Why do you suspect this?"

"Sir! She…she showed suspicious behavior."

"Such as?"

Sweat beaded on his forehead. "Her language and passport do not match."

"And this was enough for you to search her belongings?"

"I felt it prudent, sir."

"Well, she is here at my personal invitation."

The police officer gulped. "Y-Yes sir!" He turned around to Amanda. "Apologies, Ma'am." He bent down and put her clothes back into her suitcase.

The newcomer said, "Thank you, Nikolić. You must have other duties to attend to."

"Yes sir!" The officer hurried away. The newcomer watched him leave, then turned to Amanda. "Ms. Dousson?"

"Yes, that's me," she said, suppressing a chuckle at the way he pronounced her name.

He held out his hand. "Đorđe Terzić."

"Amanda Dawson. It's a pleasure to meet you."

"Was your journey agreeable?"

"It was, except for this last part. Why did he go after me like that?"

"I apologize for his behavior. It is one of the many scars of the war for the Kosovo region. Ten years ago, NATO bombed several cities here in Serbia, including Belgrade, our capital. This killed 2500 civilians, just four years after NATO had already interfered in the war with Croatia. We Serbs are a proud people. Some of us resent America for battering us into submission. Nikolić especially. You, speaking Croatian and being from America, must have incensed him."

This was quite a different view than the history Greg had given her. Hadn't the Serbians been the aggressors? And the ones responsible for various massacres? Then again, she reflected, the victors write the history books. She remembered the pain that 9/11 had inflicted on her own country. If America really had killed a comparable number of Serbians, she could understand their anger.

"I'm sorry. I didn't know."

Terzić looked surprised. "What happened was not your fault."

She was glad to know that he at least bore her no ill will. "Thanks for getting me out of that situation."

"It is no trouble. I know all the officers around here. Most of them, I trained personally. And my word still carries weight at the precinct."

"Wow. Well, thanks also for meeting me here. I know I called completely out of the blue. Can you maybe tell me where I can find a hotel and drop off my bag? I didn't have time to check for any lodgings before I left."

"Unfortunately, I do not believe there are any hotels here."

"Oh, okay. Damn. I already checked out of my place in Vranje."

"Considering the circumstances, I can offer you a guest room."

Amanda looked him over. Meeting a complete stranger was one thing, but sleeping at his house? So far, Terzić had acted very professionally. But what if it was just a ruse to lure her in? She guessed him to be in his mid-sixties, but he looked really fit. If she went to his place, she was entirely at his mercy. Her five or so karate lessons ten years ago wouldn't be much help.

Amanda reminded herself to look at this dispassionately. Profiling-wise, he seemed an unlikely candidate to be a rapist. He was keeping a healthy distance from her, so he understood boundaries. He also seemed to be a known and respected figure. Sociopaths and psychopaths tended not to rise this high. And he didn't give off a creepy vibe. Still, his generosity seemed a bit too good to be true.

"But why would you offer me a room? You don't even know me," she asked.

"The guest room is not occupied. I cannot tell you why your uncle died, so this is the least I can do."

She thought about it a while longer. *Well, it's either that or the bus back to Vranje.* "All right then. Thank you very much. I'll gladly accept."

"This way, please." He motioned toward a row of parked cars behind the bus station. He walked to an old, blue VW Golf, unlocked it, and held the door for her.

"Thanks." She forced down a giggle after slightly bumping her head. How did people squish into a car like this? It felt like a sardine can on wheels.

Terzić placed her suitcase in the trunk and drove off without another word. The silence felt awkward, but she was too jet-lagged to worry about small talk.

He stopped the car on an incline. Amanda got out and marveled at Terzić's small cottage with white-painted walls, a wooden door and, of course, a red roof. To the side, she saw vegetable patches and garden gnomes smiling up at her. Behind the house was a chicken coop and beyond that, an endless expanse of farmland.

"That's very pretty."

"Thank you. Please follow me." He unlocked the front door and stepped back so she could enter first. Amanda saw an entranceway with pairs of shoes and slippers on the side and jackets hanging on the wall. She turned around and saw Terzić open the trunk of his car and carry in her luggage.

"Oh, thank you very much. I should carry that."

"It is no trouble." He took off his shoes and put on slippers. The whole floor was carpeted, so Amanda understood why and took off her shoes too. *When in Serbia, do as the Serbians do…*

He led her to the end of the hallway and opened a door. "This is the guest room."

She entered an impeccably clean room that even included a bedside stand with an antique lamp and a small bathroom at the back.

"It's fantastic! It's like a hotel room. Thank you so much!"

"You are welcome. Are you tired?"

"Uh, yes, actually. The jetlag is pretty bad. But I'm really grateful you offered to take me to Priboj and don't want to waste your time, so if you want, we can go right away."

"I would not recommend it. It is getting late and it would be difficult to reach Priboj before nightfall."

Amanda wondered why this would be an issue. His car did have headlights. Then again, she was jet-lagged, so why insist? "All right, in that case, thanks again. If it's not too impolite, I would go to sleep now, then."

He nodded. "If you need anything, you will find me in the living room, through the right-hand door in the corridor. *Laku noć.*" He left the room and closed the door behind him.

Amanda scratched her head. Had she done something wrong? Terzić had not smiled once this whole time. He was polite, yes, but also guarded. Was that just how he was? He hadn't been talkative on the phone, either…

Amanda searched around her backpack for her phone.

*Hi Tom. Sorry I didn't write sooner. Been doing nothing but
running all over the place. Haven't been able to find the village so
far, but met someone here who knows how to get there. Tell you
more on the phone. Going to sleep. Totally jet-lagged. Love you.*

She considered adding her uncle being dead and that she was staying with
someone she had only met less than an hour ago, but it was probably better if
Tom heard that over the phone.

*

"So this is what a jet-lagged Amanda looks like." For the second day in a row,
Amanda was starting her day absolutely horrified by what she saw in the
mirror. It was even worse than yesterday.

Her watch told her it was 10 AM. *Good grief.* She rubbed her eyes. She
wanted to go back to bed, but Terzić hadn't offered her this room so she could
sleep all day. Even so, there was no way she could leave the room the way she
looked right now.

One shower and a bit of makeup later, she finally felt presentable. Her
bathroom even came with towels. All she was missing was a hair dryer, but the
weather looked warm enough not to worry about it.

The living room was surprisingly spacious for such a small cottage.
Amanda noticed a faint smell of smoke. It wasn't cigarettes, so she guessed
Terzić smoked a pipe on occasion. *At least it's not cigars...* She would forever
dread that smell after accompanying Tom to one of those high-class lounges
he and his coworkers kept going to. She shuddered just remembering that
experience.

To her left were two leather armchairs, with folded wool blankets on the
armrests. Terzić sat in one of them, reading a newspaper.

It was funny how perfectly he fit into the scene. With his receding hairline
and full moustache, Terzić looked like the embodiment of a retired detective,
satisfied with a long life of catching criminals and now enjoying his golden
years with a few less bad guys out there.

"Good morning," she said. "Sorry, didn't intend to sleep that long. The time zone difference hit me harder than expected."

"*Dobro jutro.*" He folded the newspaper. "It is no trouble. Do you need a hairdryer?"

"Oh yes, gladly."

While Terzić was gone, Amanda let her eyes wander across the room. On the opposite wall, she saw several framed awards. One of them read:

The Socialist Federal Republic of Yugoslavia proudly awards Police Officer Đorđe Terzić this commendation in recognition for his outstanding service record and excellence as an officer of the law.

The one next to it said:

The Federal Republic of Yugoslavia proudly presents this award of valor to Police officer Đorđe Terzić for his unflinching dedication and courage to his fellow officers in the line of duty.

On and on the commendations went.

Terzić entered the room again. "Here you go.".

"Thank you. Sorry to keep you waiting so long, I'll hurry it up."

"It is no trouble."

When she came back, Terzić had decked out the large dining table with tableware, plates and a variety of food and breads.

"Before going, we should have breakfast."

Terzić pulled one of the chairs out for her, waited for her to sit, then pushed her chair back toward the table. Amanda grinned at these polite gestures. But she was also impressed. In her generation, nobody cared about etiquette anymore. With Terzić, this conduct seemed so natural. She wondered how long it would take her to do something stupid and offend him. Or had she done that already without realizing? Was that why he was so aloof?

"*Prijatno,*" he said, placing his napkin on his lap. Amanda did the same, guessing she couldn't do much wrong if she just imitated whatever he did.

Looking at the food, she felt even worse about making him wait so long. It was nothing short of a feast: There were cheeses, hams, cold cuts, fruits and vegetables. Bread, hard-boiled eggs, bacon, an assortment of pastries, and a variety of jams and yogurts.

Amanda wondered why everything was so quiet, then noticed he was waiting for her to begin. *Damn, I thought the guest was supposed to wait for the host to start eating?* She hastily picked some ham and a few fruits at random and put them on her plate.

She knew she was supposed to temper herself and not act like a glutton, but as soon as she took her first bite, she decided decorum would have to wait. Everything tasted so good, it was impossible to eat in moderation. Even the most boring vegetables were amazing, especially the tomatoes—ugly and misshapen, but a flavor unlike anything she had ever tasted. Compared to the shiny but tasteless red globes sold in America, these tomatoes here were a culinary experience all by themselves.

She noticed Terzić eating only little and slowly, and became self-conscious again, wondering how she looked, wolfing down his food.

"Thank you very much. This food is absolutely delicious."

Terzić looked surprised, as if a breakfast like this was normal for him.

"You are welcome." He looked at her empty plate. "I hope it is enough?"

"Oh yes, absolutely. It's fantastic, I'd eat even more if I wasn't full already."

"I see. Would you like coffee, or tea?"

"Oh, coffee, gladly!"

He filled a cup in front of her and handed her a small milk jug and a bowl with sugar cubes. Amanda inhaled and took a moment to appreciate the aroma. Freshly brewed. It promised to do wonders for her jetlag.

She finished her cup and said, "Again, thank you. For meeting me and for this incredible hospitality."

"It is no trouble. If you are finished, I suggest we leave for Priboj soon."

"Oh, sure. I'm ready any time."

Terzić got up without a word, carrying his plate to the small kitchen in the back. Amanda took as many dishes as she could carry and brought them to the kitchen as well. "Where do I put these?"

"You can leave them here." He rolled up his sleeves, getting ready to do the dishes.

Amanda asked, "May I do that?" He looked at her as if she had asked a really strange question. She put down the plates. "I feel like I'm being a terrible guest. I've just barged in, taking up your guest room, making you wait for hours in the morning and probably eating triple what you eat for breakfast. I've given you nothing but trouble, so let me at least do this."

"Very well." Terzić stepped back from the sink. "Thank you. Then I will prepare the car."

Amanda wondered what there was to 'prepare' about that sardine can. *Maybe it's so old it needs to be wound up before it'll drive?*

She finished washing and drying the plates and stashed the leftovers in the fridge. Terzić still wasn't back, so she went to her room and called the author of the folk tale book again. Like yesterday, nobody picked up, even when she let the phone ring for a full minute.

As Amanda put away her phone, she saw Tom had replied. *Hi darling, glad to hear you're doing well. Hope you find what you need and that I'll see you soon. Love, Tom.*

She was thinking about what to reply when there was a knock on the door. "Are you ready?" Terzić asked.

"Anytime." Tom would have to wait.

"Then let us go."

Outside, a jeep Amanda hadn't seen yesterday was parked in front of the house. Like last time, Terzić opened the door and waited for her to get in.

"You have two cars?"

"No. I have borrowed this jeep from a friend."

Terzić showed no emotion, as usual. But from the energetic way he changed gears, Amanda suspected he enjoyed driving this car.

They drove through the now-familiar farmlands and open plains of the Serbian south, towards the mountains in the distance. They passed through one last village, then entered a narrow and ill-maintained road upwards. Terzić swerved to dodge the growing number of potholes.

A quarter of an hour later, the 'road' was little more than a dirt path. They drove steadily uphill, past rivers, bushes and trees. The higher they went, the denser the vegetation became. *So that's why Terzić borrowed the jeep. That poor little beetle would have broken down by now.*

Terzić had no map and there were no signposts, but he turned at every fork without hesitation. Now she understood his warnings of "the village being difficult to travel to." If she had tried to come here on her own, she would have gotten lost a dozen times over.

Eventually, they reached a tree growing in the middle of the road and Terzić stopped the car. "We must walk the rest of the way."

He took out a compass and looked at it repeatedly as they went up into the woods. The way was rough and arduous. Amanda had never been in a wild forest like this. Every step required concentration to not slip over roots or stumble on a buried rock. The trees were unbelievably dense, with barely any light reaching the bottom.

This was nothing like those cutesy US national parks, with their well-maintained gravel roads, markings on every tree, good cell phone coverage and restrooms and hot-dog stands every few dozen yards. Here, there were no landmarks, no horizon, and everything looked the same. She couldn't even tell which direction they were going.

Amanda shuddered, remembering stories of people getting trapped in wild forests and going in circles for days, even though the exit was just a five-minute walk away. Some had even died from exhaustion or dehydration. Add in mosquitos, parasites and wild animals, and heading here alone might have been a death sentence. *Thank God Terzić has that compass.*

The ascent wasn't particularly steep, but she still felt hopelessly out of shape. Constantly stepping over large roots and rocks was surprisingly exhausting. When Terzić noticed how much she was falling behind, he waited for her to catch up. As always, he didn't say a word.

To break the perpetual silence, Amanda asked, "The road we were driving on, did it used to go up to the village?"

"Yes."

"Was it just overgrown after a while?"

"Yes."

You really take terseness to an art form, huh? She tried a more open-ended question. "I'm sorry, I already asked you this over the phone, but is there nothing more you can tell me about what happened? I mean, that damn article explained nothing at all."

"It is because we, the police, could not explain it either."

"But the article didn't even mention the cause of death. You must have determined that, right?"

"We chose not to make that information public. The villagers themselves were the killers."

"Huh? Did some villagers go on a murder spree?"

"Not 'some'. As best we could determine, nearly all of the inhabitants butchered each other in a crazed frenzy. With any usable tool or weapon."

Amanda stopped in her tracks. "What?"

"That was our reaction as well."

"That's…" She tried to wrap her head around this new information. "That's unbelievable. How did you reach that conclusion?"

"The wounds on the victims' bodies were caused by many different weapons. Based on the angles of attack and wound penetration depth, the perpetrators were of dissimilar strengths and heights. We also recovered a great variety of work and farm tools with blood on them. Many of the victims still clutched them in their hands."

"But…if it was a free-for-all, wasn't there at least one survivor left standing, or somebody who hid in a closet or something?"

"No survivors ever came forward, nor were any ever found. Several victims died from self-inflicted wounds, suggesting those who did survive the massacre took their own lives."

"Good God…" She nodded that she was ready to continue. "But, why? How did this happen?"

"I do not know. I have pondered it for years."

"What happened to the dead?"

"A priest came and performed a memorial service. The victims were buried in the village cemetery. We marked the names of those few we could identify. Most bodies were so mutilated, any identifying documents we found in the houses were useless."

They kept walking, now in silence. Amanda had a hundred more questions, but decided it was best to first see the village herself.

After twenty more minutes, the forest thinned and Terzić stopped. "We are here."

They stood on a ridge, with a clearing below like a giant bowl, as if someone had used a cookie-cutter to gouge a circle from the forest. The inside, around four hundred yards across, was a flat grassland, with about two dozen buildings near the front and a lot of empty space at the back.

Amanda was amazed how well-hidden it was. No wonder none of the locals knew Priboj—even a local hiking buff might never lay eyes on this place.

She followed Terzić down. Most houses they passed were little more than overgrown heaps of wooden debris, their roofs caved in and their walls rotten with moisture. Some had decayed entirely, with only a few rectangular stones hinting at the foundations.

Wild trees grew between and even inside the houses, Nature's way of reclaiming her dominion. In a few decades more, nothing would remain of the dilapidated village.

They walked to what looked like the village center, a square area sixty feet wide. There was a well here, its walls covered with moss. Amanda peeked inside but couldn't see the bottom. She imagined this as the spot where the villagers once gathered to talk and exchange stories.

"I will wait here if you wish a moment alone. Your uncle rests there." Terzić pointed to a large building. It was as broken as the others, but from its outline, Amanda figured this had been a chapel. Behind it, she found the small graveyard. The crosses were all made of wood and in equally poor condition as the rest of the village. The first few looked straight and smooth, with names and dates. She figured these were from before the massacre.

Further back were several rows of crosses made from split planks or broken boards. They all had 'Name: Unknown' etched on them. Finally, in the last row, she found the few graves which had names.

Here lies Mirko Matijević. May God rest his soul.

She sat down in front of the grave. *So, I finally found you.* She looked at the decaying grave for a long time. This, right here, marked the end of her journey. Her feeble attempt to connect with her family. And what a depressing conclusion it was.

What was she even doing here? She could have packed her bags the moment Terzić confirmed Mirko's death. Instead, she had come up here hoping for… what exactly? There was nothing here. Except for two wooden planks, crudely hammered into a cross, and a barely legible name. But about Mirko, she still knew nothing. What had he looked like? How had he been as a person? And in his final moments, had he thought back to his sister? The sister he had never gotten to speak with again, and who was so frightened by her childhood trauma, she hadn't even come up here.

That's okay, Uncle Mirko. I came to visit instead.

At least the trip wasn't a complete waste. She could tell her mother about everything she had found. And, with Terzić's permission, give her his phone number. Then her mother could visit as well, if she could only get over her stupid fear over this absurd boogeyman.

Amanda let her eyes drift over the village. What was there to be afraid of here? After her mother's ravings about evil spirits and dismembered childhood friends, Amanda had expected more. Ghostly lights, strange sounds, or at the very least, some creepy fog over the place, like in the movies.

Instead, the village was just…sad. Broken buildings, overgrown weeds, and grey clouds overhead…a quiet graveyard nobody cared for anymore, abandoned and forgotten.

Amanda stood up and patted Mirko's grave affectionately. "Bye bye…I wish I could have met you sooner."

She walked back to Terzić. "I think I'm ready to head home. I've paid whatever respects I could."

He nodded and looked up at the sky. "Good. We must hurry. A storm is coming."

As they ascended the slope out of the village, Amanda heard thunder in the distance. A chilly wind picked up and heavy clouds filled the sky. When they reached the edge of the forest, she stopped. Was somebody whispering? She turned towards the village again. It felt…dark. The houses cast no more shadows and had no contrast, like they were melting into the earth. The trees, so green and vibrant before, were ashen and swayed sickly in the wind. There was an odd feeling of being watched.

"Forgive me, but we really *must* leave, or we will not reach the car in time," Terzić said.

Amanda looked at the village one more time, but the creepy sensation was gone. She looked at her arms—she had goose bumps all over. She laughed quietly at herself. It was amazing how some grey lighting and weird wind noises could play tricks on the mind.

She turned away and followed Terzić back down through the forest. They got to his car just as the first raindrops fell. By the time they reached his cottage, the wind had become a storm and it was raining heavily. Terzić parked as close to the house as he could, and they hurried inside.

"I will prepare dinner," he said.

"Can I help somehow?"

"No, thank you. Please, make yourself comfortable."

Amanda sat down with a thump. Thinking back, she could feel proud—she had found her uncle, against all odds and with almost nothing to go on. But, now what? She would have to tell her parents. If Mirko was still alive, that might have made up for it. But like this? She didn't even want to imagine how angry they would be. And then there was Tom. She had to concede that he had been right all along—coming here had been wasteful and pointless.

Terzić came back from the kitchen with a pot full of goulash. Amanda ate listlessly. The food was hearty and tasty, but that couldn't cheer her up right now. She needed someone to talk to. Someone who would understand her and tell her, "at least you tried!" Unfortunately, Terzić didn't seem like the best candidate to talk to about emotional problems.

Afterwards, Amanda insisted on doing the dishes again. No matter how low she was feeling, it couldn't be an excuse to take Terzić's hospitality for granted. Lightning flashed outside and booming thunder shook the house. The wind rose to an angry howl and the rain battered the windows. She was glad they had left the village when they did.

In the living room, she found Terzić in his armchair, with a bottle and two small vials on the table.

"Would you care for some rakija?" he asked.

Again with this drink? Was this some local custom? If so, she might offend Terzić by refusing. "Yes, thank you."

He uncorked the bottle and filled the two little flasks. They looked like miniature chemical beakers filled with liquid gold. Amanda sat down in the opposite armchair. It was amazingly comfy, like sinking into a stack of pillows.

Terzić raised his flask. "*Živeli.*"

"Cheers." She imitated what he did, clinking her glass with his and only taking a small sip. The taste was interesting, but the alcohol was really strong. She was grateful this apparently wasn't downed like a shot of tequila at a frat party, or she would have grimaced hard. "That's pretty good. I'm sorry for my ignorance, but what exactly is rakija and why is it so big here?"

"It is brandy, made from fruits. Plum, especially, is popular. Some would call it our national drink. Many of us make it ourselves."

"Oh wow, so this is homemade?"

"Yes," he said, a touch of pride in his voice. "May I offer you a bottle to take home?"

"Wow, that would be lovely. But I feel like I'm already abusing your hospitality so much…"

Terzić stood up. "Not at all. It is customary in Serbia to give gifts to guests,"

"Oh, I didn't know. It's a lovely custom. I still feel a bit guilty, but thank you, I'll gladly accept."

She took another sip. It was a nice drink, but she never was good at handling her liquor. She just hoped that the custom didn't require her to drink more than one of those little flasks.

He returned with a plain glass bottle full of the golden liquid.

"Thank you," she said. *This should last me over a year...*

He nodded and sat back down. "On the telephone you mentioned a newspaper article. Do you have it?"

"Yes, on my phone." She opened her photograph of the article and held it up.

He examined the article and nodded with a curious expression. "It has been quite a while since I have seen it. How did you find it?"

Amanda briefly went over her story, showing him Mirko's letter that mentioned Vranje and explaining how she had asked random people until she met the old man, then gone to the library and found the article. "Then, I called every Đorđe Terzić in the phone book."

Terzić nodded, seemingly lost in thought. He lifted the glass to his lips. Would you like to hear what the investigation was like?"

"Oh yes, please!"

"Would you mind if I smoked?"

"Not at all."

"Thank you." Terzić opened a drawer in the small table next to his armchair and took out a pipe and a tobacco pouch.

Another bolt of lightning dyed the room in bright light, followed by a deafening thunder. Amanda pulled the blanket around her shoulders and nestled into her chair, while Terzić lit his pipe and began to tell his story from the 11th of July 1995.

CHAPTER 7

The day had started well. After months of work, Terzić had finally ended the reign of a local gangster with a spectacular raid that he had personally led. Several colleagues congratulated him. When he was called to the inspector's office, he thought he might be in for a commendation.

He straightened himself in front of the door and knocked confidently.

"Come!"

Terzić opened the door and saw Luković bent over a paper on his desk. Terzić stepped in and saluted.

Luković looked up. "At ease." He looked back down at the paper and loosened the knot of his tie. His face was that of a man whose wife wasn't returning his calls. "Sit down."

Terzić's stomach tightened. What if that ominous paper was a drafting order? So far, he had avoided conscription into the ongoing war, but could his luck finally have run out?

The inspector said, "I have been notified that a local farmer called in considerable distress, saying 'many deaths' have occurred in the village of Priboj. Do you know it?"

"No, sir."

"A small logging hamlet, half an hour northwest. We do not have records of even a single crime from there. Frankly, I didn't even know it existed. Suddenly, there are 'many deaths' there. Do you see my problem?"

"Yes sir." With the ongoing wars, even a hint of dead bodies was big trouble. An invasion this far south seemed unlikely, but what if an enemy guerrilla unit had launched an attack? Then the whole region was in danger.

"I have not sent this higher. No need to cry wolf just yet. If we are lucky, the tip is false or there was an accident, or a fight that turned deadly. Take two officers and go there at once. Find out how many casualties, what killed them and who is responsible. You have three hours, not a minute more. Go!"

"Sir!" Terzić saluted his superior and went downstairs to pay a visit to the file clerk, requesting all information on Priboj the department had on record. Next, he chose two idle officers to come with him. He let his subordinate drive while he read the files he had received. Priboj was tiny, with only sixty-three inhabitants. Most were lumberjacks or craftsmen, but one also had a hunting license. Like most villages, Terzić guessed that the village had a bit of farmland, making the village self-sufficient. The village sold its lumber bi-weekly in a nearby town, where they also got their mail—since it was so remote, not even the postal office went there.

The car stopped and Terzić looked up. They were in the forest, on a dirt road leading to the village. A large tree had fallen straight into the middle of the road. The trunk was split down the middle, tell-tale signs of a lightning strike.

This was strange. The last thunderstorm had been two weeks ago. Why hadn't the villagers cleared the tree by now? They were loggers! Didn't they need this road to get out of their village?

"We will continue on foot." Terzić couldn't go back empty-handed just because of a fallen tree. At this point, the village couldn't be much farther than a couple of miles away.

The closer they got, the more Terzić's hair stood on end. The village had to be nearby, and yet, there were no trees being chopped, no children playing, no arguing neighbors, not one human sound.

"Ready your weapons."

The police officers turned to him in amazement. They had expected a simple administrative visit. After a look at Terzić's face, they drew their guns.

His order was against protocol, but something told Terzić it was best to be prepared right now.

The forest ended abruptly on a small elevation. Even from here, he could tell something was horribly wrong. Several buildings had burned down. Nothing moved. This was either an ambush, or something unspeakable had happened.

"Tomić, you guard our rear. Radić, you keep an eye on our flank. Let's go."

When they reached the bottom, the two officers grabbed their stomachs and retched. A horrible stench filled the bowl-like terrain, like an invisible lake. Terzić maintained his composure. He knew what that smell was, but he had to confirm what had happened. Stepping around one of the houses, he saw something that would forever scar his memory.

Blood-soaked corpses littered the ground, twenty, thirty—no, probably more than forty. His stomach turned upside down and he closed his eyes to refocus.

When his nausea subsided, Terzić steeled himself and opened his eyes again. Even though he was prepared for it, the sight still threatened to make him throw up. In his entire career, he hadn't ever experienced something this bad. Only one event came close—when, as a young officer, he had broken down the door of a house where a madman had killed his wife, two children and then himself. By the time the police were called, a week had gone by. All the windows had been closed, so when Terzić broke the door, the pent-up stench of decomposition burst out like a wave. It was so bad, he had keeled over on the spot, like the two officers with him now.

The stench of a decaying human body was more awful than words could describe. The best description Terzić had ever heard was 'a mixture of rotten meat, spoiled eggs and sewage'. And it stuck in your nose somehow, even hours or days after smelling it.

"Is anyone here?" he shouted, immediately regretting it when he had to draw a large breath of the foul air. There was no response. He holstered his weapon. If this was an ambush, he and his officers would have been attacked already. He looked back and saw them sitting on the incline near the forest, probably praying that Terzić wouldn't order them down again. He decided they wouldn't be much help anyway.

He took a moment to steel himself, then moved to examine each corpse in turn. It took all the strength he had. In the summer heat, the bodies had bloated and deformed. The swelling had cracked open their jaws, as if they were all silently screaming as the maggots and blowflies crawled in and out of their mouths. *Don't think about it. You have a job to do.*

From a first glance, the villagers had died just a few days ago, all of them violently. The number and variety of wounds was dizzying. On one victim, Terzić guessed at least fifty stab wounds. On another, the head and chest had been smashed to a pulp. Yet another had been turned into an unrecognizable pile of gore. Terzić even came across two children, no older than eight—no one had been spared.

When he arrived at the well in the village center, he had to lean on it and steady himself. A noxious stench rose from inside. He couldn't see the bottom, but guessed there was a corpse rapidly decomposing in the water.

Dear God, what happened here?

The murder weapons weren't hard to find—many of the dead still held them in their hands. Kitchen knives, hatchets, axes, sledgehammers, chainsaws…all with dried blood on them.

There was only one explanation—the villagers had killed each other, in a mindless and frenzied slaughter. He didn't want to believe it, but it fit everything he saw. Even more disturbing, this hadn't been a sudden burst of madness: judging by the varying states of decay, some deaths had occurred days before the others.

Whatever had killed these villagers had killed them slowly. And yet, no survivor staggering into a nearby town. No call for help.

Despite the heat, Terzić felt as if icy water was running down his back. As a police officer, he had seen victims of bombs, people shooting their brains out in front of him, even a victim of a satanic cult murder. He wasn't frightened easily, but this village made him tremble.

He couldn't investigate a crime of such scale on his own. He needed seasoned officers to comb the village for clues, and forensics experts to examine the victims in detail.

Back at the station, he went straight to the inspector's office.

Inspector Luković fell back in his chair and looked upwards as if asking God for wisdom.

"Dear God…And you are certain this wasn't a hostile army?"

"As certain as I can be, sir."

The inspector sighed and massaged the bridge of his nose. "All right. I will accept your preliminary results. Take an early evening today. I'll put a team together. You will supervise the investigation. If you find any indication this was a military attack after all, inform me immediately. Dismissed."

*

Terzić spent the following days driving to the village in the morning and staying until it became too dark to continue investigating. The team the inspector had selected was small, but well trained. Progress was slow, as Terzić insisted on entering every house, opening every drawer and every cupboard, and meticulously examining every corpse. Anything remotely promising was sealed, carefully labeled, and sent back to the precinct for analysis.

Even so, he didn't expect much of the papers and notes they found, until they entered one of the larger houses. The inside was horrendous—all the doors had been shattered and blood soaked the walls. The stench of decomposing bodies was overwhelming. One of them was a girl, no older than twelve. When he examined the room she had been found in, Terzić found something invaluable. Under the bed was a leather-cased booklet. Terzić flipped to a random page and read:

June 25th, morning
Dear Mila,

Terzić's eyes widened. This date was less than two weeks ago!

I woke up when it was still dark because people outside were screaming. Someone ran past my window. In the hallway, Papa was already putting his boots on. I wanted—

"Sir? We've managed to identify another victim. Had a letter with his name on it."

Terzić looked at the letter. "Mirko Matijević." He nodded. "Thank you. Have it sent back to HQ, along with this booklet."

"Right away, sir."

Letting go of the booklet took significant willpower. This was the first piece of evidence that looked promising, or might even explain everything. He wanted to read it on the spot. But he couldn't let his curiosity contaminate vital evidence, like fingerprints or fibers. He would read it once the forensics experts were done with it. In the meantime, there could be evidence rotting away somewhere while he wasted time here.

In the chapel, a bible lay open on the lectern. Scribbled on the first page was, *We have sinned. God, save us from the Red Dove!*

The writing was shaky, barely legible. Terzić wondered what the significance of this "Red Dove" was. An hour before, one of his investigators had found a notebook with a red bird drawn on it. Later, Terzić had found a note saying, "No way out. Red Dove won't let us go. Will die if I leave. Will die if I stay. God why have you forsaken me."

On his way home, Terzić was approached by a reporter. He told him the bare facts—they'd found fifty-one corpses, leaving another twelve registered inhabitants unaccounted for. Asked whether this had something to do with the war, Terzić calmed down the reporter and told him that it certainly wasn't. The last thing he needed now was for the paper to write the local populace into a panic about an impending invasion.

On a hunch, he decided to mention the Red Dove. None of his team had ever heard of it, but if it appeared in the newspaper, maybe somebody with more information would come forward.

Two days later, on the 15th of July, the evidence and forensics collection seemed nearly complete. As Terzić was planning to wrap things up, a member of the State Security Administration, the secret police of Yugoslavia, showed up and asked to speak to the officer in charge.

"You are hereby relieved of your command of this investigation," the official told Terzić. "The SSA will take over from here. Here is the paperwork your superiors may need."

"Can I ask why?"

"We were very displeased to learn that a massacre of this scale was not reported to us. We read your remarks to the press that this was not a military attack. We will be the judges of that. You are dismissed."

Terzić knew this was the end of his investigation. When he got back to the police station, the SSA had already taken possession of all the evidence. Everything he had so carefully collected and organized, his only hope of understanding what had happened, all gone. He cursed his own stupidity. Why had he answered the journalist's questions? He should just have told him not to speculate and come back when the investigation was completed.

Two weeks afterwards, the government finally concurred this had not been a military attack. Terzić tried to get the evidence released, but was refused. "This is no longer your concern," was all he was ever told. His only hope of ever understanding what had happened in that village was forever out of his reach.

CHAPTER 8

Terzić put his pipe down. Both vials of rakija were now empty. Outside, the storm had stopped. All that was left was the sound of soft rain hitting the roof. Amanda fell back into her armchair, having been on the edge of her seat for the last half hour.

"Poor Mirko." She shuddered, imagining her uncle's last moments, and squeezed her eyes shut to dispel the gory images. "In any case, thanks for telling me all this. What an insane story…"

"You are welcome. I only wish I could tell you more. After the investigation ended, I tried to investigate the massacre in my spare time. I still believe this Red Dove is the key, but I have come up empty. I interviewed the inhabitants of villages close to Priboj, even the farmer who had first alerted the police, but nobody knew anything about a red dove. My only explanation is that it was something only the villagers understood."

She looked up. "Huh? But, it's…"

Didn't Terzić know that the Red Dove was a local legend? Then again, there had to be hundreds of such obscure legends around here. Every country and every town the world over probably had its own folk tales, unknown even to most of its own inhabitants, much less anyone outside. Heck, even Eau Claire had its share of "haunted houses" and ghost stories. She had even visited one of them and laughed at how lame it was.

"Yes?" Terzić asked.

Amanda smiled. After all he had done for her, she finally had something to offer in return. "I can tell you about it. The Red Dove is one of those boogey-monsters to frighten children into behaving. But from what I've seen, it's really obscure. The few people who know about it all seem afraid of it. It's been around since at least my mother's childhood. It's part of why I'm here, actually—My mother already tried to find my uncle in 1998. Unfortunately, she met an old woman who I bet had read that article and told my mother that Priboj had been 'destroyed by the Red Dove.' Because of a childhood trauma she suffered, my mother panicked and flew back to the US. So, I came here to find Uncle Mirko instead."

"Did your mother's trauma involve this Red Dove, too?"

"Yeah…She was around ten, I think, when her friends discovered a 'cursed song' about the Red Dove. They decided to make a game out of reciting parts of it as a test of courage. One of them was against it, so the others teased him, until he snapped and recited the whole thing. That night, he went missing and the police later found him brutally murdered in the woods. I'm guessing it was a child molester or serial killer, but my mother of course thought the Red Dove did it."

"I understand. It must have been horrible." He stroked his chin. "Do you know this song?"

"I wish. My mother probably knows it, but she's so freaked out over it, there's no way she'd ever tell me."

"That is unfortunate. The Red Dove was clearly important in Priboj somehow… Any information about it, however small, could have brought us a step closer to solving the mystery."

"We might get lucky on that front—there's a book on Yugoslavian folk tales out there. It's a long shot, but it might contain an entry on the Red Dove. Trouble is, it's out of print. I've tried to contact the author, but so far no luck."

He nodded. "It shows good instinct on your part to research the Red Dove further. Combined with finding me as quickly as you did, you display an aptitude for investigation."

Amanda beamed with pride. If a decorated police veteran was complimenting her detective skills, her chosen career path couldn't be that far off the mark, right? "Thanks, that's very kind. I still hope I can reach the author, or find the book in a used bookstore or..." Her words trailed off as she remembered something in Terzić's story. "Speaking of books, what about that diary you found? What happened to it after the secret police confiscated it?"

"I do not know."

"Do you think it could still be lying around, in storage somewhere?"

"Possibly."

"Do you think we could get to it?"

"I have tried several times and my requests were always denied. My rank was too low and—" Creases formed on his brow and Amanda wondered what he was thinking about so hard.

"What is it?" she asked.

Terzić shook his head. Amanda wanted to know what was bothering him, but there was no use pushing him if he wouldn't answer. After a few minutes of complete silence, he looked up at a clock on the wall, and said, "You seem tired. I suggest we continue tomorrow."

Amanda wondered if she had done something to upset him. But if he needed some alone-time to think something over, she wasn't in a position to argue. Also, he was right. It was just past nine, but the jetlag combined with the liquor was making her drowsy.

"Thanks, gladly. Didn't know time zones could be this brutal."

"*Laku noć*, then."

"Good night to you as well. See you tomorrow," she said, and went to her room.

After brushing her teeth, Amanda decided to try the professor's number again. She let the phone ring a dozen times, but nobody picked up.

Why is this so hard?

She sat down and massaged her temples. There had to be some other way to make progress. But if the Red Dove was so obscure that even a seasoned investigator like Terzić had come up empty, what hope did she have?

No, I have to look at this from another angle. What strengths do I have?

What can I do that he wouldn't think of doing?

The internet! Terzić probably didn't have that in 1995. Or now, for that matter—she hadn't seen a single digital device in his house so far. She took out her laptop. Only one Wi-Fi in range and it had no password.

Probably the neighbors...Screw it. If they find out, I'll apologize later.

She found some obscure restaurants, a 'Red Dove Tavern', a business or two and even a subspecies of Asian pigeons called the Red Turtle Dove. But, nothing about a folk tale or "Yugoslavian scary story."

There was one more option... If anyone could find something obscure online, it was Greg. But, wasn't it weird to call him again, just to ask for yet another favor? Then again, the worst he could do was say no.

"Hello, you have reached God. May I take your prayer?"

Amanda rolled her eyes. "I'm curious, Greg. Do you always answer your phone like this?"

"How cheap do you think I am? I always come up with a fresh line on the spot!"

"Charming. What if you ever get a serious call? Like from a recruiter?"

"Even better! If they hang up, they aren't worthy of my genius."

"I'm sure that attitude will get you a job in no time. Ever think about writing a self-help book?"

"Several times. But it would sell too well and ruin the whole industry. I'm abstaining out of solidarity."

"How gracious of you. Listen, I need your help."

"What, again? And here I was, thinking you were a strong, independent woman!"

"Neither strength nor independence will do me much good here."

"Ah, so the plot thickens. Let's have it, I'm all ears."

She brought Greg up to speed about the last week, telling him how she had flown to Serbia, what she had learned and how she and Terzić were stuck.

Greg laughed. "Let me get this straight. Your mother tells you about a supernatural monster that wipes whole villages off the map, and your reaction is 'Cool! I have to see that up close!' Then, when you hit an inevitable roadblock and after even a veteran police detective came up empty, you now expect *me* to dig into a curse whose victims all die gruesomely."

"Exactly."

"Are you actually going out of your way to come up with weirder requests each time?"

"Anything to entertain you, Greg."

"Thanks, I guess? What favor are you calling in this time, by the way?"

"Um…coming up empty here." She put on her most sugary voice. "Pretty please?"

"Great delivery! I'll give it an A-minus, enough to melt the stoniest of hearts, except mine, of course."

Amanda clicked her tongue. "Come on! I put a lot of effort into it. Look, I'll buy you cookies, the deluxe ones."

"Ho ho, the ones from the bakery you got me for my birthday? Now we're talking."

"So, will you do it?"

"One-up a former police star by figuring out what he couldn't in years? Sure, sounds fun. Besides, my pride's still a little hurt for not being able to dig up more on your uncle. Just, um…"

"What?"

"This curse… It won't come after me too, right?"

"Please tell me you're joking."

"Half. I don't like messing with things I don't understand. And you have to admit this thing is creepy."

"Creepy? Good Lord, first my mother, then Tom, now you… Why are you guys all so hysterical about this?"

"Maybe 'cause 'we guys' have a point? I mean, the kid in the woods from your mother's childhood is one thing, but an entire village tearing itself up? Doesn't that make you uneasy?"

"No. There's obviously a rational explanation."

"Spoken like the guy who always dies first, in literally every horror flick ever."

"Yeah, you know what else those flicks are? Fiction."

"So, what's your 'rational explanation' for a whole village suddenly descending into wholesale slaughter?"

"I don't have one yet," Amanda admitted. "But just because I can't explain it doesn't mean the scary boogey-monster did it. Seriously, this is one of humanity's weirdest quirks—we need an explanation for everything, and when we don't have one, we'll just make one up. Then any new evidence that comes along gets twisted to fit the explanation we already believe, no matter how dumb it is."

"Thanks for the psychology lecture, but I already know about confirmation bias."

"Great! All the more important I point it out, then. 'Cause the people affected by it are the least likely to notice."

"Look, I won't argue with you about some curse I barely understand. All I'm saying is, better safe than sorry."

"About a dumb fairy tale? Don't make me laugh."

"Fine, fine. Whatever. I can try, but you know what I'm going to say next, right?"

"That I owe you one after this?"

"Don't be silly. What is it with you and keeping tabs on who owes whom? Although, I certainly won't say no to those cookies…"

"Duly noted. So, what were you going to say?"

"That you shouldn't hold your breath on this one. This might be news to you, but I don't actually have a crystal ball that I can consult when you come up with weird questions. If the Red Dove is as obscure as you say, the chances of me finding anything useful are slim."

"I know. I'm just trying to explore every avenue. Thanks, Greg. Appreciate it."

"Don't mention it. Talk soon."

*

Determined to wake up earlier this time, Amanda had set three separate alarms on her phone. She still managed to turn them all off without waking up. By the time she finally finished drying her hair and getting dressed, it was almost eleven. *I'll have to buy Terzić a box of chocolates for his hospitality. Maybe two— for being such an awful guest who sleeps till noon.*

She found Terzić sitting in the exact spot she had left him, with a phone book and a thick folder in his lap. His eyes were only half-open, with dark patches underneath. She wondered if he had even moved since she had gone to bed.

"Um. *Dobro jutro.* Are you okay?"

"Yes, I am fine."

"Did you have trouble sleeping?"

"No, thank you."

"It's just, well... You look like you sat here all night."

"Almost. I did not sleep much."

"Why, what's wrong?"

"I had to think about a difficult decision. Let us discuss this later. Would you like to eat?"

"Oh yes, please. I'm starving."

Amanda sampled whatever she hadn't tried the day before, including pastries with fillings of meat, cheese or jam. She wondered if Terzić was simply a great cook or if you could get all this deliciousness from the local grocer.

"Where can you buy this?" she asked after trying a delicious salami, hoping to take some home.

"I made it myself."

Amanda looked at him wide-eyed.

"It is a Serbian custom. Many families enjoy making their own cold cuts. Some even hold their own pigs for the purpose."

She nodded in amazement. The 'eat local!' crowd in America had absolutely nothing on the people here.

After a while, Amanda realized she had to stop. *If I eat any more, I'll burst.* She hoped Terzić would be more talkative now. "If you don't mind me asking again, what kept you up all night?"

"I may have a way to obtain the lost evidence we need."

"You do? That's fantastic!"

Terzić remained stony-faced and shook his head. "There are several problems with this approach. Ethical and legal. However, if the Priboj evidence can explain what happened, we both deserve to know. You, by right of your family. I, to finally conclude my investigation."

Was he planning on breaking into some dusty government vault to get the evidence back? He somehow didn't seem the type to do something so reckless.

He looked at the clock and said, "I must go visit an old friend. Could I trouble you to accompany me?"

Amanda nodded, unsure why he had changed the subject so suddenly. And what was the point of dragging her along? Didn't he want her alone in his house? Understandable, but she still wondered what she had done to earn his mistrust.

"Are you ready immediately?"

"Uh, yeah sure."

After twenty minutes, Terzić parked his car in front of a coffeehouse. Amanda could see that it was filled to bursting, even though it was a weekday. Terzić, as gentlemanly as ever, stepped up and held the door for her.

One of the patrons stood up with an expression of happy surprise. "Đorđe!"

He and Terzić exchanged a warm handshake. Then, Terzić introduced the stranger. "Amanda Dousson, Jakov Novak."

While they shook hands, she looked the man over. He was younger than Terzić, maybe late 50s. He looked like a walking stereotype of a government clerk, with a round face, thick-rimmed glasses and almost no hair left. Yet, based on his demeanor and strong handshake, she figured he was more powerful than he looked—this was a man used to giving orders.

Novak gestured for them to sit down. On Terzić's invitation, Amanda ordered coffee, still trying to understand why they were meeting this guy.

Novak spoke first, "It's been a while, old boy. How are you holding up?"

"Good, thank you. How have you been?"

"Frustrated! That's how! Every year, both the regulations and the recruits they send us get worse. When did you leave the force, again?"

"In 2005."

"I wish you'd stayed on. Honestly, the people coming from the academy these days would make you weep."

"It was not my decision to retire."

"Hah, right you are. I read what they wrote— 'Well-deserved retirement' and all that nonsense. They should have kept you on. You would have been worth ten of those modern rookies combined."

Okay, they're former work colleagues. Great. Now she genuinely felt like a third wheel.

"So, why did you want to see me, old boy?" Novak asked as if he had read her thoughts.

"I have a favor to ask."

"Oh absolutely, shoot."

Terzić's sudden tension was completely lost on the cheerful Novak. "Do you remember what happened in 1995? In Priboj?"

"Hmm...Priboj? Oh, right, that massacre. I only heard second-hand. Damn strange business, that was. Never resolved, right?"

"Yes. I am trying to solve it."

Novak roared with laughter. "Of course you are! My God, you really don't know what 'retirement' means, do you?"

Amanda was on the edge of her seat. Novak still hadn't caught on, but looking at Terzić, she could tell something serious was about to happen.

"I need to look at the old evidence," Terzić said.

"Oh sure, anything you need. I'll have it checked out for you. Do you know where it is?"

"Only that it was seized by the BIA."

Novak enthusiastic grin turned into a sad smile. He leaned back in his seat and shook his head.

"I can't."

"Is your position not high enough to give you access?"

"Theoretically, yes. But only if there were an important enough investigation for which these materials would be crucial. You know that."

"Can you not create a pretext? The evidence is old. An inquiry would be unlikely."

"I can't lie for you, Đorđe. The paper trail would kill me."

Terzić bit his lip, a gesture Novak spotted.

"Look, I'm sorry. Anything I can do for you, I will. But I'm not risking the BIA going after me just to dig up some weird story from '95. For what it's worth, it's likely they found nothing of note, so this is a waste of time anyway. On the other hand, if they found something that's eyes only, they'll throw us both in jail. Please understand."

"Amanda here is the niece of one of those who died in Priboj. This 'weird story' still affects people to this day. And they deserve to know."

Amanda fought hard not to grimace at being held up like a lost puppy in an animal shelter commercial. Not that she had a problem with such mind games, but she really wished Terzić had warned her beforehand.

Novak turned to her. "I am sorry for your loss. On behalf of the Serbian police, I personally apologize that we can't tell you what happened. I know that's little consolation, but surely, you appreciate my position. What Đorđe is asking for simply cannot be done."

Amanda nodded. What else was she supposed to do? Argue? Cause a scene? Burst into tears? No matter what she did, she was certain he wouldn't budge. He wouldn't jeopardize his comfortable life for something so insignificant to him.

Terzić sighed as he reached into his pocket and pulled out a photograph. He placed it on the table and slid it across to Novak. It showed a couple clearly having sex, through the window of a cheap hotel room.

Novak picked it up with a puzzled expression, which turned to shock and fear. His mouth fell open as if a hinge had snapped. "You…what…what is this?"

Terzić's face became hard as stone and he pulled himself closer to Novak. He suddenly looked a lot more imposing than usual. "You know what this is," he said, in a menacing tone Amanda had never heard from him before.

"How…how did you get this?" Novak stammered.

"I took it myself."

"You? But...then..."

"Yes. I knew. Ever since the failed raid, I suspected something."

"I had nothing to do with that!"

"Do you think anyone would believe you?"

Terzić leaned forward, fixing Novak with a sharp stare. The air in the room seemed to freeze solid. "I have a box with photographs, audio recordings, eyewitness reports, even a film. You may have been in a legal grey area, but your career would have been over if this had been made public."

Novak's voice faltered. "But...but so what! This is ages old! Decades! Nobody cares anymore!"

"Perhaps. But you are up to get a promotion soon. Or at least, you hope to. I am offering you a way to stop these materials from ending up in the hands of the press."

Amanda's mouth hung open in shock. She barely recognized Terzić. He actually frightened her. So this was how a criminal would have felt, face to face with this man in an interrogation room.

Novak looked at his old colleague in horror. "You are blackmailing me... because of an obsession with some stupid old case?"

"This is not merely about me."

Amanda's face burned. Why had Terzić brought her into this? Now she felt like a co-conspirator, as if she had brought this on Novak's head somehow.

Novak opened his mouth to speak, but Terzić cut him off. "These are my conditions: You will find the evidence that was taken by the BIA. In particular, I know there was a diary among the items recovered. You are to make a copy of it and deliver everything to me, in this coffeehouse, one week from now. In return, I will give you *most* of the materials I have. Do you understand?"

Novak looked like a beaten dog. He stared at the photograph and nodded mechanically.

Terzić got up and placed a bill on the table. Amanda stood up too, the air feeling so thick it might choke her. "May I trouble you to go on ahead? I will be out in a moment." Terzić told her.

She wanted to say 'Goodbye' to Novak, but then realized how awkward she would sound. "Um, I'm…sorry."

Amanda hurried outside. Through the window, she saw Terzić writing something on a piece of paper and handing it to Novak. When he came outside, he said, "Forgive me, I had to ask him something in private. Shall we?"

*

As they were driving back, Terzić remained silent as usual. Eventually, Amanda couldn't stand it anymore. "What on earth happened back there?"

"I used my last trump card."

"Which was what?"

"The story is long. Do you wish to hear it?"

"Yes."

"It goes back to 1981…after years of work, we, the Serbian police, finally had the worst crime lord of the time in custody: Ljubomir Magaš. We hoped he would be imprisoned for life, but he was sentenced to only five years. He appealed the ruling and, contrary to our expectations, the supreme court ordered a retrial. We needed stronger evidence and had little time to find it.

"In August of 1982, after months of investigations, we raided the house of one of his highest-ranking lieutenants, Kristina Mitrović. We knew she was handling Magaš' financial records and were certain she had moved them to her home. But when we arrived, we found the house empty. Devoid of anything but furniture. Even the kitchen cupboards were empty. Anything we could have seized was gone. Mitrović had been tipped off. She even laughed at us when we left her house empty-handed.

"Two months later, Magaš was granted bail. He escaped to Germany and went into hiding. All our hard work, completely undone. I was determined to find out who had betrayed us. Novak was my subordinate at the time, and had been actively involved in the raid. During my investigation, I discovered he was having an affair with Mitrović.

"Over the next two weeks, I shadowed them both. I found no evidence that Novak was a member of Magaš' organization, but felt confident he would confess to it under pressure.

"However, a few days before I could show the evidence I had collected to the commissary, Kristina Mitrović was shot multiple times and thrown into a river. I followed Novak carefully—somebody else from the organization would have to approach him, now that his main contact was dead. Yet, nothing. All his activities remained reputable and legal.

"The only thing I could prove was his affair, but not his fault in the raid's failure. If I released the materials, Novak would be dishonorably discharged and the reputation of the police force severely damaged. Why Novak engaged in the affair, I never found out. Maybe he thought he could turn Mitrović into an informant, maybe her beauty overrode his reason. Either way, with Magaš in Germany, Mitrović dead and no evidence of Novak being a traitor, I could find no value in revealing what I knew. Despite this blunder, Jakov Novak was, and still is, an excellent officer of the law. Over time, I forgot that I had kept his file and the photographs I had taken, until we discussed ways to get the diary and other evidence from Priboj."

"Wow. But if he had a lower rank than you, why would he be able to access the diary when you couldn't?"

"I was never interested in advancement. That would have meant sitting at a desk each day. Novak was different. His main goal was to reach a high position. And he succeeded. He is currently the second highest in command for the organized crime unit of the Serbian police force."

"...and that's the person you decided to blackmail?"

"Yes."

"Well, can't he arrest you? Blackmail is a crime, after all."

Terzić shook his head. "If he did, the photos would be revealed during the trial. Even if he arrested me under false pretenses, he could never be certain that I hadn't given the files for safe-keeping to a friend who would release them afterwards."

"So why hand over anything?"

"I will give him the most incriminating evidence. What I have left will not be sufficient to blackmail him again, but enough to dissuade him from pursuing me."

"I think I get it. But why did you take me with you? Novak didn't seem like the kind of guy to be convinced by my connection to Priboj anyway."

"I had to exhaust every option before playing my trump card. But even if not, I wanted you to see what happened. Should we receive the diary, I want you to know at what cost it was bought."

*

When they got home, Amanda excused herself and went to her room. She had completely forgotten to call Tom. He had to be worried sick by now. But just as she was about to call him, her phone buzzed with a message from Greg.

Dear Agent Scully, please call me ASAP. Important news.

She grinned involuntarily.

"Hello, this is Agent Mulder."

"You *really* don't look like Mulder, Greg."

"I don't know if I should take that emphasis as a compliment or an insult."

"You can ponder that while telling me the important news."

"Smooth, Agent Scully. Well, the news is, I've tried looking everywhere, and I mean *everywhere*, but there's nothing on the Red Dove. It's like it doesn't even exist."

"So why can I almost hear your grin coming over the phone?"

"Don't spoil it! So, remember how we found out about your uncle's village on a forum post? It gave me an idea. I created a script that posted messages in internet forums everywhere, asking if anyone knows something about a Red Dove or strange tales involving one."

"Wow, that's pretty cool."

"Of course it is! It was my idea after all. Most replies were useless, the Red Dove is a legend they vaguely remember, blah blah. But get this. Five replies all told the same story. A small, remote village, the inhabitants dying violently, nobody knowing what happened. Sound familiar?"

"Um, yeah?"

"Here's where it gets weird: the dates."

"The dates? *Plural?*"

"Yup. Two of those replies say it happened in 1995, both from Serbia. I'm guessing they're talking about your village. But the other three…" he paused dramatically. "Two of them say it was 1988. They're both writing from southern Ukraine. The fifth message is from someplace in Brazil and says that the same thing happened over there, in 1974. The same Red Dove, the same massacre, happened three times."

CHAPTER 9

"Isn't that crazy?" Greg asked.

She was too busy thinking to answer. The same massacre? And in such far-away places as Serbia, Ukraine and Brazil? Amanda felt ice spread around her stomach. It was like she could see the outline of a spider web materialize before her.

No! she admonished herself as she fumbled with her necklace. *I'm not wrong! Basic science dictates that there's no such thing as supernatural curses!* But the goosebumps on her arms belied her confidence in the laws of nature. She was struck with a realization: If her mother was right and the Red Dove really did exist, she had placed herself in grave danger coming here.

"Hellooo? Earth to Amanda?"

"Yeah, yeah, I'm here. Just thinking. Look, can I call you back?"

"Uh, yeah, sure. Talk to you later, then."

Amanda hung up and sat down. *Time to take a deep breath.* For all she knew, Greg's 'discovery' was the work of a few internet pranksters who had seen his messages and decided to play an elaborate joke. Even assuming the replies were genuine, those cases weren't necessarily as similar to Priboj as Greg was making them out to be. It could just be a few unexplained deaths and people attributing them to the Red Dove after the fact, like in Tihomir's case. That sure as hell sounded more plausible than some supernatural curse or monster wiping out village after village.

Now then…this is getting interesting. Her uncle had turned out to be a dud, but that didn't mean she had to go back empty-handed. No sir. She had just been given an incredible opportunity—the chance to investigate and maybe even solve a truly mind-blowing mystery. Between Terzić's long years of experience and her knowledge of psychology, she felt they had a genuine chance at cracking this. If all went well, they would soon have the diary from Priboj in their hands. And Greg had opened another avenue of investigation. Brazil was far away, but Ukraine was also in Eastern Europe, right? Just around the corner. *All right, let's get this show started.*

Trembling with excitement, she picked up her phone again. "Hey Greg, me again. So listen. That massacre in Ukraine you mentioned…can you find out where exactly it happened?"

"Why do I get the feeling you're about to do something crazy?"

"Because I'm always doing something crazy?"

"Alright, hit me. What are you up to?"

"I need to find out what happened. The police took everything useful out of Priboj decades ago. But maybe the other villages contain more clues. And since Ukraine is close by…"

"Are you serious?"

"Of course I am. Terzić asked an old friend to dig up some of the old police evidence, but we don't know if he'll come through, and I don't want to sit around twiddling my thumbs. If the villages are linked somehow, I need to know."

"But you went to Serbia to find your uncle, right? You found him, in a way. So why spend this much time and energy going after the Red Dove? What are you hoping for?"

Amanda opened her mouth to answer, but hesitated. After giving it some thought, she said, "Coming here was…depressing. Instead of meeting my uncle, I had to find out he's dead, buried in a crude grave up in some forgotten village. I know this won't bring him back, but if I can't meet him, I at least want to know what took him away."

Greg remained quiet for a long time. She wondered if she hadn't overdone it a bit.

"Fine. I'll get in touch with the people who wrote from Ukraine. Maybe they can tell me more. I'll let you know."

"Thanks Greg! Talk soon."

Amanda pocketed her phone. As she put her hand on the doorknob, her gaze fell on the wardrobe mirror. Her reflected smile slowly melted away, like a cheap mask, leaving only a face of shame. She had just lied to her best friend.

Of course her uncle wasn't her reason for staying. Why would she need to find out what 'took him away'? She didn't need closure for someone she had never even met. No, she was just excited at the prospect of solving a mystery. This investigation could be the adventure of a lifetime. The kind most people could only dream of. One she would be able to tell her friends and family about, decades from now. And if this investigation succeeded, she would be able to prove to her mother that her belief in the Red Dove was stupid. Heck, she could even put it on her CV. How many job applicants could honestly write, 'Helped solve several massacres that left the police dumbfounded'? There was no way she could let this opportunity go to waste.

But something told her that if she had been honest with Greg, he wouldn't have agreed to help her.

Amanda forced herself to smile again and turned away from the mirror. What was she feeling so guilty about? She was about to embark on the greatest journey of her life. Why let a necessary white lie weigh down her conscience?

In the living room, Terzić's expression grew heavy as she told him about the other Red Dove incidents.

"This is troubling," he said when she finished.

"Is it? Greg's information could be faulty. He's getting this from random strangers, after all."

"I know. We require more information."

Way ahead of you, buddy. "Yes. Greg's going to try and locate the village in Ukraine."

"You plan to go there?"

"Isn't that the easiest way of learning more?"

After a short while of thinking, he conceded, "It is."

"I figured that while we wait for Novak, it could be worthwhile to investigate other leads."

"I agree. Shall we go together?"

Amanda gave an imperceptible sigh of relief. After seeing how hard it was to get to Priboj, she couldn't imagine how she was supposed to reach the Ukrainian village on her own. She doubted Terzić spoke Ukrainian, but having someone with her made her feel a lot better. "Oh yes, gladly. But are you sure it's okay? I feel like I'm dragging you all over the place."

"Do not worry yourself. In every policeman's life, there is always at least one case that will keep haunting him. For me, Priboj is that case."

Amanda chuckled. She imagined how boring life had to be for this decorated investigator, with nothing to keep him busy and this case still nagging him. He probably would never admit it, but she suspected he was having fun.

She noticed tiredness creep up on her again. A look at her watch told her that it was barely 8 PM. *Damn jet lag.*

"Would you mind if I went to bed early? The time difference is still getting to me."

"I understand. Laku noć."

*

The next morning, Amanda opened her laptop to find a message from Greg.

Call me ASAP.

"Yes!" Greg *always* found something, didn't he?

"Good morning, princess!" he exclaimed.

"Now that's a greeting I could get used to."

"Sarcasm, Amanda. Sarcasm!"

"Oh come now, we all know that in secret, you worship me."

Greg laughed. "In your dreams, princess."

"So, what have you found?"

"What makes you think I found something?"

"Because you never disappoint?"

"Ah, what beautiful flattery. I feel all warm and fuzzy inside."

"Great! So talk already!"

"Har har, now this, I must savor. Are you that excited for the rabbit that I, Greg the Incredible, am about to pull out of my hat?"

She stomped her foot. "Of course I'm excited. Quit teasing me and speak up!"

"Sheesh. No patience for foreplay. Girls these days…Okay, so I wrote to the people who answered my initial messages and one of them answered back! He's from Ukraine, from a city called Ivano Frank…isk? No, Ivano Fran-ki-vs-k… Christ, how do you pronounce that name? It feels like running your tongue over a cheese-grater."

"How do you know what running your tongue over a cheese-grater feels like?"

"Silence, please. Don't interrupt my epic show-and-tell. So get this, he told me he knows the story because he grew up close to the destroyed village."

"That's fantastic!"

"Wait, it gets better. You owe me an extra batch of those cookies for this… He also told me the name of the village! It's…I have no idea how to pronounce those Cyrillic characters. Yopha Ropa?"

"Uh, probably not like that. Can you send me the name?"

"Yeah, one sec."

Her phone buzzed. *Чорна гора.* "Hmm…It's Ukrainian, so I can't be sure, but I guess I would pronounce it as 'Chorna Hora.'"

"Sounds…somewhat Spanish? But hey, it's a nice change. For once, I don't need to twist my vocal cords into a pretzel to pronounce it. Seriously, what is it with these names? First Priboj and then—"

"No, no, no. Not 'prybosh'. More like 'pre-boy.'"

"Whatever! Jesus, no wonder these villages got destroyed. If I was God and saw my creations living in places with such unholy names, I'd feel compelled to nuke them too."

"A bold theory. I'll be sure to ask God if I meet him."

"Great. Tell him I said hi. He never writes anymore. Anyway, I already checked, and the village isn't on any map. Kind of like yours. And when I asked the guy from Ivano Franki-vv-sk, he seemed reluctant to tell me how to find it."

"But you managed to find a way, yes?"

"Well, about that…" Greg paused. His voice sounded a lot less playful. "Do you know why he was reluctant?"

"No. How would I?"

"He said, and I quote, 'that village is dangerous.' He said it's unsafe, not to mention creepy. There's some weird rumors about people going there and never returning."

"Oh god, not this again. For the last time, I'm not running away from some scary children's story."

"Are you really willing to bet your life on that conviction, Amanda? Look… You know me. I'm not easily impressed. But there's something seriously unsettling about the Red Dove. A kid gets dismembered, a whole village hacks itself up with chainsaws, and now we find out this didn't just happen once? When does this stop just being a string of freak coincidences? You constantly digging deeper feels…dangerous."

Amanda clicked her tongue. "You're starting to sound like my mom."

"Maybe because she has a point? Curiosity killed the cat."

"I'm not a cat."

"Exactly, they at least have nine lives."

"Then I'll just have to make up for the difference through my superior mind."

He sighed. "Your hubris will be your downfall. I get wanting to know what killed your uncle, but are you sure what you're doing is worth it?"

"Aw Greg, you're worried for me? That's sweet."

"Of course I am! I'm…" he paused again. "I'm concerned, okay?"

"Relax. Look, I agree it's a bit uncanny. But that's just because we don't understand it yet. My bet is on some freak disease that drives people insane, like some evolved strain of rabies. Or a government experiment gone wrong? Or heck, maybe it's like Jonestown—the villagers all belonging to some crazy cult and thinking judgement day has come."

"And crazy cults, government mind-control rays and mutated rabies don't impress you?"

"Any one of those is long gone by now, so no."

"What about the fact that it happened in places as far apart as Ukraine and Brazil? Not just the same massacre, but the same cause, too?"

"We don't know that. Maybe the Red Dove just got blamed for it later. Like I said, confirmation bias is a powerful force."

"I really hope this all is just 'confirmation bias.' For your sake." Greg took a deep breath. "All right…I'll tell you how to get to the village, but only if you promise me something."

"Yes?"

"Promise me you'll be careful. That if this gets any creepier, you'll cut your losses and let this damn thing go. Oh, and also…promise me you'll keep in touch, so I know everything's alright."

"Since when are you so serious? But okay…I promise."

Greg sighed. "Alright, I hope I don't regret this. The guy wouldn't tell me how to get to the village, but when I told him I had a friend in Serbia with a family connection to all of this, he said he'd meet you to talk things over. Since I didn't know how long it would take you to get to Ukraine, I set the meeting for the day after tomorrow, May 27th. You'll be meeting in Ivano…ah screw it, Ivano-whatever. Ten o'clock sharp, in a park across from Hotel Nadiya. You can stay there for convenience. He said he'll wait on one of the benches and be wearing a brown leather jacket."

Amanda wrote everything down. "Thanks, Greg. You really outdid yourself this time."

"Good luck convincing him. Let me know how it goes. And remember—you promised!"

Amanda got dressed and stormed into the living room. Terzić, carrying a bowl of pastries, looked surprised. "I had not expected you so early in the morning."

"My jet lag is getting better. But listen! Great news! Greg found the location of the village in Ukraine. Or rather, he set up a meeting with somebody who knows."

"Your friend is very skilled. Who is this person we will meet?"

"No idea. Greg just told me how to recognize him and where to meet him."

"When is the meeting?"

"Saturday, at 10 o'clock, in a city called Ivano-Fran…something."

"Ivano-Frankivsk?"

"That's the one!"

Terzić rubbed his chin. "It is not far from here. We can drive."

"How long will it take?"

"I estimate twelve to sixteen hours. We may choose to stay for a night along the way."

"Wow. That's long! Why don't we take a flight?"

"I suspect having our own car will prove useful."

Terzić walked over to a small cabinet and picked up a telephone. When she heard a weird clicking noise, she looked more closely—Terzić was using a rotary phone. She pressed a hand to her mouth to stifle her laughter. The only time she had seen one of those was in a museum. But then again, it really fit in with everything else here.

"Good morning, Đorđe Terzić here…Yes, I require the jeep…for five days at least, maybe longer. Today, if possible… Yes… Thank you. Goodbye."

"That went fast," Amanda commented.

"Yes. We will be able to use the jeep."

"Doesn't your neighbor ever need it?"

"He had a stroke several years ago and cannot drive. Whenever I need his car, I can rely on him. In return, I drive him when he needs me to."

"Oh, the poor guy."

"Yes. Let us eat."

*

After breakfast, Terzić said, "If we wish to arrive on time, we should leave soon." He spread out a map on the table. "We are here, and Ivano-Frankivsk is here. The fastest way will be to cross Romania and stop there for a night. I suppose…Arad might be a good place to stop."

"Okay, and then tomorrow, we continue to Ivano-Frankivsk?"

"We will probably arrive in the evening. Then we can meet your friend's contact the next morning, as planned. Two nights should be all we require for now. We could be back here by Sunday."

"That sounds reasonable. Hang on," Amanda said. She went to her room and came back with her laptop. While it started up, she said, "I'll book the hotels from here, then we won't have to go searching after a long drive."

Terzić looked at her laptop with an expression that said, *this alien technology is beyond me.*

For Arad, she selected a small hotel with good ratings, and for Ivano-Frankivsk she chose the Hotel Nadiya Greg had recommended. She wondered if Greg might be pranking her by putting her in the worst red-light district hotel he could find, but the ratings looked okay and a joke like that seemed a step too far, even for Greg. She hit the button to confirm. "All done. We can leave anytime."

"The internet really is convenient. Let us begin preparations."

Amanda went back to her room. When she stuffed her phone into her bag, she remembered she hadn't called Tom once this whole time—she'd just sent him a single text message. He had to be getting worried by now. After six rings, he finally picked up.

"Tom Lewis?" he answered sleepily.

"Hi Tom, it's me. Were you asleep?"

"Yeah. Do you have any idea what time it is? It's almost 3 AM over here."

"Oh damn, sorry. Just called you on a whim and didn't think of the time zone difference."

"Plus, I've been working late. But given that I've had no signs of life from you, I'll take this over nothing at all."

"I know, I know, I'm sorry. I wanted to call you earlier, but something always came up."

"So, how are you?"

"In order of events since arriving here: Frustrated, depressed, curious and now excited."

"Does that mean you found your uncle and are now on your way to see him?"

"No, sadly. Turns out he really is dead."

"I'm sorry to hear that."

"Well, you don't know the half of it. For starters, my mother wasn't entirely wrong—Mirko really was killed in some freak massacre."

"Wait a second..." Tom said, his voice now fully awake. "Massacre?"

Keeping it short, Amanda told him of the newspaper article, her visit to the village and her upcoming journey to Ukraine. She left out the part about Terzić blackmailing Novak, figuring she didn't need Tom freaking out even more right now.

"Okay, hang on a second... You confirmed your uncle is dead and there's no more reason to stay—but instead of admitting your mother was right, you're doubling down?"

"Confirming his death isn't good enough. If he had died in the war or heck, some stupid traffic accident, I could have accepted that. But not like this. I want to know why he died."

"I get it. Sofija was right about your uncle, so now you want to at least prove her wrong about the Red Dove thing, correct?"

"That's such an awful thing to say, Tom. Imagine how you would feel if your mother died and you asked how, and the reply was 'from a super-scary curse'. That's no answer. I want to know what this Red Dove is and how and why it killed my uncle."

"Yes, yes. As usual, you have the most noble of intentions. Naturally, that didn't include calling me. Of course, for Greg, you did find time. And now you're going to Ukraine, of all places? Are you out of your mind? How many people do you know who would even find the place on a map, much less go there?"

"Okay, so it's not a popular tourist spot. What of it?"

"You don't know the language, you don't know the country or the culture, and you're chasing something your mother is terrified of. Have you at least told her?"

"I'll tell her when I get home. Then she can't freak out about evil ghosts coming after me."

"Don't you feel the least bit of shame? Your original excuse doesn't fly anymore. There's no more surprise family reunion for you to orchestrate. She deserves to know what you're doing. Especially in case something happens to you over there."

"There's no point in scaring her now. Nothing will happen Tom, I promise."

Neither of them spoke and the seconds ticked by. Finally, Tom broke the silence. "All right, I can see that you won't listen to reason. As usual."

"What the hell is that supposed to mean?"

"It means that I have to get ready for work in less than three hours and I'm too tired to argue. Do whatever you think you have to do."

"I don't need your permission, Tom, but thanks anyway. Sleep well."

"Bye," he said and hung up.

Amanda stood up and threw her mobile phone on the bed. Why was Tom even surprised that she preferred to call Greg? He could be an insufferable smartass, but at least he wasn't so judgmental and patronizing all the time.

Oh, whatever. She had a long drive ahead. No point in brooding over Tom being a killjoy. She packed her backpack with her remaining underwear, toiletries and her laptop, figuring it could be useful to look things up or change her bookings. Outside, she found Terzić loading the jeep. She was amazed at the variety of items Terzić was packing—a hammer, a flashlight, screwdrivers, a rope and even two large, woolen blankets.

"What will we need all that for?"

"Hopefully, nothing. But it is best to be prepared."

*

One quick coffee later, they set off. Terzić took the wheel, but Amanda assumed they would switch places halfway. She watched the landscape pass by, though the endless monotony of the Serbian countryside soon tired her out. She opened her backpack and took out her notebook. In spite of so much happening, she hadn't used it so far. *Some detective I am, not even writing down my findings.* On the first free page, she jotted down what she had discovered about the Red Dove—from her mother, the newspaper article, from Terzić, and from Greg. She had learned a lot since coming here, but it felt like for every answer, three new questions popped up.

After four hours of driving, she wondered when Terzić would finally stop so they could switch places. Did he actually intend to drive the entire way himself? "Haven't we passed the halfway point already?"

"Yes, I believe so."

"Shouldn't I take the wheel for a while? You've been driving for hours without a break."

"It is no trouble."

"Please, I insist. I know how exhausting it is to be behind the wheel this long."

"I will look for an opportunity to stop, then."

Half an hour later, Terzić parked at a gas station. They refueled and he bought some maps of the area. It was only then Amanda realized that the car didn't have GPS and Terzić had been driving without navigation.

As she slid behind the steering wheel, she realized her last time driving a manual transmission was years ago. She tried to look calm and in control, but immediately stalled the engine. Only on her third try did she manage to back out of the parking lot. The jeep bucked and howled as she drove back on the highway. She'd take a while to get used to this. Terzić, mercifully, didn't say a word.

*

The city of Arad was a curious mix of traditional and exotic architecture. Some buildings were old and in need of repair, others were new and fancy. Some were plain, others had elaborate domes or spires on top. There were concert halls and statues, plazas and churches. It felt like a brilliant mosaic, different from anything Amanda knew in America. She considered booking an additional night on the way back. Then again, tourism wasn't why she was here.

Since they had left in a hurry, she had forgotten to print a route to the hotel. But Terzić's maps saved the day. She was impressed at how effortlessly he guided them to their destination. *Guess that's how people got by without GPS in the old days.*

Amanda parked the jeep in the hotel's garage. When they checked in, the receptionist smiled and asked Terzić in English, "Have you been to Arad before?"

Terzić looked embarrassed and mumbled, "My English not good is."

"No, we haven't," Amanda answered for him. *No wonder he mispronounces my name so badly.*

They had dinner in a nearby restaurant, then wished each other good night. While Amanda was getting ready for bed, she remembered that she had to try calling the professor again.

She counted the rings. Ten, eleven, twelve…She was about to hang up when she heard a click at the other end of the line.

"Marković?"

Finally! "Good evening, am I speaking to Professor Dragan Marković?"

"You are."

"Sorry for calling you in the evening, I tried several times over the past few days, but I never managed to get through."

"That's quite all right. I wasn't home. What can I do for you?"

"It's about your book on Yugoslavian folk tales. I'm currently researching something called the 'Red Dove' and was wondering if you'd come across it during your research for the book."

"Hmm… It's been quite a while since I wrote that book. But yes, I believe there was an entry on it in there."

"Really? That's fantastic! Do you know where I could still buy your book? I haven't been able to find it anywhere."

"Sadly, it's been out of print for a while and there were never that many copies to begin with. But if you only need the chapter on the Red Dove, I could fax it to you."

Ever heard of e-mail my friend? "I'm currently traveling. I will ask the hotel if they have a fax machine. Would it be okay if I called you again tomorrow and gave you a number then?"

"Absolutely. That'll give me time to find the chapter."

"Thank you again. In that case, until tomorrow. *Zbogom.*"

"*Laku noć.*"

Amanda's fingers were jittery when she pressed the button to hang up. Finally, a small step forward. She just hoped the hotel in Ivano-Frankivsk would have a dusty fax machine lying around somewhere. Investigating the Red Dove really did feel like squeezing water from a rock. Before she could call the hotel, though, she saw she had received a text.

She smiled, wondering if Greg had dug up something more. Then her muscles tensed up.

It was from her mother.

Call me when you get this please.

Damn. Her mother never wrote messages like this. Amanda gulped, but decided to get it over with.

"Sofija Dawson," her mother answered.

"Mom, it's me."

"Amanda, where are you?"

Lying was pointless. First that text and now a weird question like that? Her mother probably knew everything already. "I'm driving to Ukraine to find out more about the Red Dove."

For a few painful moments, her mother didn't reply. All she heard was the buzzing of the shaky, long-distance connection. Then, her mother asked in a choked voice, "Why...Amanda, why?"

"Because, Mom...I had to know."

"You 'had to know?' We had an agreement! I told you everything! In return, you promised not to go to Serbia. You promised! Do you realize what you have done? What danger you are in?"

"Oh, enough already! What 'horrible danger'? You all keep acting like Serbia's the edge of hell. Plus, you didn't tell me 'everything.' All I got from you were pointless superstitions! Until I came here, I wasn't even sure Mirko was dead."

"But he is, isn't he?"

"Yes, but that's—"

"So, come home already! Why are you still not satisfied?"

"Because that's not good enough! I want to know why he died. I want to know what happened in that village. Spooky curses be damned!"

Again, silence. Finally, she heard sobs coming over the phone. Her mother said in a meek voice, "Amanda, I beg you. Please, please, come back. Before it's too late."

A pang of guilt hit her like a fist. She had never intended to make her mother cry. Even so, she couldn't back down now, or she would have to agree to fly back home. "Mom, I'm sorry… for not telling you earlier and for yelling like that. I know you're afraid, but look, I went to the village in Serbia. There is *nothing* scary there, I promise. I even found Mirko's grave. If you ever want to visit it, I can tell you how to get there."

"No. I hope that you are right and that you are still safe, but I cannot take the risks you have taken."

"Look, all I'm doing now is looking into it a bit more. If I'm not successful, I'll give up. And if I do see any danger, I'll stop. But so far, nothing even remotely scary has happened."

"Amanda, by the time 'something scary' happens, it will be too late. Please, I know how driven you are to always know everything, but please, *please*, give this up and come home. Some things are for God alone to know."

"I'm sorry Mom, I can't. If I leave now, all this will have been for nothing. The answers are right around the corner! And I promise, I'll be careful."

Her mother kept crying. "Will you at least call me? Let me know you're all right?"

"I will, Mom."

The call went silent again, until her mother said, "I will pray for your safety and hope God will forgive your hubris. I will let you sleep. It has to be late where you are."

"Yes. Thanks, Mom. Sleep well."

As she hung up, Amanda noticed she was fumbling with her necklace again. She finally understood why her mother kept doing that with her crucifix when she was nervous. Somehow, the gesture was calming.

She couldn't even imagine how disappointed her parents were. But were her desires truly so wrong? Yes, she had spent a lot of money on this, but it was hers, right? Her money, her time. So why did she feel guilty for using it in a way she enjoyed?

Should she abandon it all? Fly back and try to make amends? But even if she could leave right this instant, the damage was done. And it wouldn't save any money, either. All the hotels were already booked and the return flight wouldn't be cheaper just because she left earlier. Better, then, to enjoy this adventure to its fullest, and to face the consequences later. Then, at least, she would have something to show for it. Others her age were dropping ecstasy at dubious parties and waking up next to people they didn't know. Compared to that, what did she have to be ashamed of? Besides, Terzić had already blackmailed a police chief. She couldn't tell him she was backing out now.

Hang on…how did Mom find out anyway? Amanda clenched her necklace when the obvious answer came.

Tom, you little snitch.

She looked at her watch. He had to be at work now. No matter. She had a number that would connect straight to his desk. He'd told her he wasn't supposed to take personal calls and to only use this for emergencies. She also remembered a saying, 'Don't act when you're angry'. Psychology 101. *Screw that.* She was too mad to listen to fortune cookie wisdom right now.

"Tom Lew—"

"It's me."

"Amanda? Sorry, I can't talk to you right—"

"Make time. What were you thinking?"

"What do you mean?"

"Don't insult my intelligence, Tom. Why did you tell Mom?"

Tom didn't reply.

"Are your corporate overlords looking over your shoulder? Don't worry, you can tell them I'm a client. Unlike you, I won't rat you out."

He cleared his throat and said in a low voice, "I told her because you wouldn't. She had a right to know."

"*I'll* be the judge of who should know about *my* activities."

"Not when it affects other people. Do you even know how crazy you sounded on the phone? I was concerned for you."

"You have a strange way of showing concern. I hope stabbing me in the back was worth it, 'cause it changes nothing."

"What…you're staying?"

"Oh, sorry, did I just mess up your plan?"

He sighed. "Jesus, you're in a bad mood."

"I didn't take a 14-hour flight to come back empty-handed. I'll finish what I started and figure out what really happened to Uncle Mirko and those other villagers."

"Is this what this is to you? Some kind of cool mystery you're going to solve when nobody else can? You're not Sherlock Holmes."

"Don't patronize me—it won't change my decision. I'm staying."

"You called me at the office just to tell me that? Thanks a bunch, but I have work to do."

"I called you to tell you how upset I am. But yeah, your damn portfolios are way more important, I get it. Have fun at work."

She hung up. What an insufferable jerk. He had damaged her relationship with her mother, all because she hadn't come home the moment he told her to. She was so furious…if Tom had been in the room, she might have slapped him.

What a way to end the day, she thought, and buried her face in her pillow.

*

The next morning, she felt groggy. After tossing and turning for two hours, she had finally drifted into an uneasy sleep. She still felt betrayed, but she regretted calling Tom. It hadn't accomplished anything.

Then again, neither would brooding over it now. She had another long drive ahead of her and Terzić was probably already waiting, as usual. Before joining him downstairs for breakfast, she called Hotel Nadiya in Ukraine. "Yeah, hi, Amanda Dawson speaking. I have a room booked for later today and I'm expecting a very urgent fax. Would it be possible for me to receive a fax on your machine?"

"Yes, of course. We can receive your fax for you and you may retrieve it when you check in."

Amanda wrote down the number the receptionist told her, then relayed it to Professor Marković. After she took a shower, she realized she was running out of underwear. She'd need a washing machine soon, or a clothing shop as a stop-gap measure. It was strange to realize that a full week had already passed since she left Chicago.

As expected, Terzić was already waiting for her in the hotel's dining room. Amanda thanked her lucky stars that the breakfast included free coffee. It was the cheapest, most lukewarm coffee she had ever tasted, but right now, the caffeine was all she cared about.

"I suggest we leave within the hour," Terzić said. "Then we should reach Ivano-Frankivsk before 6 o'clock. Be aware that Ukraine and Romania are one hour ahead of Serbia."

Amanda adjusted her watch and said, "I'll drive the first half this time."

They finished breakfast and checked out. Before leaving, Amanda ducked into a shop and bought enough underwear to last her for another week, plus a comfy-looking shirt and pants. They weren't the most stylish clothes she'd ever bought, but they would do.

Driving the jeep felt easier than yesterday, but the endless monotony of the landscape was still a challenge. Like Serbia, Romania was nothing but fields and an occasional village in between. After three hours, Terzić offered to switch and she happily agreed.

While crossing the border, Amanda realized she hadn't looked up Ukraine's visa requirements. But, she was lucky—the Customs officer raised an eyebrow when he saw Amanda's blue passport, but ultimately waved them through when she told him she and Terzić were on a sightseeing trip.

Four hours later, they finally reached Ivano-Frankivsk. Now it was Amanda's turn to read maps, but it was much harder than she had thought. She had to constantly orient the map the right way and make sense of all the small roads with Ukrainian street names. Plus, she barely had any time before the right street passed by. She led them down a few wrong turns, but eventually, they found the right address.

Hotel Nadiya had a colorful front, painted with crisscrossing patterns of red, blue and yellow. It looked more like a casino than a hotel. Again, Amanda wondered if this was Greg's idea of a joke. But right now, she was too tired to really care.

At the reception desk, Terzić let her do all the talking. After checking in, she asked, "Has a fax arrived by any chance?"

"A moment please." The receptionist checked a filing cabinet, but came back empty.

"I'm sorry, nothing was deposited for you."

"Okay, thanks." Of course, the professor had forgotten. She would have to call him again later. Right now, though, she was hungry. Lucky for her, the hotel had its own restaurant. Terzić, as usual, didn't eat much and finished before her. They wished each other good night and headed to their rooms.

Amanda changed into her shorts and t-shirt and lay down. The drive had been more exhausting than she had anticipated. And thanks to those phone calls yesterday, she hadn't slept well, either.

If only Mom would be more rational about this…

She took out her notebook and reviewed her notes.

Red Dove
Old Serbian fairy tale? Known to Mom since childhood. Tihomir killed and mutilated after reciting song.

Priboj, logging village. Population: 67. Destroyed in July 1995.
Total massacre. Village empty on visit, nothing left. Police found
Red Dove in drawings and letters. Cause or consequence of
destruction?
    Greg discovery: Red Dove happened two more times:
    Ukraine (1988)—Name: Chorna Hora. Must ask Greg's contact
for more info.
    Brazil (1974)—No info yet. Ask Greg if Ukraine doesn't pan out.

She drank a glass of water. If—and this was purely for the sake of argument—
if the Red Dove was real, then she had to admit, a curse capable of driving all
the people in a village to slaughter each other was a scary thought. But that
didn't make it a reality. Hopefully, tomorrow would finally bring some answers
that would explain this mystery.

The telephone's shrill ringing ripped her from her thoughts.

"Good evening, a fax for you has just arrived."

"Thanks! I'll be right there."

Amanda jumped up, threw her clothes on again, and rushed down the
hallway. When the elevator took too long to arrive, she took the stairs, two steps
at a time. People she passed looked at her as if she was crazy, but she didn't care.
She was finally about to get her hands on a huge missing piece of the puzzle.

The fax was a single sheet of paper. Amanda folded it and went back to her
room. The excitement was killing her, but she didn't want to be disturbed while
reading it.

She threw herself on the bed and unfolded the paper. The copy was so bad,
the text was barely legible. It looked like a page from a dictionary, with entry
after entry on folk tales. *No wonder it went out of print.* The entries on the page
included *The Radish and the Onion*, *The Ravens of Yesterday*, and finally:

    <u>The Red Dove</u> *(or: The Curse of the Red Dove)*
    Date and area of origin unknown. Passed on mostly orally, few
    to no written textual sources.

Sometimes described as a malignant specter or demon, but most often as an omen or curse that brings death.

Written sources are often conflicting due to mostly oral transmission. Subject of a poem:

Hush baby hush,
Hurry hurry go to sleep
Quiet now and do not weep
Be still and hide your fear
Its eyes as black as coal
It's come to take your soul
Hush baby hush,
The Red Dove's almost...here."

Amanda stared at the page. *That's...a lullaby.* What sane mother would ever think of putting her child to sleep with lyrics like this? Was this the song that had ostensibly cost Tihomir his life?

Her excitement quickly faded. Aside from finally learning that damned song, there was nothing on that page that could shed any light on Priboj's destruction.

Then again...She could get *one* use out of it. She took an exaggerated breath and sang the lullaby aloud, line by line, with its strange and broken rhythm.

"*The Red Dove's almost...here.*"

A dramatic performance. Worthy of a standing ovation, if she'd had an audience. The seconds ticked by as she waited for a Red-Dovian monster to barge through the door and dismember her. Or at least for a bolt of lightning to zap her.

"Aaaaand...Nothing! Who woulda thunk it?"

At least, she would be able to tell her mother that she had sung the song and—surprise!—no Red Dove. She folded the paper up and—

"Ow!"

On her left index finger, tiny droplets of blood were pooling on a fine papercut. Amanda grabbed a tissue and pressed it on her finger until the bleeding stopped. She looked at the folded paper she'd dropped on the nightstand and laughed.

What a fearsome curse. With the power to give me...a paper cut! Maybe if I recite the song again, I'll bump my toe on the bed?

She decided to leave out the paper cut when she told her mother about reciting the poem, or she'd never hear the end of it.

CHAPTER 10

Amanda was lying on a rough surface. She stretched out her hands and felt...earth? She opened her eyes—it was still dark. She turned on her back and saw the full moon, dyed a glowing, fiery orange. She vaguely remembered that the moon changed color during an eclipse. Was there an upcoming eclipse? She didn't remember. All her memories were a haze.

She got to her knees and looked around. The moonlight illuminated a flat, endless plain. Not a single object or creature in sight. No animals, rivers, buildings or mountains. No wind, movement or sound. Just grey earth below and the red moon above.

Amanda looked down and saw she was naked. She covered herself, but then remembered there was nobody around to see her anyway. She wasn't even cold, or warm. It was as if temperature didn't exist here. But where was *here*?

Oh, I'm dreaming. But her thoughts were so vivid, so clear. It didn't feel like a dream at all. It made her uncomfortable. If it was just a dream, why did it not feel like one? Being naked also bothered her, bothered her; it made her feel vulnerable somehow.

Was this really a dream? If so, pinching yourself was supposed to wake you up, right? She grabbed her skin and twisted, wincing at the pain. But the landscape didn't change. There was still nothing but lifeless earth in every direction.

"Hello! Anyone here?"

Not even an echo. Amanda tried again, screaming at the top of her voice, but her cry simply disappeared into the emptiness around her.

She decided to start walking. What else was there to do here, after all? As she took the first step, something shifted behind her.

"Amanda…" a voice whispered.

She whirled around. There was nothing behind her. It was as if the darkness itself had talked.

"Where am I?" she asked.

"Amanda…!" the voice whispered behind her again, louder this time. The voice felt unpleasant, like a screeching violin string.

She turned around again and gasped. The flat plain was now filled with obelisks, perfectly rectangular and black, about half of Amanda's size. The stones radiated outwards and away from her in an alien symmetry.

She approached the closest obelisk, touched the black stone and instantly snatched her hand away. The stone felt extremely unpleasant, smooth and freezing cold, like touching a block of ice.

Strange runes appeared on every obelisk, glowing in the same orange as the moon. She had never seen such characters before and yet she knew what they were. Names. Names of people no longer alive. She was standing on a timeless, endless graveyard.

"Amaaaaandaaaa…" came the voice again, like a thousand fingernails scratching on a chalkboard.

This time, she knew where it came from. An obelisk about six feet away. She walked closer. It looked like all the others. The runes meant nothing to her. And yet, her fingers felt strangely drawn to them, as if touching them would allow her to read them.

Amanda drew a deep breath and stretched out her hand, wincing as she touched the icy stone. Slowly, she traced out the top row of runes, character by character. When she reached the last rune, the meaning suddenly materialized, and she shrunk back: "Mirko." It was the tomb of her uncle.

Something moved to her side. She swung around, but everything remained still. Another movement to her left. She turned, but again, she was too late.

Then it happened to her right. Every time she looked, the movement ceased, only to reappear elsewhere. This thing…or was it things? They were always just outside her vision.

"What are you?" she asked the darkness. "What do you want!"

Something moved again, closer this time. Whatever it was, it was slowly approaching her, stone by stone. The air became heavy and difficult to breathe. Sweat ran down her face as she looked around, trying to predict the next movement. There it was! Only three stones over. Something dark and foggy, untouched by the moon's light. It had no real shape, but seemed about her size and was moving in an unsettling, creeping way.

Like a living shadow.

Something moved to her left again, just two obelisks away. Her confusion turned to panic, and she broke into a run. She passed one grave after another, a different name inscribed on each. It was so hard to breathe, but she was driven on by a single thought—she had to escape. If this thing caught her…something terrible would happen.

She felt it chasing after her. A screeching noise behind her, growing ever closer. No matter how hard she pushed herself, the thing caught up inch by inch.

Something cold and sharp touched her. It pierced her ankle and pulled. She fell over and barely managed to put her arms in front of her as she hit the ground. She tried to kick with her leg and hit nothing but air. The cold, sharp touch settled on her shoulder. A flaring pain, like a spike of ice, pinning her to the ground. She was lifted from her shoulder, as if hung from a meat hook. Amanda squeezed her eyes shut. A frozen breath enveloped her as the thing's claws settled on her forehead. All she could do was scream as the claw slowly sank into her.

*

Amanda's piercing cry echoed loudly. She flailed to get the monstrous shadow off her. It took her several moments to realize she wasn't on the endless graveyard anymore. She was back in the hotel, lying on her bed.

She breathed heavily as she sat up, closed her eyes and massaged her temples. "What…was that?" She was soaked with sweat and the air was unbearably hot. She drew back the curtains and opened the window. The city lights of Ivano-Frankivsk glittered quietly in front of her. Amanda sat on the windowsill and tried to get her breathing under control. *It's all right. It was just a dream.*

But *what* a dream. She could still feel the black claws on her forehead, cutting into her. The science behind dream interpretation was flimsy at best, but even she had to wonder whether there wasn't some deeper meaning behind that nightmare. The mere thought still gave her goosebumps.

How was she supposed to fall asleep after this? She looked at her watch. 3:29 AM. She had to be at the park in a bit over six hours. She sighed and went back to her bed. It was doused in sweat. She flipped the mattress around and lay back down. *Let's hope this was the last of it.*

*

"*Dobro jutro.* Are you feeling ill?" Terzić asked at breakfast

"That obvious, huh? The room was too hot and I had a really bad dream."

"I agree, it was a warm night."

Amanda poured herself some coffee, hoping it would refresh her for the meeting later.

"The village's name was Chorna Hora, yes?" Terzić asked. "I fear it is as obscure as Priboj. This morning, I asked in the hotel and on the street, but no one who spoke Serbian was familiar with it."

"Greg's contact is our only hope, then. Oh, by the way, I finally reached the professor who wrote that book on Yugoslavian folk tales." She reached into her pocket and handed Terzić the fax.

He studied it for a minute. "Interesting. But it does not tell us much."

"My thoughts exactly. Let's hope the village isn't also a disappointment."

The park was right behind the hotel. Terzić and Amanda strolled down one of the paths until they reached the only place with benches. Amanda looked at her watch: 9:52. Just a few minutes now. She played with her necklace to steel her nerves. Would Greg's contact be able to tell them more? Would he even show up? What was she supposed to say to Terzić if this all turned out to be a prank by some moron on the internet?

No, I have to trust Greg. He wouldn't fall for something like this…

At ten, almost to the second, a short, thirty-something man walked past them and sat on one of the benches. He was wearing a brown leather jacket.

Amanda took a deep breath and walked up to him. "Hi, I'm Amanda. Are you who we're supposed to meet?"

"I believe so." He offered his hand. "Roman Kostenko. Please, call me Roman."

"Nice to meet you. I'm Amanda Dawson, this is Đorđe Terzić."

"Terzić? That sounds Slavic. Where are you from?"

"Serbia," Amanda replied when Terzić looked confused.

"Unfortunately, I don't speak the language. I hope English will do. Please." Roman motioned them to sit down. "Your friend said you were looking for information on Chorna Hora?"

Amanda was glad Roman's English was so good. He had an accent, but his grammar was great.

Roman continued, "I was surprised to see what your friend wrote. I thought nobody remembered that old village anymore. What do you need to know?"

"Anything, really. What kind of village was it? What happened there?"

"Chorna Hora was established by a coal mining company in the 70s. The company later abandoned it, leaving the workers behind. They kept working the mine illegally, selling the coal locally, until, one day, all shipments stopped. Later, news emerged that all the miners had died."

"How?"

"Nobody knows. Just that it was very violent."

"Wasn't there some kind of investigation?"

"Some of the neighboring villages tried to get the police involved, but since the miners were working illegally, the local administration wasn't interested. In their mind, a few people started a fight and the ensuing violence dispersed the village. Case closed."

"How did the Red Dove come into all of this?"

"Ever since the villagers were found dead, there have been strange rumors. Most of them mentioned *chervonyy holub*—the Red Pigeon."

Meaning Amanda's theory– the Red Dove being blamed after the fact—was still a possibility.

"Can you tell me how to get to the village?"

Roman paused for a moment. "Before I tell you, I have a question for you: What is your interest in all of this? Your friend online mentioned a family connection?"

"In 1995, the same thing happened in Serbia. All inhabitants of a village called Priboj were found dead under similar, mysterious circumstances. The Red Dove was blamed for that, too."

Roman's face darkened.

She went on, "My uncle died in that village in Serbia. Mr. Terzić here was the chief investigator of the massacre, but the case remains unsolved. We're hoping to find some answers here."

"I see. What you are saying is pretty frightening. It was similar here. I was ten at the time, living in a tiny village not too far from Chorna Hora. I still remember the miners bringing coal and selling it to my parents at discount prices. One day, they stopped coming. Later, the rumors began circulating; of the Red Dove having come and 'dozens of corpses' being found. My parents forbade me to even go in the direction of the cursed village. They said that if I did, the Red Dove would come for me, too."

A frozen tingle traveled down Amanda's back. Roman's words were so similar to her mother's, it gave her an uncanny sense of déjà vu. "So you've never gone to Chorna Hora?"

"No. Even if the rumors were false, I never had any reason to go."

"But you know how to get there?"

Roman looked up at the sky as if searching for an answer. "I am usually not in favor of disturbing the dead. I understand your reasons, but I still must advise you not to go there."

"Why?"

"I heard stories of people going up there after the massacre, like you to find out what happened, or to show some decency and bury the dead. Some of those who went never came back. Those who did were scarred from the experience and never spoke of what they saw." He shook his head. "That village is a bad place. Even the local hikers avoid the ruins."

"It can't be that bad, right?"

"I don't know. I hope not, for your sake." Roman looked into the distance and rubbed his chin. "Alright…Let's make a deal. I've been planning to visit my parents, who still live in the same nearby village. If you take me with you and promise to pick me up again in the evening when you return to Ivano-Frankivsk, I will tell you how to get to Chorna Hora."

Amanda turned to Terzić and explained what Roman had just said. Terzić nodded. She said, "Okay, deal. When can we go?"

"Right now, if you like."

"Sounds good. We're parked over there," she said and pointed toward the hotel parking garage.

*

Roman knew the area well, and guided them easily through the city. Since Amanda didn't have to read maps this time, she was able to get a better look at Ivano-Frankivsk. Ukraine didn't have the most glamorous reputation in America, but this city was charming. The architecture was simple, yet older and sturdier than anything back home. Plenty of greenery gave the city a fresh and natural look. Maybe she could return someday as a tourist, to take in all the sights in peace.

After half an hour, they left Ivano-Frankivsk behind. When Roman wasn't giving too many directions anymore, Amanda asked, "Is there anything else you can tell me about Chorna Hora?"

"I don't know all that much myself. It was built like many other villages like it—prospectors found coal reserves in the mountains and a mining company built a village to house workers and save on labor and transportation costs. The returns from the mine were never good, though. The ground here doesn't have a lot of natural resources. It was a miracle they even found the little coal they did, hence the name—Chorna Hora means 'black mountain.' Furthermore, the deeper a mine goes, the more maintenance it needs. Eventually, the costs rose so high that the company abandoned the project and fired the workers."

"That's harsh."

Roman nodded. "In such cases, the villagers sometimes disperse, leaving a ghost town behind. But often, the miners have nothing except their houses and their clothes, so they keep working. Illegal mines are a problem to this day in Ukraine, but neither the state nor the mining companies can do much against it. Not that it matters. The mines are eventually abandoned anyway."

"Do the mines just run dry?"

"No. It's because when a mine is not adequately maintained, it will eventually attract ground water. Most illegal miners don't have access to modern machines and pumps, so the mines end up flooding and becoming unusable."

"You know a lot about this."

"I studied at the university of oil and gas in Ivano-Frankivsk and now work for one of the major iron ore companies," Roman said, with a touch of pride.

"But why do the miners stay when they have to abandon the mine soon anyway?"

"Because they are desperate. They typically work in shifts of 12 to 14 hours. While one sleeps, another works, so the mine is in constant operation. The workers' life expectancy is abysmal. Toxic gases, high concentrations of dust, diseases, cave-ins, and sheer exhaustion kill even the healthiest miners within a decade. The little money they earn is used almost entirely on equipment and food. The women and children usually stay at home and make the clothing for the workers, and repair tools that can be salvaged. But at least they don't starve."

"That sounds horrible."

"It is."

Terzić gave her a confused look in the rear-view mirror. Amanda told him what she had just learned in Serbian, so he didn't feel left out. She asked if he had any questions for Roman, but Terzić shook his head.

"Please turn left here, to the south." Roman gestured so Terzić would understand. The road they turned on followed a river upstream, towards the mountains. It was a charming scenery, if a bit lonely. The jeep entered a valley, flanked on both sides by steep hills, the mountains ahead growing ever taller.

Amanda was embarrassed to admit it, but she felt uneasy. Those rumors about people disappearing in the village, that dream she had suffered…it all disturbed her more than she cared to admit. She touched her forehead where the monster had stabbed her. It felt like touching an old wound that wouldn't heal.

Roman said, "I didn't think of it before, but I hope you can still get to the village by car."

"Huh?"

"The path to the village leads through a deep gorge. The mining company dried out the river and repurposed the ravine into a makeshift road for their shipments. Since Chorna Hora's destruction, nobody has maintained this 'road'. Rocks and debris may force you to walk part of the way."

"How long would we have to walk at worst?"

"Up to three hours."

"Jesus. Isn't there another way up there?" asked Amanda.

Roman shook his head. "The village is otherwise enclosed by steep mountains."

Amanda wished he'd mentioned this earlier. They didn't have the equipment to sleep here. If the way was blocked, they'd be forced to turn back.

Five minutes later, Roman gestured again. "Please park here, Mr. Terzić." They stopped in front of a farmhouse. "Thank you, I can walk from here. Please remember these instructions carefully: First, keep going this way. After passing one more hamlet upstream, follow the river south, along a dirt road. It leads to a bridge. Don't cross it, but drive ahead, off-road, keeping the river to your left. After about two kilometers, you should see the riverbed that the mining company drained to your right. If you're lucky, you will be able to drive all the way up. If so, you should reach Chorna Hora after 15 to 20 minutes."

Amanda translated everything to Terzić, then turned to Roman. "Thank you so much for your help. When do you need us to pick you up?"

"You will return today, right? Any time is fine."

"See you later, then."

Amanda switched to the passenger seat and they drove off. Before long, they reached the dried-out river Roman had described. She could see that nobody ever came here. Trees grew haphazardly on any patch of usable soil. Terzić tried to keep to the riverbed but had to keep dodging saplings and boulders.

"This looks even more remote than Priboj," she said.

"Quite." Terzić dodged another tree. "I suggest you hold on."

It was good advice. They bounced over rocks, roots, fallen branches and molehills.

"Rough ride!" Amanda said, almost bumping her head when the car hit yet another pothole. "Good thing you borrowed the jeep."

"My car would have been insufficient," Terzić commented dryly.

Amanda smirked. *Understatement of the* century...She felt bad for Terzić's friend, though. The jeep would be in sore condition after this trip.

Eventually, the trees thinned and the sides of the riverbed grew steeper, until they found themselves in a canyon about twelve feet wide. The rock formations on either side looked imposing, if not frightening. *If one of those rocks break loose now...* It seemed to happen often—they had already passed three large boulders. Luckily, none had landed in the middle of the riverbed, or they would have had to leave the jeep behind and walk. Considering how her sneakers had barely held up on her trip to Priboj, she didn't even want to imagine her feet after a trip up here. "We're lucky those boulders missed the center, huh?"

Terzić didn't reply, but he looked troubled. After passing a fourth boulder that had fallen to the side, he said, "It isn't luck."

Amanda was about to ask what he meant when the ravine opened outwards, like the top of an hourglass. Ahead were several small houses. They had reached the village.

At first glance, Chorna Hora looked nothing like Priboj, which had been relatively level, with huts spread around the center of the village. Here, the houses were built with stones from the area, and arranged in an orderly checkerboard pattern. The terrain was also far more rocky and uneven. In spite of these differences, the empty village *felt* similar to Priboj, like time had somehow stopped here. It made her feel uneasy. There was something unnerving in how the houses were so neatly lined up, like tombstones in a graveyard. Or how cold the wind up here was, in spite of it being almost summer and the sun standing high above them.

To the left, a pine forest extended all the way to the base of the mountain. To the right, a path led to a wooden support structure in what looked like a huge, overgrown molehill. Those had to be the remains of the old mine. It looked unremarkable, and yet this dilapidated structure somehow made her hair stand on end.

Even Terzić looked tense as he slowly maneuvered the jeep towards the village. Amanda followed his gaze. A brown jeep was parked behind one of the houses, like somebody still lived here.

"We should examine it." Terzić said and parked next to the jeep.

Amanda stepped out and looked around. "Hello? Anyone here?" she shouted in English.

The jeep looked sturdier than Terzić's. The wheels were large and thick, made for rough terrain. The color was fresh, there was no rust on the rims and the tinted windows were smooth and reflective, in stark contrast to the worn-down surroundings.

"Roman said nobody ever comes here..." she murmured.

Amanda formed her hands like binoculars and pressed them against the back window. She could make out two bags and a jacket. One of the bags had a tag hanging off the top.

"Anything on your side?" she asked Terzić, who was trying to peek in from the passenger window.

"Nothing unusual."

Amanda tried the door. It wasn't locked. She opened it and leaned inside. The card on the bag read:

If found, please return to:
Liam Davis And
Morton R...

The jacket obstructed the rest of her view. As she grabbed it to read the rest, a branch snapped behind her.

CHAPTER 11

Amanda whirled around. In front of her stood a giant, a mountain of a man. He was still as a statue, without a single emotion on his face.

"Wah! Who are you?" she reflexively stammered in English. She shrunk back as his eyes settled on her. They were the most unusual color she had ever seen—a pale blue, as if they were made of ice.

"A thief should ask for mercy, not questions." A deep, strong voice, resonant with power and authority. Towering over her, he looked like he was about to squash an insect. It was like she was standing in front of a grizzly bear. "What? No...we didn't, I mean we weren't, uh...we just were trying to..."

The man did not move a muscle. "Your name?"

"It's...Amanda Dawson, and um, I..."

"Excuse," Terzić said in completely broken English.

The man turned his gaze to Terzić, who also looked unsettled, but took it a lot better than Amanda. The stranger raised an eyebrow. "You do not speak English?"

Flawless Serbian. Terzić's eyes widened, but he managed to regain his composure. "Yes, I am weak in foreign languages. How did you..."

"Your license plate. For what purpose did you open my car?"

Even Terzić seemed nervous, but unlike Amanda, he was at least able to answer, "We were told nobody comes here and wanted to investigate."

For a few painful moments, the stranger didn't reply. Finally, he said, "I understand." He took a step back and his posture relaxed. The pressure in the air eased up and that ominous, crushing aura finally subsided. His voice was far warmer now. "Apologies for confronting you with hostility. This village has me on edge."

Oh, so I'm not the only one. "I'm the one who should apologize. I shouldn't have opened your car. You have to believe me, I wasn't going to steal anything. My curiosity just often gets the better of me."

He smiled and nodded. "The impulses of youth. I understand."

Amanda could hardly believe the contrast. He seemed genuinely friendly now, like a long-time neighbor chatting across the fence.

"What brought you to this strange place?"

Amanda was about to answer, but stopped herself. As pleasant as he now was, they didn't know this man. He could be a relative of somebody who died here and take offense at two strangers trampling on his loved ones' graves. She kept it vague. "We are trying to understand the disaster here."

His face darkened. "A disaster? Please, tell me what happened."

Amanda was taken aback. If he didn't know about the massacre, what was he doing here? From his huge stature and pale eyes to his snow-white hair and stony yet oddly ageless face, he didn't look like some lost hiker. She judged him to be in his sixties, but felt she could be off by a decade or more. "How did you even find your way up here if you don't know this place's story?"

His gaze slowly wandered over the village. "My dreams of late have been very disturbing. When I consulted the spirits, they kept whispering of these ruins. I cannot ascertain what they wished me to see here, but it frightens me greatly."

Amanda's mouth dropped open. What kind of dumb answer was that? He sounded like one of those kooky mystics on a paranormal TV show.

He sighed. "You are skeptical. But surely, you feel it too? The residue of evil is so strong…observe," he said, sweeping his hand across the village.

Amanda saw what she had seen before. The ruined, mossy house walls, the caved-in roofs, the rusted metal and broken windows. No animal was in sight. The wind was the only thing moving here.

"Can you feel it? The menacing echo? The shadowy whispers in the wind?"

He sounded crazy, but Amanda had to admit there was…something here. Ever since she had arrived, she had felt out of place, like she was somewhere she shouldn't be. She had felt this way before—last night, in her dream. The images flooded back, the black obelisks, the shadowy monster…She pinched her arm, hoping the pain would snap her back to reality.

Who was this guy, anyway? A monk? A druid? A crazed loon? And where was he from? His Serbian was perfect, but so was his English. It sounded vaguely British, but with an undertone Amanda couldn't identify.

He spoke again. "Something dreadful must have occurred. If you know more, I beseech you, speak."

How would this weirdo react if she told him everything? *Better not find out.* She decided to leave the Red Dove out of this for now. "All we really know is that the villagers died suddenly, over twenty years ago. Rumors say they all went mad and murdered each other."

He shook his head. "It cannot be this simple. I have visited sites where atrocities of war have been committed. Madness and malevolence can upset the spiritual balance for a few years, but this is different. Whatever happened here was far worse. Strong enough to cause a tear between the physical and spiritual worlds."

Okay, now he was seriously starting to creep her out. Was this just a lucky guess? How did he know there was more to this?

Terzić threw her a glance and said, "Perhaps you are right. Some say a curse was to blame, called the Red Dove."

The stranger looked at Terzić wild-eyed. "That name…" He closed his eyes as if he was focusing. "That is the name the spirits kept whispering. Please, tell me more about it!"

Before Terzić could reply, Amanda decided this had gone far enough. "I'm sorry, it's shrouded in mystery. Its name is all we know."

He nodded. "Most unfortunate. You came here to find out more?"

"Yes."

"I understand, but I advise against it. Given the state it has left this land in, the curse must be mortally dangerous." After looking at the village again, he added, "Nothing good comes from digging in poisoned earth. I recommend you do not linger, lest you end up scarred." As if to reinforce his words, a gust of wind blew towards the mine. "Do not go there."

The finality with which he uttered those words reminded Amanda of her mother's words: *Some things are for God alone to know.*

"Why? What's down there?" she asked.

He pointed to the ground and slowly moved his finger up. "The tear between the worlds resembles punctured glass..." He finished his motion by pointing at the mine. "And all the cracks lead there."

Before she could ask another question, there was rustling. Amanda turned. About seventy feet away, near the edge of the pine forest, there were three piglets and a huge boar, staring at them.

She saw something move, then felt a heavy impact, as if a horse had slammed into her. The stranger had pushed her and Terzić behind his jeep. With a terrifying grunt and heavy stomping, the boar charged.

The stranger, however, did not run. He only shifted slightly so one of the houses was at his back. Motionless, he stared down the stampeding boar. A split second before it reached him, he dove to the side and rolled.

The boar slammed headfirst into the house. Caked in dust and shaking its head, the beast turned and charged once more. The stranger dodged again. The instant the boar slowed, the stranger closed the distance and something silver flashed in his hand.

An agonized howl hurt Amanda's ears and blood spurted from the creature's side as the stranger jumped back, a knife in his hand. The boar turned again, gave one last groan, and collapsed into a puddle of its own blood.

The stranger waited a few seconds longer, then sheathed his knife. Amanda stepped out from behind the jeep. Blood streamed rhythmically out of the boar, as if its heart was still beating. She was hit by a sudden wave of nausea and looked away, pressing a hand to her mouth.

"Wha—what the?"

"Forgive me," the stranger said. "I hope you did not hurt yourself."

"Never mind us!" Amanda raised her voice. "What the hell just happened?"

"We were attacked by a hog."

"I know that! But why? Why did you…kill it like that?"

"Does it upset you?"

How could his voice be so flat and emotionless? Come to think of it, he hadn't flinched once this whole time, not even when cutting open that boar.

"Hell yes, it upsets me! How could you do that?"

"Should I have sought cover instead and left you to your fate?"

"What? No! I just…It's horrible!"

She knew she wasn't making much sense. Why was she being so hysterical about this? Somehow, her rationality refused to work.

"Is it your first time in such a situation?"

She bit her lip and tried to get her hands to stop trembling. She nodded.

"Your agitation is normal. The adrenaline will pass. May I suggest you sit down?"

Amanda decided to follow his advice. Yelling at him wasn't helping. "Couldn't you just have wounded it?" she asked, a bit calmer than before.

He shook his head. "A female hog will defend its children to the death. To end the animal was safer and more efficient."

Amanda looked at Terzić. He seemed to be taking it better than she was. At least his hands weren't shaking. Then she noticed the piglets, still at the edge of the forest.

"What about them?" she asked.

"They will provide nourishment for the predators in the forest."

The piglets stared back at Amanda. They looked so cute, so vulnerable without their mother.

"Shouldn't…shouldn't we do something for them? They don't deserve to die like that."

"What another being *deserves* is not for man to judge. Their luck simply failed them when they wandered here."

While Amanda was searching for words, she saw the stranger's clothes were torn and droplets of blood dripped from his arm.

"Oh god, you're injured!"

"Indeed. A sharp rock must have inflicted it when I dodged. But worry not, the cut is minor. If you will excuse me, earlier I spotted a source of water further up. I shall go there to clean and dress the wound."

"We do have water…and a first aid kit." Amanda said.

"Thank you, your generosity is appreciated, but you should conserve these for your own use. You may yet need them." He bowed slightly and set off towards the mountains.

"Can you believe what just happened?" she asked Terzić.

"No. And I have seen it with my own eyes."

Amanda looked up. Her question had been rhetorical, but Terzić seemed to be referring to something specific.

"What do you mean?"

"Given his stature, I expected him to be strong, but he was unbelievably agile as well. Even people in the military special forces I once met are not this skilled. He must have a very eventful past."

"What do you think brought him here? Do you believe that stuff about 'the spirits'?"

Terzić took his time replying. "I do not know. I have never heard anyone talk like that before."

Don't turn on American TV, then. There's a guy talking like that on every channel.

"Maybe he just has a few screws loose," she said. "He could have heard it from someone around here, like Roman, and later convinced himself that it was 'the spirits' that told him."

Terzić cupped his chin and again said, "I do not know. He did not seem insane to me. But regardless of the reason, I am glad he was here. He took an enormous risk to save us."

"True. Don't want to imagine how that would have gone without him."

A movement in the distance reminded her that the little piglets were still at the forest's edge. They looked so lost and alone. As if they were about to cry. She wanted to tell them it was going to be all right. That she'd make up for what had just happened. She took a few steps towards the piglets, but they panicked and tried to hide clumsily behind the trees.

Terzić stepped close to her. "I do not think we can do much for them now. If you insist on helping them, I suggest you try later, when they are more tired."

She understood what he meant. It was already past noon and no matter how pitiful the piglets looked, she had something else to do, first. "Should we have a look around?"

"Yes."

*

Every house they entered was a disappointment—a mishmash of spiderwebs, shattered plates, animal droppings, rusted knives and the skeletal remains of rodents. The kitchenware, the wood, even metal items had all rotted into a grey-brown mush.

After the third house, Amanda's hands had turned the same color. "Ugh. Okay. I think there's nothing in here, either. Should we split up? Then we can cover more ground."

Amanda took the houses on the left. They were all the same as the previous ones, with everything inside slowly disintegrating. She wondered how much longer it would take for the village to disappear completely, as if it had never existed in the first place.

When she stepped through the broken door of the fifth house, something felt different. It was larger and had more furniture. On one wall was a wooden board with rusted pins, though the papers on it would long since have rotted away.

She went into what looked like the bedroom. She checked under the bed, but there wasn't anything useful. There was also a wardrobe, but the door was stuck. No matter how strongly she pulled, it wouldn't budge. She decided to save it for later.

Back in the main room, she noticed several shelves of books. She grabbed one, only for it to crumple into a moist pulp. Still, now that she thought about it, in all the previous houses, she hadn't found a single piece of paper. It was kind of obvious, too—reading couldn't have been high on the list of priorities for these poor miners.

But in this house, there were books and a bulletin board. There was even a desk, with the remains of a candleholder and a clock. The guy who lived here definitely was important somehow. She found several books and ledgers in the desk drawers. Unlike those stored outside, they hadn't decayed yet.

She opened the first one. Of course, she couldn't read it, but she could tell this wasn't an ordinary book. It was all handwritten, containing long tables, numbers and descriptions. Whoever lived here not only knew how to read and write, but had a unique job.

She opened another book from the drawer, and a paper slipped out and landed on the floor. She picked it up and turned it over. Drawn in red crayon was an image of a dove.

Her muscles all froze up. So it wasn't just rumors, or invented after the fact—the Red Dove *had* played some role here, before or while the village was destroyed. Just like in Priboj.

The drawing was simple, with no shading or depth. The hue of red uncomfortably resembled the color of blood. The more she looked at it, the more repulsive it became. While she'd examined the thing's tail, its eye had somehow changed, following her. She recoiled and dropped the paper.

Amanda took a deep breath. *Keep it together, girl.* She bent down and picked it up again. *Just a drawing. No need to freak out.*

She placed the drawing on the desk and looked over the book it had fallen out of, but all she could find were the same numbers and tables she'd seen in the first book.

Amanda went back outside. "Mr. Terzić!"

"Yes?" came from a house further down.

"Could you come here for a minute?"

Terzić emerged from a small hut and walked up to her. "What is it?"

"I think I've found something important."

He furrowed his eyebrows when he saw the drawing. Then she showed him the books with the tables and numbers in them.

"What do you think they mean?"

He looked the books over carefully. "Income and expense sheets. This house probably belonged to the overseer, who kept track of the shipments."

She nodded.

"Was there anything else here?" Terzić asked.

"Only a bedroom through that door. There's a wardrobe there that I couldn't open."

Terzić didn't have any luck with it either. "The wood may have warped over the years. Please wait here, I will bring some tools."

While Terzić was gone, Amanda picked up the drawing again. This was the first real clue they had found. She folded it up and stuffed it into her pocket. She'd look at it more closely later. If nothing else, it would make for an interesting memento in a few years' time.

Terzić came back with a hammer, screwdrivers and flashlight. Now she understood why he had packed all this in Serbia.

"Let us save the wardrobe for later. We should carefully examine this study first."

Inch by inch, they examined every drawer, every box and every piece of paper. When they got to the bulletin board, Terzić said, "This may have held a map of the mine, once."

Amanda saw what he meant. A big chunk of the rusted pins formed a rectangle about the size of a poster. But just knowing that a map might have been here once wasn't much use.

They resumed their search, but after an hour of combing the house, all they had found were useless trinkets and more account books.

That left only the wardrobe. "Please stand back," Terzić said and positioned a screwdriver at the edge of the door like a chisel. After a few blows from the hammer, the door cracked and shifted.

"I believe we can try it now."

Amanda wasn't optimistic, but this was the last place that could conceivably contain anything useful. They both grabbed the handle. Terzić looked at her. "On the count of three. One. Two. Three!"

The door swung open and a huge plume of brown dust enveloped them. Amanda tried to stop herself from inhaling, but it was too late. An old, musty stench forced its way up her nose and down her throat. She ran outside and fell to her knees coughing as hard as she could. It was like trying to clear her lungs from a sticky sludge, every cough dispersing a brown cloud from her mouth.

After over two minutes and with tears in her eyes, her throat was too sore to cough any more. No matter how many breaths she took, the awful smell just wouldn't go away. Terzić had also fled the house, but wasn't having any coughing fits. *Guess he was smart enough not to breathe at the worst possible moment.*

Back from the house, dust was billowing from the door, as if there was a fire inside. Then Amanda noticed that her t-shirt and jeans could now be mistaken for brown overalls.

"Are you all right?" Terzić asked, as she slowly got up.

"Yeah… ugh. Somehow. Jesus, that must have taken at least ten years off my life."

"Are you able to head inside or should I go alone?"

"You want to go back in there?"

"Once the dust clears out, yes. We have not examined the wardrobe yet."

Amanda groaned. Right now, that wardrobe could have contained a magic wish-granting device and she wouldn't have wanted to go back in. But Terzić was right. She couldn't let her lungs be ruined in vain. She shook her clothes and plumes of dust fell out.

Terzić held out a handkerchief. "Use this to breathe inside."

"Thanks, that's very considerate. But, what about you?"

"I will hold my breath. Please illuminate the wardrobe for me."

She turned on the flashlight and they headed back inside. The dust hung thick in the air, making her eyes water. When they reached the wardrobe, she saw only a huge pile of dirt inside. Terzić bent down and dug around in the heap, but quickly looked up at her and shook his head.

Amanda went back outside. "Fuck this!" She had just ruined her clothes and turned her lungs into a toxic waste dump, all for a pile of dirt? Terzić stepped out, looking sullen but not angry. She wondered how he managed to stay so composed in the face of such miserable failure.

"Fuck," she said. "I've never seen that much dust and filth in one place. Why was there so much in that wardrobe anyway?"

Terzić awkwardly looked away.

"Mr. Terzić?"

"I have seen something similar before, but I believe…you would not like hearing this."

"What? No, I want to know."

He took a slow breath, as if to give Amanda time to change her mind. "When I examined the dirt pile, I felt many hard and brittle objects—bones, most likely. The dust in that closet could be human remains that have turned to powder over the years."

Amanda blinked a few times, hoping for some sign he was joking. Then she remembered Terzić had never joked about anything so far.

"So, I…I breathed in a dead person?"

That weird smell was still up her nose…

Amanda sat down on the hard soil and stared off into the distance. She had no words to describe the emotion she was feeling. She just…really wanted to hug her teddy bear right now.

As the minutes ticked by, she wondered whether her eyes had adopted that infamous 'thousand-yard stare'. The thought would have been funny, if she didn't also feel like on the verge of a nervous breakdown. Terzić, at least, had the tact and patience of a saint and waited quietly.

Amanda wanted to keep sitting until the shock and disgust finally subsided, but she couldn't keep Terzić standing there forever. As she got up, he asked, "Are you well?"

"No, not at all. But it's way past three and we still have houses to search."

"You can wait in the car. I will examine the remaining houses."

"Thanks, that's very considerate, but we'll be faster this way."

She forced a smile to convince him she was feeling better, even though her brain was stuck trying to decide whether to cry or throw up.

Terzić nodded. "In that case, I shall examine these houses over there."

For all the good that will do, she thought as they split up again. After an hour of searching, she emerged from the last house. As expected, there had been nothing useful there either. Zilch. Nada.

She clenched her fists. *To sum up: we almost get killed by a boar, we search and dig around in grime the whole afternoon and I inhale a fucking corpse, and what do we get out of it? A fucking kid's drawing of a fucking red pigeon!* Amanda kicked a stone at one of the houses. It made a satisfying smack, but unfortunately didn't do any damage. She would have liked to demolish the whole place right about now.

Terzić emerged from another house and shook his head.

Amanda went over to him. "You had as much luck as I did, huh?"

"It would seem so."

"So, we have nothing."

Terzić looked around the village. "The massacre happened too long ago. In any investigation, speed is paramount. Vital clues begin degrading mere hours after a crime. And here…"

"…we're two decades too late."

He nodded. "Shall we head back?"

They walked to the car in silence. Amanda had never been so annoyed in her life. She couldn't remember ever having put in this much time, money, and effort, and being rewarded with such a humiliating failure. She knew it was pointless to stay, and yet part of her just couldn't accept that all she had gone through today had been for nothing. There just had to be *something* here that would make all this worth it.

In the distance, she saw the small mound marking the entrance of the old mine. She thought back to the drawing and which house she'd found it in. She turned to Terzić. "Before we go, can we take a look into the mine?"

He looked at her with alarm. "That would be ill-advised. After decades of neglect, the mine might be structurally unsound. Also, we do not have a map, and I doubt we would find much."

"But we can't just leave with nothing to show for it! The drawing of the Red Dove was in the overseer's house; doesn't that strongly suggest something might be down there? If we just leave now, all the time and money we sank into this will have been for nothing."

"Better to waste time and money than our lives."

Before she could think of a good reply, they had reached the jeep. As usual, Terzić courteously opened the passenger door for her.

"Is police work always like this? You work your ass off and get zilch in return?"

"Sometimes, yes."

He closed the door. Amanda looked out the window at the mine again. Was Terzić seriously prepared to just walk away? What if Novak didn't come through? What if the Priboj evidence had been destroyed? Then she would have to fly home completely empty-handed. And she would always hate herself for leaving this last stone unturned. Years from now, she'd still ask herself, *What if I had found the answer down there?*

Terzić was busy putting away his tools in the back of the car. But she still had the flashlight in her hands. Amanda fumbled nervously with her necklace. This was practically fate winking at her. The thing hadn't collapsed so far, right?

Screw it.

She jumped out of the car and ran towards the mine.

"Ms. Dousson! Wait!"

Amanda kept running. "I just want to have a quick look!" she shouted back. If he was too afraid, he could just wait in the car. But she couldn't.

The closer she got, the larger and more intimidating the opening to the mine grew. What had looked like a molehill from a distance soon looked like the rotting maw of a prehistoric monster, with only blackness beyond. The stranger's words came back to her.

"Do not go there."

But she couldn't stop now. Not after coming this far. She fought back the fear creeping up on her and took the last remaining steps inside.

The ground felt soft under her feet, like moist earth. Amanda turned on her flashlight and saw two rusted metal cables at her feet. Probably used to pull coal out of the mine. The mineshaft itself looked completely unremarkable. It was just a rectangular tunnel, about eight by eight feet wide, extending down at a slight incline. This was the "tear between worlds" she was supposed to be so afraid of?

She heard footsteps and Terzić arrived behind her. "I will accompany you," he said flatly.

She could tell he wasn't happy. "I promise, I just want to have a quick look."

Amanda walked ahead, Terzić placing a hand on her shoulder and following behind. Soon, they had left the light of day behind them, the flashlight now their only source of illumination.

They passed several doors and smaller tunnels leading away from the one they were in.

"Ms. Dousson, if we get lost, we could die."

"If we just follow this main tunnel, we'll be fine."

The air kept becoming drier and colder, and an ancient, earthy smell made breathing unpleasant. The ceiling, though still high enough for them to stand, grew lower. Everything felt increasingly cramped. By now, they had to be under a thousand tons of earth and rock. If anything caved in, they would never get out alive. But since this mine had survived over two decades, she wasn't particularly worried.

After passing another three side tunnels, Terzić asked, "Are you satisfied? I urge that we leave immediately."

"Just a bit further."

She couldn't believe how monotonous this mine was. There was nothing but tunnels full of earth, rock, and those repetitive wooden support columns. Was there really nothing down here? Not even one message on one of the walls? Not one hastily scribbled note? *Speaking of notes…* She remembered she still had the drawing of the Red Dove in her pocket. It felt uncomfortable, as though glued against her thigh.

As she pulled out the paper, her steps gave off a heavy sound. She wasn't stepping on earth, but on…wood? Why was she stepping on wood?

"Look out!" Terzić's voice pierced the silence, but he was too late. Under Amanda's feet, the wooden boards she had stepped on snapped in two. Her desperate scream faded quickly as she disappeared into a black void below.

CHAPTER 12

She couldn't see. Something was wrong with her eyes. And with her ears, too—there was this loud ringing. Why was she feeling so dizzy? Had she suffered a concussion? Before she could try to piece together the last few seconds, Amanda bent over and threw up.

"Ugh," she groaned.

It was unbearably cold and she was sitting on a floor made of jagged rocks. Everything hurt. The pain on her right temple was especially bad. She touched it and felt something warm and sticky.

Then it all came back—the strange sound of her steps, the wooden boards breaking under her, the dancing cone of the flashlight and her scream as the world went black.

She had fallen for so long…How was she still alive? She remembered sliding on something rough. Maybe the hole she had fallen into was not fully vertical. That had saved her life. She tried to get up and a bolt of pain flashed through her right leg.

"Ow!"

Amanda collapsed again.

I broke my ankle.

What now? She was lost in an abandoned and unstable mine, she needed medical attention and there wasn't even a speck of light to guide her. Amanda's stomach tightened up and her breathing turned ragged.

She frantically patted her surroundings. With just a bit of luck, the flashlight had fallen alongside her. Crawling around randomly, every inch made the pain worse. Her pants were torn all over and she kept scraping her knees on the stone floor. Several times, her hands ended up in her own vomit. Disgusted, she tried to wipe it off on the floor and kept searching. At last, her hands settled on a cold, metal tube.

Please...please! She pressed the switch. Nothing. She tried a couple more times, but the light stayed off. She touched the front section—the glass was shattered.

Damn it!

Maybe Terzić was still up there? If the fall hadn't been deep enough to kill her, he could well be within earshot. She raised her head and screamed, "Hello?"

No answer.

"Mr. Terzić? Can you hear me?"

Her echo was the only reply. How long had she even been out? Minutes? Hours? Heck, a day could have gone by. *No, wait, that's not possible.* She would have died from the cold by now if she had been unconscious for that long. But if only a few minutes had gone by, why was Terzić not answering?

"Hellooooo?"

Amanda let her head sink again and started shaking. All she could do at this point was crawl randomly. But for what? This place was a maze and the only way up might be blocked or have collapsed already.

No. She grit her teeth. She couldn't let her fear take over. As long as she could move, she had to keep going. First, was there anything she could use to get her bearings? To figure out what kind of room she was in and how large it was?

Then it hit her: Her phone! She wouldn't have any reception down here, obviously, but...

She took it out of her pocket and pressed the power button.

"Haha! Yes!"

The display was cracked and only showed gibberish, but it still provided some illumination. Amanda smiled triumphantly and waved her phone around. She was in another tunnel, extending into the darkness in both directions. It was different from the mine entrance, which had been earthy and smooth. Here, the walls and floor were made of stone and were choppy and uneven, as if someone had haphazardly hammered a hole in the mountain.

Her watch told her it was 5:32 PM. She hadn't been out that long. But she had to get going fast. The air was really cold and her torn clothes weren't helping. Hypothermia was a serious threat. And the wound on her head needed a bandaid, even if it wasn't too deep.

She turned the phone upward and could almost make out the hole she had fallen through. With her sprained ankle, there was no hope of climbing out that way.

Amanda decided to head left. It was hard to see in this light, but she thought she could see a slight incline. She crawled along the tunnel wall, trying to keep track of the distance. If she could somehow get a mental picture of this place, it might help later. After crawling about 60 feet, the blue light of her phone illuminated the outline of a door.

She reached up to the handle and pushed. Nothing. She tried pulling, but the door didn't move. She pushed and pulled, stronger each time, but the door wouldn't budge.

"Fuck."

Her flashlight was broken, her head was bleeding, she was cold and getting thirsty. Now the tunnel that might lead out was locked. Why was everything against her?

"Why? Why?" she cried, louder each time. "Why!" Amanda slammed her fist against the door over and over. "Why did I have to be this stupid? Why did I just *have* to be this stupid?"

She collapsed and beat her trembling hands on the stone floor. "Why did I come in here? Why didn't I listen!"

She abruptly sat up and slapped herself across the face.

No! Don't waste your strength! Stop pounding the floor and think! Just think...

She looked the door over. It had no lock. Like the wardrobe in the village, it had probably warped over the years and become unopenable. But, the woodwork looked makeshift and relatively thin. With the right tool, she might be able to break this open.

She crawled again. Twenty, forty, sixty. Now Amanda was back where she had started. She had only one hope left—follow the tunnel downwards in the other direction, and hope to find a hammer or pickaxe somewhere.

She'd crawled only a few feet when she saw a door to her left.

Amanda sat up and tried the handle. The door scraped along the floor. With enough strength, she could open it. But, it looked too small to be important and she had to conserve her strength for now. *Maybe later.* She resumed crawling, but after another minute, she froze. A feeling of dread overwhelmed her, as if she'd just touched a hornet's nest. The tunnel suddenly angled sharply downwards and from below came a horrible stench, like something rotten was hidden in the depths. In the silence, she heard a sound. Like something monstrous breathing deeply. Or was it growling?

What's down there? Oh God, what's down there? Her instincts warned her not to run. *Don't move, then it won't notice you.* She held her breath, worried that exhaling might give her away.

She remembered the jammed door from earlier. *Had* its wood really warped? Or had someone bolted it from the other side? To hold back whatever was down here?

The heavy sound continued unabated. After a minute of waiting, her legs finally started moving again and she crawled back. She turned her head several times, but nothing came after her.

She had one goal: To reach that small door she had passed before. She crawled as fast as she could, suffering the constant pain of banging her knees against the rough floor.

Panting from exhaustion, she finally saw the outline of the small door. It opened slowly at first, then swung open with a horrible screech. Amanda froze up. What if that…something from below had heard? She hid her phone, scared of the light leading it here.

Nothing happened. When she listened closely, she could still hear the rumble, but it wasn't getting closer. Amanda allowed herself to exhale and closed the door behind her. She saw there was a bolt, which allowed her to lock herself in, if need be.

Mercifully, the floor here was more even. The light of her phone illuminated a closed room, the outline of a wall barely visible on the opposite side. She could make out a desk, wooden chairs, shelves and tools. Had this been an office? A break room? *Never mind that now.* She crawled to the wall opposite the door and leaned against it, trying to catch her breath. Crawling on all fours was surprisingly exhausting.

It's looking at you. She didn't know why, but her hair was standing on end. *It's looking at you!* Over and over that thought echoed in her head. What the hell was this? Why was she feeling so...watched?

Amanda turned her phone to the right-hand wall. Illuminated by the glow was a chair, with a pile of tattered clothes and bones on top. A skull sat on the dirty-white heap as if on a throne, a wide grin on its face, fixing her with empty eyes.

Then the bones stirred. Like a jittering, crawling mass of insects, pushing and pulling, reassembling themselves into a monstrous skeleton. It rose to its feet with disjointed and jerky movements. The skull's disgusting grin widened, its empty eyes fixed on its prey. Cracks and creaks echoed through the room as the skeleton moved towards her.

She jumped up, followed by a searing flash of pain in her leg. Amanda fell back down and dropped her phone, plunging the room into darkness. The cracking grew into a maddening cacophony, as the skeleton came ever closer. Amanda crawled away, but the thing kept getting closer. She hit her head on a wall—she had nowhere left to run. She squeezed her eyelids shut and prayed for a miracle to save her.

Cold, bony fingers closed around her neck. Amanda's scream turned into a rasp as the thing pressed down on her throat. She gagged and clawed at her neck, trying to pry the skeleton off, but its grip was like iron. It cackled as it slowly squeezed the life out of her.

Then, its grip loosened. Amanda tried to kick it away, but her feet hit nothing but air. The pressure on her neck and the cracking noises disappeared. She coughed violently, finally able to fill her lungs again.

Where had the skeleton gone? She reached out, but there was nothing. Her phone! Where was her damn phone? She groped blindly, until her fingers finally closed around her only light source. As she lifted it, it slipped out of her sweaty hands. She gripped it again tightly, shone the light up and—

The skeleton was gone. The heap of bones was back on the chair.

Amanda gripped her sweaty forehead. *What…was that?* Had she just hallucinated the whole thing? But she didn't have any family history of psychosis. Then again, given the situation and the amount of adrenaline she was under, anything was possible.

She took a deep breath. *It's alright. No undead monsters here…Just calm down.*

Her neck hurt. She touched it and an icy fear ran over her…why could she still feel the imprints left by those bony hands? A dark snickering rose from the chair. On its heap of bones, the skull was looking at her again, its teeth arranged in a sickening grin.

She tried to crawl towards the door, but the skull's eyes followed her and the pile of bones stirred once more.

Her hands found a rock. She threw it as hard as she could. There was an ear-shattering noise as the bones crashed to the floor and shattered into a plume of dust.

What the hell is this? What the hell kind of place is this!

As if to answer, she heard whispers in the darkness. Indistinct at first, they slowly became louder, speaking a language she couldn't understand. They enveloped her like a cold blanket, coming from everywhere and nowhere.

"What are you?"

The whispers didn't reply. They only kept talking in that strange language, the sound like a nail scraping on glass. Finally, amid the cacophony of whispers, she heard something else—a broken, rhythmic chant that she recognized. It was the lullaby she had sung in the hotel room.

Amanda turned on her phone at one of the corners, where the whispers were loudest. The darkness moved strangely, like a thousand creeping shadows rearranging themselves to stay just outside the light's reach.

She recognized that movement, and that voice. It was the monster she had seen in her dream.

Now she understood her nightmare—in the endless graveyard of the victims of the Red Dove, naked and unprotected, chased and murdered by living shadows. Had that been a warning? Or a promise? Was this how the curse of the Red Dove started? Had all its victims suffered this same nightmare?

She hugged her knees to stop what little warmth was left from disappearing. "Please, spare me." But the whispers continued unabated, scraping at her ears like razorblades.

She recalled the stranger words. He had warned her of the "shadowy whispers." And as usual, she hadn't listened.

Just...why didn't I listen?

The whispers turned into a snicker. Every dark corner of the room laughed at her. Was it funny how pathetic and stupid she was? Well, they weren't wrong. She giggled. It really was laughable. She would freeze to death here, mocked by the same curse she used to make fun of. And it was all her own fault.

Her laugh became louder, almost in sync with the whispers. *I'm dying. Why am I laughing? What's so funny?* It grew worse by the minute, till her body was laughing uncontrollably, while her conscious mind stood removed, powerlessly watching in shock.

Desperate, she struggled to regain her sanity. She couldn't die here, Not now. Not like this. But her body continued laughing. Amanda focused all her willpower on her breathing. If she could only get that under control...*in, out. In, and out again.*

Her laughter slowly subsided, finally turning into a whisper and then dying down completely. Her eyelids felt unbearably heavy. She wasn't moving and yet everything was spinning. She fell face forward, barely managing to put a hand in front of her head before hitting the stone floor.

Amanda raised her head. She thought only a second had passed, but as her senses returned, she knew she had fallen unconscious again. Her body was deathly cold, the icy floor having sucked away what little warmth had remained.

With the last strength she had left, she pulled her knees to her chest, trying to warm herself. Her teeth clattered as she rocked back and forth, while the whispers kept talking and chanting the Red Dove's song in their strange language. From every dark corner they came, on and on without end.

"Shut up," Amanda said to the darkness. The whispers didn't care. They multiplied ever more, drowning her beneath a flood of noise.

"Shut up! Shut the fuck up!" Amanda screamed, squeezing her ears shut.

Maybe I should just bash my head in…if I do it hard enough, it might even be painless?

Amanda pulled her hair so hard it hurt. *What am I thinking? What the hell am I thinking?* She had to get out of here. Now. Before those things killed her.

With her phone, she illuminated the tools she had seen before. The shovels, bags and screws were all useless to her. But there was a pickaxe. This might do the trick for the locked door outside.

Amanda held her phone with her teeth, pointing the light downwards. She grabbed the pickaxe with one hand and used the other to crawl forward.

It was almost unbearable. The massive pickaxe felt like dragging a boulder behind her. When she finally reached the door, she cried out in pain as she shifted her weight to her knees, scraped raw and bleeding at this point. With slow, mechanical movements, she lifted the pickaxe. But just as she felt she had it high enough, her strength failed and she dropped it. The whispers laughed and became louder.

"No…No…Can't give up. Can't give in."

Exhaustion swept over her like a wave. It was strange. Amanda knew she was cold, but she couldn't feel it anymore. All that was left in her was a cozy tiredness. *Must not sleep. Must not sleep…* If she did, she knew she'd never wake up. The cold would kill her.

Her body didn't listen and her eyes closed against her will. With her last effort of will, she slapped her knee. The pain burned like fire, but the tiredness receded.

Amanda pushed herself up for another try. She grabbed the handle, but the pickaxe had grown so heavy she couldn't even lift it. She wanted to sleep so much. The whispers approved. Every time she closed her eyes, they became quieter, less grating. Maybe if she huddled up into a ball, she wouldn't die after all? Then she could recover her strength and—

A loud boom came from the door in front of her.

She froze up. Everything went silent. Even the whispers ceased. But she knew she had heard this. She had even felt it.

Another boom made the door tremble. As if a bull had slammed the door. For a few painful seconds, everything went quiet again, then another bang shook the tunnel. Dust and rock chips fell from the ceiling.

Amanda's stomach twisted inside out. Shaking uncontrollably, she crawled back inside the room, closing the door behind her. Panting from the pain, she raised herself up and threw the bolt.

Another explosion outside, followed by the sound of dozens of splinters hitting the stone floor. Whatever had been slamming the door had broken through and was inside the tunnel.

Amanda grabbed a hammer from one of the tables and crawled to the opposite wall. Something pushed against the door of her room. She could hear it, feel its murderous intent, its heavy breath.

What was that? What on earth had just smashed a solid wood door to splinters? She cowered against the wall, readying the hammer. For a few seconds, everything was quiet.

She whispered, "Please don't let it find me. Please don't let it find me. Plea—"

Another loud boom shattered her hopes. *What's out there? God what's out there! Please let the door hold!*

The thing slammed against the door once more. The door cracked and rocked in its hinges.

"Oh no. Oh God. Oh no. No. No. Please!"

Again, the terrible beast outside slammed against the door. The entire room shook from the violence of the impact. The bolt now hung loosely, barely holding on.

Amanda lifted the hammer, ready to throw it. This was all she had left. *God, save me!*

With a deafening blast, the hinges flew off and the door burst open. A blazing light pierced her eyes like a dagger. She wanted to scream, but even her vocal cords were paralyzed. With the last of her willpower, she threw the hammer. It disappeared into the light. There was no sound. It didn't drop to the floor. The monster had simply swallowed it. The last thing that could have saved her, was gone.

Behind the light, she could make out a dark, enormous shape.

Delirium swept her. *I'll die. I'll die. I failed. I failed. I'll die. I'll die. I'll die. I failed.*

CHAPTER 13

A deep, familiar voice spoke to her, "Miss Dawson. Your luck is enviable."
Amanda looked up, her mind reeling.

The huge figure said, "Ah, please forgive me," and shone the light at his own face. There, holding the hammer in his left hand and a flashlight in his right, stood the stranger they had met earlier. And behind him…Terzić.

"Aha- ahah- aaaahhhhh!" Amanda cried, sobs interrupting every breath. "You- you-I- ahhaahhh!"

"Apologies, Miss Dawson," said the giant. "Had I known you were here, I would have called out to you."

More tears shot up her eyes and spilled down her face.

"Mr. Terzić informed me of your accident. Are you injured?"

"Ughm—uh—Ankle…broken, I think—concussion, maybe," she managed to cough up between sobs.

The giant placed the lamp on the table and leaned down. "Excuse me."

He twisted her leg slightly, and a lightning of pain traveled from Amanda's foot up her spine. "Aaaahhhh!"

The stranger nodded. "Your ankle appears sprained, but not broken." He put his hand on her forehead. "Your temperature is dangerously low. We must head outside. Can you stand?"

Amanda shook her head, still sobbing in pain and relief. The stranger picked up the light again and shone it around the room, pausing on the chair and the broken bones. He turned and said, "We must improvise."

He took her hand and pulled her up, putting an arm around her so she could lean on him. She winced at every step, but the wish to escape pushed her on.

The flashlight gave the tunnel an eerie outline. He paused and his expression turned grave. She could clearly hear the faint growling from before again. Was it coming closer?

"We must leave. Now," the stranger said. Turning to Terzić and handing him the flashlight, he added, "Please illuminate the way for us."

Without warning or waiting for Amanda's approval, he lifted her in his arms and dashed through the splintered door that had blocked her way and up the tunnel. It felt awkward being carried bridal-style like this, but she was in too much fear and pain to stand on her pride.

The stranger's strength was practically inhuman. She weighed at least 140 pounds and he was running uphill. Yet, he ran so fast that Terzić had trouble keeping up. The ceiling was high at first, but soon lowered. After a while, the stranger had to crouch to not hit his head. Carrying Amanda, the strain on his legs had to be enormous, but he did not slow down.

Bits of dust shook loose from the stranger's clothes and lit up in the cone of Terzić's flashlight. They passed several doors, many of them broken open. Amanda couldn't imagine how many tunnels they'd searched and doors they'd broken down to reach her.

The minutes trickled by, the stranger rushing up the tunnels as if he could see in the dark. Terzić was breathing heavily behind them, but the stranger pressed on relentlessly. Past another door, Amanda recognized the shape of the walls again: They were in the main tunnel. Not long after, she could finally see daylight in the distance. She thanked every god she could think of. This dreadful mine had almost become her tomb.

The giant put her back on her feet and she grimaced. The stranger took out a pocket watch. "The sun has already set. Twilight will fade soon. You should depart swiftly."

Amanda couldn't agree more. The thought of being here after dark was terrifying.

Terzić handed the flashlight back to the stranger. "Thank you."

"Goodbye, Miss Dawson, Mr. Terzić."

He turned to leave, but Amanda held him back by the arm. "Thank you… Thank you, I…"

She struggled for words. She wanted to convey how grateful she was for the unbelievable rescue, but the words just weren't coming. Nothing she could say would make up for what he and Terzić had done for her.

"Miss Dawson…You were blessed with extraordinary good fortune today. Providence has decreed that you shall live, for now. Treasure it, and waste not the life you so narrowly managed to keep. Farewell, and good luck."

He turned and walked to his jeep, not looking back again.

Terzić extended his arm as a crutch as they walked to their car. By the time Terzić started the ignition, the stranger's jeep had already disappeared down the ravine.

As Terzić drove off, Amanda's stomach clenched together. Even though they were leaving the village behind them, something felt wrong. How the air felt heavy and the dark pine trees moved strangely in the cold wind.

She looked back at the village and saw a nightmare emerge. A glob of black vapor grew from the mine, swallowing everything like a growing void. It had no eyes, but she knew the growing mass of darkness was looking at her. "Oh god…Oh god!"

A second later, Terzić turned a corner and the village disappeared from view. He looked at her in alarm, slowing the car.

"Am I driving too fa—"

"No! Drive! Please drive faster! Get me away from here!"

He looked puzzled but stepped on the gas. Amanda looked back repeatedly, but the black mass wasn't following them.

Halfway down the ravine, Terzić said, "Excuse me, I must stop for a moment."

Alarmed, she turned around, but the liquid darkness was nowhere to be seen. She kept checking, terrified the thing would emerge behind them. When Terzić finally came back, he was holding two wool blankets.

"You may find these useful."

Amanda nodded and wrapped herself up. Looking down, she finally realized just how torn up her clothes were—and how cold she was. The warm and fluffy blankets allowed her to take a few deep breaths and get her nerves under control. Outside, the remaining light was fading quickly. How much time had she spent in that mine anyway? She checked her watch: 5:32.

What? She stared at the watch for a moment until it finally hit her. *No...No, not this...*she begged. *Not grandma's watch.*

She tried shaking it and adjusting the time forward and backward, hoping the movement would get it working again. But the watch remained perfectly still. Amanda clenched her fingers and pulled the blanket tight around her. She had broken it. She had broken her grandmother's last memento. Fresh tears filled her eyes and quietly dropped on the blanket. Terzić drove silently and pretended not to notice. She thanked him inwardly for his sense of tact. The last thing she wanted right now was a stupid remark like "It's going to be okay."

As if waking from a daze, she finally realized how insufferably she had acted and what she had put Terzić through. She shouldn't have gone into that mine, just like he said. But as usual, she hadn't listened, and put both of both of their lives in danger.

And yet, he had come back for her. The flashlight had vanished with her, so he would have had to find his way out of that mine in complete darkness. And once out, he had set off to her rescue, despite the danger. Despite her being such an unbearable brat.

"Mr. Terzić, I..." she started, but he stayed quiet. She felt the tears come again and her breathing became ragged. "I'm so sorry—I didn't—I mean—I shouldn't have–",

"I understand. Do not worry yourself. I am relieved you are unharmed."

Amanda nodded and allowed her tears to flow freely again.

"It was fortunate that odd man hadn't left yet."

Right, the stranger. Without him, Terzić wouldn't have had a light and couldn't even have attempted to save her. And she would have been long dead before a proper rescue party could have made it down there.

Terzić continued, "When I found him and told him what happened, he went straight to his jeep and picked up a flashlight, then down into the mine without another word. I think he would have gone all by himself if I hadn't followed him. Inside, he said we had to memorize every door and every distance we traveled. Then he worked his way down methodically, door by door, until we found you."

She furrowed her brow. Something was missing from Terzić's explanation.

"Hang on…he only went in with a flashlight?"

"Yes."

"How did he break down all those doors along the way? From my side, it sounded like a bull was pounding the door. What tool did he use?"

"His bare hands," Terzić said.

Amanda wondered if he was joking, but his face showed he was serious.

And I couldn't even find the words to thank him for it…god, how pathetic I am.

"Should we go to a hospital in Ivano-Frankivsk?" Terzić asked.

"No, thanks. I'll be fine." Her ankle still hurt and she had hit her head hard enough to cause a gash and a concussion. But she had no desire to explain her injuries in a country she didn't know the language of. Not to mention the headache of figuring out whether her insurance would cover a stay in a Ukrainian hospital. Also, she was insured through her dad. If her parents found out what had happened, her mother would panic. *Better to just bear the pain.*

Five minutes later, Terzić stopped the car and went to knock at Roman's house, something she had completely forgotten about. She muttered a small greeting as Roman opened the back door and got in.

Except for the few times Roman gave directions, none of them spoke during the drive back. She hadn't looked into any mirror, but she knew she had to look bad. Really bad. She thanked her lucky stars that both Terzić and Roman had the rare gift of knowing when to shut up.

Amanda felt a wave of relief seeing Ivano-Frankivsk. After over an hour driving on blackened roads, the lights of a city had never looked this good.

In front of the hotel, Roman bid his farewell. "It was a pleasure meeting you. Take good care of yourselves."

She shook his hand. "Thanks. You too." She didn't mean to be rude with such a lackluster farewell, but it took all her willpower just to remain halfway composed. In the hotel, she quickly wished Terzić good night and hurried to her room.

As soon as the door closed, Amanda threw herself on the bed and allowed herself to cry freely. Finally, she didn't have to worry about anyone giving stupid remarks or looking away awkwardly.

When the tears subsided, her pillow had turned a greyish brown. "Ugh." She stood up and went to the bathroom. She turned on the light and stepped back in shock. For a second, she hadn't recognized herself. Her face was covered in blood and dirt, the only clean spots were the streaks where her tears had flowed. Her hair had turned from its usual shiny blonde to a grey piece of gluey goop. Even her eyes had somehow lost their vibrancy.

Then there were her clothes, or what was left of them. She had seen the holes and rips in the car, but hadn't fully realized how bad it was. Her pants were little more than loosely hanging scraps and her shirt and bra were torn all over, with parts of her breasts showing. Now she understood why Terzić had handed her the blankets.

Disgusted, Amanda tore her clothes off and turned on the shower. She winced as the hot water burned her cuts and bruises. But she didn't turn the temperature down. She didn't care if she scalded herself. Anything but this ghostly cold from that mine that had dug into her very bones.

The grey sludge gathering at the drain sickened her. She emptied the hotel-provided bottle of shower gel, and it still didn't feel like enough.

Half an hour later, the heat was making her dizzy and she had to step out of the shower.

As she dried herself and put on her necklace, she looked at it closely—it had lost its shine and was scratched all over.

"No…Not this too."

She couldn't face Tom like this. She couldn't tell him that because of her stubbornness, his beautiful necklace was ruined. Using the bathroom soap bar, she scrubbed the metal and the sapphire until her fingers hurt. It wasn't perfect, but the original brilliance did come back a little.

When she looked back up at the mirror, she saw the hot shower had reopened the wound on her temple. It was larger than she had imagined, over an inch long. She could only hope the scar wouldn't be too bad. She clutched the necklace in her hands. "What have I done..." she asked the emptiness of her room.

Amanda went back to the bed and let her head fall into the pillow. *The piglets at the edge of the forest...* After escaping that mine, she had forgotten all about them. Now they would die, alone, in that awful place, just like she almost had.

"What have I done?" she repeated. Why was she, of all people, so lucky? Terzić and the stranger should just have let her die. *Someone as stupid as me doesn't deserve to live.* Her sobs shook her like heavy coughs.

When her tears finally subsided, she was left with a crushing headache. She combed through her backpack until she found her aspirin. She took two tablets, then fell back on the bed. Exhausted, she turned off the lights.

The night had been unbearably hot moments ago, but now, a strange chill crept into the room. Amanda pulled the covers over herself and huddled into a ball.

What the hell? Did the AC turn on and—

She heard something. It was indistinct, at first, but she recognized it immediately.

"No...they followed me here? Oh God no, please, no!"

Snickering whispers filled the room. Mocking her and chanting their broken song in that strange and alien language. Then something touched her foot. A claw, cold and hot at the same time, as if made of burning ice.

Amanda desperately hit at the wall, the whispers laughing at how pathetic she was, until she finally found the light switch. The shadows retreated, slithering back into the darker corners of the room. Her heart pounded. *Oh God...it followed me. It followed me!*

She kept shaking, though the light seemed to keep the whispers at bay, for now.

Hours passed. Her exhaustion became overwhelming, but she didn't dare to turn the light off, or those awful monsters might return. Eventually, she started to drift off in spite of the bright lamps.

As soon as sleep took over, the nightmares came. Shadows, materializing from the darkness, surrounding her. Murderous villagers all chanting the cursed lullaby. The Red Dove's deformed grin staring down at her. Cackling skeletons strangling her and formless horrors slicing her open. Over and over, she died one gruesome death after another.

It was the longest night she had ever experienced. When the sun finally came up, she was so exhausted she had trouble even lifting her arm. She wanted to keep sleeping, but soon, there was a knock on the door.

Amanda jolted awake. "Who's there?"

"Đorđe Terzić. Are you feeling well?"

"Oh, uh. Sorry, no, not really."

"I have brought something for your wounds. May I enter?"

"No, sorry. It's really kind, but I'm not dressed."

"I understand. I shall leave it here. Should I wait for you with breakfast?"

"I'm not really hungry."

"Rest well, then." Terzić's footsteps went away.

She felt bad for acting like this. He had probably waited hours downstairs before coming up here. But she didn't have the strength for this right now. She could barely even keep her eyes open.

Her body felt like a robot made of scrap metal as she stumbled to the door. Terzić had left her a first aid kit, with disinfectant and bandaids. Even after she had caused this much trouble, he was still thinking of her well-being…and she had sent him away without a word of thanks. Amanda closed the door and sank to the floor. "What a fucking jerk I am."

She drifted to sleep against the wall but was startled awake moments later by another knock at the door.

"Oh god, what the hell?"

"Pardon me," she heard Terzić's voice, "but I have important news."

"Sorry…you startled me."

"Novak called. He has the evidence from Priboj in his possession."

Amanda looked up at the alarm clock on the bedside stand. Two hours had passed since Terzić's breakfast invitation.

She was dead tired and could have stayed like this the whole day. But then again, the faster she was out of Ukraine, the better. "I'll get ready."

"I will wait downstairs."

"Alright. And Mr. Terzić?"

"Yes?"

"Thank you. For everything."

*

Half an hour later, they were on the road again towards Romania. As usual, Terzić didn't talk. Not that Amanda minded. She spent the journey drifting in and out of sleep, always on the edge between dream and reality.

When she woke up, Terzić had stopped at a gas station. Her head felt awful, as if an anvil was pressing down on it. And she felt incredibly cold. While Terzić filled the gas tank, she retrieved the blankets from the trunk and wrapped herself up. Terzić gave her a curious look, but didn't say anything.

By the time they arrived in Arad, Amanda was shivering all over and her teeth were chattering. All she wanted was to go up to her room and disappear under the warm covers, but Terzić held her back.

"Excuse me." He put his hand on her forehead. It felt cold against her skin, even refreshing. "You have a fever. I suggest going to a doctor."

She smiled. *Why couldn't you have been Mirko? You would have made such a great uncle...* "Thanks, but I think I just need some rest."

"Will you join me for dinner, at least? You have not eaten for the last thirty hours."

"Really?" She hadn't been hungry once this whole time.

"Yes. If you do not eat, you will lose your strength, and your fever may worsen."

It was kind of awkward that he'd been keeping tabs on when she'd last eaten. But she knew he meant well.

163

She joined Terzić in a nearby diner, but the salad she ordered tasted awful, like she was eating last week's leftovers. Amanda mouthed it down anyway. Sending it back would only have dragged the whole dinner out.

Back in her room, she opened her laptop and wrote,

Hi! Sorry for not being in touch. Broke my phone and couldn't text. Will return home soon.

She sent the same message to Greg, Tom and her mother. It felt wrong not telling them what had happened, but what would be the point? She'd only worry them, and they couldn't help her anyway.

In bed, her hand hovered over the lamp switch. Would the Red Dove come back? Or had she moved far enough away from Chorna Hora? Did the physical distance to the village even matter? She closed her eyes and flipped the switch. The room fell into darkness. She breathed heavily as the seconds passed, but the room stayed silent.

Thank God. It's not here. It's gone and—

"Amandaaaa..."

Right next to her ear. She jumped up in terror and hit the light switch again.

The room was empty. Amanda slumped to the floor and pulled at her hair. It had followed her. All the way here. Would the whispers from the dark continue forever? Would she never be safe without light again?

She started crying once more. Her mother had tried to warn her, and she hadn't listened. Tom had warned her. Greg, Terzić, Roman and even that stranger, they had all warned her and she had ignored all of them. This had to be her punishment. Her just deserts for her arrogance.

When the tears stopped, she folded her hands together and, for the first time since her childhood years, she prayed.

CHAPTER 14

She barely got any sleep. At least her fever had gone down. It allowed her to convince Terzić that she didn't need a doctor after all. He drove the entire way again, Amanda brooding and occasionally falling asleep. Instead of driving back to his home, Terzić first drove to the same café where they'd met Novak a week earlier. He slid a thick envelope from his bag. "Would you like to stay in the car?"

"No, I'll come."

She winced every step of the way. Her ankle was swollen and painful. Still, she had to go. After everything they'd been through together, she couldn't leave Terzić on his own at a time like this.

When Novak saw them enter, his expression soured, until his eyes drifted to Amanda. He was so shocked, his mouth dropped open. She turned her head away. She knew how bad she looked; he didn't have to make it this obvious. It also told her that her attempts at covering up the bruises and cuts with makeup weren't fooling anybody.

Novak regained his composure. "I found what you requested, including that diary you wanted so badly. I took a look at it. I suggest you read it while sitting down."

He handed Terzić a large bag. Terzić, in return, gave Novak the envelope he was carrying. Novak opened it, took a few photographs out and immediately pushed the contents back inside, his face flushing red.

He looked at Terzić. "We've known each other for a long time, so I know this must be important to you. But what you did is still blackmail. Don't ever contact me again."

Terzić nodded and extended his hand. "I hope you will understand my reasons one day. I wish you all the best in your ambitions."

Novak reluctantly shook the offered hand and nodded.

*

Amanda had really missed the rustic little cottage.

"I will prepare dinner," Terzić said. "Will *prebranac* be alright?"

"I don't know what that is, but yes, of course. I'm not picky."

"Prebranac is bean casserole."

"Can I help somehow?"

"It is no trouble."

He really loves saying that. She sat down in his armchair again. It was just as comfy as when she had left it. She had to get one like that in Chicago.

A quarter of an hour later, Terzić said, "It is ready."

The food looked and smelled amazing, as usual. She wondered if Terzić was a great cook or if this was just the standard Serbian people expected of their meals.

"*Prijatno,*" Terzić said.

Amanda still wasn't hungry. But she knew she had to eat. Plus, she didn't want to be rude and let his great cooking go to waste.

She took a bite and her face contorted. The food tasted horrible, as if it was moldy. She had to fight hard not to spit out the entire mouthful.

Why? It looks so good!

She tried some of the bread Terzić had put on the table, but the result was the same. It was just like that salad yesterday…Nothing tasted good anymore. Amanda looked at the darkness outside. Was this the Red Dove's doing as well? Were those whispers and endless nightmares not punishment enough? Was there no joy in her life it wouldn't take away?

She stared down at her plate. There was still so much to finish…but she had to eat. She gripped her spoon and mechanically shoveled the beans into her mouth. Every spoonful tasted worse. It was like eating maggots suspended in a sludge of liquified ash.

When she was finally done, she could barely hold back her nausea. "I'm sorry, I think I'll go to bed early."

"I understand. Let me get the diary for you."

He opened the bag Novak had given him. "Good. Novak did make a copy. I suggest you take the original." Terzić handed her a small booklet.

"Thanks. Goodnight, Mr. Terzić."

"*Laku noć.*"

Amanda went to her room, locked the door and rinsed her mouth clean. At least water was still tasteless. She sat motionless for several minutes. How was she supposed to live like this? First her sleep, now her food…just how much more would it take from her?

She turned her eyes to the small, leather diary. It had multiple stains and smelled musty, with traces of mold on the edges. Stitched into the cover with dirty, golden thread were the words *Jelena's diary*.

It felt surreal holding it in her hands. After all she had been through, this brown little book might finally answer all her questions—about the Red Dove, Priboj and, if she was lucky, her uncle.

Just a week ago, she would have jumped around at this point, giddy with excitement. But now? Now her hands were shaking so strongly, she couldn't even hold the diary still. What if this book was like the song? What if, just for opening it, the Red Dove would make her suffer even more?

She didn't even know what she had done to invite its wrath in the first place. Amanda had mulled it over on the drive from Romania—why was it going after her, but apparently leaving Terzić alone? What had she done that he hadn't? He had also read that song. He had also gone into both villages and that cursed mine. In fact, he had been looking into the Red Dove way longer than her. *So why me?*

Was it because of her arrogant belief in her textbooks and her 'science?' Was this the Red Dove teaching her a lesson? But that didn't ring true. The timing of that first dream, in the Red Dove's graveyard—it hadn't been a coincidence. She had *done* something to call the curse on herself. But...what?

If she didn't know what she had done wrong, wasn't it safer to leave this book closed? After the many horrors she had already suffered, she shuddered at the thought of how much more the Red Dove might do if she opened this diary.

Yet, this was also the only connection she was ever going to have to the other victims of the Red Dove. The only ones who could understand what she was going through. For all she knew, she couldn't escape her fate anyway. If she was going to be haunted for the rest of her life by those maddening whispers, or sliced to pieces by the shadows, like her mother's friend Tihomir, she at least didn't want to feel completely alone.

She turned to the first page and began to read.

CHAPTER 15

June 7th, 1995

Dear Mila,

I hope you like the name I've chosen for you. You'll be keeping all my secrets and they have to stay between us!

There's already big news. My birthday is coming up! The day after tomorrow, I'll turn twelve! Papa says it's one step closer to being an adult. I can't wait! I was only supposed to get you then, but Zora was full to the last page. Papa was really sweet and gave me you as an early present. Oh, Zora's my old diary, by the way. I had so much to tell her, I reached the last page before I knew it. But don't be jealous! I'll have a lot to tell you as well. In fact, you're really special! See, there's no pretty diaries like you in our tiny village. Papa asked for a favor so he could go to the city on one of the wood shipments. All just to buy you! Isn't Papa great?

I'm so glad to have you and can't wait to tell you all the exciting things in my future.

*

June 8th

Dear Mila,

I'll get to sing in church on Sunday!

It all started when Mama asked me to get water from the well. Thank God our house is so close. Old Slavna lives near the forest and always has carry that heavy water so far. I don't know how she does it. Anyway, at the well I met Father Viktor. He's our priest. He's been away on a long pilgrimage, but he finally came back yesterday. Mama was really happy he didn't decide to move elsewhere. She says there are villages three times our size who don't have their own priest. For mass, they have to walk or drive long ways.

Father Viktor said, "Ah, Jelena, greetings." It's how he always says hello. He put down his bucket and took a drink from that flat metal bottle he always has on his belt. As usual, he asked how Pavle and my parents were doing. And if we were saying our daily prayers. "Yes, Father," I told him every time. He smiled and ruffled my hair and told me my parents had raised me well.

He picked up his water bucket, but then turned back around and asked if I'd like to sing *Aleluja* on Sunday. Mr. Kralj had told him I was talented. Mr. Kralj did once tell me I should sing in church, but I never thought he'd talk to Father Viktor about it. But they're good friends, so maybe that's why. I was so happy, I agreed on the spot! Now I'm really nervous. I've never sung for the whole village. What if I make a mistake? I'll have to practice hard!

*

June 9th

Dear Mila,

Today was a great day. It was the best birthday I've ever had! Did you notice how pretty my writing is? That's because one of my presents was a pen. Yes, Mila, a real fountain pen, with a small ink bottle! It takes me longer to write, but it's so beautiful...I could do this all day.

Mama also made me a cake. Her cakes are the best. But don't tell anybody! I always have to pretend to enjoy the boring cakes from Andjela's mother. I wish Mama would make cakes more often, but she says Pavle and I will get spoiled if we eat too many.

Andjela is my best friend, by the way. She always knows every answer in school and she helps me with homework. She came for my birthday, too. She even brought her dog, Tomo. He was a stray they found during one of the wood shipments. He's so sweet and follows Andjela everywhere she goes. I hope I can have a dog too, some day.

Can you guess my second present? It was a music sheet book! Now I can finally practice my singing. Maybe with Mr. Kralj's help, I can even write my own songs.

But the best gift of all was that Slavko was here! I was so nervous when I asked him to come. I feel a weird tingle in my stomach whenever he talks to me. Mama once told me his name means 'Glory'. It suits him so well. I can't stop thinking about him. He has such a pretty face. And his hair...Mila, if you could see him you would understand.

*

June 11th

Dear Mila,

I was so nervous in church today. I practiced a lot yesterday after my party, but my hands still shook when I walked to the altar. But everything went well! The whole village clapped. Even Father Viktor congratulated me! After mass he said, "Jelena, you have the voice of an angel."

When I told Papa on the way home, he laughed and said he hoped Father's breath hadn't made me drunk. Mama got really angry and told Papa that Father Viktor was a man of God and if he drank from that flask on his belt so often, he had a good reason for it.

Papa and Mama kept fighting all the way home. But I don't care what Father Viktor drinks or how much. He's always so kind and he knows so much! I'm sure he meant what he said. "The voice of an angel." It still makes me smile.

If singers always get this much praise, I want to be one later! Maybe like the ones who sing on Papa's radio. Can you imagine that, Mila? Being heard by thousands at the same time? Making so many people happy? I need to practice a lot so I can become a singer too.

*

June 14th

Dear Mila,

I'm so sorry I didn't talk to you for three days. It's not because I don't like you. I said nothing because there was nothing to say, at least until now. Life in this village is always the same. I often wonder how life is elsewhere, with more people.

I mean, there are only four kids around my age here. Me, Andjela, Slavko and Srecko. Maybe Miljan, but he's fifteen already. Imagine how many friends I could have in a big city. It would be so much fun!

Do you think cities are quiet? Here, it's unbearable. You hear a chainsaw or somebody using a hammer almost every day, except Sundays and when it rains. It's so annoying. I can't even hear myself sing.

Then there's school. I have to spend so much time there. But Mr. Kralj always says we have to study and that "education is important."

Papa says I should listen to him, because he's very smart and knows a lot. Kind of like Father Viktor. But Father Viktor at least talks about interesting, far-away places. All Mr. Kralj teaches is *so. Boring!*

But today was different. Not because of Mr. Kralj. He was boring as usual. But Slavko passed me a note! Oh Mila, when he gave me the note, he touched my hand! The place he touched still feels tingly. He asked if I want to meet tomorrow! I'm so nervous, Mila. I'll have to write a reply and pass it to him in class tomorrow as well. But I must make sure nobody sees it, or the whole village will know. People gossip so much here. Mila, I can't wait to give him my reply!

*

June 15th

Dear Mila,

I'm still shaking all over, I can barely write. You won't believe what happened!

You remember how I told you about the note Slavko passed me? Well, today, while Mr. Kralj's back was turned, I passed him my reply. He seemed really happy that I'd meet him. I couldn't wait for evening the whole day. Time went by so slowly!

When it was near seven, I walked to the forest. I didn't tell
Papa and Mama where I was going, or they wouldn't have let
me. They keep saying it's dangerous and I might get lost. But I'm
twelve now. How bad can it be if I take a few steps outside the
village?

Slavko was already waiting for me. He took me uphill, until we
could see the village from above. I didn't know about this place,
but it has such a pretty view!

I was so nervous, I didn't know what to do. It was just me
and Slavko, alone together. In the end, we just sat under a tree
together and talked. About what we want to do later in life, what
other people in other places are doing right now, and how big
the world is. It felt like we talked about everything. I don't know
how long it was, but I never got bored!

And then, Mila…while we were both sitting against the tree,
his hand touched mine! I was so surprised, I pulled it away. He
quickly apologized, but he looked so sad! I didn't want to make
him sad, so I put my hand on his. It felt so strange…like it was
on fire. I was so insanely nervous! But so happy! I don't know
how long we stayed like that. We didn't move, we didn't talk. We
just looked into each other's eyes.

And then, it just happened so fast! He leaned forward a bit,
and then a bit more, and then slightly more… I don't know why,
but I closed my eyes. And then…our lips touched!

Oh, Mila! If only I could tell you how it felt! My lips tingled
all over and they got hot and cold at the same time! When we
separated, the first thing I saw were his big, brown eyes. They
were so close! And so beautiful, like shiny acorns.

Then, when he moved a bit further away, I realized the sun
had already set, and I was supposed to be home already! It was
so unfair! We quickly said goodbye and agreed to meet again
another day. I hope it'll be soon. Mila, I feel so lonely right now.

I keep thinking about him. I've never felt like this before. I'm so happy, I think I'll burst! But I also feel guilty. I don't think we were supposed to do what we did. Mama always told me, "A woman's lips are sacred. Only the man who marries you is allowed to touch them." Does that mean we did something wrong? Mila, did we sin?

*

June 16th

Dear Mila,

Something bad happened. I was getting ready for school and had my window open. I heard shouts and saw people running around. Papa and Mama also didn't know what was happening, so we went outside together.

Everyone was standing outside Mr. Kralj's house, looking really upset. I got curious and squeezed through the crowd.

There was a bird on Mr. Kralj's door, and it was covered with blood! So much there was a puddle under it! It was stuck to the door with a big nail and a piece of paper coming out of its mouth. It was so disgusting! Why would anyone do this?

Some people said it was a bad joke, or an animal hater. Some even said it was an evil spell. But nobody really knew. When Papa saw it, he told me to go back inside. Mila, it was so awful. I hope they find who did this!

*

June 17th

Dear Mila,

School was strange today. Mr. Kralj kept looking at us like we had done something bad. Papa said some people thought a

175

child killed the bird yesterday. Because children sometimes don't know right from wrong.

I was so angry. Of course we all know that's wrong. None of us would ever do something like that. I'm sure of it!

Papa also told me the bird was a dove and the piece of paper in its mouth was some kind of poem. How cruel is that, Mila? Killing a dove for a stupid joke like that!

I wanted to cheer myself up by singing along to the songs on the radio, but it wasn't working. There was only noise coming out. Papa said they can only fix it in the city. I hope we'll make another delivery soon.

*

June 18th
Dear Mila,

Ever since that dove showed up, the village feels different. It's hard to explain, but everyone seems worried somehow. Even mass wasn't the same. I was hoping to sing again today, but Father Viktor didn't ask me. At the end of his sermon, he said "Be vigilant! We must guard ourselves against the devil and pray fervently the killer of the dove is found. God help us!"

We were all so confused. Father Viktor is always gentle and kind. The way he talked was so unlike him. As we left church, he and Mr. Kralj were talking. Their faces were really serious. I wanted to listen, but it would have been too obvious. What do you think they were talking about?

*

June 19th

Dear Mila,

As if the dove hadn't been enough! School had just started when Branko burst into the classroom and asked Mr. Kralj to come and help. Branko's always so nice. He sometimes gives Pavle and me some apples or even milk from his farm. I've never seen him so angry.

Mr. Kralj said he was busy teaching, but Branko wouldn't leave. Mr. Kralj told us to sit still, and they went outside to talk. Slavko and I looked at each other, but this wasn't about our secret. Something way worse was happening.

We all huddled together at the door. It was hard to hear, but it went something like:

"...and she was my best cow!"

"Calm down. Are you sure it wasn't an animal?"

"Don't treat me like an idiot, Kralj! No animal could have done that."

"What makes you say that?"

First, there was no reply. We wondered if they had left, but then Branko talked again. He was so quiet I could barely hear. "She was torn up... ...never seen anything like... ...sliced open... ...entrails strewn around the farm... ...and her eyes! Gouged out..."

Andjela jerked her head away from the door and knocked over a chair. Branko stopped talking and Mr. Kralj opened the door. He scolded us for eavesdropping, but he didn't punish us. He told us to go home and stay there. I told Papa what happened and he went to Branko's farm to see if he could help.

When Papa came back in the evening, he said nobody suspects us children anymore of killing the dove. What happened to Branko's cow is something none of us could have done.

But then, Mila, what did?

177

June 21st

Dear Mila,

There's only bad news to tell you lately.

It was my turn to get water from the again. While I was lifting the bucket, Mr. Kralj shouted that all the adults should go to Branko's farm.

Papa told me to stay inside while he was gone. He came home late and told Mama that more of Branko's animals were dead. He and a few others spent the whole day helping Branko build a strong fence. When I asked Papa if Branko's cows were safe now, he said yes, it would take a bear to break the fence they built.

I told Papa that while he was gone, Slavna told me she knew what happened. Last night, she was sitting by the window and saw a large, dark shape creep toward the farm. Papa said Slavna was very old and her eyesight was bad. He thinks it was a wolf or a rabid fox and there's nothing to be afraid of.

But Slavna has lived here for so long. Even with her bad eyes, she would know a fox. What if it's something else? What if it's not over yet?

*

June 22nd

Dear Mila,

I met Slavko today! It was only for a short while, though. I wanted to talk about what happened in the forest, but Slavko said somebody might hear us. His parents don't want to let him out of the house anymore, but he'll try to slip out and come over. I can't wait!

Papa is in a good mood. He says it was just a wild beast after all and the fence is working. I so hope he is right! Mama says it's too soon to celebrate, just because nothing has happened for a day. But Papa won't take her seriously.

In the afternoon, Ratko, our hunter, asked everyone to come to the well. Like Mama, he thought that whatever killed Branko's cows was still out there, and could kill one of us next. He would go into the forest to track the creature down. Until then, he said nobody should leave their house after dark or go into the forest.

The Lukic brothers complained. They were already behind on the next shipment and needed to cut more trees. But Mr. Kralj agreed with Ratko and asked them to stay inside the village. He would explain the delay to the buyers in the city when it was safe to go out again.

Father Viktor wished Ratko good luck and blessed him. It was so strange. Ratko never received a blessing for a simple hunt before.

Ratko said he was setting off right away. Since the beast only attacked at night, it could take him long to track it down. But he promised he would be back in a day or two. Then, he picked up his backpack and hunting rifle and left towards the forest.

After seeing all this. I'm a bit scared, Mila. Why did Father Viktor bless Ratko? Does that mean even Father Viktor is scared?

*

June 23rd

Dear Mila,

Oh Lord. Oh God. Mila, it's so horrible! Ratko is dead! When I went out to get water, many were standing at the well, like when that awful dove showed up. Everyone seemed upset, some were shouting. Then I got close and saw it.

Ratko was lying there, on his back, with a circle of blood drawn around him. His face was...destroyed; it was all just

179

red goo. His legs and arms were snapped and twisted like
tree branches. His breast was ripped open, like the center of a
crooked star.

It was so awful! I threw up when I saw it. Just thinking of it
makes me sick. I didn't know humans looked like that on the
inside! And the smell! It was so disgusting, I couldn't even
breathe. When I stepped back, I saw Slavko. He didn't know
what had happened and his parents were trying to stop him
from going closer. He pretended to give up, then slipped past
his mother. He stumbled and fell right in front of Ratko's open
breast. His face turned white and he screamed until his parents
took him away. His eyes in that moment, Mila…they were so
wide and bloodshot. For a second, he didn't even look human.

Then, Father Viktor arrived. When he saw Ratko, he fell on
his knees and crossed himself. He unhooked his flask from his
belt and emptied it in almost one go. His hands were shaking so
much he spilled half all over himself. He looked up and shouted
"God, have mercy on us!"

Papa took me back home. Since then, I haven't been allowed to
leave. I hope Slavko is okay. He probably won't be able to come
visit me now.

At dinner, Papa told us that Ratko would be buried tomorrow.
They also found his hunting rifle next to him. They didn't
recognize it at first, because it had been sliced into thin strips,
like it was made of paper. That really scares me, Mila. What in
the world can cut steel like that? Papa says nobody knows, but
many suspect a crazy and evil person from outside. Mama said
this was too wicked and is something far worse. Oh God, what if
she is right?

*

June 24th

Dear Mila,

Nothing happened today! I'm so relieved to be able to write this. I was even allowed outside again. But everything feels so different now. Everyone is walking so fast and looking over their shoulder all the time. Nobody is cutting trees anymore. The monster that killed Ratko could still be in the forest, after all!

In the afternoon, went to Ratko's funeral. It was so sad. All of us were there to say goodbye. Father Viktor said a prayer as the Lukic brothers lowered the coffin. I hope Ratko is in a better place now. After the burial, Father Viktor asked everyone to come to church tomorrow so we can pray for strength and guidance together.

Slavko was there, but before I could talk to him, his father took him by the hand and led him away. He kept staring into the distance the whole time, like nothing mattered anymore. It scared me.

When I went back to Papa, I saw Father Viktor talking to Mr. Kralj again. They both looked so scared! It was like when the dove showed up. I wanted to know what they were saying, so I walked as close as I could. Father Viktor said something like, "… and if so, we are in grave danger."

I couldn't hear what Mr. Kralj replied, but Father Viktor said something about "find where the…" but then Papa grabbed my hand and pulled me away. He asked how often he had to tell me that eavesdropping was wrong and took me back home.

I'm so frustrated. What do you think they were talking about? If only Papa had given me a few moments longer. Now I'll never know.

*

June 24th, night

Dear Mila,

I can't sleep. I hope writing to you can calm me down.

It all started after dinner, when Pavle and I were cleaning up the kitchen. There was a knock at the door. "Who's there?" Papa shouted. There was a reply and Papa opened.

It was Mr. Kralj and Father Viktor. Mr. Kralj leaned close to Papa and whispered something. Papa's face grew stiff, but he stood aside and let them enter. Everyone's faces looked so grave. Mr. Kralj and Father Viktor went around, closely looking at everything we owned. Every chair, shelf and table. I wanted to ask what they were looking for, but I had a feeling Papa wouldn't want me to speak up.

Then, Father Viktor asked if he could see my bedroom.

I looked at Papa, but he nodded. Father Viktor came into my room and carefully examined everything. Even my bed and my dolls! I was so scared he would find you, but thank God, I hid you well.

After a few minutes, Father Viktor took a gulp from his bottle. He seemed relieved for some reason and smiled at me. He said I had a beautiful house and that I should "guard it well."

I didn't understand what he meant, but I knew something was wrong. I wanted to ask him why he was acting so strange, but he went back to Mr. Kralj before I could. They both thanked Papa and left.

From my window, I saw them go to the next house. When I went into the kitchen, Papa and Mama stopped talking. I asked if I could go outside and ask Mr. Kralj and Father Viktor what they were doing. He said no, because it was getting dark. I tried to ask again, but Papa yelled at me to go back to my room and sleep.

Why was Papa so angry? I don't understand. What did I do wrong?

I looked out of my window a long time and saw Mr. Kralj and Father Viktor enter and leave two more houses, then it got too dark for me to see. What is happening here, Mila?

*

June 25th, morning

Dear Mila,

I woke up when it was still dark because people outside were screaming. Someone ran past my window. In the hallway, Papa was already putting his boots on. I wanted to go too, but Papa told me to stay inside with Mama and Pavle. He even threatened to beat me if he found me outside!

Papa came back an hour later and told us there had been a fire. It was at one of Branko's old huts, where he used to store his hay. The village built him a bigger one a year ago, so nobody was using it. People are wondering how the fire could have started in the first place. At least nobody got hurt.

*

June 25th, evening

Dear Mila,

We finally know what's happening. Oh Mila, it's so horrible!

During mass, Father Viktor looked so exhausted. His eyes were drooping, and his hair was all sweaty and tangled. He was shaking the whole time! It only stopped when he drank from his flask.

After our last prayer, Mr. Kralj stood up and loudly asked for our attention. He walked up to the front and told us we didn't have to be worried about the abandoned hut that burned down. He said he and Father Viktor found out what was happening and asked us all to listen carefully.

Father Viktor raised his hands and said, "We are in grave danger! Evil has come to this village!" He reminded everyone of the death of Ratko and the murdered animals and then said, "All began with a dove, drenched in blood!"

We all looked at each other. He was right! Everything was fine until we found that dove nailed to the door. Ever since then, bad things started to happen. Father Viktor then explained what was happening:

"A white dove is the avatar of the Holy Spirit. Defiling it has long been how devil worshippers have sought favor from the dark prince, to bring agony and destruction to their victims. What happened is proof that a Satanist, a traitor to us and to our Lord, resides here.

"Yesterday, Kralj and I went out to find the sinner and his lair. Hidden inside the abandoned hut was a foul shrine, with devilish symbols, black candles, gutted ravens and worst of all, a satanic book, filled with witchcraft and black magic. This unholy shrine was sacrilege. It had to be destroyed. That is why we burned it to ashes. But we were too late. The evil is already upon us. Before burning the shrine, we examined the unholy book. It described a foul ritual, and the curse that now haunts us. It was the Satanist who spilled the blood of a white dove, the symbol of our lord, and nailed it to our door with an unholy incantation. In so doing, he called forth a horror of the evil one, called the Red Dove, the harbinger of madness and death.

"Heralding its arrival are the Dark Ones—moving, living forms of darkness and terror. They lurk in the shadowed spots, where the sun's light cannot reach them. It is they who slaughtered our cows and poor Ratko. Kralj and I have already drawn a ring of holy water around the village to ward them off. However, the Dark Ones will only grow stronger and bolder as the Red Dove draws closer every day. Once it arrives, nothing can save us—it will drag all of us to hell.

"But there is hope! By God's eternal decree, Satan cannot hold power in this world on his own. As with Judas, the devil requires someone to invite him into his soul and act as his tether. If we can find this sinner, this Satanist, this betrayer, we may yet be saved.

"Do not wander at night, when the Dark Ones move. Stay inside and sprinkle holy water onto your doorstep and windows to ward off the foul demons and await the cleansing sunlight. We must remain strong in our faith. With God's grace, we may yet find a path to salvation."

Mila, you should have seen the helpless faces of everyone in church. Nobody knew what to say. Mama even fainted and Papa had to carry her home.

I am so scared of the dark now, Mila. I am scared that I'll run into one of those monsters. Do you end up in hell when these... Dark Ones kill you? Does that mean Ratko is in hell now? Will they take all of us?

I don't want to die. I don't want to go to hell. God, save me!

*

June 26th

Dear Mila,

Nothing happened today. Could Father Viktor have been wrong? Could the shrine he and Mr. Kralj found just be a stupid joke? Oh, I so hope he is wrong!

The village has become so quiet now. When I went to get water from the well, I barely met anyone. Everyone is staying inside. I saw Slavko near school and tried talking to him, but he kept turning around to look behind him. He was biting his nails and talking about who the devil-worshipper could be. He even said he had a few 'suspects', but he wouldn't tell me who. Mila, what happened to him? Where did his warm smile go?

*

June 27th

Dear Mila,

There was a heavy storm today. We were all supposed to meet by the church to discuss what to do next, but it's not safe outside right now. I'm scared, Mila. The storm is so strong, it doesn't feel natural. Is even the weather against us now? Or do you think this is the Red Dove's doing, too? Has God forsaken us?

I tried singing to pass the time, but it just makes me nervous and I feel like I'm annoying Papa and Mama. What am I supposed to do?

*

June 28th

Dear Mila,

After the storm we found someone else dead, at the edge of the forest. Like Ratko, his face was destroyed. But none of us are missing, so it's someone from outside. Some think it was a hiker who got lost, or maybe a visitor. He didn't know the Dark Ones were in the forest. Oh Mila, what should we do? If we go into the forest we'll die, but if we stay, we'll die too!

Papa doesn't talk much anymore. He just sits in the kitchen with a bottle of Rakia. He doesn't drink from it, he just sits there and broods. The whole village now feels like this. The only one who still smiles is Mirko, the craftsman who makes those pretty jewels and wooden toys that sell for so much in the city. Papa once said that without him, we'd all be a lot poorer.

I really don't understand it...Mirko lost his leg in an accident a long time ago, he should be sad. But he's always so kind and happy, always trying to help someone. I hope he stays like this. You can only smile when you have hope, right? So, maybe there's still a way out of this?

*

June 29th

Dear Mila,

Branko is dead. It's getting worse every day. Like the others, his face was gone. Why? What do they take people's faces for? Papa said that, like the hiker, they found him at the edge of the forest. Why did Branko go there? He knows how dangerous the forest is! We have to stay inside the ring of holy water Father Viktor and Mr. Kralj made. But how long will it last, Mila? Father Viktor said the Dark Ones would only get stronger. Every moment the betrayer is free, more of us might die. If only time would stop! The old clock next to my bed is ticking so loudly. I never realized how loud it is. It's scaring me. Every tick makes our end come closer. And it's so loud. Mila, make it stop!

*

June 29th, 1995, evening

Dear Mila,

I broke my clock. It was so loud I couldn't hear anything else anymore. I threw it down on the floor and it stopped ticking. At least I don't need to hear time pass anymore. The clock in the kitchen is also loud, but if I close my door, I don't hear it anymore.

Papa came back from a meeting with some of his friends. He

said Pavle and I had to stay inside from now on. But Papa still seemed happy, for the first time since Sunday. He explained he and his friends have formed a group to protect the village. They even thought of a name: The Five Watchmen. Starting tomorrow, they will look for the betrayer together. I hope they find him before it's too late.

*

June 30th

Dear Mila,

I want to go out! It's the most beautiful weather today. Even Father Viktor said it's safe to be outside during the day. So why do I have to stay inside?

All the adults had a big meeting in the afternoon. Papa stayed longer to talk with the other Watchmen. He told me to keep this secret, but the Watchmen have written a list of people who have acted suspiciously. They will talk to those on the list, and test how they react to holy symbols. He patted me on the head and said they would find the betrayer in no time.

Papa also told me what happened during the big meeting in the afternoon. Mr. Kralj had the most to say. He told everyone that with Branko and most of his cows dead, we would quickly run out of food. If we didn't do something, we would all starve to death. Some suggested slaughtering Branko's remaining two cows, but Mr. Kralj said it would only buy us a couple more days at most. The only way was to go to the city and buy food. Of course, everyone told him it was suicide to go into the forest.

Mr. Kralj agreed and said he was really scared, but there was no other choice. Somebody asked if this was an excuse to run away and leave the rest of us to die. Mr. Kralj and his friends got really angry and a fight almost broke out. Papa said that Father

Viktor was the one who calmed everyone down, explaining that it didn't matter what Mr. Kralj did—as long as the betrayer wasn't found, nobody could escape the Red Dove

Then Mr. Kralj asked if there were any volunteers who would come with him. Only two raised their hands: the Lukic brothers. They are very strong. They are our best lumberjacks and they have a big car. If anyone can get through the forest, it's them! Father Viktor said he was very scared for Mr. Kralj, but that he understood the need to go. It would be best to leave at noon, he explained, when the devil was weakest. He would bless them and pray for God to guide them through the forest.

I really hope they will make it. Our last meal was tiny, and Papa told us that with Branko dead, we would have to 'tighten our belts'. Oh Lord, please watch over Mr. Kralj and the Lukic brothers.

Papa also wrote a letter to a friend who works for the church. He hopes someone outside knows more about the Red Dove, or how to find the betrayer. Usually, Mr. Kralj or Father Viktor take our mail to the nearest town, but since the Red Dove came, we haven't been able to send any letters. If Mr. Kralj can deliver Papa's letter, maybe we'll get help.

Tomorrow is the big day. Oh Mila, I so hope they come back safe. If they can bring food and deliver that letter, I'm sure everything will be fine.

*

July 1st

Oh dear Mila,

All hope is lost! I'm sorry my writing is so bad, but my hands are still shaking. Mr. Kralj and the Lukic brothers are dead. Oh God, Mila, they are dead. They died right in front of us!

We all gathered near the well, where the Lukic brothers had already parked their jeep. Father Viktor sprinkled holy water on it, then we all sang a prayer for the three to get back to us safely.

They all got into the car, and then…and then…there was a ball of fire! I was standing with all the others when everything went bright and the air became really warm, like a hot wind blowing past me. I fell down somehow and then Papa dragged me backwards.

When I looked up, everything was burning and Father Viktor was trying to smash one of the windows with a rock, but the fire was too hot to get close. Then I saw that Mr. Kralj and the Lukic brothers were still in the jeep.

Their screams…weren't human. The worst sound I ever heard. I can still hear it when I close my eyes. And then, there came this smell! Like when Mama roasts pork. I wondered who was cooking dinner, until I finally understood.

When the screams stopped, Father Viktor fell to his knees and raised his arms to heaven and cried for God to forgive us for our sins. Slavko's parents shouted something and carried him away.

As they passed by, I saw his face. It was red all over and his lips were black. And his hair, Mila, his beautiful brown hair, it was all gone.

Then someone pushed me and I fell. Everyone was running and screaming. I tried to get up, but someone kept shoving me back down. Thank God Papa pushed them away and lifted me up.

"Run!" he shouted behind me.

When we got back home, I turned around. The jeep was still burning. Only Father Viktor was left, still kneeling and his hands folded in prayer. Why did something so bad happen? I prayed so much the last days, why won't God help us? Is he angry? What have we done?

July 2nd

Dear Mila,

I'm still sad about what happened yesterday. I couldn't sleep.

Papa was out in the morning with his Watchmen friends, but came back annoyed at everyone's "lack of cooperation." Nobody wants to talk anymore. It was the same in church. Everyone looked so cold. Nobody held hands for prayer.

Father Viktor looked so pale! Like he got 10 years older. But he still did his best to smile as he greeted everyone. He said he would bury Mr. Kralj and the Lukic brothers today. That makes six burials in just a week, Mila. It's so sad. And nobody wants to attend, so he'll have to do everything by himself.

He asked us for forgiveness that he was not strong enough to banish the evil himself. But he said we needed to stay strong in our faith and that he would pray as much as he could.

I wanted to go visit Slavko, to see if he's okay, but Papa told me not to leave the house. He won't even let me sing. He says it might bring "unwanted attention". All I'm allowed to do is sit around and wait. I feel I will go crazy.

That's why I asked Mama if I can go to the funeral of Mr. Kralj and the Lukic brothers, while Papa is out with his Watchmen friends. She didn't want to, but when I said she should come with me and that the sun was up, she agreed. We'll head out soon, so I have to stop here. I'll write to you more later.

*

July 2nd, evening

Dear Mila,

As Mama and I walked to the cemetery, we met Father Viktor. He was carrying four buckets of water. Four, Mila! He looked like he would collapse any moment. Mama and I offered him our help, but he said, "This is nothing, compared to the burden of the cross our Lord had to bear."

When I asked him why he was carrying so much, he said it was for holy water and that he had used "great amounts" lately.

Papa sprinkles holy water on all doors and windows on our house every evening. Father Viktor must be spending so much time making enough for everyone…maybe that's why he looks so tired? But why does he think we'll need even more? Is what we do not enough?

The burial was lonely. Only Slavna and Mirko were here besides Mama and me. We helped Father Viktor lower the coffins. He spoke a few prayers, sprinkled holy water over them and then covered them with earth. Before we left, he told us, "Thank you for being here. May God watch over us all."

Now we are back home. We were lucky, Papa didn't see us leave the house. He just came back, but the Watchmen made no progress. Nobody trusts them, nobody wants to talk. Oh Mila, how will this end? How are we supposed to find the betrayer if nobody trusts each other? Our food is running low and Slavna even told me she had seen the Dark Ones at the edge of the forest after dark! I hope Papa manages to convince everyone to cooperate, before it's too late!

*

July 2nd, night

Dear Mila,

I can't sleep. I'm so scared, writing to you is all I can do right now. I hope you'll comfort me. It all happened so fast, but I know it happened!

I was having a horrible nightmare. I was in the forest and the Dark Ones were all around me. They wanted to take my face, like the others. I was so glad when I woke up and saw it was only a dream. But then, something moved outside my window. I looked and there was a Dark One! Right in front of our house! It looked just like the satanic book said! Like a deformed, moving shadow! It had no eyes, but when I looked at it, it moved like it wanted to get inside!

I screamed until Papa came running into my room and turned the lights on. I told him everything and he shone a light outside, but everything was quiet, nothing moved. He pulled the curtains and told me it was all just a bad dream, but he was lying! He was scared too! I could tell! And it wasn't just a dream! I know what happened! I saw it! I know I saw it! And I know it saw me! It was looking at me!

The Dark Ones are here! They are in the village! They are not staying outside anymore! Mila, what can I do? I am so scared! What will they do next? What if they come into the house? What if Papa misses a spot with the holy water? I'm so scared...Mila, please don't leave me!

*

July 3rd, morning
Dear Mila,

Woke up to see Papa head outside through my window. There were lots of people at the well. Everyone was talking or shouting.

Then, Father Viktor came, accompanied by Borislav and Josif who pointed at a bucket. When Father Viktor saw it, he shrank back and took a drink from his flask. He and the others talked for a few minutes, then everyone left.

When Papa came home, he looked so scared! I asked him what happened, but he said he will talk to all of us later. I think I'll go crazy. I want to know what's going on!

July 3rd, noon

Dear Mila,

Papa called me and Pavle into the kitchen. Mama was crying while Papa finally told us what happened: The water in the well has turned black! That's why everyone was shouting outside before.

Borislav and Josif went to get Father Viktor. When he recovered from his shock, he told everyone that the Dark Ones must have cursed the well. Nedeljko then said he had seen a shadow move from his window at night! See Mila, it wasn't just a bad dream! There was a Dark One next to my window! And it did something to our well!

Father Viktor said that the ring of holy water he and Mr. Kralj created around the village must have weakened and he said he would go out at noon and strengthen it again. Then he told everyone to stay indoors. He would prepare as much as holy water as possible and that all of us, including the children, should gather at 6, while the sun was still up, so we could pray together for God to forgive us and purify the well. Until then, no one was allowed to drink the black water.

Papa said we have to be careful and only drink when we are thirsty and that we have to "hope for the best." But Mila, what are we supposed to do if God doesn't help us? That well is our only source of water!

Papa told us something even more scary—after the others left, Papa and the other Watchmen went to talk with Father Viktor. He told them he hadn't said much because he didn't want to scare everyone, but our time is running out. If the Dark Ones can breach the holy barrier around the village, it means the Red Dove is almost here. Even if Father Viktor adds more holy water to the barrier and cleanses the well, it will only buy us a few days at most!

I've been praying ever since. If only God helps Papa and the other Watchmen…maybe we can all still escape from this!

*

Dear Mila,

I keep thinking about Slavko. He got hurt so badly when Mr. Kralj and the Lukic brothers died. It was only the day before yesterday but it feels like so long ago. I want to visit him. I keep praying that he will be alright. But what if God doesn't listen because Slavko and I kissed? It was a sin, wasn't it? Maybe this is all my fault? The curse of the Red Dove started the very next day! If I had just pushed Slavko away, do you think God would listen to my prayers and show us mercy?

I'll ask Papa if I can go to church. Maybe if I confess my sin to God and ask for forgiveness, maybe all this will stop?

*

July 3rd, afternoon
Dear Mila,

I just came back from church. At first, Papa didn't want me going outside, but Mama saw how important it was and said it was a holy place and there was nowhere safer. Papa didn't look happy, but he agreed. After checking outside that all was quiet, he let me go.

The church doors were open, like they always are. There was nobody inside. I sat down in the front bench and confessed my sins to God. I asked him for forgiveness and mercy and promised that I'd never do something so awful again. I don't know if that's enough. I was going to pray more, but then

195

the door to Father Viktor's room opened. "Who goes there?" he shouted. He looked really scary, but when he saw me, his expression became much softer.

"Ah, Jelena. What a pleasant surprise," he said.

I tried to apologize but lost my breath midway when I saw him step into the light of the window. He used to look so healthy and strong. Now he has a thick stubble and dark rings under his eyes, it's like he's thirty years older.

He said, "Sorry, you startled me. What brings you here, my child?"

I told him I needed to pray and he said, "That is most commendable. May I join you? I will need the Lord's strength today."

We sang the Lord's Prayer three times. When we were finished, he looked at the small clock on the wall. I hadn't noticed it before. At least this one didn't tick so loudly.

Father Viktor rubbed his temples and unhooked his flask. I remembered Papa's silly face back when he made fun of Father Viktor and I giggled before I could stop myself. Father Viktor looked at me and asked, "Do I have something on my face?" I wanted to lie. I was worried he would get angry. But lying to a man of God was probably a sin, too, and I had just promised God I would never sin again. So, I told Father Viktor that Papa once said he drank too much of the Communion Wine.

Father Viktor frowned, but then held up the flask and looked at it. He turned to me with a sad smile. "He is not wrong, I suppose."

I asked him why he drank so much.

"Well, it is the blood of Christ, my child. It makes me feel closer to God. Also, a good wine makes you live longer." He smiled and held out the bottle. "Would you like to try?"

I was taken aback. I'm only twelve and Papa never let me try the beer he drinks. But I didn't want to say No to Father Viktor. He always drank so much, I thought it had to taste pretty good. I managed two gulps, but when the taste crept up my nose, I spit out everything. It was so awful! Like a mixture of bitter grapes and herbs.

I swallowed badly and had to cough a lot. Father Viktor laughed and patted my back with his large hand.

"Forgive me, child. This was a cruel jest," he said.

I saw I had spit the wine all over the bench. I told him I would go get Mama's cleaning tools and hurry back, but he held me back and shook his head.

"Do not worry yourself. The stains are immaterial now." He looked at the old clock again and said, "Well then, I better return to making holy water."

Father Viktor did his best to smile, but I've never seen him look so weak and exhausted. God, please give Father Viktor strength! If something happens to him, I don't know how we'll manage.

*

July 3rd, evening
Dear Mila,

I have been crying for an hour now. Why does God hate us so much? Why can't he show us the tiniest bit of mercy?

We all met at the well at six. Father Viktor arrived last, carrying a large bucket. He crossed himself and asked us to form a circle around the well. We all held hands and Father Viktor began his prayer. "Almighty God, our Lord who sits atop the heavens, blessed be thy name. We are gathered before you to ask for your forgiveness and mercy. We beg you—though this water has been tainted by darkness, let your light restore its purity and save us from the vile abomination that torments us. Though we walk through the valley of the shadow of death, we shall fear no evil, for your light guides our way. Amen."

He picked up his bucket of holy water and poured it into the well.

We all hoped that Father Viktor's prayer had worked, but none of us wanted to be the first to try. Father Viktor said, "I see you are afraid. But God's mercy is eternal for those who have faith. I will prove it to you!"

He brought up the bucket. A few gasped when the bucket came up. Just like Papa had described it, it was completely black! It looked like ink! Father Viktor wiped his brow and looked at us. His voice was shaky when he said, "Please, remain calm. It may look tainted, but have faith. This water *is* drinkable."

Of course, nobody believed him. Even Father Viktor himself didn't seem to believe it. He must have been so scared…his hands were shaking. He took the flask from his belt and emptied the remaining wine in one gulp.

Father Viktor said, "T-then…I will p-prove it to you…"

He filled his flask with the black water, crossed himself, and drank. We all watched in silence. As he lowered the flask from his lips, Father Viktor seemed normal. Nothing happened!

We all started cheering, some falling on their knees and thanking God for the miracle he had bestowed on us. We were all so happy that God had not forsaken us after all.

Father Viktor beamed with pride. "You see? You see? The Lord provides!" At that last word, he started coughing. "Put your— trust in—the Lord."

His coughing got worse and worse, but he didn't stop.

"You—will be—saved—if—if—!"

Mila, if only you had seen us…The terror on everyone's faces as Father Viktor gasped for breath, his eyes terrified with fear.

He fell down, coughing and shaking. He made horrible gurgling sounds and clawed at his neck and twisted his head upward, like he was asking God for help.

When Father Viktor threw up blood everywhere, everyone screamed and ran. I didn't look back. I couldn't look back. The gurgling sound was so horrible, I pressed my hands to my ears.

Mila, why is God so cruel? If He didn't even save Father Viktor, what hope do the rest of us have? We still have a little bit of water in the house, but what are we supposed to do when it's used up? I'm scared. I'm so scared.

*

July 4th

Dear Mila,

The first day without water. The entire village is quiet. Everyone is hiding for now.

After lunch, Papa went out to meet the other Watchmen. When he came back, he told us something really scary. The Watchmen wanted to do what was right and bury Father Viktor. Except, there was nothing to bury! All they found at the well was Father Viktor's blood-soaked cassock, but no body.

When the Watchmen went to the graveyard, they found something even worse. All the graves of those who died from the Red Dove were broken up, and the coffins torn open. Just like with Father Viktor, the clothes were still there, but the bodies were gone. What is the meaning of this, Mila? I am so scared! Why are the dead not in the earth anymore? Where are they now?

*

July 4th, evening

Dear Mila,

Papa came back from another meeting with the Watchmen and told me and Pavle to go to our rooms. A quarter of an hour later, he called me back into the kitchen. Mama looked so frightened!

Papa asked me strange questions. How old I was, what I remembered from the past two years and even what songs I used to sing when I was little. Then he put some holy water in the shape of a cross on my forehead and asked me to say the Lord's Prayer. When I was done, he smiled and looked relieved. He sent me to bed and called Pavle into the kitchen.

I don't understand, Mila. Did Papa think I was the betrayer? How can he think that! Do others think so too? Will someone try to hurt me? I'm innocent!

*

July 5th, morning

Dear Mila,

The old water tastes so bad and I'm so thirsty. My mouth feels like it's filled with sand. We still have some food, but it's salty. If we eat it, we'll just get more thirsty. Pavle cried all night. I know he's thirsty, I am too. But it's keeping the rest of us up. Why can't he just shut up!

I have nobody to talk to except you. Papa and Mama sent us to our rooms to talk alone in the kitchen. I eavesdropped a little. Mama said, "Is there any hope left?"

"Yes. We Watchmen have agreed to do what we should have done from the beginning. We'll go through our list of suspects and interrogate them. By force, if we have to. Once we find the betrayer, we'll hang the bastard. Father Viktor called him the devil's tether, so once he's dead, everything will go back to normal."

"You can't just hang someone who won't talk! What if you kill an innocent?"

"Then we'll continue down our list until we get the right one."

"This is madness! Murder is a sin! You would—'"

A chair scraped and Papa yelled, "Don't raise your voice at me! Stupid woman. Do you think this is easy for me? I am trying to save us! We tried to be nice and thanks to that, we're all dying! Do you have a better idea?"

"No. I just—"

"Then shut your useless mouth! *Jebo ti pas mater!*"

I heard Mama sob and run out of the kitchen.

It's all going so wrong...how long until the Watchmen start killing people? Papa already thought I could be the betrayer! What if I am on that list of suspects? Will Papa stop the other Watchmen? Or will he be the one to kill me?

Mila, how did all this happen? I keep thinking of my birthday. It was only three weeks ago, but I can barely remember how happy I was. There was Mama's great cake, and Andjela was there, and then Slavko...Do you think he's doing okay?

I'm so thirsty. God, please forgive me. I know I shouldn't have kissed Slavko. I know it was wrong, so please, have mercy! Just please, a tiny bit of water, that's all I ask for. Just one raincloud in that hot blue sky!

I've always been a good girl. I always prayed in church, even when it bored me. God, why are you so mad at me? Will you let me die? I don't want to die. God, please don't let me die.

*

July 5th, noon

Papa was out all morning searching for the betrayer with his Watchmen friends. He is looking so desperate, Mila. Time is running out for us. The Watchmen split what little water they found amongst each other. I even got half a cup. Drinking felt so good, but now I'm even more thirsty than before.

*

July 5th, afternoon

Sorry for the tearstains, but I can't stop crying. Papa headed out again and a few minutes later, I heard screams. When I looked through my window, I saw Andjela with her father and Ivan. Her dog, Tomo, was tied to the well and she desperately tried to undo the leash. Her father brought up some black water and poured it into a bowl. Andjela kicked the bowl away. She was sobbing so loud I could hear it. Her father shoved her hard and she fell.

"Keep her away!" he yelled and his friend Ivan grabbed her and held her down.

Andjela's cries were so terrible, Mila. "No please! Don't do this! Please! No!" she shouted.

Her father ignored her and filled the bowl again. Tomo looked so happy as he gulped down the water. Andjela screamed, trying to get Tomo to stop, but Ivan covered her mouth with his hand.

Andjela kicked and thrashed, but Ivan didn't relent, even after Tomo finished drinking all the water. I prayed that God would at least spare poor Tomo. He was innocent! But then, he started making strange noises, like coughing and barking at the same time.

Andjela broke free and put her arms around Tomo. He bent forward and puked blood everywhere.

I looked away, but I could still hear Tomo throwing up and

making those strange sounds. When it got quieter, I saw Tomo collapsed in a pool of red vomit. His coughs grew silent and then he stopped moving.

Her father said, "Well, at least we know we still can't drink the water."

Andjela screamed and ran at him. He slapped her so hard she got knocked down.

"You would raise your hand against your father? Over a stray mutt? You insolent little shit. Get back into the house if you know what's good for you!"

She clenched her fists as she got up again and stumbled to the well. But she didn't go to Tomo. She heaved herself up and sat on the edge of the well. Her father's face turned white and he shouted, "Andjela, don't!"

She yelled, "I hope Satan puts you next to me in hell, so I can watch you burn forever!"

Ivan and her father both ran, but they were too slow. Andjela smiled as if she didn't have a care in the world…then let herself fall. There was an awful crack and a splash.

Her father yelled, "Andjela!" then fell to his knees. When Ivan put a hand on his shoulder, her father stood up and screamed down the well, "Fine, rot down there, you ungrateful brat!"

Mila, why was Andjela's father so mean? What if it had been me? Would Papa have done the same if I had a dog? Would he have said the same things? I'm so scared.

*

July 5th, noon

I saw Ivan outside again. He was arguing with Mirko. I didn't see him before, but from how they were talking I think Mirko saw what happened with Andjela. I opened the window and heard Mirko say, "Come on, Ivan. This wasn't like you. How could you hold Andjela down like that? The water was black, wasn't that proof enough?"

"We had to make sure! It was just a stupid dog."

"It wasn't *just* a dog. He was so precious to Andjela, she killed herself. We have to hold together if we want to get through this."

Ivan punched Mirko in the face without warning. Mikro fell down, then Ivan kicked one of Mirko's crutches away and shouted, "Fuck you! We're dying and you're talking down to the men making the hard choices? Crawl back to your hut, you stupid cripple."

Ivan left Mirko to drag himself to his crutches and struggle to get up on his own. I don't understand, Mila. Isn't Mirko right? Why are we fighting? Why is everyone so nasty?

*

July 5th, afternoon
Still no water and now Slavko is dead.

It happened after I asked Mama if I could stand outside, just for a little while. The air was so stale, sitting by my window was making me go insane. Mama said it was too dangerous. I should have listened…when Pavle cried in his room and she went to see him, I put on my shoes and slipped out.

I saw Nedeljko, Borislav and Josif trying to dig a new well. Nedeljko looked up when he heard me. His face looked so dry. Like it was made of leather. What was the point of wasting his strength like this? Papa helped dig the first well, before I was born. He often told me how difficult and time-consuming it was. Nedeljko worked on it too, so he had to know how hopeless it was. Maybe they were hoping for a miracle, or maybe they just couldn't stand around doing nothing. I wondered if I should help them. At least it was better than sitting at home.

Then I heard laughter. When I turned around, Slavko was limping toward our house. I barely recognized him. His hair was all gone and one side of his face was all red and yellow and blistered. In spite of that, he was laughing. It sounded so strange, so broken, it made me feel cold.

He screamed, "Hello, betrayer! I found youuuu!"

Then I saw he was dragging a large axe behind him. The way he looked at me scared me so much. I stepped back and stumbled. I wanted to get up and run back into the house, but my legs weren't moving. Slavko kept laughing and walking towards me.

Nedeljiko shouted "Hey! Stop!" and ran over between me and Slavko. "Slavko, calm down!" he said. "What happened to y—"

It happened so fast, I didn't even really see. But suddenly, the axe was in Nedeljko's head. Slavko was covered in blood and laughing even harder. He laughed so much he let go of the axe and Nedeljko fell over like a sack of grain.

Slavko kept laughing, even when Borislav and Josif ran over and tackled him. Borislav held Slavko down while Josif pulled the axe from Nedeljko's head. He looked so angry, he didn't even blink when he swung down the axe on Slavko's neck. I closed my eyes but still heard this disgusting…thump.

When I started crying, Josif said, "You're safe, quit your damn bawling."

Between sobs, I asked why they had killed Slavko. They already had him pinned down! Josif shouted, "Are you stupid? He killed Nedeljko and he was going to kill you! Show some fucking gratitude. *Govno jedno!*" Borislav nodded and said they did the village a favor.

Why, Mila? First Ivan punching Mirko, now this. Why is everyone so cruel? Why are we all killing each other?

God, please, save us!

July 5th, night
Dear Mila,

I can't sleep. I still see Slavko, laughing and swinging his axe. There's still no water. The heat is so stifling. Everything is dry. Why won't God give us a single cloud?

I tried to sing *Aleluja* again. Maybe God would like it and give us some rain? But my voice is hoarse and my throat hurts with every breath. The song started to come after a while, but just when I started to feel better, Papa came home. He wouldn't tell me if the Watchmen found the betrayer. When I tried to sing again, he shouted "Stop making noise! Annoying brat!"

Why won't he at least let me sing? It's so hard, it feels as if today was the last time. My voice will be gone soon. Then I'll only have you, Mila. You're the only one I can still talk to now.

*

July 6th

So thirsty Tired all the time Trouble writing Mila you'll understand me

one of the Dark Ones was standing in my room holding slavko's head i was too weak to run so i closed my eyes Dark One is gone now where is slavko's head

josif killed someone right outside my window
borislav?
after josif bent down and slurped up dead man's blood

will this make josifs thirst better? will Josif leave me some?
could go outside and have a slight drink
why am I thinking this? Mila help me.

Mila,
chainsaws now
is someone cutting trees?
      keep hearing screams   screams and chainsaws
                so loud
    papa sitting behind front door lots of knives around
him
        grinning like slavko
why is everyone laughing?

Dear Mila,
        getting dark
   Dark Ones everywhere in the forest
      waiting for night
thousands
    sun is setting
chainsaws so many   screams not so many
papa mama?
mila you are all I have   maybe this my last message

dead one outside stinks
        so thirsty
when will betrayer die

Still alive.
Don't want to die.
Want to stay alive.   God don't let me die.
                          God give me water.
Mila
something gnawing   doesn't stop
                                                    so dark

      gnawing   louder
          gnawing so loud   be here soon?
      end must be near
must hide you   keep Mila safe

              will miss you

CHAPTER 16

A ll the remaining pages were blank.

Amanda let the diary drop to the floor. Was this how it would end? Cut to pieces like Tihomir and those who tried to escape? Or driven mad by Dark Ones? Now she finally had a name for the shadows whispering in the dark and haunting her dreams.

The minutes passed as she stared into nothingness. *Why me?* What had she done to draw the ire of a monster like the Red Dove? In Priboj, the betrayer had cursed the village deliberately, with that blood-soaked dove nailed to the door with the cursed lullaby. But neither she nor Tihomir had killed any dove and—

Wait.

Amanda slowly raised her trembling hand and looked at her left index finger. *Oh God...*

Blood. Father Viktor had explicitly mentioned it as a condition for the curse. The dove in the village had been nailed to the door with the lullaby *and* been soaked in blood. Tihomir had shouted the full song after a day of playing in the woods. He could easily have scratched or bruised himself. And she...she had sung the song and then cut herself on the paper.

Amanda collapsed into her pillow. All she had suffered, all she would suffer...all because of a stupid little paper cut? Just how cruel was this? But then, she only had herself to blame. If she hadn't been so arrogant, if she had listened to her mother and all the other people who had warned her, she would have left this thing alone. But no, she just *had* to go on her stupid detective "adventure" and figure out what "really happened." And guess what? She had gotten exactly what she wished for. Now, the toll had simply come due. She had dug up the past at the expense of her future.

Amanda curled into a ball and cried.

*

She barely got any sleep. Every time she drifted off, the nightmares began. She was forced to watch the death of everyone in the diary, in nauseating detail, over and over, the Dark Ones whispering all throughout in their strange and broken language.

When she finally got out of bed, it was 11:27 AM. Amanda was dizzy, wondering whether she might drop unconscious.

She looked out the window. What was she still doing here? Why hadn't she booked her return flight already back in Ukraine? She missed home. Her parents, Tom, Greg… She didn't know how much time she had left, or what the Red Dove was planning to do to her, but she wanted to with her loved ones as long as she could before that.

She opened her computer to check for flights. Three e-mails were waiting. Her mother and Tom had both written essentially *Okay, let me know when you arrive.* Greg's e-mail was different.

> *Yo, princess! Is everything ok? Your e-mail didn't sound like the Amanda I know. You still in Ukraine? What's going on?*

Amanda ran her finger over the screen. *Greg, if only you knew…* But she didn't want to explain what happened in a text. Hopefully, she would be able to tell him in person.

> *Hi Greg. Yeah, still alive. Busy preparing for the return trip. I'll catch you later.*

She booked a 9 AM flight for the next day. She would have to get up at four to be at the airport in time. She checked, but no buses drove that early. *Guess I'll take a bus today and stay in a hotel at the airport.* Then she could sleep a bit longer.

She found Terzić in the living room, sitting in his usual armchair, smoking his pipe.

"*Dobro jutro,*" he greeted her.

"Good morning."

Amanda sat in the other armchair and wrapped the blanket around herself. Neither of them spoke. When Terzić finished his pipe, he said, "I shall make breakfast."

Same as yesterday, the food tasted rotten, like she was eating straight out of a compost bin. Fighting her nausea, Amanda forced the food down, hoping to get enough nutrients to keep going for the day.

Terzić ate silently. Even though he was taciturn, she had expected him to want to talk about the diary. All the better for her, though; she was in no mood to revisit this awful story.

After almost a quarter of an hour of complete silence, Amanda said, "Mr. Terzić. I would really like to thank you for your hospitality. I've never been treated so well. But I think it's time I went home."

"I understand."

"Is there anything I can do to pay you back?"

He shook his head. "There is no need."

"Well, if you're ever in the United States, let me know. I know it's not much, but I can offer you a place to stay, if you're near Chicago."

"Thank you. You are very kind."

After cleaning up and helping with the dishes, she told Terzić she was planning to leave in the evening.

"I will drive you to the airport," he said. "The hotels are very expensive."

"Thanks, but you've done so much for me already, it's really not necessary."

"It is no trouble."

Amanda didn't have the willpower to stand on principle. Having a ride

211

to the airport meant not having to sit in a cramped bus, or explaining her destination to a confused taxi driver.

"Thank you, Mr. Terzić. For everything. I mean it."

He nodded. "You should try and get some rest. You look very tired."

*

At 3:36 AM Amanda felt like little more than a zombie. Mechanically, she arranged the room to how it was before. 'When visiting, leave things as you found them,' her mother always insisted.

In the living room Terzić was already preparing a small breakfast. She choked down a few necessary bites of the pastries and salamis, then helped put away the dishes before they set off.

Aside from the headlights of the car, everything outside was pitch black. No moon, no streetlamps, no oncoming cars. Even the occasional village they drove past didn't have any lights on. By the time she saw the first bluish tint in the sky, they had nearly reached the airport parking garage.

As they walked through the airport, Amanda wondered how she should say goodbye. She didn't think Terzić would ever visit the US, so this was farewell. But she had so much to be grateful for...and so much to apologize for. What should she say to someone who had not only been an exceptional host, but had stuck with her every step of the way; even risked his life for her? Words could never fully convey her gratitude.

When they were at the gate, she said, "Mr. Terzić, I know I can't really express it, but I want you to know how grateful I am. I'm so sorry for all the pain and work I put you through."

"It is no trouble."

No. Stop saying that. This wasn't good enough. She had given him nothing *but* trouble. She couldn't just run off now without properly expressing herself.

She was still trying to put together the right words, when Terzić reached into his coat pocket and withdrew an old, yellowed envelope. "Forgive me for being selfish and not giving this to you sooner, but with Novak's help, I was able to acquire a parting gift."

He handed her the envelope. Amanda turned it around and immediately recognized the calligraphic handwriting.

If I die, please give this to my little sister Sofija—Mirko Matijević

She looked up at Terzić, fresh tears coming to her eyes.

He extended his hand. "It has been an hon–"

Amanda threw her arms around Terzić and hugged him tight. Fighting back her sobs, she said, "Thank you Mr. Terzić! Thank you so much. For everything. I really don't know how, but I promise, I'll repay you some day!"

Terzić gave her an encouraging pat on the back. "You owe me nothing. It has been an honor."

*

Amanda switched planes in Istanbul and collapsed into her seat. She passed out several times during the flight, but was repeatedly knocked awake by heavy turbulence. She wondered what would happen if her sleep deficit got any worse, then realized she had learned it in her psychology classes. Except, she couldn't remember it right now.

She decided she had to keep herself awake somehow, as crazy as it sounded. This constant passing out and being shaken awake was making her nauseous and giving her the worst of headaches. She went to the bathroom and splashed some water on her face. Her bruises were still visible, but makeup would hide most of it, and with her hair down, she could hide the nasty cut on her temple. Hopefully, Tom wouldn't notice anything. He wouldn't understand anyway, and being forced to recount what she had gone through was the last thing she wanted.

Back at her seat, she took out the envelope Terzić had given her. Her hands moved to tear it open, but her eyes fell on the writing: "Please give this to my little sister." Meaning, it wasn't for her. Sure, if her uncle had known about her, he might have addressed a letter to her as well, and he might even be fine with her opening this. But even so...it wasn't for her.

She put it back into her backpack.

When the turbulence quieted, Amanda let herself drift off again. It wasn't long before she was woken up again, this time by the flight attendant telling her they would be landing at O'Hare soon.

Tom was waiting for her. "Welcome home, darling."

"Hi Tom."

He gave her a kiss and took her bag. Once they were in the car, Tom asked, "So, how was the journey?"

"How do I look?"

"Exhausted?"

"There's your answer."

"You barely kept in touch, you know?"

"Yes, Tom, I know. Can we discuss this some other time? I'm jet-lagged, my head feels several sizes larger than it should be, I might throw up any minute, and I really just want a bed."

"Wow, okay, sorry I asked."

Amanda leaned back in the car seat and looked at the passing skyscrapers. She thought of Mirko's farewell letter again. At least one good thing had come out of this awful trip.

Delivering it meant facing her parents. She couldn't imagine how angry they had to be with her. But it had to be done. Her mother had waited thirty years for this, even if she didn't know it yet.

*

She went to see her parents the next day. In hindsight, she wished she had caught up on some much-needed sleep, first. But putting this off wouldn't make it any easier, either.

"Amanda," her father said, when they were all seated at the kitchen table, "What you did is deeply troubling, not to say hurtful. I hope you won't debate that. But we're not looking to make you apologize in front of the class like a schoolgirl. We want to know what prompted this."

"I…I just…" She had rehearsed her apology half a dozen times on the way here, but it felt fake and useless now. "I just wanted to meet Uncle Mirko." *God, how pathetic I am.*

Her mother looked sympathetic, even though she had the most reason to be angry. Maybe she felt something was wrong.

Her father wasn't so generous. "We understand that, but to go so far off the rails? We know you're a little headstrong, but you've never spent money impulsively, which is why we felt comfortable letting you have your own credit card in the first place. Good grief, Amanda. What were you thinking? Sofija begged you to let this go. And what did you do? Booked the first flight you could find and burned through several thousand dollars, just to prove her wrong."

"That's not true. It wasn't to prove Mom wrong. I...I thought Uncle Mirko might still be alive. I wanted to meet him and reunite him and Mom."

"You could have done that with a phone call. Or at least owned up to your mistake when you found out you were wrong. But no, you double down instead, and Sofija has to learn what's going on from Tom. How do you think she felt when she got that call?" He shook his head. "I don't think you appreciate just how disappointed we are."

Amanda closed her eyes to stop her tears from flowing. *This is the price I have to pay for what I did.* She wondered if he'd be this harsh if he knew the whole story. But telling them to garner sympathy would only hurt her mother more. So, she kept her mouth shut and let her father's words fall on her like rocks.

"Honey, I'm also upset, but I think she understands that," her mother said.

Amanda nodded slowly and kept staring downwards.

Her father sighed deeply. "Sofija is far too lenient with you. Frankly, when I heard what was going on, I was going to block all your accounts and get the Serbian police involved. Sofija stopped me, and now again, she wants to let you off easy." He sighed again. "Did you at least find what you were looking for?"

"I think I found enough," she said.

Her father gave her a curious look. *No, please don't ask any questions. The last thing I want is to lie again.*

Amanda bent down and unzipped her backpack. A feeling of déjà vu hit her. Weeks ago, her "adventure" had started right here, in this very chair. Now she had come full circle, her story ending the same way it began—handing her mother a letter from Mirko. "It wasn't all in vain. I found this."

She pulled the letter out of her backpack and slid it across the table.

Puzzled, her mother picked it up, then read the front. "What…what is this?"

"I don't know. I didn't open it."

Her mother looked at her, then back down at the letter. With trembling hands, she slowly ripped open the envelope and pulled out a piece of paper. It was only a few lines long. Her mother looked at it for a few seconds, then clenched the letter in her hands and started to cry.

CHAPTER 17

"What is it?" Amanda asked. "You've been standing there for...eight pages."

"I was wondering if you would react at all. Nicholas Sparks? Again? How many romance books have you gone through this past month? Ten?"

"Thirteen, not counting this one."

"Jesus."

"What can I say? I want something simple and carefree right now."

"I thought so. That's why I'm taking you out to dinner."

She turned a page. "No thanks, I'm not hungry."

"Have you been on a diet or something? If so, you can stop. You're getting way too thin. Besides, I've already got the reservation."

"Damn it, I told you, I prefer to stay home."

"Exactly why I want you to go. You'll go crazy in here! You're like some basement-dwelling gamer kid who never sees the sun."

"That's not true. I went to church on Tuesday."

"Okay, but aside from that, you truly never leave the house. And since when are you so religious, anyway? You hate Christians."

"I don't *hate* them. My mother is one, remember? I've just...rethought a few things."

"God, I wish you would stop being so cryptic and just talk straight with me. Anyway, I'm not canceling now, they would charge a fee."

"What a drag… When's the reservation?"

"Six."

She checked her phone. "Can you move it to five?"

"Why? Do you have something else planned?"

"No, but I want to be back by eight."

"Why does that matter?"

"I don't want to be out after the sun sets."

Tom shook his head. "This again. Can you please talk already? What is it with you and your obsession with avoiding the dark?"

"Tom, please, I told you, I don't want—"

"Yes, yes, you don't want to talk about it. Guess we'll never sleep with the lights off anymore and I'll have to use a sleep mask the rest of my life. Whatever. This isn't worth another fight. I'll call the restaurant. Get ready, we don't want to get caught in traffic."

When Amanda was done curling her hair and putting on makeup, she checked the small vial of holy water she wore as a pendant. She'd gotten the idea after a particularly bad night. Father Viktor had told everyone in Priboj to sprinkle holy water on every house entrance to keep the Dark Ones at bay. Amanda had done that, but figured it couldn't hurt to carry some close to her. Tom had looked somewhat sour that she was wearing a second necklace beside his, but ever since, her nightmares and the whispers had gotten a bit better.

She checked the time. Going out in the evening was making her uncomfortable. Still, the vial looked fine. None of the water had evaporated. She just had to make it back before the sun set.

*

Half an hour later, Tom parked near the Chicago Stock Exchange. Amanda gave him a confused look. What were they going here?

He put his arm around her and pointed to the top of the skyscraper. "See that place up there? That's the Everest Restaurant. And it's not called that for nothing. Just wait till you see the view."

He talked to a receptionist, then took her hand and strode confidently towards the elevator. Just before stepping in, Amanda froze. Something was wrong. It was something about the geometry of the elevator, or was it the lighting?

"You coming?" Tom said.

"Um…do you think we could take the stairs?"

"It's forty floors up." He laughed. "The restaurant's called Everest, but you don't have to take it literally."

Amanda gripped the vial around her neck. *It's just my imagination. Just my imagination…It'll be fine.*

They stepped into the elevator and Tom pressed the button for the 40th floor. The doors closed slowly. Tom was smiling. Gentle music played in the background. And yet, Amanda just couldn't shake her discomfort.

She looked down at her arm and saw her hair was standing on end. What was bothering her? She was all alone with Tom, yet it felt crowded. As if something else was taking up space.

The light in the elevator flickered. She checked the display. 12th floor. *Why is this thing so slow?*

The light kept flickering. Every time it did, the room became darker, but Tom didn't seem to care. And then there was this noise—the rumble the elevator made on its way up, floor by floor. It kept growing louder and heavier, overpowering the soft music. It scratched at her memory, until she finally realized what it was: that terrible breathing…down in that dreadful place.

Amanda fumbled with the vial around her neck. 22nd floor. The rumble grew to a menacing growl and the air grew icy cold, till her very breath turned white. The lights flared and darkened, casting deformed shapes into the corners of the elevator. She felt Tom shaking her shoulder.

"Darling? What's happening?"

"I don't know!" she coughed out between breaths. She clutched the vial hard. "It's not working! It's not working!"

Dust fell from the ceiling, as the walls turned to ancient stone and the elevator door to wood.

"No! Not here…Anywhere but here!"

She heard screeching noises above. Something was on top of them and scratching at the ceiling. Amanda threw herself against the corner and pressed her hands to her ears as the scratching turned to an ear-ripping screech.

Tom knelt in front of her and shook her shoulders. "What the hell is going on? Answer me!"

Black claws pierced the ceiling and ripped it in two. A monstrous arm lowered itself into the elevator. Amanda squeezed herself into the corner, but there was no escape.

"No! No!" She squeezed her eyes closed. Bony fingers closed around her neck once again.

"Aaaaaaaaaaaaaaaahhhhhhhhh!"

While she slowly choked to death, there came a sound, barely audible, like in a distant fog. *Ding.* They had arrived on the 40th floor.

Amanda thrashed and the monster loosened its grip. She scrambled out of the elevator and collapsed on the carpet outside. The air out here was warm. The skeleton had let her go. Between ragged breaths, she laughed and sobbed with relief.

She felt Tom's hand on her shoulder and looked up, expecting him to be as relieved as she was. Instead, his expression was a strange mixture of pity and embarrassment, or was it disgust? She looked around at several well-dressed patrons and a waiter. None of them spoke—their faces said enough.

As her senses returned, she noticed her hands were sticky with dark blue smears. Even without a mirror, she could tell she'd smeared mascara all over her face. Her dress had dark, wet spots all over it and her hair was sticky with sweat.

Her relief gave way to crushing shame.

"I'm sorry Tom, I…I'm sorry." She stumbled to her feet and found the emergency exit. Pretending not to feel everyone's looks on her, she walked into the stairwell.

On the way down, Amanda had time to herself where she could think. *What…was that?* What had happened in that elevator had been worse than any of her nightmares. And it had happened during the day, in a well-lit room, while she was wearing her holy water.

She pulled out the vial around her neck. Had its protection weakened somehow? For over two weeks now, it had kept her nightmares from worsening. So why would it fail now? How had she messed up? She had to get home as quickly as possible.

Hopefully, Tom was waiting for her down in the lobby. She wondered what he thought all this was. In that elevator, for a brief moment, she had felt like he could see it too. It would have been so comforting, to know she wasn't so alone. *What an empty hope.* Tom hadn't been stupid enough to curse himself with that vile lullaby. From his perspective, she had just gone completely nuts for no reason, messing up his evening in the process. Still, did he really have to have that look of disgust on his face?

When she reached the lobby, a full quarter-hour later, Amanda felt as if her legs would give out at any moment. There was no sign of Tom. She checked her phone, but he hadn't messaged her.

Tom, I really need to go home. Are you coming? Else I'll take a cab.

The reply came within seconds.

You go. I need to deal with something here.

He had to be really mad. She thought about calling him and talking it out, but she couldn't stay here, not one minute longer.

The moment she got home, her phone buzzed again.

I'll stay out a bit longer, feel free to go to bed without me.

Not the slightest hint of concern. Not even a simple: "Are you okay?" She knew Tom was mad, that he had been looking forward to that dinner, but did he not care at all what had happened to her? Was she really this alone?

"Aaaaahhhhh!" Amanda thrashed. She tried to run, but the shadow kept stabbing her leg and—

"Amanda! Amanda! Wake up!" Something shook her shoulders. She opened her eyes and saw Tom beside her.

"Are you okay?"

"It's getting worse. It's—" Amanda put a hand over her mouth. She rushed to the bathroom and put her head over the sink, trying to breathe steadily. The nausea slowly subsided. *At least I didn't throw up this time.*

She looked at her watch. 2:45 AM. She was so glad it was working again. After coming back, she had taken it to a watchmaker and the only damage had been a jammed spring. This had been her only good news since coming back. At least her stupidity hadn't destroyed her grandmother's last memento.

She felt a tingle and looked up into the mirror. A shadowy serpent was slowly creeping up her face.

She cried out, jumped backwards and slipped. The door to the bathroom flew open and a dark and monstrous figure towered over her. Amanda shrieked and shrank back in terror.

"What the hell?" Tom stepped into the light, looked around the bathroom, and shook his head. "Okay, I think you and I are due for a chat."

She breathed raggedly. "Tom, right now is really a bad moment. And I told you, I don't want—"

"No! I'm sick of that excuse. I've been hearing it for over a month. This… thing that's happening to you, whatever it is, it's affecting me too, okay? I can't get a single good night's sleep because we have to leave the lights on, or because you start screaming and thrashing all of a sudden. I can hardly focus at work anymore."

"I know, and I'm sorry."

"I've tried to be patient, but I think the time has come for you to visit a therapist."

"Excuse me?"

"Don't give me that. Look at what happened in that elevator! That wasn't normal. You just…snapped. You need help."

"This isn't something a therapist's couch will solve, Tom."

He gave an exaggerated sigh. "How did I know you would refuse? You realize that if you keep going like this, you'll ruin everything, right?"

"What's that supposed to mean?"

"Do you seriously have to ask? Look at yourself, look at us! I feel like I hardly know you right now. We don't talk, we don't go out, we don't even make love anymore! Ever since Serbia, you've been a different person and you won't even tell me what's wrong. We can't keep going like this. Or look at your internship! A month ago, you couldn't wait for it to start, now you quit before even a single day on the job!"

"They wanted me to work night shifts."

"This again…." He sighed. "So you threw away a fantastic opportunity all because you refused to seek help. It's sad, honestly. I don't think you appreciate how much damage your stubbornness has done to your future."

Amanda grimaced. *Way more than you could possibly know.*

*

The next day, after Tom was gone, she recited her morning prayers and wiped down all the windows and the door with holy water. This sequence had become something of a morning ritual. Praying or holy water hadn't saved the people of Priboj, but they were making her nightmares a bit better, at least.

When she finished praying, Amanda took a magnifying glass and examined her vial closely. There wasn't a scratch on it and it was still full. If the water really had helped before, the only explanation for things getting worse was that the water was somehow losing its power. Like a shield breaking from constant onslaught.

The timing was great, because she had just used up all her remaining holy water and it was almost noon, the safest time to go out get more.

Since the weather was nice, she decided to walk, but regretted it halfway through. The weather was unbearably hot and the water bottle she had brought along was half-empty by the time she passed by Daley Plaza. The scene there was the same as always; people strolling around, talking on their phones or having a late breakfast. On one of the benches, a couple held hands and gazed into each other's eyes. Once, she and Tom had sat here, looking just the same. She even remembered the exact bench, over there, second to the right. Where she and Tom had kissed for the first time. It felt so distant now, like she was remembering a half-forgotten movie.

There were also the ever-present pigeons, eagerly picking up leftovers from rushed eaters and careless kids. Amanda suddenly felt ill. She had never noticed before, but that motion…the way the grey animals bashed their heads into the pavement to suck up crumbs…it was disgusting.

One of the pigeons stopped and looked up at her. A second later, all the pigeons scattered in a panic. Passers-by were visibly shocked. When Amanda looked down at her hand, she realized she had thrown her water bottle at the pigeon. She had barely missed. If she had hit it, the bird might have been severely injured, or killed.

What…just happened? How had she thrown that bottle without wanting to or even being aware of it? She clenched her shaking hand and hurried away, anxious to reach the safety of the church.

When she stepped into St. Peter's, she could finally lean against a wall and take a deep breath. She should be safe here, from…whatever had just happened. She looked at her hand. First the elevator, now this? Why were things getting so much worse all of a sudden? She urgently needed that holy water.

She walked down the aisle and crossed herself before the altar, then sat on the front pew and folded her hands. Amanda began to recite the Lord's Prayer, but stopped herself. She looked up at the huge figure of Christ on the cross and closed her eyes.

Lord,

I'm sorry for changing my prayer today. Mom always taught me not to pray for selfish things and not to ask for favors from You. I've tried to follow that advice ever since I started talking to You again. But today, I have to be selfish.

My nightmares are growing worse every day, holy water isn't helping anymore and there's no one I can turn to. Tom already thinks I've gone crazy. I haven't even spoken to my parents because I'm scared Mom will find out and it'll break her heart. You're my last hope. If you don't help me…I don't know how long I can last like this.

She kept her eyes closed and waited, but God didn't answer. The church was quiet as ever.

I know I only have myself to blame. I dug in places I wasn't supposed to and got what I deserved. I know pride is the worst of the deadly sins. I promise, I'll do better from now on. I'm sorry for always making fun of Mom for believing in You. I'm sorry I lied to my parents. I'm sorry I was such an insufferable idiot. I'm sorry for all I ever did that may have offended You. I know I don't deserve Your help, but if you have any compassion left for me, I beg you…save me!

When Amanda opened her eyes, she saw Father Wesley standing next to her. "Father, I'm sorry, I didn't notice you."

"Amanda, please, call me Bill already."

"Sorry, Mom hammered it into me to never address a priest by his first name."

"Very polite, but it feels a bit outdated these days. Mind if I sit down?"

Amanda moved over. The priest sat down and crossed himself. "Are you all right?"

He held up a handkerchief as she felt a tear run down her cheek. Embarrassed, she took it and wiped her eyes. "Thanks. No, I guess I'm not."

"Would you like to talk about it?"

She wanted nothing more, but even if he was a priest, she wasn't sure he would believe her if she told him everything. Also, she didn't want to defile this holy place by uttering *its* name here.

"Let's say…your friend was afflicted by a horrific curse that was slowly killing her. Would there be anything you could do to save her?"

Father Wesley raised his eyebrows. "I must confess, this is not my area of expertise. Just to confirm, you are not talking about demonic possession?"

"Hm, no, not really. It *is* a satanic curse, but not like in The Exorcist."

"That's not quite how exorcisms work anyway…but, on curses, all I can offer is some generic advice. If it really is satanic, confession and frequent prayer may help, especially with a rosary. I'm sorry if that's not much help."

Amanda shook her head. "It's fine. Thanks for asking how I'm doing."

"Is there something else I can do for you?" Father Wesley asked.

"Could I have some more holy water?"

"Again? You need a lot. But, of course. Please, help yourself." He pointed to the basin.

"Sorry, but would you have a bottle somewhere? I...lost mine."

"Of course, give me a moment."

A minute later, he came back with a bottle full of holy water. "Here you go."

"Thank you, Father. For all your help."

Amanda was reminded of the diary. Similar to Amanda right now, Jelena had also gone to church and prayed, and found a bit of comfort talking to a priest. She shuddered remembering what had followed for Priboj, and what that might mean for Amanda's own future.

Father Wesley interrupted her thoughts. "Anytime. I wish I could do more. I'd better get back to my duties. Happy Fourth of July."

"Thanks, you too. At least the church looks less busy today." *Come to think of it, didn't Jelena also go see Father Viktor around the fourth of July?*

"Oh yes, but in return, things will get really crazy on the seventh."

"The...seventh?"

Why did everything feel so...wrong? Something about what Father Wesley said, or was it that strange connection with Jelena?

Father Wesley said, "Yes, we are completely swamped with wedding requests. Lots of couples want to tie the knot. You know, the seventh of the seventh? Makes remembering anniversaries easy, I guess. Plus, it's a lucky number and...Amanda, is everything alright?"

She was reeling. 'The seventh of the seventh.' That number. Seven. The more she thought about it, the more she saw that number everywhere. Jelena's last diary entry was on the evening of July 6th. So everyone in Priboj had also died on the seventh of the seventh. When had the Red Dove first appeared? June 16th. 1 plus 6 equaled seven. And June 16th was twenty-one days before July 7th, or three times seven.

The pages of her little notebook flashed before her eyes, where she had written down the dates of all the massacres. She saw the dates before her and realized what she had been missing the entire time—how many years they were apart.

1974—Brazil

1988—Ukraine, fourteen years later, or seven times two.

1995—Serbia, seven years later.

And finally...July 7th, 2009, again fourteen years later.

The seventh of the seventh, every seven.

"Oh God," Amanda said, and ran out of the church.

CHAPTER 18

Amanda slammed the apartment door and turned the key. She sprayed more holy water on the door and slumped down. How had she not seen it? She should have known from the start that there had been more than three massacres. In hindsight, it seemed so obvious—in that first nightmare, she had seen the black tombstones of the Red Dove's victims, stretching infinitely into the horizon. There had to have been hundreds, maybe thousands of massacres.

Now she understood why she had been allowed to live for a whole month, why her dreams were getting worse now, and what that nightmare in the elevator meant—the seven-year cycle was nearing its zenith. Like the villagers of Priboj, she was living on borrowed time.

She felt so terrified, so powerless. On the 7th, in just three days, the Red Dove would come for her. All the praying and holy water in the world hadn't helped the people in Priboj, so what hope did she have?

Her phone buzzed.

> Hi babe. You back from church yet? I met up with a few pals from work for a July 4th celeb. Are you coming too?

She stared at her phone. Why did Tom have to write something like this, now, of all times? She dropped the phone, not having the energy to type a reply. Judging by his message, he was drunk, and wouldn't be back for a while. She had no clue how she was supposed to tell him. Or her parents, or Greg. How did you tell your loved ones that you only had three more days to live?

"I don't want to die." Amanda fell to her knees and crossed herself. "I don't want to die. Please, God, I don't want to die. I'll do anything, just please, spare me!"

But as usual, God didn't answer.

"I don't want to die! I don't want to die!" she choked out between her tears. Her stomach hurt with fear, like a lump of hot coal burning her insides. What had she endured all this suffering for, this past month? It had all been for nothing from the start.

Amanda touched the scar on her temple. If only back then she had hit her head a little harder... And to think she had sobbed with relief when Terzić and that stranger had come to her rescue!

They should have just let me die.

Why had that stranger so selflessly rushed in to help her? Even he had seemed terrified of that place. Yet he had come anyway. And all it did was delay the inevitable. If only he could have saved her from the curse, too...

Can't he? Amanda sat up. She remembered his strange knowledge of the spiritual. He'd sensed the village's history and the danger from the mine. If she could get in touch with him, if she told him everything that had happened, couldn't he maybe help her? Give her some advice on how to survive the 7th? It was a long shot, but if there was *any* way to survive the curse, he was the only one who could possibly know.

As quickly as the faint glimmer of hope rose within her, it was snuffed out by a cruel realization—she had no way of contacting him. She had briefly seen that card in his car, with two names: "Liam Davis" and "Morton R." How was she supposed to find him with nothing but that? She didn't even know what country he was from.

But, there was someone who might be able to find the stranger, even with such little information. She looked at her phone. Out of laziness and fear, she hadn't talked to him once since coming back from Serbia. But...if anyone could find the stranger, if anyone could get her to survive the 7th, he was her only shot.

*

Greg was busily typing on his computer when his phone rang.

"Hi…"

"I'm sorry, who is this?"

"I know. I know I should have been in touch. And I'm sorry. Had…a lot on my mind since I came back from Serbia."

Greg rolled his eyes. "I really hate that excuse. 'I was busy' is pretty much the grown-up's version of 'The dog ate my homework.'"

"It's not like that. Can we talk about this in person? Like, at 3rd Coast in thirty? My treat."

"Wow, aren't you in a rush. Is the world ending?"

Amanda paused. "You're not far off."

"Is being this dramatic and cryptic really necessary? Fine, fine. But this had better be good."

"Thanks. See you."

Before Greg could say anything more, she hung up.

When Greg entered the café half an hour later, he didn't notice Amanda at first. It wasn't that she looked all that different, but rather as if she was a different person. In this bustling and happy café, she radiated a lonely aura of misery. Even the other patrons seemed to avoid her. She had also lost quite a bit of weight.

She looked happy to see him, but she barely talked. She didn't even eat. She used to have quite an appetite, especially in this place. But now, every time she put food in her mouth, she grimaced, like a toddler being given spinach. After a while, she stopped eating entirely and just spent the whole time cutting her salad leaves into strips. By the time Greg ordered his dessert, her plate had become a green mush.

"Are you on a diet now?" he asked.

"No. Just, some trouble eating lately." She gave him a smile that looked painfully forced.

Finally, when Greg was already biting into his cake, she said, "Look, Greg, the truth is…"

"You're in trouble and need another favor?"

"Is it that obvious?"

"Are you kidding? You look like a prisoner on a hunger strike and just spent the past fifteen minutes turning a fantastic salad into a modern art masterpiece. Doesn't take Sherlock Holmes to figure out something's up. What do you want?"

"I need your help to find somebody."

"Contact a PI, then."

She grit her teeth. "I don't have time to go through a detective agency. This is really urgent and I know almost nothing about the man I'm trying to find."

"And why is it so 'urgent' to find someone you don't know?"

"That's…Please don't ask." She looked down, avoiding his eyes. "Will you help me?"

"No."

"But—"

"Nope, don't want to hear it. You heard me the first time. Good luck on your own. Honestly, I feel stupid for having come here at all."

Amanda shrunk back, as if she had just been handed her divorce papers. "Why?" she asked, her voice flat.

He folded his hands on the table. "Because, plain and simple, I am angry at you. Livid, really. I'm surprised you actually had the balls to ask me out here just to get me to do more dirty work for you. Are you even conscious of how much of an asshole you've been?"

Amanda gave him a blank look.

Greg sighed and shook his head. "I spent the last four weeks waiting to hear from you. Four, fucking, weeks. And you didn't call *once*. You couldn't even be bothered to put in five minutes for me. The only time I ever get a call is when you have a problem you need resolved."

"Greg, that's not true. Please, listen—"

"No, *you* listen for a change. You promised, remember? You *promised* to call me and to tell me how things were going. But the moment I set up that meeting in Ukraine, I wasn't even worthy of a single text, except for that

231

dismissive one-liner you sent. Even now that you need something again, I'm apparently not important enough to know *why* you need to find your mystery man. I'm just supposed to shut up and do as I'm told. Well, sorry. If that's all our relationship means to you, I'm not interested. Find somebody else to be your lackey."

Amanda didn't speak. She didn't even move. She just stared down at her plate. Then, amidst the bustle in the café, Greg heard a strange noise; like the clinking of raindrops. When he looked, he saw tears falling on Amanda's plate. Softly, as though talking to herself, she said, "There's no point struggling, is there?"

Greg's mouth dropped open. He had never seen the strong and proud Amanda look so broken. She put her hands on her temples and dug her fingernails into her head, as if she was trying to rip her hair out. She swayed, repeating, "No…no…no…"

Greg stood up and went to her side, putting his hand on her shoulder and saying, "Amanda what's—"

"No!" she screamed, and pushed him away with surprising force. Greg lost his balance and toppled to the floor. The entire café fell silent. He got back up and straightened his clothes, feeling everyone's accusing looks. Amanda avoided his eyes, staring empty-eyed into her plate.

Greg pulled out a fifty-dollar bill and placed it on the table. Way too much, but right now, getting out of here was worth any price. As he turned to leave, he felt a tug on his sleeve.

"Don't go," Amanda said meekly.

He turned, ready to knock her hand away, when his eyes fell on her face and on the nasty scar on her right temple. Her hair had hidden it before, but after her outburst, it was impossible to overlook. He was certain this was new. Something truly bad had to have happened to her. *It doesn't matter. She's obviously crazy. Leave, leave and never look back!*

"Greg, please…"

Her entreaty was heart-wrenching. It gave him a curious impression—that if he left now, he would cut the last string still animating her. Greg stood still for a few seconds, then gave an annoyed sigh and sat back down. *Stupid things, feelings.*

Amanda looked at her shaking hand. "I'm sorry. I didn't mean to do that. That's the second time now…I'm running out of time."

She wasn't making any sense, but he waited for her to finish. She wiped her tears. "I'm sorry, Greg. For everything. You're right, I should have told you everything from the beginning. I should have called you. But I'm a coward A shitty, pathetic coward. Something…really bad happened when I was in Ukraine. I was scared you would ask questions and I didn't want to relive what I went through. But if anyone deserves to hear it all, it's you. Especially since my life depends on you."

He furrowed his brows, but one look at her told him this was not hyperbole.

"You were right, when you called me in Serbia. I shouldn't have messed with it."

"You mean…this all has to do with the Red Dove?"

She winced, as though stung by a wasp. Amanda retrieved a small vial from under her shirt and squeezed it tightly, then took a deep breath. "I'll tell you everything."

Her story of what had happened in Ukraine and Serbia, and the diary she had found, was so unbelievable, so harrowing, Greg found himself wishing this was all an elaborate joke, but he knew she would never do something this nasty. Also, her scars, both visible and invisible, bore witness to the hell she had been through. It was terrifying to know that a monster like the Red Dove existed in this world.

Amanda told him how empty and painful her life was; how even food tasted rotten and she could barely eat anything anymore without throwing up; how, as soon as the lights were out, the "Dark Ones" would start their maddening, whispers, how she had spent the past month locked up at home with meaningless books and TV shows, trying to distract herself from her miserable life and the unending nightmares, where she would be hunted, tortured and murdered, over and over. And she told him what had happened in the elevator and her terrible discovery in the church, and why she was here now.

Greg fell back in his chair and closed his eyes. "Jesus, Amanda… just… Jesus."

He had no words. How was he even supposed to react to her telling him that she'd be dead in three days? What could he even say to something like this?

Amanda wiped her eyes. "I'm sorry. I should have told you all this before."

"No, I'm sorry. I had no idea what you…I mean, I just…I shouldn't have talked to you that way. If I'd known…"

Amanda smiled and placed her hand on his as a tear ran down her cheek. "It's okay. I'm just glad you didn't hang up on me and that I was able to see you again." That smile…it was so angelic and yet so sad. Greg felt tears come to his own eyes.

A movement of her finger made him aware her hand was still on his. Embarrassed, he pulled away. Wasn't she still with Tom? She looked unsettled as well, as if she had just come out of a trance, and her hand moved as if to hide a beautiful necklace.

Greg took a deep breath. At least this brief awkwardness allowed him to gather his thoughts. He was still overwhelmed by what she had told him, but he could mull it over later. Right now, all that mattered was that Amanda had one hope left, a hope that rested entirely on him. He had to find that strange mystic or whatever he was. Given how little Amanda knew about him, it seemed impossible, but as long as there was even the slightest chance of success, Greg had to give it his all.

Greg took his laptop out of his backpack. "I swear, when this is all over, you'll owe me a whole truckload of those cookies you keep promising. Better call to see if they'll give you a bulk discount."

"Thank you Greg. Thank you so much." There was that heart-wrenching smile again, and those tears in her eyes that glittered like crystals.

He looked away. *Come on Greg. Don't bawl now. Focus!* "Anyway," he said. "The name of that guy was either 'Liam Davis' or…?"

"Morton R."

"Let's just try it." He searched for 'Liam Davis and Morton' but found nothing useful. Searching only for 'Liam Davis' turned up millions of hits.

For a quarter of an hour, he checked out random Liam Davises, hoping that the man they were looking for was a well-known spirit medium or something similar, but nothing turned up.

Amanda looked on in silence.

"Well, didn't expect much, but it was worth a shot." Greg scratched his forehead. "We need to restrict this search somehow. Just knowing which country he's from would help. Was there anything distinctive? Some of his stuff maybe?"

She thought about it, but shook her head. "No, I'm sorry. Everything looked completely ordinary."

"His car? Was there anything special about that?"

"I never checked the plate, but I guess it was a rental."

"Damn it. We need *something* here. Was there really nothing that stood out? Any detail could help, no matter how tiny."

She cupped her head. "I can't think of anything. But maybe..." Amanda took out her phone. "I'll call Terzić. Haven't spoken to him this past month either, but maybe he saw or noticed something I didn't."

Greg nodded and waited. She smiled when Terzić's voice came from the other end of the line, but her tone of voice felt somewhat formal, as though she was worried she might be annoying him. Greg tried to at least get the gist of what was being said, but it was hopeless. Croatian was just too different from English. Amanda talked for about ten minutes. *"Hvala, doviđenja,"* she ended the call.

"Any luck?"

She shook her head.

Greg did his best to smile encouragingly. "Ah well, this wouldn't be fun if it was easy, right? Still, gotta say, Croatian sounds much nicer spoken than written."

Amanda chuckled. "That's because you keep pronouncing things wrong."

He looked back at his laptop. He had to admit, things were looking pretty grim, given her friend also hadn't come up with anything useful. He had racked his brains while she had been on the phone, but without anything to narrow down the search, how could he make progress?

Greg swayed back and forth on his chair. "It's kind of weird that there's two names on that card."

"Maybe Morton and Liam are business partners?"

"What, like a law firm? 'Johnson and Johnson?' Really doesn't work with those names, though. 'Liam Davis and Morton Rockefeller, spiritual mediums at law.'"

She giggled. "Greg, what would I do without you?"

"Live a sad life devoid of stupid remarks? Anyway, I don't think they're business partner and we...hang on..."

He had an epiphany. What if the answer was far simpler? "What exactly did you see on that card? Be precise."

"Just what I told you. 'Liam Davis and' on the first line, 'Morton R-' on the second, the rest was covered."

"The 'A' in 'Liam Davis *and*'. Was it capitalized?"

"It...might have been. I don't remember."

"Screw it. Give me a second."

He typed into his computer. After ten minutes, he finally found the right page. Greg clapped his hands in excitement. *Don't disappoint me now...* He typed 'Liam Davis' into another page, hit search, then felt a sheepish grin grow on his face.

"What?" Amanda asked.

"Okay, so, I figured...What if the 'And' is not an English 'and' and what if Morton R- is not the name of a person, but, as usual on a card like that, a place name? Check this out!"

Greg turned the laptop around. It showed: "Morton Ridge," in Alberta, Canada. Amanda looked wide-eyed, but Greg wasn't done yet. He felt like a magician pulling an impossible second bunny from his top hat as he opened the second webpage. It was an online phonebook, and the search result read: "Liam Davis Anderson, Morton Ridge, BC, Canada" together with his telephone number.

She jumped up. "Yes! Greg you're a genius!" She typed in the number that

Greg held up to her. "Oh God, please let this work, please let this—huh?" She looked confused. "Greg, are you sure this is his number?"

"Yeah. Why?"

"I think it's disconnected. Can you get me a neighbor's number? Maybe they'll know how to reach him."

"Yeah, sure. Give me a sec. Let's just pull up a map, and...hey, this is easy. The place only has a single street. Okay, try 'Mary Sinclair.'"

When he looked up, Amanda's face had changed to a kind of nervous urgency. Her hands shook as she typed the number and held the phone to her ear.

"Uh, Amanda, are you okay?"

She gave him a thousand-yard stare. Slowly, as if afraid to break it, she moved the phone to his ear. A mechanical voice said, "We're sorry, but the number you dialed cannot be reached now. Please try later."

"Um. What?"

"Greg, where is Morton Ridge located?"

"Let's see...some remote corner of the Rocky Mountains."

"And it's a village so small there's only a single street?"

"Yeah, but so wh—wait! You don't think..."

She nodded gravely.

"You mean that's why the phones don't work? How does that make any sense?"

Amanda put a hand to her chin. "Remember the diary I told you about? After the Red Dove appeared, nobody was able to leave or enter Priboj. Anyone who tried died horribly. Maybe the same applies to all forms of communication, and—" She gasped. "Jelena even wrote that the radio stopped working, right after the village was cursed!"

"Wait, wait, hang on, this is just ridiculous. From the millions of places the curse could be hitting, you think we just happened to stumble on the *one* where the Red Dove is right now? That's way too much of a coincidence."

"It's not." She fumbled around with the vial on her neck. "The name the spirits kept whispering..."

"Huh?"

"That's what Anderson said when Terzić told him about the Red Dove. Oh my God, he even said something about his dreams having been really frightening! And that when he consulted the spirits they whispered the Red Dove's name and told him to go see that village in Ukraine. Dear Lord, they were trying to warn him."

"Jesus…"

Again, Amanda gripped her hair and pulled. "Damn it! It was so obvious! The answer is *always* staring me right in the face! Why do I never see it?"

"Come on, don't beat yourself up. Hindsight is always 20/20. How were you supposed to notice something like that at the time?"

She shook her head. "I didn't notice it because I was so stubborn. If I hadn't been such a diehard rationalist, I might have connected the dots then and there."

"Yeah, but it's normal to be skeptical at something like that. Especially for you."

Her shoulders slumped. "If not for that skepticism, I could have warned Anderson, and I might not have cursed myself. That beautiful 'skepticism' has cost me my life."

The longer she talked, the more her eyes lost all expression. "There's just nothing I can do, is there? And it's always my fault."

It was painful seeing her like this. What could he say that could help her? That would give her at least some strength back? "Maybe there's another person like Anderson somewhere else? Or maybe if you stay far enough away, you'll survive the seventh? Look, in the diary, only the people inside the village died, right? You're over a thousand miles from the place."

"It won't help. The priest in Priboj confirmed it—once you're cursed, there's no escape. It's over for me."

"But…"

She stood up and gave him a hollow smile. "It's okay Greg. You don't have to cheer me up."

"Where are you going?"

"To pray. That's about all I've got left."

As she mechanically walked past him, Greg was hit with an absolute certainty—if he didn't say the right thing now, this would be the last time he saw her. He grabbed her wrist. "Amanda, I refuse to let it end this way. I'll keep searching. And I promise, I *will* find a way to help you. So, sit tight and don't do anything stupid, you hear me? I'll contact you as soon as I find something. And if anything happens, call me, okay? You don't have to face this alone."

She bent down and gave him a kiss on the cheek. "You're sweet. I'll see you."

CHAPTER 19

After leaving the café, Amanda wandered aimlessly through the streets. She didn't care where she would end up—it didn't matter anyway.

She checked her watch. 3:29 PM. Half past midnight in Serbia. Terzić had asked her to call him if she managed to find Anderson. So he could "send a thank-you note." She decided to call him tomorrow—she had probably woken him up when she called before, no reason to do it twice.

She wondered what Terzić would say about the seven-year cycle. He had seemed so relaxed on the phone. Meaning the curse really was only affecting her. Amanda looked at her left index finger. There wasn't even a scar to show the little cut with which she had doomed herself.

It felt so insulting. To suffer and die because of something so mundane. But maybe that was the point—to humiliate her, to make her suffer both physically and mentally. Like those constant bait-and-switches: Every time she found the tiniest hope to cling to, the Red Dove invariably crushed it later. When she'd escaped from the mine, when her dreams had started getting a bit better, when Greg had found Anderson...every time things seemed to be getting better, they had only ended up getting worse.

Actually, wasn't this how the Red Dove had killed everyone in Priboj too? It hadn't just murdered everyone quickly and painlessly. It had taken its time, tormenting the villagers for three whole weeks before finally ending it all. Like Amanda, Jelena had repeatedly been given a faint glimmer of hope, only for that hope to be brutally extinguished the next day. Apparently, killing people just wasn't enough for the Red Dove, they had to be sadistically tortured as well.

She crossed the street to Millennium Park. She used to come here often, especially to soothe her nerves before exams. That was so long ago, now. Worrying about an exam…what a happy and innocent world she used to inhabit.

In the center of the park, a woman threw a pack of breadcrumbs and a large flock of pigeons quickly gathered. Again, this disgusting motion as they picked up the breadcrumbs. But there was something else about them—the way they kept looking up at her between mashing their heads down, the way the sunlight caught unnaturally in their necks, throwing strange and unworldly colors.

All in unison, the birds stopped eating and raised their heads. As their black and empty eyes settled on Amanda, the sounds around her died down as an overwhelming dread settled on her. She tried desperately to run, but her legs lost all energy and she fell to her knees. Those horrible, dead eyes…the longer they stared, the more her strength left her. Even her lungs weren't spared. Every breath became harder, until she was gasping for air.

"P-p…please…"

A grin spread over the pigeons. Red dots appeared on them like raindrops, until their coats were dyed the color of blood.

"Amandaaaaaaa!"

The grin on them grew monstrous and deformed. They took a step towards her.

No, God, please…

A few more steps.

Save me!

The world around her faded, becoming darker and emptier, until she knelt in an endless blackness. Out of the darkness, shapes materialized. She recognized them. There was Tom, holding an axe. Her mother with garden shears. Her father with a hatchet. Greg with a saw.

"No! I'm sorry! Please, no!"

They all surrounded her, looking down at her with the same sick grin the doves had. Tom struck first, slamming the axe into her shoulder. She screamed in pain, while her father followed up with his hatchet. Then her mother and Greg. Over and over, they cut and hacked, tore and ripped.

Amanda convulsed and struggled, begging to die, but her loved ones only laughed and kept torturing her. She screamed until she was stifled by a red-hot mud filling her mouth. Time vanished and was replaced with nothing but a raw, searing pain.

*

An eternity later, the torment finally subsided. Amanda heard the fluttering of wings and the pain dissipated slowly. When she opened her eyes, she saw an unknown man above her.

"Hey! Are you okay?"

She blinked. She was back in the park. The pigeons had flown away and a crowd had gathered around her. Except for the man above her, all were standing at a distance. Some snickered, some were pointing at her, some were tracking her movements with their phones.

As her senses returned one by one, Amanda noticed that she was lying on her back on the pavement. She tried to sit up and coughed hard. She could barely breathe and the hot mud from before was sticky and wet on her face. When she touched it, she realized it was her own vomit.

"Christ, are you okay?" the man asked.

"It's…I…"

She tried to get up. The man above her held her back. "Wait, you shouldn't move. Did you OD? That looked really bad. I called an ambulance. Stay put, it'll be here any moment."

An ambulance? OD? What was he talking about? She had to run away. Before it came back.

"Thanks, um, I really…"

The man shook his head and gently pressed against her. "Wait till the ambulance gets here, at least."

The pigeons were gathering again. *Oh God.* Amanda tried to get up, but the man still wouldn't let go, as more and more pigeons landed around her. One of the birds looked up and flashed a grin.

"No! Please! No!"

"Hey, hey, easy now," the man said.

She put all her strength into her right arm and swung, hitting him square in the jaw. The shock made him let go. Amanda struggled to her feet and ran, shoving through the circle of onlookers.

"Fuck, my teeth! You bitch!" the man shouted after her. She kept running. She couldn't stop now. If those pigeons gathered again...

She turned around a few times, but the pigeons didn't follow her. She clutched the small vial. *It's no use. It's no use!* It had attacked her while the sun was up and while wearing the holy water. At this point, she had nothing left that could protect her. She was at the Red Dove's mercy.

Several times, she tried to hail a cab home, but the drivers always drove away as soon as they got a closer look at her. Amanda knew she looked bad, but couldn't at least one of them show her a bit of kindness?

An hour later, she finally opened the door to her apartment. Her hair, her blouse, even her jeans, everything was soiled. She threw all her clothes into the basket and went into the shower. She wiped her face clean and watched the water turn greenish-yellow.

She wanted to feel disgusted, or even afraid. But everything was numb. She felt only exhaustion, more than ever before in her life. All she wanted to do was sleep. And hopefully, to never wake up again.

Why didn't it just kill her already? Did it really enjoy torturing her that much? Or was it hoping her brain would snap under this endless torment? Amanda looked down at her knuckles, still hurting from hitting that man. She had never punched anyone before. Good grief, she had even shoved Greg. How much longer did she have before she lost herself? Before she started laughing hysterically while hacking people up, like that boy, Slavko, from Priboj? She slumped to the tiled floor. Her eyelids felt so heavy. With the last of her strength, she heaved her head outside the shower, away from the falling water, before the world went dark.

When she woke up again, Amanda saw by the light through the small window that it was already nighttime. The water was still falling on her. She was grateful the apartment had a tankless boiler. Otherwise, she'd have spent hours under an icy cold shower.

She dragged herself to bed and pulled the covers over her head. Even though she had just spent several hours unconscious, she was still as exhausted as before.

Just as she began her prayer, the door to the apartment opened.

"Honey! I'm home!"

Why did Tom's timing have to be this bad? Then again, if he'd come twenty minutes earlier and seen her passed out in the shower…

She closed her eyes as Tom entered the room. He sat down next to her and kissed her cheek.

"It's a shame you're already asleep," he whispered.

From his breath, Amanda could tell he and his buddies had sampled at least half the bars in Chicago. It was surreal—she had maybe two more days to live, and here was Tom, drunk and trying to come on to her.

She kept her eyes closed and her breathing regular until Tom had gone to the bathroom. Then, Amanda quietly recited her evening prayer and waited for the terrible dreams to come.

*

The morning greeted her with the sun in her eyes and with a pounding headache. She had suffered so many nightmares, she wondered if she had slept at all. Amanda forced herself out of bed and closed the curtains. She found Tom in the living room, bent over a stack of papers from the bank. *Right, it's Sunday.*

"Oh, good morning honey," he said.

"Hi Tom. Didn't notice you coming home."

He smiled. "Yeah, it got a bit late. By the way, you look pretty tired. Is everything okay?"

"No, actually. It's…Yesterday was kind of rough."

"I understand. Well, I got assigned new clients and wanted to get an early start on their portfolios. I'll be here all day, so let me know if you need anything."

"Yeah, thanks," she said and left Tom to his work. He was being oddly nice. Typically, new portfolios stressed him out. But she wasn't about to complain.

She found herself some yogurt and cereal in the kitchen. It tasted even worse than usual, like she was eating liquid drywall with mildew. Why was she still doing this to herself? In two days, it would all be over anyway.

Amanda stirred the mush in front of her. How low she'd fallen. Just a month ago, she'd been enjoying Terzić's wonderful breakfasts. And now…*Oh right, I still need to call him.*

She went back into the bedroom and closed the door.

"Đorđe Terzić," he answered as usual.

"*Dobro jutro*, Mr. Terzić."

"*Dobar dan*, Ms. Dousson."

"You asked me to call you if Greg and I found the man we met in Ukraine. We got lucky. His full name is Liam Davis Anderson. He lives in a small village called Morton Ridge, in Canada."

"Very impressive, Ms. Dousson. You and your friend would make great detectives."

"Thank you. Unfortunately, we're too late. There's something else I need to tell you…"

There was a long silence when she finished explaining the seven-year cycle and that the curse was happening right now, in Anderson's village.

"This is frightening," Terzić said. "But thank God there is still time."

"Time? For what?"

"Canadians speak English, yes? Have you contacted the police?"

"Huh?" *What police? And what for?*

"In Canada. Have you informed the police about the massacre?"

"Um. No. I haven't. But why?"

"The police may still be able to evacuate the villagers, before it is too late."

Amanda shook her head. She understood his faith in the police, but this was silly. "Mr. Terzić, you've read the diary. You know what happened to those who tried to enter or leave the village. Sending anyone in there would be tantamount to murder."

"Then you must warn them of the danger."

She tried hard not to sigh. "They would never believe me. Even if I could somehow convince them, they can't do anything."

"We cannot know that for certain. What other choice do we have? If there is even the slightest hope to save even one person, we and the police there have a duty to try."

We? How was this her duty? Or, for that matter, the duty of the police? She knew what he meant—police officers or firefighters often risked their own lives to save others from burning buildings and the like. But nobody, no matter how heroic, could be expected to run into a building that was seconds from collapsing. There was no glory in dying a senseless death.

But, she could tell Terzić wasn't going to take no for an answer and was determined to get the police involved. "I'll try. But I can't promise they'll listen."

"Let us hope they do. *Srećno,* Ms. Dousson"

Amanda hung up. What a mess. Convincing the cops to go wouldn't be hard. She just had to call and act like a resident in Morton Ridge who had just seen somebody get shot and the killer was banging at the door. But no way would she send innocents to be torn apart by the Dark Ones. Terzić was delusional if he thought she would put that on her conscience.

Luckily, all she had to do was to call Terzić in a few minutes and tell him she had tried, but that they hadn't believed her. Even so, the thought of having to lie again left a bitter taste in her mouth. Lying was the source of all her suffering, her punishment for breaking her promise to her mother. If she had kept her word and not gone to Serbia, Amanda would be blissfully ignorant of the Red Dove right now, enjoying her safe and easy life. What if lying again caused even more suffering? Was there no other option?

Amanda chewed her nails. She could tell the truth, but then Terzić might try getting the police involved by himself and might succeed. Telling him she'd tried and failed was as white a lie as she could imagine, a moral necessity.

She took a deep breath to settle her nerves, then picked up the phone.

"Mr. Terzić? Hi, it's me again. I screwed up. The police didn't believe me."

"I see. What happened?"

"I told them there was a massacre, but they wanted to know why. I stammered when I tried to tell them about the curse, since I realized how stupid it sounded. They thought it was a prank call and hung up on me."

"That is regretful. The officer should have taken this more seriously."

"Maybe, but it's understandable if he thought it was a joke. I'm…I'm really sorry I couldn't be of more help."

"Do not blame yourself. May I please call you back later?".

"Uh, sure."

There was a click and the call ended. *What are you up to?* She prayed that Terzić would not try to call the cops themselves. Thirty minutes passed and Amanda was sick with worry. *Please let nothing bad happen. Please let nothing bad happ—*

Her phone rang.

"*Dobar dan*, Ms. Dousson. I have good news. I have reached out to a travel agency and asked them for a way to get to Morton Ridge."

Oh God. No. Why? Why!

"They were able to reserve a flight for me tomorrow morning," he continued. "It will land at 16:10 in Edmonton, which is only 300 kilometers away from Morton Ridge."

"Mr. Terzić," she stammered. "You can't go there. It's suicide."

"If nobody will believe us, then it is up to us to make a difference."

There it was again. "Us." What was he thinking? Him rushing straight to his death was one thing, but did he seriously expect her to say, 'Great! I'll meet you there'? Did he even understand what he was asking? No matter how much she had suffered here, she couldn't imagine what nightmarish horrors awaited her if she went to Canada.

This was a sacrifice nobody could be expected to make. She had to tell Terzić that if he wanted to go, he was on his own. Anyone faced with her situation would do the same. So why was her mouth so dry? She felt like she was betraying him somehow. But she couldn't let her guilt trick her into jumping straight into the deepest pit of hell.

Amanda mustered her courage and drew a deep breath. "Look, Mr. Terzić…"

"Yes?"

She gave herself the final push. "I…I'm sorry, but I can't come with you."

A painful, awkward silence followed.

"I understand," Terzić finally said. "You have your safety to consider." His words were calm, but his voice had shifted. "I wish you the best of luck in your future. It has been a pleasure meeting you. Farewell."

"Wait!" She checked her phone. He hadn't hung up yet. "I'm sorry, I didn't mean to shout. I just… Please, rethink this. You'll just end up killed."

"I know the danger is great. However, the villagers have nobody else to help them."

"But you can't help them! All you're going to do is add one more victim. You read the diary."

"It is because I read the diary that I must go. I know what awaits these people if they are not rescued."

His tone made it clear he was determined to see this through. "Please excuse me, I must begin my preparations."

"Mr. Terzić, please don't," Amanda said with a broken voice. Sure, it was his life, he could do whatever he wanted with it, but she didn't want to see him throw it away so pointlessly.

"I am grateful that you are so concerned for me. But please understand; I cannot leave the villagers to their fate. As long as there is the slightest hope of saving but one life, I must attempt it."

Her vision became blurry. She knew there was nothing more to say between them. "Good luck, Mr. Terzić."

"Thank you. *Zbogom.*"

Amanda heard the click of his old telephone and knew this was it—the last sound she would ever hear from him. She heaved herself into bed and hugged her teddy bear. *If this is another bad dream, can I please wake up now?*

By the time her tears stopped, a heavy exhaustion was hanging over her like a cloud. She drifted in and out of consciousness, but mercifully, she had no dreams, this time. When she finally opened her eyes, everything was spinning and a heavy nausea made her sit up, scared that she would throw up. As the spinning stopped and the nausea subsided, she saw on the alarm clock that several hours had passed and it was already afternoon.

In the living room, she found Tom still working on his computer. She watched him as he studied his figures and balance sheets. She opened her mouth several times, but the right words wouldn't come. After how badly talking to Terzić had gone, she really wanted to avoid this talk. But, as desperately as she hoped Greg's parting words would come true, that he would miraculously find a last-minute way to save her, her rationality told her it wasn't going to happen. She had to tell Tom, and later her parents, what lay ahead. Even if they didn't believe her, at least she would have told them the truth.

"Tom?"

He turned around. "Oh. Sorry, didn't even notice you. How are you feeling?"

"Um…not too good, actually."

"Do you want to talk about it? Here, let me make you a coffee. You look like you could use one."

"I don't think caffeine would help right now."

"Then how about a cup of green tea?"

"That sounds great, thanks."

She followed Tom into the kitchen, remaining silent while he boiled water. It felt strange, knowing she would finally tell him the whole story. Would he be as shocked as Greg was? Would he even believe her? Either way, she would have to apologize for everything she had put him through the past month.

Tom sat down and placed the steaming mug in front of her. "So, what's bothering you?"

"Quite a lot. It's a long story."

"That's fine, take your time. I'm not going anywhere."

Amanda resisted the urge to raise an eyebrow. Something about his friendliness felt off. She had expected a comment like, 'will you finally tell me what's going on?' Not that she minded him being understanding, but she wondered what brought it on. *Maybe he got a raise?*

She took a sip. "Remember when I called you from Serbia to go to Ukraine?"

"Yeah. Sorry for being such an ass back then, I was just really scared for you."

"That's sweet, but it's not to chew you out. I just want to tell you what happened after—"

She was cut short by an aggressive buzzing. Tom took out his phone. "Goddammit. Now of all times…sorry, I have to take this."

"Go ahead."

"Mr. Chen, yes, good day. How is your family?"

Amanda went back into the living room and closed the door to give Tom some privacy. His client portfolios were stacked high on the desk. How did he even manage dealing with so many of them simultaneously? This job would seriously grind him down one day.

A book at the back of the desk caught her eye, nearly hidden among the client portfolios. The paperback stood in odd contrast to the otherwise uniformly sized papers. Tom didn't read novels; was this one of hers? But this book had dozens of post-it flags, something she never used.

She looked back towards the kitchen, but Tom was still talking. She moved the papers out of the way and picked up the book. *When Someone You Love Has a Mental Illness—A Handbook for Family, Friends and Caregivers.*

What…the? With trembling hands, she opened the table of contents and saw chapters marked with bright, neon yellow. *Chapter 4—Handling Hallucinations and Delusions. Chapter 6—Coping With Your Own Feelings.* On the first page was a handwritten note:

> *Hi Tom. This is the book I told you about. It may give you some*
> *more insight into what your girlfriend is going through. If you can*
> *manage it, it would be great if I could see her in person.*
> *All the best, Susan.*

Her stomach felt like she had swallowed a rock. Was this why he was being so nice to her and asking her how she was doing all the time? Because he had written her off as a delusional maniac and some damn shrink had told him to "build rapport" with her?

"Thank you, Mr. Chen. You too!" came Tom's voice through the door.

Amanda quickly put the book back and arranged the papers how she'd found them. Her shaking hands made it difficult not to knock everything over.

The door opened and Tom came in. "Sorry, a client called. What were you going to say? I put the phone on mute."

"It's fine, Tom…it's fine." Amanda grit her teeth so hard it hurt. "Sorry, I'm still feeling really tired from last night. Can we talk about this some other time?"

"Oh yeah, sure. No rush. Sleep well, darling."

She closed the door behind her and lay down, grabbing her teddy bear and hugging it tight. "Sorry, you're being abused quite a lot lately…"

As sad and bitter as she was, at least she had dodged a bullet and not told him anything. God knows what he might have done if she had opened up to him.

Her phone buzzed with a message from Greg. A nervous jitter ran through her.

Yo. Wanted to let you know, I'm searching for another spirit medium. Anderson can't be the only one, right? Most are frauds, obviously, but I've found two who seem promising. I'm tracking them down now, should have something in a few hours. Hang in there, okay?

Oh Greg… Amanda ran her fingers over the screen. He really was a sweetheart. But his message only depressed her even further. She doubted any of his "promising" leads would pan out. How many people with Anderson's gifts could there even be? And how many of those could be found online? She somehow doubted Anderson had ever advertised his skills on the internet.

4:55 PM. Meaning it was almost 2 AM in Serbia. Terzić had probably already left his little cottage and was on his way to the airport, and his inevitable demise. All because of one stupid phone call.

Amanda hugged her teddy close and closed her eyes, hoping never to open them again.

CHAPTER 20

There were no streetlamps on this road. The only illumination came from the moon and a lonely car as it sped along highway A1.

Terzić rubbed his eyes. He had never been fond of driving at night. Driving tired with limited visibility was an accident waiting to happen. He looked at his watch. 2:45. He was well on time. Barring a tire blowout or other major impediment, he would arrive at the airport half an hour earlier than planned.

Blue lights appeared in his rear-view mirror. He hoped there was some emergency elsewhere, but the police car pulled in front of him and blinked to the right, signaling him to pull over. Terzić was certain his car had no broken lights or an obstructed license plate. He had always driven under the speed limit. There was no good reason to stop him.

Anxious, he pulled over and stepped out of his car. "Yes, officer?"

"Good morning sir, will you please show me your license and registration?"

Terzić's heart sank. He could tell from the slimy voice and false deference, this was the worst kind of officer he could have run into. Probably he was bored out of his mind, had seen Terzić drive by and pulled him over just to have a distraction. The officer was young, obviously hadn't seen much action, and being placed on traffic duty at an hour like this had certainly been a bad way to start the week.

Terzić understood the young man's boredom—he'd been on graveyard shifts his first years in the force, wondering what the point of it all was. But

Terzić had always taken every assignment seriously. He had never performed pointless traffic stops just to kill time.

"Sir? License and registration, if you please."

Terzić went back to his car, opened his glove compartment and took out the requested documents. He wondered what he could do to end this quickly. If he just submitted himself to the whims of this young hotshot, it could mean losing anything from a few minutes to over an hour, depending on how nasty he decided to be.

There was no use telling the officer there was a plane to catch. In fact, this might make him waste even more time, just to show Terzić who was boss. Saying he was a retired officer himself also wouldn't help. He didn't know this man and there was no way to prove it.

"Could you please spell your first and last name and give me your birthdate?"

"T-e-r-z-i-ć, D-j-o-r-d-j-e, 3rd of November 1946."

"There is a smudge on your license, Mr. Terzić. The expiration date is a bit hard to read. I shall have to confirm with the department of transportation that your license is genuine. May I see your registration?"

The pointless harassment, the faked politeness, the smug grin…what a contemptible man. Becoming a police officer meant representing and upholding the laws of the land, not lording over innocent civilians and playing silly power games.

At this rate, Terzić could be here for several hours and miss his flight. Dozens of lives hung in the balance. Lives that would be lost to the whims of a bored rookie.

Terzić decided that he wouldn't be able to talk himself out of this. That meant he only had one option left. He had never enjoyed having to pick the lesser of two evils, but with this many lives at stake, there could be no hesitation.

"Sir? Your vehicle registration, please."

He stretched out his hand to give the officer his registration papers. The moment the officer grabbed the booklet, Terzić delivered a blow to the man's stomach.

The officer stumbled backwards. Before he could recover, Terzić moved behind him, put his arm around the officer's neck, locked his elbow and squeezed. The man gasped for air, then quickly lost consciousness.

Moving quickly, Terzić took the officer's handcuffs and shackled him to a nearby guardrail, wiped off any fingerprints, then threw the keys into the field beside the street.

He opened the police car and looked inside. It was a standard highway patrol car. Terzić deactivated the dash camera and pocketed the digital memory card. Again, he wiped down all fingerprints,, then locked the car and threw away the keys as well.

The officer would get help as soon as another car passed, which would be within one to three hours, given the time of day. If Terzić was unlucky, the officer would remember his name and he would face punishment when he came back from Canada. *If* he came back from Canada. He went back to his car, turned on the ignition, and slammed his foot on the gas pedal. He had lost far too much time already.

*

He was walking on a road paved with human bones. The air was thick and oily. The bones cracked under his heavy steps. There were no stars, no moon, just a faint, red glow covering the landscape like vapor.

In the distance lay the village, a dark cloud shaped like a dove hanging over it. The cloud turned towards Terzić, eyeing its prey.

No.

If he had turned back, he might have lived, but he was too stubborn. With his typical determination, he took the last few steps towards the village.

No, don't.

Everything was silent. All the inhabitants lay face down in the blood-soaked dirt. Nothing stirred as Terzić made his way to the center of the village. He stopped and examined something on the ground. A grin spread over the Dove in the sky.

No, no! Go back!

The villagers began to stir. They twisted and contorted, rising to their feet like marionettes pulled by invisible strings.

Please, run!

Terzić didn't hear. He was still fixated on whatever had caught his attention before. The villagers shuffled towards him, their skin lifeless and grey, their eyes black as tar.

"Mr. Terzić!" she screamed.

Finally, he heard her and turned. As if waiting for that moment, the villagers fell on Terzić like a swarm of wasps. He screamed helplessly as the villagers held him down and readied their farm tools.

Amanda tried to run. Maybe she could still save him. She got within a few steps from him, when a sharp pain tore through her chest and stopped her movements. She looked down and saw a black claw sticking out of her rib cage. She screamed, but her blood-filled lungs only produced a pathetic gurgling. Everything faded to black once more.

*

Slowly, the world came into focus. She saw her nightstand to her right, her teddy bear to her left and the white ceiling above. She checked her alarm clock. 6:44 AM. *So…early.*

Amanda let herself fall back. This had to be the fifteenth nightmare in a row. Every single time, she had seen Terzić. Getting cut open, cannibalized, decapitated, or torn apart. And every single time, she had been helpless to stop it.

She was so tired…and so thirsty. "Tom?"

She waited, but there was no reply.

"Tom! Are you here?"

Of course not. It was Monday and he was at work. How had she forgotten something so simple?

As she tried to get up, something obstructed her movement. Like heavy, invisible chains holding her down. A horrendous fear rose in her when she realized it wasn't just her imagination. She struggled desperately to escape, but the more she fought, the tighter the chains got, cutting into her skin, burning and freezing her wherever they touched.

No! Let me go!

Above her, a shape materialized. Misshapen and grinning, the Red Dove looked down at her. It drew a deep breath and sucked all the air from the room. Amanda gasped and ached, her lungs trying to catch the last slivers of oxygen. She wanted to beg for her life, but the surrounding vacuum smothered her words. She became aware that her beloved teddy bear had vanished. The bed, the nightstand, the walls, everything was gone. She was shackled in an endless nothingness.

Out of the shadows, the Dark Ones emerged, forming a ring around her.

Please, spare me! I'll do anything! she pleaded in her head, hoping the Red Dove would hear her. It didn't answer, it only widened its grin.

One of the Dark Ones moved closer. It raised one of its claws and stabbed Amanda's hand. She screamed, but there was no sound in this airless world, and the chains trapped her firmly in place.

Another Dark One stabbed her knee. Then another stabbed her neck, yet another stabbed her stomach. Every stab hurt more than the last. She prayed for mercy, she prayed to die, but her consciousness never faded. Over and over and over, the Dark Ones' claws burned into her. Her vision faded to a searing, white oblivion. Minutes turned to hours, hours to days. There were no more thoughts, no emotions. There was nothing but pain. And it was never going to stop.

*

After an eternity of torture, there came a sound. A loud, repeated beeping. Slowly, the Dark Ones vanished and the endless agony receded. The walls and ceiling came back. Amanda was in her room again.

Had this...been another dream? Was she finally awake? Or was the Red Dove just giving her yet another fake hope before plunging her into an eternity of torture again?

The beeping continued. Amanda rotated her head towards her nightstand. Tom was calling her. As she willed her hand to pick up the phone, the ringing stopped.

Her throat was so dry it hurt to breathe. Carefully, she sat up and waited for the room to stop spinning. Five minutes later, she finally had the strength to stand. Every step felt like wading through cement. The trip to the kitchen had never been this long.

When she finally had her glass of water, she collapsed into the kitchen chair.

Even though the torture had lasted for weeks, the kitchen clock told her only an hour had passed. And it wasn't even the 7th yet…maybe tomorrow, time would lose meaning altogether and her suffering would stretch to infinity, her whole existence becoming nothing but torment. Or maybe she would wake up eventually, her mind destroyed, ready to grab the nearest weapon and murder everyone around her.

Her phone buzzed with a message from Greg.

Hey. The other two didn't pan out. I'll keep searching. Be in touch.

Amanda let her phone drop on the table and raised her eyes to the kitchen counter. An idea had just occurred to her—a way to escape the eternity of suffering the Red Dove was going to trap her in. She opened the top drawer and took out one of the steak knives. The light from the window reflected off its smooth edge; the shining key to her salvation.

She sat back down and put her hand on the table, gently pressing the knife on her wrist. She had expected the steel to be cold, but she could barely feel it. She pressed harder. There was an uncomfortable tingle, a sensation warning her something sharp was touching her.

Amanda pulled, gradually, her hands steady as a surgeon's. There was some pain, but it was laughable compared to what she had been through. She watched a steady trickle of blood flow down her hand and felt a warm sense of relief wash over her. Finally, she would know peace. She wondered why she hadn't done this sooner. She watched the drops fall on the table and decided this was too slow. She placed the knife on her wrist again and prepared to cut once more, along the vein this time.

Out of the corner of her eye, Amanda saw Terzić's still-unopened bottle of rakija on the kitchen counter. It was funny—after everything they had been through together, it was fitting that they both ended up committing suicide on the same day, neither of them having accomplished anything and yet both determined to see it through.

She paused. He said he would arrive in Edmonton at 16:10. He wasn't dead yet. She looked back down at the knife in her hand and the blood flowing from her wrist. Why had he seemed so disappointed when she told him she wouldn't go? Because he thought they were in this together. Because he thought they could achieve more as a team, or he would have simply gone on his own from the get-go.

And why had she refused? Because of the silly hope that if she stayed far enough away, if she waited for Greg's miracle, she might somehow be saved.

But Greg's miracle hadn't occurred and the Red Dove had no trouble trapping her in an eternity of torture, right here in Chicago. The result was the same as if she had gone with Terzić.

She dropped the knife.

God, what a selfish asshole I am…

If she was going to kill herself anyway, why do it in such a pathetic and useless manner? There was no escape for her, but Terzić? He wasn't affected by the curse, his fate wasn't sealed. If she could do something, anything…like take a fatal blow in his stead, then her death at least would have meaning. In Ukraine, down in that mine, he had risked his life to save hers. If she had nothing left to lose, why wasn't she returning the favor?

But, wasn't she already a danger to others? She bit her lip and looked down at her right hand. She had already shoved Greg and punched that man. What if something worse happened in Canada? Then *she* might end up being the one to kill Terzić.

She bit her lip. *Stop making excuses.* She and Terzić were doomed either way. The worst that could happen was that she would fail to avert the inevitable.

Terzić was going to the village because he believed in the possibility of someone being saved. Therefore, she too would put her faith in the hope that she could still do some good with the brief life she had left, no matter how slim the odds.

She went to the medicine cabinet and bandaged her wrist. Then, she searched for her laptop. For some weird reason, she found it buried under a folder on Tom's desk. He did sometimes make a mess while working from home, but he always left it clean when going to the office. Maybe he had woken up late and left in a hurry?

After some searching, she found she was in luck—there was a flight that would leave at noon, nonstop to Edmonton. She selected one of the last available seats and entered her credit card information.

She checked her watch: Almost 08:40 AM. She had to hurry. She got dressed, took her backpack out of the closet and packed her passport, her wallet, her phone and her jacket. Other than that, nothing looked useful for this last journey she was about to embark on.

As she passed by the kitchen, she realized how frightening it looked, with her blood smeared all over the table. She didn't have much time, but she couldn't leave it like this for Tom to find in the evening. She wiped the table as clean as she could, then rushed to the front door.

Just as she touched the door handle, she heard a click in the lock and the door flew open. Tom stood in the doorway, his breathing rapid and his brow moist.

"Tom? What are you doing here?"

"The damn client portfolios! Left them here!" he panted while running into the living room. He took the stack of papers from his desk and stashed them in his briefcase. When he came back, his eyes fell on her backpack. "Where are you off to?"

"I…I've got an errand to run."

"Ah all right. Well, I'll see you this evening!" he said and gave her a hasty kiss.

"Um, Tom!"

He stopped by the door. "What?"

"I, um…might not be back by this evening."

"Huh? But what about the dinner?"

"What dinner?"

"*The* dinner, Amanda! Don't tell me you've forgotten!"

"I...Uh..."

"God damn it! The company dinner! At Alinea! The one I RSVPed for both of us back in fucking May!"

Amanda turned her eyes to heaven. *God, why do you hate me so much?* Why did this stupid company dinner have to be today of all times?

All she had to say was, 'Yeah, sorry, just slipped my mind. I'll be there, bye honey!' But she didn't want to lie again. Not this time.

"Sorry, I can't. It's about the Red Dove. A friend of mine needs my help."

Tom blinked several times and his mouth dropped open. "You have got to be kidding me."

"No, I'm not. I'm sorry."

He gripped his forehead and rubbed his temples. "Amanda, I beg you, please don't do this. Susan warned me something like this might happen, but you can't seriously wreck everything I've worked for just to satisfy some deranged fantasies. Just...let me get you a pill, or something, okay?"

"Thanks, Tom. That's...so sweet. And who's this Susan? Your shrink?"

"Yes! Never thought I'd need one, but you were so depressing, I was starting to feel low just being around you. She told me you probably have PTSD or even schizophrenia, so I've tried to be patient, I've tried to be sympathetic, but it's clear that you need treatment."

"Jesus. You're really not holding back, are you?"

"Well, forgive me for being a little upset that you're blowing off the most important event of my career to go help some imaginary friend."

"Wow...just wow. If only you knew how hurtful you're being. I'm sorry, but I can't discuss this any longer. Sorry about your dinner."

Amanda had walked past him when Tom said, "Yeah, and don't bother coming back."

She stopped in her tracks. Had he really just said that?

Tom rolled his eyes. "Come on, does that really surprise you? Sorry, but I just can't deal with this anymore. You're burning down everything to chase those crazed delusions of yours and I can't be a part of that. The Amanda I know is gone."

His words hit her like a brick. Their relationship hadn't been great since she came back, but did he really hate her this much? All because she was haunted by something he didn't understand?

Her watch was tugging at her wrist like a leaden weight. If she stayed any longer, she would miss the flight, and Terzić would have to face the Red Dove alone.

Amanda walked back into the kitchen. She reached behind her neck, unhooked Tom's necklace and placed it on the table where she had nearly bled to death minutes ago. "I'm sorry, Tom. I'm sorry I couldn't be the carefree girl you used to love."

And she rushed past him out the door.

*

She cried all the way to the airport. Her tears just wouldn't stop, no matter how much she hated all the awkward stares. On a rational level, she didn't understand why this was hurting so much. She had a few more hours to live at best. How did any of this still matter?

Past security, she could finally flee into the bathroom to get her tears under control. How pathetic the woman she saw in the mirror looked. She hadn't taken any makeup, so there was no way to cover up her puffy eyes and red nose. She grabbed some toilet paper, moistened it with cold water and patted her eyes with it, hoping to get the swelling down. A woman washing her hands saw her and asked, "Boy trouble?"

"Yeah. In a way."

"What happened?"

"It's a *really* long story."

"You wanna talk about it?"

"Thanks for the offer, you're very kind. But I can't miss my flight."

The woman shrugged. "Alright. See you around."

Not in this life, Amanda thought as she made her way to the gate.

CHAPTER 21

In Edmonton, she still had some time before Terzić's plane arrived. Since the airport had Wi-Fi, she decided to look up Morton Ridge. There wasn't much to find. It seemed to be a relatively isolated community. Like Greg had commented, all houses had the same street name. There were some scattered reviews by hikers about the 'charm of the place' and that you could stay for a night or two. She also found praise for *Zoey's Groceries*—'small but well-stocked.'

To get to Morton Ridge, they had to drive through a larger town called Jasper, the closest place that had a police station, probably the one she would have called if she'd told Terzić the truth. She saved the map on her phone. When she checked the announcement boards again, Terzić's plane had just landed.

Fifteen minutes later, he walked out of Customs with a small bag slung over his shoulder, looking surprisingly well-rested. She could guess how tired he was after that flight, but he looked just like when she had left him. It was only a month ago, but it felt like decades had passed.

He looked surprised when he saw her. "*Dobro veče*, Ms. Dousson."

"Mr. Terzić...I'm so sorry. For abandoning you like that and...and..." She wanted to say more, but everything she had planned on saying suddenly sounded dumb to her.

He shook his head. "Not at all. I understood. Nevertheless, I am glad to see you. Why are you here?"

She smiled, glad that he wasn't mad at her. "I…had a change of heart. You came with me when I went into that mine. So if this is something you feel you have to do, I'll come with you too. Even though I'm not sure how much use I'll be."

Again, he looked surprised, but Amanda also saw the faintest smile.

Terzić nodded. "That is very kind of you. I appreciate it." He checked his watch. "Shall we?"

"How will we get there?"

"One of my friends speaks acceptable English. I had him reserve a vehicle."

On the way to the rental counter, Terzić also bought a street map of Edmonton.

Half an hour later, they finally had the keys to the car. Amanda insisted on driving. Given that Terzić had driven the whole way from Ukraine back to Serbia, this was the least she could do, especially given how tired he had to be right now. Once they had navigated out of Edmonton, she told him there was no more need to use the map. "I looked it up—all we have to do is follow this highway west until we hit Jasper."

Terzić nodded but remained quiet, as usual. *Just as well,* Amanda thought and focused on the road.

The view outside was a sight even the best camera couldn't capture. There were blue lakes with crystalline water, lush, vibrant forests, and rivers sparkling in the afternoon sun. And ahead of them, rising majestically in the distance, were the Rocky Mountains.

A couple of months ago, this scene would have taken Amanda's breath away. To rent a motorhome here, drive along this road…it would have been heaven. But now? It all seemed so fake. Just over there, in those deceptively beautiful mountains, a monster was lurking, ready to again massacre an entire village of innocents. It made her wonder—was the Red Dove the only thing of its kind out there? Or were there other, maybe even more dreadful horrors, all hidden in those pretty lakes and mountains?

The thought made her shiver. Terzić gave her a curious look, but as usual, didn't pry.

Finally, past 8 PM, they crossed Fiddle River, the stream that marked the entrance of Jasper National Park.

Soon, the first buildings came into view.

Terzić motioned to an empty parking spot. "Please stop here."

"Aren't we driving straight to Morton Ridge?"

"You called the police here, correct?"

"Yeah," she lied reflexively.

"I am hoping we can still get them to act. Our chances are not high, but we must attempt it."

Amanda grimaced. What a situation she was in now...Her reasons for lying to Terzić before hadn't changed—convincing anyone to go to Morton Ridge was basically committing murder. Terzić had to know this, too, yet he kept insisting they get the police involved. Then again, him even being here suggested that he thought he could somehow get into the village and save someone from the curse. Where was this coming from? Did he have some kind of ace up his sleeve that he hadn't told her about? Like a way to shield himself and others from the Red Dove? Was that why he wasn't bothered to send someone up there?

She took a deep breath. *I really hope you know what you're doing, Mr. Terzić...*

Amanda started the car again. They stopped by one pedestrian after another, until one of them was able to tell her the way to the police station.

Five minutes later, she parked the car in front of a small wooden house, with a tiny sign indicating they'd arrived at the right place. She took a moment to settle her nerves. If she wanted to get someone up there, she would have to lie, yet again. And to the police, no less. If she got found out, would they be detained and charged with a crime? No matter what, she wasn't allowed to mess up here.

She turned to Terzić, "Let's go."

*

Behind the front desk sat a police officer with a broad face and big moustache.

265

His nametag read "M. Jones" and based on the imposing-looking stripes on his shoulder, he was a higher-up. He was typing on his computer and didn't seem remotely interested that two people had just come in. Amanda cleared her throat.

"Yes?" he asked without looking up.

She took a deep breath and prayed that the act she had cooked up in the car would work. "Thank God we found you, we need help!"

"Yeah? What happened?" he asked, with a tone of voice that said, 'Damn tourists getting excited again because they saw a moose.'

"We were out driving when we heard gunshots and screams for help."

He looked up. "You...what? Why didn't you call immediately?"

"Cellphone was out of juice, I'm sorry. Please, you have to come quickly!"

"Okay, slow down, slow down. You said you were driving around here?"

"Yes."

"And you heard gunshots?"

"Yes, several!"

She wanted the guy to act quick, not ask questions. She was trying her best to appear shocked and frantic, but she was starting to wonder how good her acting really was.

Jones drew out a map of Jasper National Park. "Do you know where?"

She looked at the map for a while, pretending she was trying to find the right place. "Pretty sure it was..." She pointed close to Morton Ridge. "Around here?"

Jones looked at it, then back at her, then back at the map.

Please don't make him second guess me, please don't make him second guess me...

"And you're sure you heard cries? It wasn't just some kids playing around with birthday crackers?"

"Yeah, I'm sure. People were desperately calling for help. And it wasn't firecrackers. My dad took me to the shooting range several times. I swear, those were gunshots!"

She mentally apologized to her gun-hating father. Truth be told, she had never witnessed a gun being fired in her life. She just hoped Jones wouldn't start asking about her favorite caliber or something.

"How long ago was this?"

Amanda was glad that she had looked up the travel distances at the airport. "Around thirty minutes ago?"

Jones looked down at the map and shook his head.

Please, stop asking questions already! If he kept picking apart her story, she would eventually mess up. Her throat tightened up. This entire act was like dancing on a razorblade.

"Can you drive back to the exact place where this happened?"

"Yes, I think so."

He nodded. "Robinson! Westen!" he shouted.

Two young officers entered the room. One was a tall woman, with short, blonde hair and a fiery look, standing perfectly erect, like a soldier. Next to her and in sharp contrast was a short and thin man with black hair, also standing at attention, but not as rigidly as the woman next to him.

"Sergeant?" the woman said sternly.

"Allow me to introduce you. These are officers Robinson," he pointed to the woman, "and Westen. And your names are…?"

"Amanda Dawson and Đorđe Terzić," Amanda said, holding out her hand.

Jones raised an eyebrow at Terzić's weird name, but he didn't ask any more questions. "Robinson, Westen, you will accompany these two to a place due west, about half an hour from here. They claim to have heard gunshots and a shout for help. Take a squad car, drive behind them until you reach the spot and find out what happened."

"Yes, sir!" Officer Robinson said, flashing Amanda a look that said, *Thanks for ruining my evening.*

Amanda strained to put a smile on her face.

Jones turned and asked, "So, is that fine by you, Ms. Dawson?"

"Sure."

"All right, good luck."

As they were about to leave, Jones said, "Oh by the way…" Amanda's guts clenched. Jones continued. "When you guys are done with this, you can take the night off."

"Yes, sir!" Robinson said. Amanda wondered if Robinson ever said anything else, while breathing a sigh of relief the plan had worked, at least for now.

Amanda showed the officers the rented Jeep and said, "We'll wait for you here, okay?"

"Sounds good," Westen said, speaking up for the first time. *Lovely voice,* Amanda thought. *Seems way more laid back than that Yes Sir lady.*

Amanda and Terzić got into their Jeep and waited for the officers to get their car.

"What happened?" Terzić asked.

"I told them I heard cries and gunshots somewhere close to Morton Ridge. I'm hoping we'll be able to get the police officers to understand something is wrong, then they can call for reinforcements."

Terzić nodded. She got that he wanted a full-scale evacuation, but Amanda hadn't been able to think of anything that would have made that happen. Who would believe her if she told them what was really happening?

Amanda put on her seat belt and made a silent prayer for God to forgive her for lying again and to spare those two police officers and Terzić. *Please, let them get out of this alive.*

She took out her phone to open the map to Morton Ridge and saw a message from Greg waiting for her.

Heya. Couldn't find much, but have a few new leads. Meet up and discuss next steps?

It was sad to see how hard he was fighting for her, all in vain. Still, it was a bittersweet comfort to know she'd made the right choice coming here—there really never had been any hope.

Greg had also called four times. She could only imagine how worried he was. She wanted to respond, but the police car pulled up behind them and flashed their headlights.

Amanda clenched her teeth. She couldn't risk the officers seeing her making a call after she'd told Jones she had no battery. What if one of them had overheard the conversation? She gave the phone to Terzić. "This map shows the route we have to take."

After they had left Jasper, Amanda considered telling Terzić to give her the phone so she could call Greg. The police car was far enough behind them to not see it. But if she called, she would have to tell Greg that this would be the last time they spoke. They'd only have like ten minutes. Amanda had so much to say to him, so much to apologize for. How was she even supposed to start?

"Excuse me, I believe someone is calling you?" Terzić said. He held up the buzzing phone.

Greg...You really have a sixth sense, don't you? She gulped. Did she really have to take this call? She could just vanish quietly, without such a hard conversation. All she had to do was to let it go to voicemail. But Greg didn't deserve that. She couldn't be a coward. Not this time.

"Amanda? Oh thank God you picked up. I'm standing in front of your place and feared the worst. Did you read the message? I wanted to...wait, what's that sound, where are you, anyway?"

"I'm in a car...in Canada."

There was a pause. "Amanda, please tell me you're joking."

"No. I'm sorry."

Another pause. "Why, Amanda? Just why?"

"I...had no other choice. My friend from Serbia insisted on flying over here, hoping to rescue some of the villagers. We are heading there now with two police officers from a nearby town."

"Isn't it suicide to go into the village?"

Of course it was. But something stopped her from telling Greg that she had no intention of returning. It felt embarrassing somehow, like she was abandoning him.

After a minute of silence, Greg asked, "Why didn't you tell me you were going?"

"Wouldn't you have stopped me?"

"I would have tried, obviously. Or I would have come with you."

"Are you serious?"

"Of course I am. Did you think I would let you go to a place like that on your own?"

Amanda tightened her other hand on the steering wheel and blinked a few times to stop her eyes from blurring. "Thanks Greg. That means a lot."

"So, how can I help?"

"What?"

"You can't expect me to just sit around, right? I'm asking what I can do to help."

"That's very sweet of you, I really appreciate it, but there's nothing that…"

Then she remembered—in all this rush and confusion, she had forgotten something very important. "Wait, there is something. In case… in case I don't come back, can you please call my parents and tell them what happened?"

"You mean they don't know?"

"I know, I'm a horrible daughter. I haven't told them anything about what's going on. Mostly, I wanted to spare my mother the grief of losing someone else to the Red Dove. Now I wouldn't even know how to start."

"Don't worry, I get it. When should I call them?"

"If you don't hear from me by morning."

"And what should I say?"

"Just…tell them I'm sorry."

"All right. But can I ask for something in return? You know, for all the times I helped you and all the cookies I never got?"

"What is it?"

"I…don't want this to be our last conversation. So please…don't die."

A warmth spread around Amanda's heart, a feeling she had almost forgotten existed. This was a voice she had never heard from Greg before. He sounded close to tears.

"I can't make a promise that I don't know how to keep."

"I don't care. Promise me."

God…A selfish piece of trash like me doesn't deserve someone like him. "I promise I'll try," she said as her vision clouded.

"I'll hold you to it. Good luck, Amanda."

She gave Terzić the phone back and tried to focus on the road again.

"He is a good friend," Terzić said.

"You understood that?"

"I did not have to."

Up ahead, Amanda noticed a fork in the road. Terzić hadn't had the map during the phone call, but she remembered this part. Left, then left again at another fork, and then straight up to the village.

When she reached the second fork, Amanda slammed on the brakes at the last second. A landslide had buried the road under tons of mud and debris. Beyond that stretched a large, dark forest.

Amanda got out of the Jeep.

"This is troublesome," Terzić said, as the police car pulled up behind them and Robinson and Westen got out.

"Is this where you heard gunfire?" Robinson asked.

"Ah no. It was further up."

"So it's not reachable by car? Why didn't you tell Sergeant Jones about this?"

"We hiked up," Amanda lied, thanking her stars that Officer Robinson apparently hadn't listened in on her conversation with Jones.

Before Robinson could reply, Westen spoke up. "Abby, don't you think it's strange the way is blocked? Morton Ridge is up there. They should have complained about this already."

"Is there another way up?" Robinson asked.

Westen shook his head. "The rest is just mountains. This road here is the only way."

"All right. We'll take the flashlights."

Amanda spun around, eyes wide with shock, but Robinson seemed serious. Westen nodded and went back to the police car. She turned back toward the forest. If she hadn't decided to come here, she would have bled to death in the kitchen at this point. It was silly to get scared now. And yet, this dark forest felt alive, hostile. Driving through in a car was one thing, but on foot, with nothing but a flashlight?

The landslide and forest behind it looked like the edge of the abyss. If she went in there, how long would she have until the Dark Ones came for them? Or…what if the Red Dove drove her insane while they were hiking up? What if she attacked Terzić and the others?

"Are you ready, Ma'am?" Robinson asked sharply, flashlight in hand.

Amanda looked at Terzić. He stood with his head held high, showing not even a hint of hesitation. If she was hoping to save him, she had to go in there with him.

Her backpack was still inside the Jeep. When more police would come looking tomorrow, they would at least find her passport and be able to identify her body. *If there will even be a body left to find…*

She clenched her fists and looked Robinson in the eye.

"Yes. Let's go."

CHAPTER 22

Night was falling fast. The similarity to the forest around Priboj was uncanny—trees so large and vegetation so thick that barely any light reached the forest floor. Soon, the officers' flashlights became their only illumination.

Robinson swung her flashlight right and left. The trees threw eerie shadows that appeared, vanished, then reappeared. Every time, Amanda thought their branches were hanging deeper and closer. Even the rocks seemed to move as the light swept across them, like she was in a den of crawling insects.

She wanted to ask Robinson to stop swinging the light around, but her voice might awaken something. Something that, so far, was merely watching them. No matter how often Amanda told herself that she couldn't escape anyway, that there was no point in being scared at this point, she could barely bring herself to keep going. Every fiber of her being wanted to run away.

Through the canopy above, she could barely see the moon rising. The further they walked, the denser the trees and foliage became, as if they were slowly being swallowed by the forest. Malicious intent permeated the air. Even Terzić looked around repeatedly, as if searching for some kind of movement.

"How much further up?" Robinson barked, making Amanda give a small shriek. Why did she have to be loud!

"Um. Uh. By the village," she stammered.

"Ugh. Really not our lucky day," Westen complained. Robinson remained quiet and swung her flashlight left and right again.

At the last swing, Amanda saw something move by a bush, a couple yards away. When Robinson swung her flashlight again, Amanda saw another shadow disappear up a tree, closer this time. She knew that motion—unnatural and creepy, slithering always just out of sight.

She felt something strange and looked down. Her left hand was moving weirdly, as though animated by another consciousness. It wanted to reach for Robinson's gun. *No. No!* She used her right hand to hold it in place. Fighting an invisible force, Amanda pulled her left hand back, towards her vial. *Please work, please work...I can't lose myself now!*

Pressing her left hand against the holy water, it calmed down. She muttered every prayer under her breath she could think of. Anything to hold on to her mind a bit longer.

At the next swing of Robinson's flashlight, the tree beside her bent unnaturally and a dark shape materialized behind it, less than three feet away Just as Amanda drew a large breath to scream for them to run, the trees thinned before them.

The road stretched across the open plain like a black snake, with houses dotted on either side. Not a single light was burning. For a moment, she doubted her senses. Had they really reached *the* village? How?

"Hey, Abby. You see that?"

"Yeah."

Both officers were on edge.

"What's wrong?" Amanda asked.

"Morton Ridge has permanent street illumination. See those lamps over there? They shouldn't be turned off like this."

Amanda looked down, but her hand was steady. *What's going on?* Why hadn't the Dark Ones attacked? Aside from the wind, everything remained deathly quiet. Were they too late? Had the last villager just died? Was that why her hand had stopped shaking?

For a moment, Amanda found herself wishing for that outcome. With everyone dead, maybe the Red Dove had already left. Then the Dark Ones would also be gone, meaning Terzić and the police officers were safe. And since she was still alive, maybe that meant even her life had been spared!

An inhuman scream pierced the silence; an agonized howl, like an animal being skewered. The shock made Amanda freeze, but Terzić dragged her behind a tree. She stumbled and Terzić struggled to stop her from falling.

When she pulled herself up, the two officers had taken cover as well.

"What the hell is going on here?" Robinson said. "Call it in!"

Westen pulled up his radio. "Jasper command, this is Westen, come in."

There was a long silence. Westen tried again, "Jasper command, do you copy?"

Amanda checked her phone. No reception. Her hunch in the café had been correct—like in Jelena's diary, not even radio waves made it outside. They were on their own. Although…wasn't that a good thing? Since the Red Dove was still here, calling for reinforcements would only result in more needless deaths.

Robinson tried her radio as well. "Jasper command, this is Robinson, come in."

Westen shook his head. "This is really shady. No way both radios stop working at the same time. Something's interfering with the signal."

"Okay, we're going in," Robinson decided. "Sir, Ma'am, you stay here. Do not enter the village."

Amanda looked at them in disbelief. "Wait, wh—" she started, but her voice broke down. "What about us?" she finally managed to ask.

Westen smiled reassuringly. "You two go back the way we came. Here, take my flashlight. Get to the car as fast as possible, then drive back to Jasper. Tell them that the road is blocked, that police radios don't work, and that Westen and Robinson need help in Morton Ridge immediately."

Terzić looked surprised when Westen and Robinson both ran into the village. He watched them until they disappeared behind one of the houses. "Why did they go alone? This leaves both them and us vulnerable."

"Since the radios aren't working, they want us to go back to the car and get help in Jasper."

Terzić shook his head. "Going back to that town and returning with

275

reinforcements would take over an hour. Staying together would have been the better option."

Could they even return to Jasper at this point? Amanda looked back at the forest. An overpowering dread emanated from the wall of black trees and shifting shadows. She was certain the Dark Ones were waiting, ready to pounce if they tried to escape.

But why hadn't the Dark Ones already killed them on the way up here, like that unlucky hiker in Jelena's diary? The only explanation Amanda could think of was that the Red Dove hadn't killed them because it *wanted* them up here. Meaning, by accompanying Terzić, she had played straight into the Red Dove's hands.

Amanda sank to her knees. If only she had bled herself to death in Chicago… that would have been the easy way out. But no, she had tried to play the hero and only made things worse. Now she was trapped and could only wait to see what the Red Dove had in store for her.

Terzić was still observing the village. The monstrous danger they were in didn't seem to faze him.

"Mr. Terzić…How do you do it?"

"Do what?"

"Be so fearless all the time. I'm so scared I'm not even sure I can move. But you look so calm."

"In truth, I am not." He saw how incredulous she looked and continued, "I am frightened, as you are. It is natural to be afraid here. But I must overcome this, or I will be of no help."

Amanda nodded. How different the two of them were…while she was completely useless and only thinking of herself, he was unflinchingly staring death in the face, all on the slim hope of saving people he had never met. She had already found out in Serbia, but Terzić was truly impressive. Both as a police officer and as a person.

He turned his attention to the village again. "We must go in."

"What?"

"We are not accomplishing anything here. We must catch up with the officers and stay together." He looked up at the sky and added, "We are unfortunate with this full moon."

"Why? At least we can still see something."

"It also means that we ourselves will be seen."

Amanda looked at her hands, dyed silver in the moon's light. She doubted the Dark Ones needed light to see, but Terzić was right: anyone—or anything—could see them.

Sounds came from the forest. Breaking branches, rustling bushes and stirring leaves.

"Let us go, now!" Terzić started towards the closest building.

"Hey! Hey!" she gasped.

Amanda's legs wouldn't move. The forest sounded like a hive of insects coming alive.

Move. Move! MOVE!

There was a fierce growl, less than 20 yards away. Amanda saw the flash of a monstrous silhouette rising among the trees, twice as tall as her, before a cloud hid the moon and plunged everything into darkness. Her legs finally reacted and she was able to run.

Terzić stood at the corner of the nearest house.

Amanda looked back, but the monster wasn't following her. "You can't leave me behind like that!"

"Quiet!"

She swallowed her complaint. A door flung open and heavy steps moved away from the house. Amanda pressed her back against the wall, suddenly noticing how awfully loud her breathing was.

What was that? What was walking out of that house? The steps were irregular and heavy. Whatever it was, it wasn't one of the officers. The steps grew fainter and died away. Terzić leaned around the corner, then slowly exhaled. Amanda looked, too. Something monstrous had happened here. The street in the village was broken all over, with dozens of protruding bumps, like big molehills. As if something had broken through from below.

Between the bumps, she saw a human figure shambling down the road.

"Who was that?" she whispered.

Terzić put a finger to his lips, his eyes telling her that now was not the time for questions. He was so different from the calm retiree she knew. The way he moved and checked his surroundings reminded her of a SWAT officer.

"Do you have the flashlight the officer gave you?" he whispered.

Amanda nodded. He took it, but didn't turn it on. "Let us inspect the house."

She followed him around the corner and through the front entrance. Terzić opened the first door and stepped into a small bathroom. With no room for two, Amanda opened another door.

A dense, putrid smell punctured her nose. There were two windows across from her. The moonlight outlined a table, chairs and a kitchen counter. She took a step, but her foot hit a soft bump and she tripped into a wet, warm puddle. When Terzić came into the room, she said, "There's something here."

He turned on the flashlight. The thing Amanda had stumbled over was a woman, judging by her dress. Her body was mangled with dozens of bite-sized holes, as if a hungry animal had chewed the flesh from her. As Amanda's eyes wandered upwards, she realized that the woman had no head—there was only a mash of red, brown and grey pieces.

Amanda threw her hand over her mouth. She barely made it to the bathroom before emptying her stomach.

No matter how bad her nightmares had been, they were nothing compared to the real thing. The sound the body had made when she tripped over it, the warm, sticky puddle, the smelly mush where the woman's head should have been…

Amanda took some toilet paper and wiped her lips clean, then leaned against the door to steady herself. Her hands were still smeared with blood. After some fumbling, she found a towel and wiped her hands.

She found Terzić in the bedroom. All the drawers had been opened and Terzić was busy checking the last one.

"What are you looking for?" she asked.

"I heard that many Americans keep firearms in their bedrooms."

"That's only in the US. And even there we don't all have guns under our pillows."

"A pity. It would have been extremely useful."

"What about her?" Amanda nodded towards the kitchen. "Shouldn't we... do something for her?"

"We can do nothing for her right now. Let us leave."

They checked the street through one of the windows. The houses stood bleak and lifeless along the dark street.

"Follow me and keep watch behind us," he said.

Terzić kept to the shadowed side of the road, where the moonlight was blocked by the houses. Amanda followed close behind and turned repeatedly, hoping to spot a possible surprise attack in time. After what she had seen in that house, she knew what awaited them if they weren't careful.

Out of the corner of her eye, she saw movement. For a split second, between two houses, she thought she saw a small girl, with black hair, a red dress and skin so pale it looked like snow.

Amanda blinked and the girl was gone. Was that...her imagination? A ghost? Some new horror she didn't know of? She kept checking where the girl had been, but she didn't reappear. *What was that? What the hell was that?*

She wanted to warn Terzić, but noticed he was focusing on those bumps in the road. She followed his gaze to the nearest one and realized what was wrong. "Mr. Terzić...are those?"

"Yes. It seems we are too late."

The 'bumps' actually were human bodies—the whole street was littered with corpses. Dark trails led from the bodies to the houses, where the doors lay broken and splintered.

Some of the dead had bear traps stuck to their legs. Like the woman in the house, the bodies were chewed all over, as if a pack of wolves had descended on them. Scattered around and between the bodies, like discarded trash, were knives, ice picks, hammers and saws. All wet with blood.

A horrific, metallic stench crept up Amanda's nose, as if she'd inhaled a cloud of poison. When she realized it was the smell of the dead, something stirred in her, a hungry mass of worms coming alive in her stomach.

A tidal wave of horror enveloped her as the worms began to spread. Devouring everything inside, they only left behind a cold emptiness.

When the squirming mass reached her legs, she lost her balance and fell to her knees. She begged God for mercy as they kept spreading, moving up towards her head. A strange noise came from inside her, like the final sounds of a broken clock. *Click click, click click.*

Before long, the worms were in her neck and kept crawling further up. She tried to scream, to warn Terzić to get away from her before they reached her brain, but all that came out of her mouth was a broken cough.

In front of her, she saw a teenager with singed hair and a half-burned face. *Slavko.* His lips contorted into a hideous grin. He held up his axe, inviting her to take it.

With her last vestige of will, she closed her hands around her neck and squeezed as hard as she could. She had to crush her windpipe, before she turned into a crazed murderer like all the others.

Through a haze, she saw Terzić gently laying his hands on her shoulders. When she strained her ears, she heard, "…and try to feel the ground you are standing on. Breathe steadily."

His calm and reassuring voice finally gave her a bit of warmth and slowed the spread of the worms. They stopped just above her nose. Amanda relaxed her grip and struggled to get her ragged breathing under control.

Terzić took off his coat and placed it around her shoulders. Even though it was just a piece of cloth, it was strangely calming. Her senses slowly returned. She hadn't noticed, but she was incredibly cold, the sweat on her body and the wind having sucked away all her warmth. She also realized that the weird clicking sound she had kept hearing was the sound of her own chattering teeth.

"Steady yourself," Terzić said calmly.

Amanda nodded. She remembered his words at the edge of the forest. He was also scared. But he was still holding on, still fighting. So she couldn't give up, either. If she went mad now, if she screamed or attacked him, she and Terzić would both be found and killed.

Terzić put an arm under her shoulder to support her. "Can you walk like this?" he asked. "We must find cover."

"I-I-I-I'm t-t-t-traa-traayii-nng."

Amanda forced one foot in front of the other, as if she was learning it for the first time. *Mustn't give in. Mustn't look around. Mustn't give in.* Terzić kept serving as a crutch for her while she stared at the ground, careful not to look at the dead bodies again.

Then Terzić stopped moving. Reflexively, Amanda looked up. In front of them was a strange building, much taller and wider than the others, with all ground-floor windows boarded up. A sign read 'Zoey's Groceries'. Why had Terzić stopped here? Then, she saw he wasn't looking at the building, but at a tree to the left of it. In its shadow was Westen's body. Even in this darkness, the uniform was unmistakable.

As if through a dream, she saw herself running to him, dropping Terzić's coat.

"Wait! Ms. Dousson!" he whispered behind her.

Amanda's body moved as if by itself. She knelt down and shook the officer like a doll. "Mr. Westen," she whispered. No reply. She looked him over. No wounds, no blood. She checked his ribcage and saw he was still breathing.

Thank you, Lord…thank you. If they could wake him up, they would be three people. Then they could find shelter somewhere and—

Behind her came a sound like a bag of rice being dropped. She turned and saw Terzić face down on the ground. Something enormous stood over her. There was a sharp pain and something cold spreading in her neck. Her last sensation was of falling forward, and the cold earth embracing her.

CHAPTER 23

When Amanda woke up, she felt as though all her muscles had turned to rubber. She had an awful taste in her mouth and breathing was unnaturally hard.

Her eyelids were so heavy, they seemed glued together. When she pried them open, she was in a large, barren room, like an empty storehouse, sitting on a hard, wooden chair. The only illumination came from the moonlight outside, falling through a row of windows to her left.

How did I get here?

She tried to move, but her limbs barely reacted. A sudden pain reminded her of the sting she had felt on her neck, just before losing consciousness. She ran her hand over the spot and felt a slight protrusion, like a mosquito bite. Had somebody injected her with something? Was that why she had blacked out?

She blinked a few more times, straining to adjust to the darkness. Ahead of her was an empty chair and a small table with a desk lamp. Beyond that, the room seemed to stretch to infinity. She could barely make out several boxes and a support column, but nothing more. To her right, Terzić sat tied in a chair about a step away, a white cloth stuck in his mouth. She looked down and saw Robinson and Westen on the floor. Both were still moving, but like Terzić, they were bound and gagged.

Fear rose in her once more. What was the meaning of all this? Who had drugged her and brought her here? She listened intently, but everything was quiet. She tried to move again, but her muscles felt heavy and sluggish. The only thing she could confirm was that she wasn't tied up like the others.

Looking back at Terzić, she noticed there was something to his right in the shadows. Painfully, she turned her head as far as it would go. She saw several clothes hangers, with multiple coats, furs and animal skins. Behind that, she could make out a few mannequins, dressed up in a variety of clothes. All were staring at her, their empty, glassy eyes reflecting the moonlight from outside. She turned her head back, unable to bear the creepy, doll-like stares.

A rustle came from behind. Amanda uttered a cry reflexively. What was behind her? A Dark One? A villager? Something worse? Her instincts warned her not to turn her head.

The seconds ticked by. Nothing moved. Whatever was behind her wasn't doing anything. Her hands began to shake. Why was nothing happening? What did her captor want from her?

She couldn't take it anymore and turned her head. Behind her sat a large, shadowy figure, mostly hidden in the darkness. It looked human, but it didn't move. Like those mannequins, it simply stared at her. But she was sure it was alive.

When she couldn't bear the silence any longer, she whispered, "Who are you?" The figure did not respond. "Who are you?" she repeated, louder this time. Still, no reaction. "Who are you!" she cried. The dark shape rose and grew monstrously large. A menacing aura engulfed the room. Amanda immediately regretted the way she had spoken.

"I see your method of introduction remains unchanged, Miss Dawson."

Serbian. And a deep, powerful voice that Amanda instantly recognized.

"You?"

The figure walked around her, his slow, heavy footsteps echoing around the large room. He sat in the chair opposite her, crossed his legs and looked at her.

Even in this low light, there was no mistaking his gargantuan stature and domineering voice. Anderson, the stranger they had met in Ukraine.

He flipped a switch and the weak desk lamp sprang to life. Her body trembled. How was he still alive when everyone else was dead? Why did he seem so...relaxed? Was he the one who had drugged her and tied them all up? Just *who* was he and what did he want with her?

After several agonizing minutes of silence, he said, "You look frailer than when we last met. What brings you here?"

Amanda didn't dare to find out what might happen if she didn't answer.

"I...that is, we...we came looking for the Red Dove."

The briefest smile flickered across his lips. "Not the wisest course of action, Miss Dawson."

Again, he remained silently fixed on her. His stare grew increasingly unbearable. Amanda felt as if his eyes were gazing straight into her soul. *Talk, please, just say something!*

Finally, unable to endure it any longer, she again asked the question to which she had never received an answer. "Who are you?"

"I am what you have been looking for."

"Um..." She struggled to understand his cryptic words. "What?"

"You came looking for the Red Dove. And you have found me."

What is he saying? Did this mean what she thought it did? Was he the one serving as the devil's tether in this village? Had he called the curse here?

"Are you...are you the betrayer?"

Again, that smile flashed across his lips. "You are trapped in a hall of mirrors, Miss Dawson. This is not Priboj."

His words hung heavy with meaning. How did he know Priboj? She was absolutely certain she had never mentioned it to him. She hadn't even told him there had been multiple massacres. And yet...he knew.

Was he really *the* Red Dove? In human form? In that Ukrainian village, had she actually been speaking to the Red Dove the whole time? But then why had he warned her to stay away? Even rescued her from the mine? And what did he want with her now?

Amanda's brain felt like a strained muscle. Nothing made sense anymore. Was any of this even real? Maybe this was just another one of her dreams that she couldn't wake up from? A hundred fragmented thoughts contradicted each other as her mind cracked like glass. If only she could find a single thread of reason to latch onto…

Anderson remained silent, looking at her like a teacher who had given his student a clever hint, and was waiting to see whether she was smart enough to figure it out.

With her last shred of focus, she went over his words. *A hall of mirrors.* Was he saying that she was seeing her own reflection? *Think back. What do I really know for certain?*

She went through her story again, from before she'd even heard of the Red Dove, through her adventures in Serbia and Ukraine, her return to Chicago, and all the events that had led her here.

It still didn't make sense. She couldn't see anything that would explain what was going on, or his strange comment. She forced herself to go over it again. No matter what, she didn't want to lose this last sane thought she was hanging onto. She reached the end of her story again and still there was nothing.

What am I missing?

In spite of the minutes passing by, Anderson hadn't moved an inch. He kept looking at her with that same, strange look, partly curious and partly analytical.

Maybe the problem was that she was too focused on herself? Was that what 'hall of mirrors' meant? He had mentioned Priboj by name—maybe the key wasn't her own story, but Jelena's. But she had gone over it several times now— the fall of Priboj didn't shed any light on what Anderson had said.

One more time. In her head, Amanda went over every page of the diary, remembering how the Red Dove had made its first appearance, drenched in blood and nailed to a door with its cursed song. Shortly after, it had started killing - Branko's cows first, then the villagers, in increasingly gruesome fashion, culminating in the poisoning of the well and Father Viktor's death.

After that, as far as she knew, the Red Dove hadn't killed anyone—the villagers themselves had taken over that job, slaughtering each other trying to survive and find the betrayer.

She went over this same story, again and again. But no matter how often she revisited Jelena's story, Anderson's words remained an enigma. *What am I supposed to see here, damn it? The story won't change no matter how—hang on.*

One detail stuck out. So strongly that she wondered how it hadn't bothered her before. On July 4th, after the poisoning of the well, Jelena's father had told her that all the people killed by the Red Dove had vanished, their graves open and empty.

But…why? Why would a supernatural curse feel the need to make a few bodies vanish? Jelena didn't mention seeing them again afterwards and none of the other victims disappeared, otherwise Terzić and his men would have found an empty village. So what was special about those first few victims?

She turned her head back to the clothes hangers, with those coats and folded animal skins. And those dresses and mannequins…

She felt a click in her head. The story from the diary flashed before her eyes again and suddenly, all the puzzle pieces fell together. She saw the deaths, each more brutal and demoralizing than the last. She saw every new horror the villagers suffered, meticulously choreographed, fanning their fear from a small spark into a blazing terror that consumed everything.

She could see the strings on which everyone had danced. And the hand holding those strings. Everything fit perfectly…except one detail.

He died.

But she couldn't be wrong. Not after all this. It explained everything, including why Anderson had mentioned Priboj, specifically—because it had been a dead giveaway: Priboj had been the only village where there had been a "betrayer." It all worked out so perfectly, so why did this one detail not fit? Was her sudden epiphany nothing but an illusion? No, there had to be something she was still missing.

She went back to the most important day. July 3rd. The day the well had been poisoned. Jelena had gone to church and met Father Viktor there. After praying with her, he had spent the day preparing holy water. And finally, in the evening, after downing the last of his beloved wine, he drank the black water and died, in front of everyone's eyes.

Later, Andjela's dog died when drinking from the well, so the poison was definitely—*Wait! The flask! The wine!*

Amanda snapped back to reality. Her spine turned icy cold as she finally saw the whole picture and understood just who was sitting in front of her. "Oh God. You…You are…"

No, there was no mistake. She knew she was right. "You are…Father Viktor."

CHAPTER 24

The man in front of her flashed that brief, eerie smile again. "You may call me that if you wish."

There it was. The words she needed. After all this time, the fog had finally cleared. Her head sank as the full force of her discovery washed over her like a wave of chilly water.

There was no Red Dove, no supernatural curse.

Humiliatingly, Tom and his therapist had been right: her misfortunes *had* been of her own making—a bad case of PTSD-induced delusions and hallucinations. And yet, the truth she had just uncovered was, if anything, even more incredible than the lie she had convinced herself of.

All the massacres were the work of just one man, one brilliant puppet master who had carefully orchestrated the destruction of every village. A serial mass murderer whose victims by now had to number in the hundreds. And that man was sitting right in front of her.

She looked at him again and felt her head spin. She still couldn't believe just who, or what, this man was.

"How did you reach your conclusion?" he asked.

It was like a noose settling around her neck. After the brief exhilaration of having that epiphany, fear rose in her again. Was this why he hadn't killed her yet? Because he wanted to figure out how she had found him? To stop others from doing the same? That meant that if she told him, he would have no further use for her.

Her studies came back to her. She knew what the theoretical 'best' way to handle a situation like this was: get him talking at all costs, appear sympathetic, build rapport. Above all, keep humanizing herself. Make him see her as a person, not as a victim. It all sounded laughably academic and useless right now, but it was all she had.

Amanda clenched her fists and took a deep breath. "We found a diary," she said, trying to make her voice sound flat and composed.

"Whose?"

"Jelena's."

"Ah, the talented singer?"

"Yes."

"Please, do continue."

"I'm embarrassed to admit it, but after what happened in Ukraine, I really did start believing there was a curse. It got so bad, I started suffering full-blown paranoid hallucinations and attributed those to the Red Dove. But, after your comment, I remembered something strange that Jelena had written—that the bodies of the first few victims had mysteriously disappeared. Why would a supernatural curse bother with this? It didn't make any other bodies disappear. It gave me an idea: what if it was to hide the fact that one of the victims was still alive? It happened right after the priest died and he was the only one who wasn't buried, so he was the most likely candidate.

"That made me wonder—what if there had been no priest in Priboj? As kind and caring as Father Viktor was, he was always connected to every major event. If he hadn't been there, nobody would have known what to make of the blood-soaked dove. It was Father Viktor who 'discovered' that satanic shrine and that book that described the Red Dove, and it was he who first mentioned 'the betrayer', the bogeyman who made everyone suspicious of everyone else."

He flashed that smile again, thin like a knife. She was on the right track. She had to keep talking.

"Then, I saw the whole sequence of events in a new light. It all started with vague unease about the murdered dove and farm animals, and escalated slowly to a full-blown, murderous paranoia. Every death was more gruesome than the last, every time things seemed to get better, they only ended up getting worse. A hope-despair cycle carefully calculated to steadily break down everyone's mental state. That's when I figured out the supernatural wasn't actually necessary to explain what happened.

"Jelena wrote about those 'Dark Ones' everyone kept catching glimpses of, but when I saw those puppets here, I figured those could just be costumed mannequins, strategically placed to scare people from going into the forest. The few who tried anyway were killed, with their mutilated bodies put on display as an example to the others. This also explained why the Red Dove villages are all so similar—small, isolated and surrounded by ravines or forests, each with only one way out, making it easy to catch someone trying to escape. With everyone scared of leaving, and mistrusting each other thanks to the 'betrayer', nobody thought of escaping together, the only thing that might have saved them.

"Finally, when the well was poisoned, the massacre was all but guaranteed. Mad from fear and thirst, the villagers hunted each other down, desperate to kill the one responsible and end a curse that didn't exist.

"The only thing that didn't make sense was Father Viktor dying gruesomely, in front of the whole village. Coughing up blood and collapsing could have been done with some good acting and red food coloring, but the water from the well was undeniably lethal. Andjela's dog died to prove that. So, how had Father Viktor survived drinking it? That's when I remembered the flask. With a wine that Jelena weirdly described having an 'herbal' taste. Father Viktor took a big gulp from it just before drinking the poisoned water. Was that an antidote?"

"Excellent, Miss Dawson. Most excellent."

She thought back to Jelena's encounter with him in the church. "Wait! That means…since Jelena drank a bit of the wine in the morning, she might have been able to drink from the well too!"

"Well, I *did* tell her that a good wine would make her live longer."

His smile chilled her to the bone. Even the most heinous serial killers she had read about hadn't played jokes this cruel. Or was it really a joke to him?

Maybe he had tried the same with Jelena as he had with Amanda—giving her a tiny hint to see what she would do with it.

She waited for Anderson, or rather, Viktor, to say more, but he remained as silent as before. Again, his eyes grew unsettling. The air was dry and dusty, but he never seemed to blink. Her heart pounded. Was he waiting for her to say more? But what? And what would happen if she didn't say anything?

I can't afford to find out. She had to keep the conversation going, and maybe she would find a way out.

"Mr. Viktor…If I can call you that…Can I ask something?"

"Naturally."

"Over thirty years ago, there was a boy called Tihomir, in today's Croatia. Did you kill him too?"

"What makes you think so?"

"He recited the Red Dove song and died the same day, so his classmates thought the Red Dove had come for him."

"Most intriguing…Let me assure you, I had no hand in that. It may help to clarify that I did not invent the Red Dove, nor its lullaby. It is merely a folk tale I came across in my travels."

Meaning Tihomir's death had just been a sick, random murder, just as Amanda had suspected when she had first heard the story from her mother.

Come on, Amanda. Don't let the conversation die down.

She didn't know where to go with this or what she was hoping for. But all her textbooks and lectures on criminal psychology told her to keep him talking.

"What's the significance behind the number seven?"

"There is no significance. Like the Red Dove itself, it simply suited me."

She couldn't keep up a conversation if he kept his answers this short. She needed something open-ended, something that would take time to answer.

"What were you doing when we met you in Ukraine?"

"Before I begin anew, I like to visit my destinations of the past. Nostalgia, if you will."

Meaning he had probably been to Priboj, too. It was weird to imagine she'd just missed him by a couple of days.

"But why tell us all this nonsense about spirits and rifts in reality and shadowy whispers and so forth?"

"It was a way for me to discover how much you knew, how close you were to the truth, without revealing anything myself. It also allowed me to see how credulous you were, and to give you some advice."

"Advice?"

"You have a rather perilous sense of curiosity, Miss Dawson. As I told you, nothing good comes from digging in poisoned earth." His eyes narrowed. "As you now understand all too well."

She bit her lip and turned her head away. 'Lest you end up scarred.' Those had been his words in Ukraine. It reminded her just how painfully visible those scars were. But it gave her an idea.

"Why did you save us from that boar? And then rescue me from the mine?"

He *had* saved her life, after all. If she reminded him of that, maybe she could convince him to spare her and the others. That, and she really wanted to know why a mass murderer would risk his life to save a nosy college student looking into his secret. Twice.

"You are the first I encountered who recognized that more than one village had been destroyed and who expended the effort to investigate it. It would have been a waste to let you die."

Would have been? Meaning it wasn't anymore?

"You have been attempting to free yourself for thirteen minutes now," Viktor said, with a voice that cut like a razor. "You ought to have succeeded after at most two."

Amanda followed his gaze and saw Terzić's eyes wide with shock.

"Oh no, please," said Viktor. "Do continue. I am curious what you plan to do once free. I am merely remarking on your sluggish progress."

Terzić hung his head, his groan muffled through the gag. How had Viktor even seen that? Amanda hadn't noticed a single movement or sound.

He kept staring at Terzić. Amanda racked her brains for something that would draw his attention back to her.

"How many?" she asked. "How many times have you done this?"

"This is now the sixth time."

"Six times? That's...dear god. So many people...But, why? Why are you doing this?"

"There is no reason."

"Um..." What was she supposed to do with that answer? "But, then...uh." She wanted to ask 'then why do it?' but realized that she would just be repeating herself. He had to have a reason for inflicting all this carnage, right?

"You appear confused."

"Well, yes..."

He nodded. "Your bewilderment stems from a common symptom of the human condition. Have you ever observed, that when faced with an evil, society desires, nay demands, a rationalization for the deed? Gratifying this need, a cornucopia of 'experts'—psychologists, doctors, pundits, leaders—will unfailingly emerge, to announce that the man who committed the evil did so due to mental illness, an abusive childhood, a radical ideology or a brain tumor.

"Sometimes, these pronouncements may well be true. That is incidental, however. Their purpose is not to be correct, but to soothe your anxiety. To convince yourselves that if you diagnose every psychopathy, excise every brain tumor, treat every trauma and provide a good childhood and education for everyone, you may yet be shielded from the dark side of human nature.

"But this is an illusion, maintained at great cost. It makes you underestimate the danger and fail to take proper precautions. Yet, maintain this illusion you must, to ward yourselves from the truth: that there will always be those who bring about destruction and have no reason for it. Who need no reason for it. Who simply *do* what you dread."

Amanda sat wide-eyed as the last hammer blow of his words rained down on her. This struck deep. As if he really had looked into her soul and decided to make a mockery of everything she believed in. All the books she had read, everything she had studied, her entire chosen career, were all built on the presumption that she could achieve mastery over the mind of evil, and in so doing, defeat it. Yet, here in front of her sat evil incarnate, scoffing at her hubris.

Her precious textbooks, her university lessons, what good were they here?

Her attempts to keep talking and 'build rapport' looked downright pathetic now. What could a puny college student like her hope to achieve against a monster like him? Her father's words came back to her. Today was the day "when you look someone in the eye and find nothing but a bottomless void, staring back at you."

Was he going to kill her now? Torture her first? Maybe if she begged him for a quick and painless death, he would indulge her? The seconds turned into minutes. She felt cold sweat drip down her chin and soak her clothes. Viktor had to see it, yet he made no move.

Once again, the silence grew too much for her to bear. If he wanted to kill her, he should just get it over with. As she was opening her mouth, she heard a groan and saw Westen, struggling to readjust his position. How much time had the two police officers spent on the hard floor already?

She had completely forgotten, but it wasn't just her life at stake here—Viktor had no reason to spare anyone here. Any witnesses could prove troublesome later, when he moved to a new village and...

Oh, right. It was even bigger than the four of them here. In seven years, he would do this all over again, and dozens more would die.

She didn't want to let that happen. She *had* to do something. But all she could think of was bound to fail. She would never win a fight against him. A charging boar had stood no chance. Even if she somehow managed to free everyone here, he would probably still win with ease. She had no leverage, no way to manipulate him, nothing to negotiate or bargain with.

Amanda gritted her teeth. She felt so useless. She had the murderer of hundreds right in front of her, who might kill hundreds more, and she was powerless to stop him. With Viktor still observing her quietly, she decided to do the only thing she could think of.

She steeled herself for what might happen and took a deep breath. "Is there anything I can do that will make you stop with the massacres?"

It was downright stupid, but it was the only thing she could come up with. With nothing to lose, what harm could it do?

He cupped his chin and lowered his head. Then, he flashed that disturbing smile again. "Unexpected, but most engaging."

She had expected him to laugh or to kill her outright for her insolence, but he seemed to take it seriously. Was he honestly going to stop killing just because she asked nicely? There was no way it would be that simple.

As if to confirm it, he asked, "But are you certain you wish to make this request? You should know that pacts with the devil exact a heavy toll."

His voice chilled her to the bone. But, her life was already hanging by a thread. If he was really offering to make the massacres stop, she *had* to go for it.

"Yes, I'm certain."

He remained seated for a few meaningful seconds, then stood up. "Excuse me, I shall return shortly."

He disappeared into the darkness of the room, until only his footsteps could be heard. Amanda threw a glance at Terzić, who looked just as confused as she was. She could see him struggling against his binds more overtly now, but from what she could tell, he wasn't making much progress. His hands were too constricted.

Something wooden and heavy was dragged across the floor. There was a noise like a box of glasses being moved, and a series of indistinct thuds.

Then, a monstrous growl, as if a huge wolf was prowling the shadows. By the time the shock passed and Amanda dared to breathe again, the sound was gone. Viktor emerged from the darkness, carrying a glass of water. He placed it on the table and sat down in front of her again. Amanda wanted to ask about the growl, but Viktor seemed so relaxed, she wondered if this hadn't been another hallucination.

Viktor reached into his coat pocket, then opened his hand under the light. In his palm was a glass tube with a cork. Inside was a thick, dark-green liquid.

"As you have observed, I am knowledgeable in poisons. I utilize them regularly. This is a formulation of my own devising—a potent, delayed-action toxin."

Amanda's eyes remained fixed on the liquid.

"Similar to the amatoxins in poisonous mushrooms, there are no symptoms for approximately half a day. Then, the alkaloids slowly destroy the internal organs, causing ever-greater pain. There is no antidote and death comes only after hours of unremitting agony."

Amanda looked at the small cylinder with revulsion. She couldn't believe something this awful even existed.

"You have found me here and discerned my identity. As a token of my respect, I shall honor your request and offer you a choice: You may either leave this village, unharmed and with your life intact, or…"

He removed the cork and emptied the contents of the tube into the glass. The water turned green and there was a heavy odor, like a mixture of herbs and honey.

"Or…" Viktor pushed the glass towards her. "You drink this. In return, I vow never to enact another massacre."

CHAPTER 25

Amanda heard mumbling from her right and saw Terzić, violently shaking his head, the gag muffling his words.

She looked down at the glass, then back at Viktor. She wasn't dreaming, right? He'd just offered to let her go. To let her live! To take back everything she had lost. The mental scars of her trauma were deep, but now that she knew her nightmares were products of her own mind, she could get professional help. She could resume her studies, maybe even try to get another internship, put everything back on track.

Yet…at what cost? If she went on living, he would go on killing. How many more times could he do this before dying from old age? Three times? Maybe more? Her heart ran cold imagining the mountain of corpses he would leave in his wake. This was her one chance to stop it.

But why should she believe him? He was a master manipulator, who had tricked six villages into wholesale slaughter. She wanted to ask him, *Why should I trust you?* But she knew it was a stupid question—if he wanted to kill her, he could have done that any time he wanted. If she didn't trust him, she could always take him up on his offer and leave. But if there was even a chance that he was honest, wasn't that a risk worth taking? Hundreds of lives could depend on it.

She wondered if she had any other way of ending the massacres. If she ran away, she would have a full seven years, right? Couldn't she come up with something in the meantime? No, she knew it was hopeless. If he moved to some far-off country, how would she ever find him again? Greg's genius and a lot of dumb luck were the only reason she'd even gotten this far.

And she knew nobody else would stop him, either. He had done this six times now, in different places, languages and cultures. Yet, he hadn't failed once. If he could be stopped, somebody far more capable than her would have done it by now. Nobody could end this. Nobody, except her. She alone could save all those people who had no idea what kind of horror was coming for them.

The green water glowed menacingly in the incandescent light. Could anyone really expect her to suffer a slow and painful suicide to save a bunch of people she would never meet? Somebody braver and less selfish would have shown no hesitation. But she wanted to live. She wanted to live so badly that she was prepared to throw away hundreds of lives for it.

Except, what then? How would she live with herself? She could see how it would end. Popping anti-depressants like candy, she would tell her sob story to anyone who would listen, desperate to get them to say that, of course, it wasn't her fault, everybody else would have done the same. All while the guilt slowly ate her up.

She remembered that sanctimonious speech she had given Tom when they were discussing serial killers. She had felt high and mighty back then, insulting those who pretended to be oh-so affected by the tragedies around them, and their silly candlelight vigils and fake shows of virtue.

Well, here was her chance to prove that she wasn't like all the candle-carrying hypocrites she had condemned so self-righteously. This was her chance to *do* something instead of just talking big.

Save everyone or save yourself. One life for hundreds. The choice was clear. A life bought at the expense of so many others couldn't be worth living. Slowly, as if in a dream, she reached out her hand. Her fingers curled around the glass. She lifted it slowly towards her mouth.

An agonized moan came from her right. Terzić was screaming into his gag and thrashing violently, trying to undo the binds. Amanda bit her lip. Why was Terzić making things so hard? She didn't want to do this, either. But wasn't this better than running away and accomplishing nothing? Didn't Terzić understand how much was at stake?

She thought back to the diary, to Mr. Kralj, Branko, Andjela and Slavko. To Uncle Mirko, her very reason for being here. And to Jelena. Poor little Jelena.

In some village out there, there were other people just like that. If she didn't drink now, another, future Jelena would suffer for weeks before dying a lonely and horrible death, all because Amanda had been too selfish to do the right thing.

She ignored Terzić's thrashing and looked up at Viktor, still fixing her with the same, emotionless stare.

"May I ask one last question?"

"Of course."

"I originally started looking into the Red Dove and Priboj because my uncle lived there, but Jelena's diary doesn't say what happened to him."

"His name?"

"Mirko. Mirko Matijević"

"Indeed? I remember him fondly. Truly, a great man. He had lost the use of his legs in a farming accident, yet worked tirelessly every day to brighten the lives of those around him. As luck would have it, I witnessed his final moments.

"Three days after the well was poisoned, in the early morning, he attempted to carry Nina, a six-year old girl, out of the village. Despite the danger, despite missing his legs and being severely dehydrated. His strength and determination impressed me greatly. I considered making an exception for him and letting him leave. Alas, before he reached the forest, two crazed villagers found him. Though it was futile, he died defending the girl's life. Even as he lay bleeding into the mud, he fought to the bitter end. You may consider yourself proud to be his kin."

Amanda looked down at the glass and smiled. "Then, at least if there's a heaven, I won't have to be ashamed when I meet him."

She tightened her grip around the glass, closed her eyes, and gulped down the green liquid in one go. It tasted strange, but surprisingly good. Like tea with honey and peppermint syrup.

She put the glass down. Terzić had stopped thrashing. The look in his eyes was one of grief and pain.

I'm sorry. I had to.

She looked back at Viktor.

"An impressive deed, Miss Dawson. Most impressive. You have my word. There shall be no further massacre by my hand."

Amanda took a deep breath and let the tension drain out of her. Now, all she had to do was wait. The thought of spending hours in agony frightened her, but she remembered the endless torture her own mind had put her through. At least this time, she knew the pain was temporary and that her suffering had meaning.

Then she realized she'd forgotten to ask something important. Something she should have clarified before making her decision. "May I ask you one more favor?"

"You may."

"Could you please spare Mr. Terzić and these two police officers?"

He looked at them, then back at Amanda. "They shall live." An ominous beeping came from his pocket. He stood up and walked over to the row of windows and peeked outside.

"What? What's wrong?"

"Recently, five particularly vicious killers in this village banded together, slaughtering anyone they could find. They are surprisingly efficient at it. The sea of corpses outside is mostly their doing."

Amanda remembered the Watchmen from Priboj and shivered.

"It would appear they have not turned on each other yet. A most unexpected development." He turned around. "They are on their way here. They must have seen the light through the windows."

It took a moment before Amanda understood the full meaning of those words. "They are coming here? Will they—"

"Do not move."

He walked past her and disappeared. Soon, his footsteps vanished, and she couldn't even tell if he was still here. The entire place seemed abandoned except for Terzić, Westen, Robinson and herself.

Had he retreated somewhere safe and left them to their fate? Why tell them to 'not move'? Was he seriously expecting them to sit still with a group of murderous villagers at the door?

She looked at her companions. It didn't matter anymore if the villagers found her, but there was no reason for Terzić, Robinson and Westen to die. She went over to Terzić's chair. She still felt sluggish, but at least now she could move.

Terzić's hands were tied behind his back. The knot looked incredibly intricate. She didn't even know where to begin. Terzić mumbled something and she removed his gag.

"It is hopeless. I have tried for fifteen minutes and couldn't even loosen it. You must find a knife."

"Where am I supposed to find that?"

"This seems to be his hideout, he must have something sharp *somewhere*. His stubble was less than two days old, so you might be able to find a razor."

She nodded and went to check where Viktor had gone to get the poison, hoping he kept all his equipment there.

She was met with dozens of boxes. The moment Amanda tried to open the first box, a devastating roar came from her left. She shrieked and fell back. In front of her, an enormous figure rose, growing to over seven feet tall, baring sharp fangs and teeth. She covered her face, expecting to be torn to shreds any moment.

But the blow never came. When she opened her eyes, she noticed that the monstrosity was moving weirdly, as if it was stuck in place. *Wait, is that…*

"Ms. Dousson! Are you alright?" Terzić yelled.

"Yes!"

She pulled out her mobile phone and turned on its flashlight. The thing in front of her was a werewolf, straight from the movies, with thick black fur and blood around its yellowed teeth. It moved menacingly, without taking a single step towards her. She approached it, but its movement pattern didn't change.

She looked down and saw gears at the monster's base. *Incredible…*She touched its fur, amazed at how real it felt and looked. It was like in a ghost-ride: a proximity-triggered animatronic monster. She had heard this growl before—at the edge of the forest, just before she and Terzić ran into the village. A dark monster had risen up there, too.

So this was how Viktor had kept people out of the forest. If someone came close, a werewolf monster like that would spring to life and scare them into running away, or at least distract them long enough to allow Viktor to find and kill them.

A loud bang ripped her back to reality. The sound had come from below. The villagers were here.

Amanda prayed Viktor had fortified his hideout somehow and opened the first box to her right. She found a stack of newspapers from "The Jasper Local," with an enormous headline: "BEASTMEN ON THE LOOSE—Human-wolf hybrids whose DNA was spliced in a secret military project codenamed "Red Dove" have broken out of their containment facility. Residents are warned to remain indoors in well-lit areas and to avoid forests at any cost."

Amazing. So that's the story he used for a modern, secular village…

She opened the next box, as another loud bang came from below. There was so much stuff around here. She remembered how long it had taken her in her parents' attic to even get through a few boxes. She didn't have that kind of time. She took the box and emptied it. Nothing but clothes fell out. She grabbed the next and turned it upside down. A flood of glass bottles shattered on the floor and a jumble of thick, sweet smells engulfed her.

"Ow!"

She shone her light down at the sudden pain and saw a glass shard in her leg. She pulled it out and watched the blood trickle down. *Wait…that's it!*

She searched through the glass shards to find the biggest ones. When she had found four of them, she tried a test cut on one of the carton boxes. It sliced clean through.

She rushed back to Terzić as the sounds from below grew louder and more aggressive.

"What happened?" he asked.

"I'll explain later. Hold still, please."

Cutting through the rope still took effort, but eventually, Terzić managed to pull his hand free. She gave him one of the glass shards and went over to free the two officers.

They got up surprisingly fast. *Thank God they're fit.* She wouldn't have been able to get up that quickly after being tied up in the same position for that long. Terzić gestured to their left. Amanda understood immediately.

"What the hell just happened?" Westen asked.

"There's people coming to kill us," Amanda said in English. "We have to get out of here!"

Both officers nodded. Terzić opened one of the windows. They were on the second floor, the ground below them shrouded in shadow. But further on, they could see grass, so their impact would be softened. The banging on the door sounded far away. This was as safe as it was going to get.

Robinson jumped first and landed rolling. Westen went next. The heavy pounding from below was getting worse. Terzić said, "I will jump last. Go ahead."

"There's no point, Mr. Terzić. It's over for me. The worst they can do is kill me faster than the poison."

"It is not too late, yet. You must get to a hospital."

"For what? You heard him—There's no antidote. Besides, if he finds out I tried to bail on the deal, he'll keep killing."

"That is his choice. It is *he* who kills, not you. You are not responsible for his actions."

"But he's offering to stop! If I try to break the deal now, any deaths *will* be my fault. This is hard enough, so please, stop trying to dissuade me when it's already too late. Just go already."

Terzić clenched his hands into fists. He looked as if he was about to shout, but then took a deep breath. "If you wish to commit suicide, I cannot stop you. But what about your loved one?"

"My what?"

"The man you spoke to on the phone."

"Greg…" Amanda whispered. If she died here, she would never see him again. Her vision blurred. She had promised him, hadn't she? A promise she wouldn't be able to keep now.

But…if she escaped with Terzić and the poison really did take half a day to kill her, she would at least have time to call Greg and tell him how sorry she was…for everything. And she would be able to talk to her parents one last time. If there was no antidote, surely Viktor wouldn't begrudge her making the most of her final few hours, right?

Amanda looked at Terzić. "That was really below the belt, by the way, bringing Greg into this."

She turned towards the window and jumped.

CHAPTER 26

S he didn't know how to land like those two officers and the impact hurt a lot, but compared to her pain in the mine, this was nothing. Terzić landed next to her soon after. The slamming on the door was still audible. By the sound of it, the villagers weren't making much progress.

Amanda recognized this place. She was standing a few yards from the tree where Viktor had drugged them. Meaning this building was Zoey's Groceries, the last house in the village. All they had to do was follow the road straight back to the forest. Yet, for some reason, Robinson and Westen were busy patting the ground.

"What are you doing? Why aren't we running?" Amanda whispered.

Westen looked up. "I woke up just in time to see him throw all our equipment out the window. Pretty simple, but effective. That means our guns are around here somewhere."

Amanda's mouth dropped open. They wanted to stay longer so they could search for guns in the dark? "These people banging at the door are coming to kill us. We have to run, now!"

Robinson hissed, "We're only in this because of you! When we get out of here, you'll have some serious explaining to do, mark my words—"

"Got one!" Westen interrupted.

Robinson bent back down and continued looking.

"Don't you have a mobile phone?" Westen asked Amanda.

"If I turn on a light and someone sees it, we're done for! Please, can we just go already? Almost everyone in this village is dead anyway! The only ones alive are the killers at the door! I'll answer all your questions, but please, we have to go!"

Westen gave Robinson a meaningful stare. The only illumination came from the moon and they were standing in the building's shadow. It was pure luck that Westen had even found one gun. The police officers nodded to each other.

"I'll go first," Westen said. "Then you two. Abigail, I'll leave the rear to you."

Amanda translated, and Terzić nodded and gestured for them to get going.

They moved quietly on the street. Even though they weren't running, they were going much faster than was comfortable for Amanda. Her legs still felt sluggish and she could tell she was slowing everyone down. They passed the corpses on the road, and their awful smell of rusted iron. She tried to breathe through her mouth but it didn't help much to suppress the nausea.

She looked back. The five villagers were all bunched up at the entrance of Zoey's Groceries. One was maniacally hitting the door with what looked like a hatchet. Amanda was grateful the ground-floor windows were boarded up, or she and the others would be dead already. The door's cracking sound told her the villagers were only a minute or two away from breaking it down and storming inside, up to that storage room on the second floor. She didn't even want to imagine what would have happened if she hadn't found that box of fruit juices.

A sharp pain pierced her stomach and she stopped.

"What's wrong?" Westen asked.

She shook her head. "Just need a moment."

Was this the poison acting up already? But she was supposed to have half a day before the symptoms started! At this rate, she'd never to talk to Greg again. This wasn't fair!

She clenched her teeth. They didn't have time to wait. She would just have to bear it and hurry out of here. As she turned to Westen to tell him to keep going, something in the distance caught her eye. By the steps of a house, about

60 feet away, lay a small figure face down in the dirt. She recognized the bright red dress and the black hair. *So that girl wasn't a hallucination.*

Amanda looked more carefully. There wasn't any blood around the girl. Could it just be that…

Westen whispered, "Are you okay? We should—hey! Hey!"

Without waiting for him, Amanda ran to the girl. Her hair was clotted with dirt, her face devoid of color and her eyes glassy. But her chest was still rising and falling, like a breathing doll.

"She's alive!" Amanda exclaimed quietly to Westen and the others. She shook the girl. "Can you hear me?"

She whispered something Amanda couldn't understand. Did she even realize what was happening around her? Amanda lifted her into her arms. She was frighteningly light, as if she hadn't eaten in weeks. Amanda had lugged around shopping bags heavier than this. "I think I can carry her."

"You must be exhausted," Terzić said. "I can carry her."

"That's nice of you, but if there's a fight, I'm useless anyway. You three stay unencumbered. Let's go, she needs medical attention." Switching to English, Amanda said, "I'll carry her. That will leave your hands free if something happens." Westen and Robinson exchanged looks again, but they seemed to understand this wasn't the time to argue.

"I'll go first again," Westen said.

Robinson nodded. "Let's stick to this side, where it's darkest."

Amanda was glad none of them insisted on carrying the girl. She didn't want to admit it, but she *had* to do this. Otherwise, all she was doing was slowing them down. Plus, Uncle Mirko had also tried to save a little girl. This was Amanda's way to try and make his wish come true.

The villagers were still loudly bashing against the door of Zoey's Groceries. Whatever Viktor had done to fortify that place, it seemed to be giving the villagers quite a bit of trouble. Amanda looked ahead and saw the forest was getting nearer. *Just a bit longer!*

Westen stopped and put up his hand. She followed his gaze across the street. Ahead of them, beneath one of the houses, was a man crouched on all fours, his back to them. He was busy with an odd motion, moving his head down for a few seconds, then moving it up quickly and staying there for a while, before going back down.

She had seen that man before, walking away from that house she and Terzić had entered…with the woman with bitemarks in the kitchen, whose head had been beaten to a pulp.

When she squinted, Amanda recognized the object the man was leaning over. A human body. And the man was making chewing sounds.

She pressed the girl's face to her chest, hoping she wouldn't wake up and be forced to see this.

"What kind of hell are we in here?" Westen whispered.

"Be thankful he's busy and keep moving," Robinson replied.

They all nodded to each other and continued as quietly as possible. Amanda's heart felt as if it would rip apart from the pressure. Less than thirty feet lay between them and a murderous cannibal.

After ten painful seconds, Amanda allowed herself to exhale. When she took another step, a metallic snap pierced the silence, followed by a half-stifled cry of pain. Westen's leg was caught in a bear trap, blood spurting from the wounds.

She slowly turned her head. The cannibal's eyes were settled on Westen. However, he didn't react. He just calmly kept chewing, his face that of a man being interrupted during a fine dinner by some curiosity outside the window.

Amanda prayed the cannibal was too busy with his food and would go back to eating the mangled corpse in front of him. But then, the cannibal turned towards Amanda. Or, rather, the girl she was holding. His face contorted with maniacal rage. Snarling like a rabid dog, he jumped up and dashed towards her with terrifying speed.

Robinson and Terzić ran to intercept him.

"Police! Get down on the—"

The man didn't slow down or even turn his head. He charged past Robinson as if he was possessed. Terzić grabbed hold of the man's arm. He growled and tried to shake loose, but Terzić held fast. With his free hand, the man threw a vicious punch, hitting Terzić square in the jaw and knocking him into the dirt. A moment later, Robinson caught up and tried to force the man into an armlock, but in spite of his ghoulish appearance, he was surprisingly strong. The cannibal caught both Robinson's arms and held them in an iron grip. Robinson kicked the man's knee. He stumbled, held on to Robinson and took her down with him. They fought on the ground in a chaotic tumble of punching and scratching.

For a second, Robinson was winning. Then the man threw his mouth open and dove for her neck. With a sickening sound, he ripped his head away. Blood gushed from Robinson's throat, nearly black in the moonlight. She pressed her hands to her neck, trying helplessly to staunch the flow. The blood shot out remorselessly between her fingers, forming an inky puddle in which she kept thrashing.

The man looked around wildly, flesh and blood still falling from his mouth, until his eyes settled on Amanda again. He charged like a wolf, ready to tear his prey to pieces.

He was almost upon her when a deafening blast ripped through the air. As the echo died, Amanda looked dumbfounded at the man in front of her: wide-eyed, his mouth open, teeth blackened by Robinson's blood. For a second, he didn't move. Then, he keeled over like a cut tree, his head hitting the pavement.

Westen was holding his gun in his hands.

There was a loud ringing in Amanda's left ear, but another sound was missing now. Her brain was desperately trying to catch up, trying to figure out what it was.

Oh… The banging on the door. She looked back at Zoey's Groceries. The five villagers stood there, all looking at her. For a terrible, drawn-out moment, nobody moved.

The first of the five villagers was a woman dressed in tattered clothes, the one who'd been hacking at the door with a hatchet. Next to her, a teenage girl, no older than sixteen. She was standing barefoot in a blood-soaked nightgown, holding a cleaver larger than her head. The third was a tall man in a black jacket and ripped jeans, holding a large pitchfork. Next to him was a small, bearded man, with a shovel over his shoulders. The last of them was a teenager with blond hair and a dirty shirt, holding a large kitchen knife.

And they were all looking at her.

Westen's voice tore Amanda out of her stupor. "Run!"

She turned towards the forest and took off. As if they'd been waiting for that signal, the five villagers dashed after her. Amanda was out of breath within seconds. The girl in her arms, who had been so light before, now became a crushing strain on her knees. She kept running, pushed on by a single thought—*get to the forest or the girl is dead.*

On her left, Terzić was on his feet again and had caught up with her.

"Faster!" he shouted. "Keep going!"

Another shot rang out. Amanda glanced back and saw Westen firing his gun, still immobilized in the bear trap, as the villagers rapidly closed on him. Another two shots, but they kept coming.

Two more shots. The small, bearded man with the shovel stopped dead in his tracks, grabbed his stomach, and fell face-first into the pavement.

Another shot, and the man holding the pitchfork stopped briefly, then resumed his pursuit, limping. Yet one more shot, but nothing happened.

Westen fired again. The woman with the hatchet fell down. Each shot made Amanda more hopeful: The closer they got, the easier it was for Westen to hit them. One more shot rang out. The young man holding the knife twisted around, but kept running. His T-shirt started blackening from the shoulder down.

Incapable of running anymore, Amanda slowed down. Not that it mattered—she was certain Westen would hit all of them now. They were just a few steps from him and he had a clear line of sight.

But there were no more shots. Westen's gun was empty.

"Run!" Westen screamed after her.

The tall man in the leather jacket limped up to the defenseless Westen and brought the pitchfork down.

"Do not look back! Go, go!" Terzić shouted.

Amanda looked away, but couldn't avoid hearing a nauseating sucking sound, followed by an agonized cry. It took all of her strength not to throw up on the spot.

Her muscles were screaming for air. Her legs felt as though stung by a thousand needles, every breath burned inside her lungs. The forest looked further and further away, and the girl felt heavier with every step.

Terzić looked behind him, then pushed Amanda violently to the side. She barely caught her balance, then saw the blond teenager, his knife stuck where she had been just a moment before.

"Keep running!" Terzić cried.

Amanda wanted to disagree. Terzić shouldn't sacrifice himself like this. But the weight in her arms reminded her that she had insisted on carrying the girl. If she didn't escape now, they'd all die. She clenched her teeth, turned and started running again.

Hysterical laughter came from behind her. Amanda knew she had to keep her attention in front. Any step could land her in another bear trap, or she'd trip over something. But she kept turning her head in spite of herself.

She saw the blond boy swinging his knife erratically at Terzić. After several crazed swings, the boy lost his balance. Terzić caught his arm and flung him around, grabbed the knife and threw it away into the dark. The boy punched, but Terzić dodged, gripped the boy's other arm, and threw him to the ground, pinning him with his knee.

Amanda looked forward to check her path, then back again. It had taken her only a second, but while Terzić restrained the boy, the girl with the cleaver had snuck up behind him, lifting her weapon high above her head. Amanda wanted to cry out to Terzić, but it was too late.

The teenage girl brought the cleaver down into his shoulder full force. Terzić gave a horrific cry and fell to his side.

Amanda tried to look away, to keep running. But her body wouldn't listen and her steps slowed down. She couldn't make herself run as the man who had helped and saved her so many times, her friend, bled to death in the street.

The teenage girl gripped the cleaver and tore it out, ready for another swing—but there was no need. Terzić wasn't moving. She looked down at his lifeless body and snickered, her laughter becoming louder and more hysterical until she was cackling maniacally at the dead man before her.

The young boy got up again and fixed his eye on Amanda. A shock of electricity ran through her, making her legs move again. Heaving under the strain, she cursed herself for ever slowing down and looking back.

Her legs were burning up and the small girl's weight had increased tenfold. But Amanda couldn't slow down. Not now. Not after Terzić, Westen and Robinson had all died to allow this little girl to live.

Amanda heard mumbling and looked down. The girl's eyes were still glassy and unfocused, but her mouth was moving. "Mommy? Mommy, I'm sorry. I didn't mean to let him in."

Amanda's shins slammed into something soft. Her momentum carried her forward, airborne, and the girl was ripped out of her arms. A burning pain flashed up Amanda's knees and wrists as she scraped along the street.

She looked behind her—she had tripped over a corpse. The last one in the village, and it just had to lie straight in her path. In front of her, the forest was less than thirty yards away. Pain pulsed through her as she struggled to get back on her feet.

Strong hands grabbed her shoulders and flung her to her back. The blond boy had caught up to her. Amanda struggled, punching and kicking at him wildly, until he grabbed her head and knocked it into the pavement.

A burst of bright flashes and twinkling lights exploded in front of her. It felt as though her skull had been slammed through her face.

The boy straddled her. His eyes were bloodshot and wide, like a crazed psychopath. He breathed heavily as his lips contorted into a hideous grin. He started laughing, like the teenage girl over Terzić's corpse. His hands tightened into fists.

This is it. This is where I die. He'll pummel me till my head is just red mush.

As if time slowed down, she saw the boy draw back his fist, charging it like a spring. *Mom, Dad, Greg…I'm sorry. Maybe—*

Something in her periphery moved. There was a loud crack and the boy on top of her was blown away, flying off her and crashing headfirst into the street, blood dripping from his head.

Amanda strained her dizzy eyes.

Viktor was towering over her.

Why save me, yet again? Can't he stand having someone else kill me?

Viktor shook his head. "I told you not to move. You would have been safe in the store."

She saw a white dress behind him. She wanted to scream, but her lips wouldn't move. Viktor read the warning in her expression and whirled around, just as the teenage girl swung her cleaver. He dodged, but she still slashed across his left arm. Like Terzić, Viktor hadn't heard her. Barefoot, she was deathly quiet.

Blood flowed from Viktor's arm. Despite the gaping wound, he didn't even wince. The teenage girl raised the cleaver once more, as the man with the pitchfork jumped out of the shadows on Viktor's left. Giving him no time, the two villagers attacked simultaneously. Viktor twisted and jumped backwards. The cleaver missed him completely, but he couldn't dodge the pitchfork. It made that horrible sucking noise again as it pierced his abdomen and his leg.

Before the girl could take another swing, Viktor turned, grabbed the pitchfork and pushed himself loose. The man with the black jacket was thrown back and stumbled, reflexively grabbing the gunshot wound Westen had inflicted.

The teenage girl slashed at Viktor again, but he caught her arm mid-swing and yanked her into the air like a weightless doll, slamming her into the street. The teenager gasped as the air was knocked out of her. Viktor grabbed her hand and tore away the cleaver.

As if he had eyes in the back of his head, he turned just in time to dodge another stab from the pitchfork. A moment later, Viktor had already slipped to the man's side and slammed the cleaver into his skull.

The man's head jerked upwards, as if pulled by a rope. Without wasting an instant on freeing the hatchet, Viktor took the man's pitchfork and skewered the teenager on the ground. She gave one last groan, then stopped moving.

Viktor checked his surroundings, but all the villagers were dead. He fell to one knee, holding his abdomen. Blood trickled from the pitchfork wound.

*He really is a monster...*He had just sustained wounds that would kill an ordinary man and still defeated two armed lunatics. He hadn't even blinked when he had ended their lives. Same as with that boar in Ukraine—with no mercy or emotion, like disposing of trash.

Amanda propped herself on her elbow. Her vision wobbled, but she spotted the girl she had dropped, lying in the street, unmoving.

God really did hate her, it seemed. Everyone had given their lives to save this girl, and it had all been for nothing. Amanda turned her head back to Viktor.

"Aim ssssoweee fow wunning awwwae. Auw deal..." Her speech was so broken, she couldn't even understand herself.

But Viktor seemed to get what she was asking. "I gave you my word. I shall keep it."

Amanda tried to smile, unsure if her facial muscles were working correctly. At least, it hadn't all been in vain—she would be the Red Dove's last victim.

Her elbow gave out and she fell on her back again. Darkness grew slowly from the edges of her vision. High above her, the stars glittered. She had never seen so many before. It was like an ocean of glowing sparks. And there was something else. Like...curtains of light, with a soft touch of green, swaying gently in the wind. More beautiful than anything she had ever seen before. She couldn't believe how wonderous the world could be. She wished she could stay here, just admiring the sky above, but the darkness grew inexorably, soon covering all but a tiny sliver of her view.

Just a bit longer...

But the darkness didn't stop. Soon, she couldn't see anything, and a cold sleepiness smothered all her thoughts.

CHAPTER 27

Everything was awash in light. Her eyelids twitched at the blinding glare. Her head felt heavy and her thoughts were hazy. Had she just woken up from a dream? She couldn't remember what it was about, but it hadn't been a pleasant one.

Amanda tried to shift position, but every movement was accompanied by a stinging pain across every muscle.

Where am I?

When her vision slowly adjusted, she saw this wasn't her bedroom. The ceiling was white and uniform, with square tiles. Her body lay at a slight incline, and the pillow was several sizes too large for comfort.

Why was everything so bright? It came from the left, outside her vision. She turned her head as if rotating rusted cogwheels. A row of windows. The sun was rising, seeming to rest on top of massive, distant mountains. It bathed the entire room in a golden orange. Beautiful, but…

"There are no mountains in Chicago," she said.

"What an astute observation."

She turned her head.

"Yo."

Amanda laughed, even though it hurt her chest. "Greg, what are you doing here?"

"Nothing. I just spontaneously decided that sitting in a chair next to you was my new hobby."

Greg turned his head away as a tear slipped down his cheek. He faked a yawn, amazingly poorly, and covered his mouth with his hand, using the opportunity to wipe his face and rub his eyes. "Sorry, a bit tired here."

Never try to become an actor, Greg. Amanda wondered what brought on this strong emotion. If there was ever a person who was always cheerful, it was Greg. She turned towards him, but a sharp chest pain stopped her. "Ugh," she said, and leaned back.

"Take it easy, princess. You're really beat up."

"What happened?" It felt awkward to look at the ceiling while talking, but this was the least painful position.

"You don't remember?"

"I...don't know. It..."

It feels like I'm forgetting something important. That dream of hers, what did she remember? *Let's see...*She had gone to Canada, yes. To Edmonton. And she had met Terzić. They had gone to Jasper. And from there, they had driven to...

Then it all came back. Her journey through the woods, the village, her meeting with Viktor...and her bargain.

"Oh God." The sun! She had taken the poison sometime after midnight. Half a day ago. She looked at Greg. "Thank God you're here. I get to talk to you one last time. I don't have much longer."

"Wait, what?"

"The sun is rising. I have an hour or two, tops."

Greg looked at her dumbfounded. "Okay, slow down—"

"Not now, Greg. If I have time, I'll explain later, but I have so much to say, before it's too late."

"But, Amanda..." He looked embarrassed.

"God damn it, what?"

"Okay...First of all, this window faces west. The sun isn't rising, it's setting."

She turned her head. Greg was right. The sun had already dipped below the mountains.

"And second, about that 'an hour or two, tops'...it's July eleventh."

"What?"

"You've been in a coma for four days."

Amanda looked back up at the ceiling. How was she still alive? The poison was supposed to kill her 'after half a day'. Did Viktor make a mistake? No. He was far too meticulous for that. So then... "That stuff...really was just syrup? But why did he..."

"Amanda, you're making no sense. As usual."

It made no sense to her, either. Viktor had tricked her. To entertain himself? No. Then he wouldn't have put his life on the line, yet again, to save her from those villagers. It was a disgusting feeling—owing her life three times over to a mass murderer. But why did he care so much if she lived? Why put her through that torturous choice of whether to drink the 'poison' and then go to such lengths to keep her alive?

Unless...that was the whole point. A test. Would she selfishly run away, or make the ultimate sacrifice? He had praised her uncle for being selfless, even in the face of mortal danger. Was that something he respected? Was that why he had saved her again?

Amanda looked at the disappearing sun. "So, I'm still alive."

Greg laughed. "Give a medal to Captain Obvious. Though, your surprise is warranted. When they brought you here, you were in very, very bad shape. I couldn't understand half the words the doctors used for you. Whatever you did, it's not something the kids should try at home."

"Where am I?"

"At the hospital in Jasper."

"How come you're here?"

"After you called, I was up all night, sick with worry. When I couldn't take it anymore, I called the police station here. I figured, since the seventh had come, the curse should be over, right? Luckily, you told me you had two cops with you. Sergeant Jones probably would have hung up on me if I hadn't told him two of his officers were in trouble in Morton Ridge. When he couldn't reach either of them, the cavalry got going pretty fast. Long story short, they found you collapsed in the street, heart barely beating anymore. I called your parents and we flew over together."

"Wait, my parents are here too?"

Greg nodded. "Yeah. They sat here and watched you 21 hours straight. They finally went to get some rest and I took over watching Sleeping Beauty here. I considered going in for a kiss to see if that would wake you up."

"But of course, your sense of decency stopped you, right?"

"Naturally. Besides, if kisses woke people from comas, the world would be a much simpler and happier place."

"How long have you been here?"

"Since lunch. But it paid off. Looks like I'm the lucky guy who gets to ask you first: What the hell happened?"

"Don't you know more than me already?"

"How would I? There are newspaper stories out, but as usual for the Red Dove, everything's a mystery. The police aren't talking. Rumor has it they found some pretty grim stuff in that village. But the investigation can't have gotten far yet, since it took the firefighters two days just to put out all the burning buildings."

Amanda furrowed her brows. "Burning buildings?"

"Around the back of the village, from what I heard."

*Where Zoey's Groceries was…*Nothing was burning when she was there. Meaning Viktor had gone back after she had passed out to destroy the evidence. She couldn't imagine how he'd survived being stabbed with a pitchfork, but then again, with him, nothing seemed impossible. She wasn't even sure if he was really human.

"The police have been itching to talk to you, by the way. I think they know the story you told them to get them there was BS. Guess they want to know how you knew what was going on before they did."

"Great, just great."

"Oh yeah, and Chicago PD apparently also wants to talk to you? They phoned your dad. Something about a battery charge in Daley Plaza?"

"What? Oh crap…" The man she had punched after her hallucination with the pigeons. She remembered people filming with their phones. No wonder they had managed to identify her.

"I called a friend who studies criminal law," Greg said. "He told me to warn you not to breathe a single word to the cops without a lawyer. But don't worry. I'm sure your dad can afford some cocaine-sniffing trailblazer from Harvard who can get you off. That, or you'll just have to tell the truth. Whatever gets you less jail time."

"Thanks, you're very encouraging."

"One of my underappreciated talents." He flashed a winning smile and winked. "But enough of that. What *did* happen up there? How come the curse didn't kill you?

"That's a long, long story. I'll tell you when I feel a bit better. But you don't need to be worried about the Red Dove anymore."

"Aww, come on. You can't end on a cliffhanger like that."

Amanda laughed again, but her laughter turned into a cough.

"Easy, easy," Greg said.

They remained silent for a while. It gave Amanda time to think back to her escape. She remembered Robinson and Westen, both killed so violently. And Terzić, too…They all had died to save her. And that little girl.

"Greg, did…did a young girl survive?"

"Oh right, nearly forgot. Yeah, they found a kid curled up next to you. She seems to have a severe mental trauma. But at least her physical injuries were pretty minor. Compared to what you suffered, anyway. Hey, at least she's alive, right? Was it you who saved her?"

Tears ran down Amanda's cheeks. "No…not really. "

"Speaking of survivors, there's also this other guy who—"

"Wait…" Bearing the pain, she sat up. "What guy?"

"The only male survivor. Had quite a nasty wound, too. An officer told me a couple hours ago they finally managed to talk to him. Since hearing you were alive, he keeps saying he wants to talk to you."

"Oh God, he's here, in this hospital? What the hell does he want from me?" Was Viktor going to tell her he didn't mean what he said? He'd just been messing with her and now he'd keep killing? Then what would she do?

"Uh, no idea. Look, if you don't want to talk to him, you don't have to."

Amanda shook her head. The gnawing fear that had finally subsided rose in her again. If Viktor wanted to talk to her, she had to go right away. God knew what he might do if she didn't. She tried to push herself up, but the pain stopped her again. "Goddammit, I need to…"

"You need to lie down and rest." Greg gently pushed her back down.

"No, you don't understand. I need to talk to him. Right now."

"You make no sense at all," Greg said. "A second ago you were terrified of the guy, now you want to rush into his arms?"

"Of course not, don't be stupid. But if he…ugh. I need to go."

Greg's look asked *Are you sane or do I have to restrain you?* After a few seconds, he shook his head. "Fine, if it's that important to you, I'm guessing you have a good reason. Wait, let me get something for you."

He left the room for a minute, then came back with a wheelchair and helped Amanda into it. She winced. Every movement brought new spikes of pain.

When she was finally seated, Greg moved the wheelchair left and right, as if testing a new car. "Haha, this is fun. I get to cart you around."

"Glad you're enjoying yourself so much."

"Don't get me wrong, it's not my next passion, but compared to your usual crazy requests, it's a nice change."

He took Amanda to an elevator and to another floor, then looked up and down the room numbers. "Aaaand…right here."

Greg knocked on the open door, but there was no reply. "Guess that means we're invited." He pushed Amanda into the room. She saw the sleeping man and gasped. Heavily bandaged and breathing steadily through tubes while machines beeped, was Terzić. Tears blinded her vision.

She gestured for Greg to leave. If Terzić was sleeping, she didn't want to disturb him. In the hall, Greg put a hand on her shoulder as tears streamed down her cheeks.

"I'm so happy…Greg, he almost died for my sake. God, everybody died for my sake. Robinson, Westen…If I hadn't gotten it into my head to…" Her sobs interrupted her speech like hiccups and she began to shake again.

"No idea what's going on, but I guess it's a good thing this guy's alive?"

"What are you people doing here?" came a stern voice from her right.

"Uh-oh. Hello again, doctor." Greg smiled. "Fancy running into you here."

"Save it. When did she wake up? Why didn't you call me to examine her? What is she doing here?"

"Sorry, doctor. Amanda insisted and would not be dissuaded."

The doctor opened his mouth, but when his eyes fell on Amanda's teary face, he shook his head and heaved an exaggerated sigh. He pointed into the room. "Well, you seem to be well enough…is this man a friend of yours?"

"Uh-huh," Amanda managed between sobs.

"Hallelujah. You have no idea how infuriating he's been. Imagine how hard it was for the police to get a Serbian interpreter. And then all he did was ask how you were and that he wants to see you. He's refused to say anything since."

"Will he be okay?"

The doctor's face stiffened. "Your friend has been through a lot. His right shoulder was practically pulverized and part of his lung was torn. The surgery took hours, but we stabilized him." His tone grew somber. "He'll never be able to lift his arm again. Still, he was incredibly lucky. His shoulder muscles lessened the blow. During surgery, we found that the wound he suffered stopped just short of an artery. If it had been a quarter of an inch deeper, he would have bled to death in seconds."

The doctor paused for a moment. "Actually, the blood loss would still have killed him if you hadn't put that bandage on. Or he might have suffocated if you hadn't sat him upright. That was amazing work, by the way. Few would know what to do in a situation like that, or how to apply a ripped-off piece of cloth so skillfully. Are you in medical school, by any chance?"

Amanda looked up. Apply a bandage? Sit Terzić upright? There was only one person who could have done all that…but why? Why would Viktor go out of his way to save her and Terzić's life? For 'no reason', just like his massacres? Because he felt like it? Or maybe there was a reason. She remembered his reply when she had asked him to spare Terzić and the others: 'They shall live.' Was saving Terzić his way of keeping that promise?

"Well, never mind," the doctor said when Amanda didn't answer. "You must be tired. You should rest. I'll inform your parents that you've woken up and come by for a checkup later on."

"Thank you, doctor." She felt as if she hadn't slept in days.

As Greg pushed her back to her room, he said, "You have to promise me to tell me later what happened. I want to know how you escaped and why you started to cry when you saw that guy and—"

"Yes, Greg. I promise you'll hear more of this than you ever wanted to know. But now, I just want to sleep."

Loading Amanda back into her bed proved challenging. Every movement sent fresh bolts of pain through her. Greg had to kneel down so she could use his shoulder as a crutch.

Amanda blushed when she felt his hand around her waist as he helped her up. In spite of being in so much pain, she felt a tickle in her stomach. A bit like when she had jumped out of that window from the grocery store.

"There we go," he said as he eased her into the bed. She immediately felt sleep wash over her. As Greg tried to pull back, she held his hand.

"Can you stay a bit longer? I want you close to me."

Drifting away, she saw him shake his head and smile. He caressed her hand and said, "I'll be here."

ACKNOWLEDGEMENTS

How is a book written? One romantic image is that of a Shakespeare or Dante – a lonely wordsmith, surrounded in his candle-lit study by towers of papers. His muse-inspired words flow from the quill in his hand onto the pages before him, night after night, until, one day, his pen finally traces out the magic words "The End".

As you might have guessed, the reality is a bit more mundane. Quills and candlelight aside, writing may indeed sometimes be lonely and done in the middle of the night, but none of us ever manage to do it truly "alone." As every author knows only too well, our work is greatly indebted to innumerable people, without whom our books would never have ended up the same, or possibly would never have been written in the first place.

This is certainly true for The Red Dove. I can state for a fact that, without the people mentioned below and their invaluable contributions, this book would not exist. I'll probably fail at expressing the full extent of my gratitude, but I'd like to at least give it my best shot. These few lines here are my admittedly feeble attempt to thank those who left their mark and helped make The Red Dove what it is.

*

First and foremost, I must of course thank my parents, Wolfgang and Maria. Since they were the ones who raised me, I am who I am in large part thanks to them. Therefore, it's obvious that this book, and any I might still write, could not have existed without them. Moreover, even long after I moved out and was no longer dependent on them, their constant moral support and advice was what kept me going through the long years of writing this book. This in spite of the fact that they had no idea what I was doing – I kept my writing a secret from them, hoping to make it a unique surprise to them when I finally finish, though that took a bit longer than anticipated.

To you both, Papa, Maman, thank you for making this possible. I hope this is as big a surprise for you as I always envisioned it to be. I also hope you'll enjoy it, even if this is probably not the genre you usually read.

*

To Elina, once again, my deepest gratitude. I have attempted to convey my thanks in person, several times, but it always fell short of the appreciation I actually feel. After all, she gave me so many things to be thankful for: First, Elina was the only one who was kind enough to read nearly all the drafts of The Red Dove, front to back, in spite of how repetitive this must have become after a while. Her feedback over the years was always both impassioned and valuable beyond measure. Most importantly, though, I can confidently say that, without her, The Red Dove wouldn't exist. You see, in the early days of this novel, my writing was not merely awkward, but outright hideous. I blame nobody for dismissing my early efforts after reading past the third sentence. Yet if nobody had taken an interest in the early chapters back then, I am certain I would eventually become discouraged and stopped writing altogether. Only Elina kept reading the bits and pieces I published on social media, egging me on to write more. It was her enthusiasm and encouragement that kept me going and allowed me to write the book to its completion.

So, to you, Elina: thank you. Thank you so incredibly much. You have no idea how much your friendship and your encouragement have meant to me. I don't think I'll ever be able to adequately repay you (you never asking for anything doesn't help, either). But, I want you to at least know that what you hold in your hands right now would not have been possible without you.

Like every author, I am also incredibly indebted to my editor. Therefore, a great big thanks goes to Allison, for all her proofreading and advice. Yes, she returned the book each time with over half of it crossed out or critiqued. And yes, I did have to rewrite it, almost in its entirety, three times because of her feedback, but…I can honestly say that The Red Dove would never have been what it is now without her. I believe that, as authors, we always feel alternating waves of anger and despair when our editors decimate our beloved books, but we also have to admit that, in the end, they are right about almost everything. This was certainly true here.

Therefore, a big thanks to you, Allison, for helping to polish The Red Dove and to make it what it is now.

Then there's Elsa. Especially in the later stages of writing this book, I frequently turned to her for advice, often sending an almost identical paragraph to her for proofreading over and over. And yet, she's never once, to my knowledge, deleted my number. While not a professional editor, she has been no less ruthless in her criticisms. However, here as well, I begrudgingly had to admit that her insights and feelings were rarely wrong. Through this, she has helped me improve the book in all sorts of ways, when I was still writing it and when I was getting it ready for publication.

My thanks to you, Elsa, for our friendship and for all the help you gave me.

Next up, Zinus. Back in my student days, I used to live in a dorm. Zinus was one of the many interesting people I met there. He began writing his own book roughly around the same time I did. It was always a pleasure meeting in the ground floor dining room and discussing the various storytelling problems we faced in our respective books, bouncing ideas back and forth, and trying to find solutions for the impossible twists and turns we wanted our stories to take. While The Red Dove changed enormously from the first draft we discussed so much, many of the ideas we came up with survived all rounds of editing and are still in the book today.

For that, many thanks to you Zinus, and for all these wonderful discussions we had. I hope you are still writing on your book and that I'll get to read it soon.

*

A big thanks also goes to Veronica. She was also kind enough to read several drafts of the book, even though I know full well what a chore this becomes after a while. But, like the others above, she asked for nothing in return and never complained. The hilarious comments she often left in the margins were always a joy to read.

Thank you, Veronica, for everything you did to help me with The Red Dove. If you have the patience to read it yet again, I hope you'll enjoy it in its final and completed form.

*

Then, there's Nevena. While I was putting the finishing touches on my book, I was thrilled to learn that one of my coworkers had grown up in Bosnia and knew Serbia well, both in its language, countryside and culture. I immediately thrust my latest draft onto her and pestered her for her opinions and feedback. She was kind enough not to report me to HR for making such an outrageous request on her free time. When she was done reading, her comment on how I had described Serbia ("oh my God, yes! It's totally like that!") was a joy to hear. Her notes in the book, as well as her encouragement, both then and afterwards, meant a lot to me.

Therefore, also to you, Nevena, a big thank you. The draft you read was a pretty final one, so there will be little you don't know in this version, but maybe you'll enjoy it all the same. I hope I can come to you for advice again in the future, even if the next book will probably not take place in Serbia.

*

Let me also mention Mark, who arranged the book's interior design and formatting. In addition, he also provided fantastic advice on a whole host of other topics, for which I am especially grateful. Cheers to you, Mark! I hope you'll get to bless many more books with your talents.

*

Similarly, there's Jeff, whose amazing work was probably the first thing you saw about this book—he was the one who designed the cover. I'm especially grateful for the high quality of his work and for bringing to life one of my favorite scenes in the book. Thanks a lot, Jeff! If I write another book, I hope you'll do the cover for that one, as well.

*

I should also thank my cats, Lume and Lili. They will, I fear, never be able to read these lines, so this might feel like wasted effort. However, I cannot express how invaluable it was to be able to lie down and pet them when I was feeling especially frustrated or unable to come up with a single coherent sentence anymore. In addition, they also helped to keep my book short, by always managing to lie down on my keyboard in just such a way as to press the backspace button. Doing so, they managed to delete more text than even the harshest editor could ever dream of. As such, a big thanks to them both, for their unpaid editing services and tireless moral support.

*

Finally, and most of all, I would like to give my greatest thanks to you, my dear reader, for letting me share this story with you and for indulging me in this acknowledgements section. I hope Amanda's little tale kept you guessing all the way to the end, and that you enjoyed following her adventures.

I wish you all the best from my small Swiss town, wherever and whenever you might be. Perhaps until next time and thank you for reading!

ABOUT THE AUTHOR

A.K. Spalva was born and raised in a tiny mountain village in Austria. He moved to Switzerland in 2007 to pursue degrees in science and IT and has stayed there ever since. When he's not penning new stories, he works as a consultant. In his spare time, he enjoys cooking, discovering new languages and taking landscape photographs.

He can be reached through his website at *https://www.akspalva.com/*, or through social media under *@akspalva*.

Printed in Great Britain
by Amazon